SHIELD OF LANTIUS

David C. Corbett

TABLE OF CONTENTS

CHAPTER 1

The Harrier leaped into North Carolina's night sky. At the controls, Major Dar Fantin slowly eased the nozzle control lever forward . . . the "jump jet" gathered speed into the darkness.

"Mars Two Two airborne," Dar spoke distinctly into his oxygen mask. "Climbing for fifteen thousand."

"Roger, cleared for fifteen, and entry into training area Bravo," Mainstay Control responded.

Dar settled back into the confines of the ejection seat, shaking off the tensions of a night STO (Short Takeoff). This was his first night hop in over a month, and though he enjoyed the closeness of the stars once he reached altitude, he had to readjust his flying habits to accommodate for the darkness. A light blue haze, emanating from the instrument panel lighting, filled the cockpit,. The soft glow brought a smile to his ruggedly handsome face. He loved flying, and was one of the Marine Corps' best. Still, night flying a Harrier after a long layoff was something he took very seriously.

As the aircraft passed ten thousand feet, the vast diamond studded sky opened like a heavenly ocean. *They actually pay me to do this*, he thought, as a million stars reflected off his clear, night flying visor. Gently, he lowered the nose of the small fighter, pulled the throttle back to 85% and, with quick professionalism, his pale blue eyes scanned the instrument panel for anything that might be out of order.

"Mainstay, Mars Two Two leveling off at fifteen thousand in training area Bravo."

"Roger, Two Two, we have you on radar. Switch to button nineteen, and contact Cherry Point Approach Control for your TACAN penetration.""Switching button nineteen, and thanks for the follow. Y'all have a nice evening." Dar spoke lightly, rightfully assuming the ground controller was swallowing slugs of lukewarm coffee from a much used, heavily stained mug.

Snapping on the autopilot and setting a heading for Cherry Point's tactical air navigation (TACAN) approach fix, he relaxed into the familiarity of his jet, instrument flight, and the night sky above. Since his divorce from the wicked witch of the north two years prior, he had given every ounce of his soul to becoming the finest fighter pilot in the Corps. The Harrier had, over the past ten years, become an extension of himself, and he knew it. *I'm going to be VMA - 542's executive officer in two weeks,* he let the pleasure of that thought wash over him with gratification. He smiled inwardly, *I am a good leader, a good pilot, and I am having a ball.*

Major General Harold Moore sat comfortably on his overstuffed couch watching television. At fifty, he still had a muscular six foot frame, though a small paunch was beginning to show when he viewed himself in a mirror. As the Commanding General of the Second Marine Aircraft Wing, he was the leader of over thirty thousand men.

The phone next to him rang. It was the blue phone, his direct line to Washington D. C.. Setting down the scotch he'd been sipping, he reached out to stop the incessant ringing. "General Moore," he answered.

He listened intently for several minutes, then said, "Yes, sir. I'm on my way."

"Mars Two Two, this is Mainstay. Over."

The excited voice shook Dar from his self-adulation.

"Mainstay, this is Mars Two Two. What's up? I haven't contacted Approach Control yet."

"Two Two, say fuel state and time on station."

The ground controller sounded frantic. "Mainstay, Two Two has six thousand pounds and about an hour and fifteen minutes on station. What's going on?" Fantin's eyes swept his instruments. Instinctively he knew something was up, and wanted to make sure his bird could handle any assigned task.

"Two Two, we have an unidentified flying object approaching the coast. The Air Force has scrambled four F-16's from Seymour Johnson and two F-15's from Myrtle Beach, but they can't reach the predicted coast in point for this thing before it crosses the ADIZ."

Dar felt the first effects of adrenaline hitting his system. It wasn't often that the Air Force went to general quarters when an unknown tried to penetrate the Air Defense Intercept Zone. "Roger. I'll have a look. Give me a vector and an altitude."

"Steer one-three-five, climb to angels three-five, and go Buster," a new Mainstay controller interrupted. "Say weapons aboard?"

Dar knew by the sound of the new and obviously older controller's voice, whatever was approaching the North Carolina coast should not be there. "Negative on the weapons, Mainstay. What am I looking for?" His question came as he simultaneously banked hard to the left, shoved the throttle to 100%, and started a climb for thirty-five thousand feet.

"Two Two, we have no idea. The only thing for sure is that it isn't an aircraft. Whatever it is, it's big and it's fast. We're tracking it at better than Mach three on our scopes, and Seymour had it at Mach five a few minutes ago."

"Jesus H. Christ," Dar blurted out. "What am I supposed to do if I even see it . . . get a license number?" The Harrier was passing thirty thousand at 490 knots. "The best I can get out of this bird will be around five hundred knots at thirty-five thousand."

"Roger, understand. Take up new heading of one-three-zero for intercept. Bogie has now slowed to Mach one."

Dar swung the aircraft on to its new heading and leveled at thirty-five thousand, surveying the night sky above, ahead, and below. Nothing! No hint of anything out of the ordinary, but that could change in a heartbeat. When you are closing head-on with another aircraft at better than 1200 miles per hour, a sneeze can ruin your whole day. "Steady one-three-zero, and level at angels three five. Nothing in sight. Say distance and altitude of bogie," his voice was steady and professional.

"Bogie at One-two-eight, passing angels eight-eight."

"Passing eighty eight thousand feet?" Dar could not hide the skepticism in his voice. "What've you got me chasing, a damned spaceship?"

"Mars Two Two, we have no idea, but it's there and it's heading straight for you. Distance two hundred miles, speed now six hundred."

"Roger," Dar replied absently. He was busy making calculations. If the "thing" was two hundred miles on his nose, it would be eight to ten minutes before they ran into each other. He checked his fuel . . .

4000 pounds and going down fast. To go "Buster" meant keeping the throttle at 100%, which burned JP-5 fuel at a very rapid rate. Heading out to sea, as he was, required a higher bingo than what he might have decided had he been over land. He'd crossed the beach five minutes ago, and intercept would be in ten minutes . . . *I'll fudge it for momma*, he thought . . . fifteen minutes at five hundred knots puts me one hundred and twenty-five miles off shore, plus another thirty-five to Cherry Point, and an approach. "Yeah," he mumbled to himself, "a two thousand pound fuel remaining bingo will work."

"Two Two, bogie one-two-nine, range one-two-five, passing Angels six-zero. Still slowing. Now at five hundred fifty knots."

"Roger, Mainstay. I'm looking."

The glow surprised Dar. He didn't expect to see anything for at least another five minutes. Nevertheless, there it was . . . a ball of orange surrounded by shimmering blue. The light was growing fast, and so was its size.

" Mainstay, I can see it. Say again distance and bearing."

"Bearing one-two-nine at one hundred miles. Speed five hundred. What do you see?"

Dar tried to describe the phenomena, but words came hard. He was busy flying his jet, and trying to assimilate the sight growing rapidly before him.

"Mainstay, this thing is one huge beasty, and it sure as hell isn't any aircraft known to man. What do you want me to do?"

"Hold course and speed, Two Two." There was a short pause.

"This is Shaker, Cuda," Shaker was Lieutenant General Moore, and he was addressing Dar by his call sign . . . Cuda. "Dar, get in there as close as you safely can. Get a look and get out. I just got a call from the Pentagon. Fighters are missing all over the world. I don't want you making a hero out of yourself."

"Roger that, Shaker, but I'm telling you this thing is huge. I'll try to get as close as I can, but my perceptions are all screwed up. It's just so damned big. I'm going to have to slow down soon."

"Do what you have to do, Cuda, and good luck."

"Thanks, General. Mainstay, say distance to bogie."

"Fifty miles and closing. Bogie now down to two hundred and fifty knots."

"Mainstay, I'm slowing to three fifty." He pulled the throttle to 85%, checked his instruments for the hundredth time, and stared back at the orange and blue light now filling his entire windscreen. He wanted to turn. Just rap his bird up into a 90-degree, 5G bank, and get the heck out of this particular airspace, but Mainstay insisted the object was still fifty miles away. He had always considered himself as brave as the next guy, but now it was all he could do to contain the fear welling up from his gut. He took three deep breaths from the pure oxygen the AV-8B was feeding him, shook his head to clear the tension, and resolved to fly ahead. "Say distance, Mainstay."

"Two Two, distance to bogie twenty miles. Speed ~ you're not going to believe this ~ speed fifty knots and slowing at Angels three-eight."

Dar momentarily stared straight ahead in disbelief. Stopping in mid-flight was simply not possible at thirty-eight thousand feet, but that's what this thing was doing. He pulled the throttle to idle, slowing the jet even more.

"Mainstay, I'm slowing to two hundred fifty. This thing is nothing but light . . . orange light surrounded by blue. I can't see any definition other than a huge ball. There appears to be nothing but light."

"Understand, Two Two. You're at seven miles. Bogie at angels three-eight-zero, speed zero. I say again, zero speed."

Dar, heart pounding, suffered real tinges of fear, as he drew ragged excited breaths. The light had a hypnotic effect on him. *What on God's Good Earth can this thing be*, kept playing over and over in his mind like a stuck needle on an old phonograph record. He could not look away. With astonishment, he realized he was not flying his aircraft any longer. He stared ahead.

"Mars Two Two, come in, Mars Two Two."

Dar seemed to awake from a dream. "This is Mars Two Two," he replied as if drugged.

"Two Two, turn NOW! Distance to object five miles. Turn left to three-three-zero."

Dar didn't hear the panic filling the ground controller's voice. The burly gunnery sergeant was rapidly realizing his intercept was going sour. Two Two was going to hit whatever was out there. He saw a white tube of light form around his aircraft. *It's a dream*, Dar thought, *nothing but a dream*. The aviator in him could not understand what the white light was, only that it completely illuminated his small AV-8B. Now only semi-conscious, Dar, no longer reacting to his surrounding, allowed the beam of electronic antigravity pulses pull his aircraft into a vortex of orange light.

"Two Two, vector three-three-zero, "Sergeant Jones screamed into his lip mike. "Two Two, turn to three-three-zero."

There was no response from Fantin.

On the ground, General Moore stared into the radar scope. "My God, he's gone. He's disappeared from radar. What happened, Sergeant?" He turned to the man sitting in front of the radarscope, his face wrapped in green light.

"I don't know, sir. He just disappeared into that thing. Holy shit!" Sergeant Jones yelled. "Look at this! It's moving again. Christ, it's already doing over Mach 1 in less than a mile. No! Mach 3. Holy shit, Mach 5. It's gone."

The Carolina sky was empty when the Air Force F-15's arrived two minutes later.

CHAPTER 2

Dar's dream continued. He felt the Harrier around him move, but he wasn't at the controls. Lights, hundreds of multicolored lights, surrounded him, hypnotizing him. He could see movement through the windscreen and canopy, but what the motion was he could not discern. Nothing made any sense. Then darkness . . . sudden and complete darkness.

Dar shook his head. The cobwebs clouding his mind persisted, "but at least the old brain housing group is still functioning," he mumbled.

A red flare exploded behind his eyes, and with it Mainstay's last desperate call, "Turn to three-three-zero."

Grabbing the stick, he gave it a yank aft and to the left. Nothing happened. Dar looked out of the cockpit for the first time. Snapping upright in the ejection seat, realization of where he was slammed home like a Harrier hitting the deck of a lurching aircraft carrier. He was on the ground.

"What the . . .!" Dar yelled in confusion. The Harrier was still running. He could feel its rumbling power in his rear. He checked his instruments. The tachometer showed 28% power, oil pressure and Jet Pipe Temperature within limits, and the throttle at idle. Bewildered, Dar looked out at his surroundings, giving the area careful scrutiny.

His head still foggy with the dream, Dar made himself concentrate on his new surroundings. There was not much to see. Like his head, the space outside the safety of his cockpit was swirling with a gray-white substance not unlike a cloud. There was a soft ring of light glowing through the cloud from above, but that was all . . . no stars, no moon, no night.

"Night! I was night flying. Chasing something huge." Dar's memory was returning in bounds now, and it scared hell out of him. "Orange light surrounded by blue, Mainstay vectoring him onto a . . . something extraordinary." It all came back in a flash, and just as rapidly he knew where he was. The orange ball had sucked him up like grape through a straw. "I'm sitting inside the darned thing," Dar exclaimed aloud. "Well, I'll be a son-of-a-bitch."

With his head clearing rapidly now, Dar poked himself several times. *I'm alive. That's a lot more than I would've figured*, he thought. Mechanically, he pulled the throttle to the shutdown detent. "That was a dumb thing to do," he said aloud, immediately regretting his actions. *Now the engine driven Onboard Oxygen Generator will shut down. I won't be able to breathe. Stupid. Stupid*, his thoughts swirled like the fog outside the windscreen.

The engine turbine blades rattled to a stop as Dar unsnapped his oxygen mask, letting it dangle from the right side of his helmet. Staring with mild awe at the eddying smoke, he realized the only oxygen he'd have left now would be what was trapped the confines of the cockpit. He pulled the ejection seat safety handle up, snapped open the Koch fittings at his shoulders, and unfastened the lap belt.

"Well, pally, what are you going to do now?" He spoke aloud, as he often did when flying. Hearing his own voice question his actions always seemed to put a tight situation in perspective. "Can't sit inside this bubble forever. The big question is, can I breathe out there?"

Consciously holding his breath, Dar pulled the canopy unlocking lever. The bubble cracked, then quietly moved fully open. With a shove on the canopy rails, he stood up on the ejection seat. His face grimaced as sore muscles pushed him upward. *I wonder how long I've been sitting here*, he thought. He stretched his five-foot ten-inch frame, shaking out the kinks, and pulled his helmet off, throwing it into the cockpit. The smoke curled around him as he took a tentative sip of air.

"I'll be damned, it tastes like a morning breeze blowing across the Eisenhower's flight deck," Dar said with pure astonishment.

"We tried to make it that way for you, Major Fantin," a disembodied female voice echoed through the enclosure. "Please, try to relax. No harm is meant you."

"You've got to be kidding. I have no idea where I am or what I'm doing here, and y'all want me to relax?" Dar dropped to the floor and went into a crouch, assuming a "ready-for-anything" stance. His eyes darted around the smoky enclosure, searching for the voice in the thick haze.

"We assure you, Major Fantin, we mean no harm to you. We understand your confusion, but all will be explained in due time. Please step this way." As the words ended, a tunnel began to appear through the opaque vapor.

Dar wrestled with a flash of fear, but they hadn't hurt him yet, and God knows they could have. He ran fingers through sandy brown hair, a vain attempt to be more presentable, and took a tentative step for the tunnel. He walked slowly away from the Harrier, alert for danger, yet not really expecting it. Grinding gears stopped him in mid stride.

With an athlete's agility, Dar pivoted around to meet the new danger. His jaw dropped in astonishment, as he watched the Harrier begin to disappear. It was literally vanishing into the floor . . . no door, no crack, and no hole ~ just quietly slipping from sight.

"We assure you, Major Fantin, your aircraft is quite safe," the voice said.

"Yeah, I'll just bet," Dar said in a whisper.

"Please continue for the hatch, Major Fantin," the voice urged.

Running his fingers through his hair once more, Dar turned and began walking. The tunnel opened slowly with each step. Silently, he counted his paces to get an idea of the size of the room. At one hundred and fourteen, head down counting, he ran into the wall.

"Damn it!" Dar exclaimed. A small bump was already rising on his forehead.

"Please wait one moment, Major Fantin," the voice intoned.

"You could've given me some warning, lady," Dar yelled. Waiting, he figured the size of the room to be 342 feet from his aircraft to the wall. If the Harrier was in the center, this wasn't a room. It was a hangar!

A soft hissing sound, followed by a panel sliding to his left, jolted Dar out of his silent calculations. He stepped through the hatch, entering a small white room. The door hissed shut behind him. The complete whiteness of the enclosure dazzled his eyes. White upon white upon white, with the only distinguishing feature being the outline of another door straight across from him.

"Major Fantin, we do not wish to alarm you, but in a moment a blue electronic field will open around you. The field will not harm you, but you may feel a mild sensation of tingling. This field is to rid your body and clothes of Earth-borne contaminates which may be harmful to us. Do you understand?"

"Yeah, I understand," Dar said. "Do what ya got to do."

The white of the room gave way to a shimmering blue. Dar felt the tingling of a million tiny shocks, not unlike the accidental zaps he'd received while installing phones for the Florida Telephone and Telegraph at age sixteen. As suddenly as it started, it was over. The blue light extinguished leaving only white walls, as the door opposite him hissed open.

"We welcome you, Major Fantin," said the most beautiful woman Dar had ever seen.

Dar stared unabashedly, trying to get his tongue into working gear. "Thank . . . I mean where . . . Thank you, I think," he stammered out the words. He was completely caught off guard by the beauty before him. The woman, maybe an inch shorter than he, was dressed in a loose fitting, white tunic. A purple sash, its edges stitched in gold, gathered the material at her slim waist, pulling the tunic down across ample breasts. Though her legs were not visible, for the tunic touched the floor, Dar could imagine their shapeliness. For all that, it was her face that totally captured and twisted his tongue into incoherent speech. Heart shaped, framed by corn silk golden hair hanging to her waist, her face would take the breath away from any man alive. Her full lips were a shade Dar could not describe, but the hue was perfect against the total whiteness of her skin and the grey-green of her eyes.

"We would like to welcome you aboard the Nanta. We are called Littia. We shall be your guide while you are with us. We recognize the confusion you must feel, but all will be explained. However, there is one final procedure that we must request of you."

No longer echoing from unseen walls, the voice sounded young and fresh. Dar fought to regain control of his emotions. "I've come this far, I guess one more step won't hurt," he said.

"We thank you. If you will follow me, please," Littia said, as she turned and walked away from Dar.

Dar followed close behind, drinking in the beauty of the woman before him. "Well, I guess she's a woman," he laughed to himself.

"We beg your pardon, Major Fantin. What did you say?" Littia asked.

Dar's face colored. "Nothing. I'm sorry, I was just talking to myself." Littia looked at him curiously, but said nothing. She continued into a large room with Dar close behind.

Unlike the other rooms he'd been in, this enclosure was colorful, almost cheerful. Not overwhelmingly large, it was nonetheless expansive. Multicolored lights created shadows which played on the walls forming an artistic atmosphere. In the center of the chamber stood a console panel filled with instrumentation Dar could not comprehend. The console faced a bank of tubes, each at least ten feet tall with a diameter over six feet. What caught Dar's attention immediately, sending warning signals up his spine, were the forms inside the canisters. Obviously human, eight of the nine tubes were occupied. He looked at the encased forms and back to Littia several times.

"Yes," she said, again answering the unasked question, "they are terrain's like yourself. We ask you to join them in the remaining Educator."

"Join them? Educator? Are you serious?"

"We are, as you put it, very serious. It is vitally important to us that you are properly educated, for without the use of our language and history, how will you function while you are among us?" Littia spoke to him as if he were a small child.

Thoughts of his flight and abduction raced through his mind, mingled with out-and-out fear. He wanted to run, to hide from whatever was rushing to overwhelm him. The idea of being shut in one of the tubes was terrifying. *Still, why would they harm me now, when they had every chance already? What could I do about it anyway? If I refuse, they'd just force my education some other way, and that might be worse than accepting it now.*

"Well, I said I'd go through with this. Sooo . . . educate me," he said, trying to sound casual about the whole affair.

"Thank you, Major Fantin. Please remove all of your clothing while we prepare the Educator." She paused. "Yes, Major Fantin, all your clothes, and yes, in front of me, and yes, we have seen others like you. Your species is so very concerned about their bodies," Littia said and smiled.

"Right," Dar said. He began stripping off his flight gear, then boots and flight suit. Standing in his skivvies, he hesitated a moment before pulling them off as well. As he stood naked before the most beautiful woman he'd ever seen, the red in his cheeks betrayed his discomfort.

"Major Fantin, if you will now step into the Educator, we will begin. Once the outer shield is down, the Educator will be filled with a sweet smelling gas. You will go to sleep, and you will dream. The dream will be of us, the Lantiusians. You will learn our language and some of our history. In the final stages, you will begin to understand the reason you are here. When you awake, we shall be there to answer any questions you might have. Are you ready?"

"Yeah, I guess so." Dar was uneasy. Standing naked in front of a lovely lady, getting ready to be put into some sort of trance and be "educated" did not make him feel warm and fuzzy all over. "Let's get this over with. Hell, you hypnotized me in my plane, sucked me into some huge ball of light, and blinded me with smoke. I figure if I don't cooperate you'll just stuff me in that thing anyway." With that, he stepped under the clear cylinder, outwardly showing a lot more confidence than he felt.

The tube slid down silently around him. As it snapped audibly into place, the smell of summer lilacs washed through the container. Dar blinked once, and fell into a deep sleep.

CHAPTER 3

Like a living film directed under the tutelage of a master, Dar's dreams drifted through the long historical background of his captors. Spinning in an orbit several hundred light years from Earth, the small planet of Lantius was warmed by two suns. From the primordial slime, a race of humanoids, not unlike mankind, had evolved to hold lordship over the resource rich world.

As scene followed scene, Dar became a part of the growth of a civilization, feeling its struggles to master nature. Social structures developed slowly but relentlessly, religions blossomed to fade into antiquity and a mind politic grew meeting the needs of the people. Long before the first microbes appeared on Earth, Lantiusians had developed a universal religion whose precepts they tenaciously held throughout continued social growth.

Even in his dream state, Dar squirmed at his first site of the grotesque effigy of The God of Many Arms. The stone sculpture, depicting a sitting demon with multiple arms reaching out as if to scoop an unwary passerby into its hollow belly, towered thirty feet above him. The head was reptilian, fearful looking until he looked into its eyes. The God's eyes reflected an entirely different image.

The immense silver-blue eyes shone through Dar's mental images revealing the theological meaning of this ancient religion. The basic core, the shining discs explained, was that all sentient life was sacred. No intelligent being could directly be killed by another. Beyond that basic premise, The God of Many Arms gave free will to its disciples. Unlike Dar's Christian beliefs of a loving God, the Lantiusian deity set few "laws," leaving that to those who believed. Rather, it was upon a Lantiusian's death that he fully became, in a quite literal sense, part of the God's conscience. The God would receive and assimilate the spirit of the departed as part of His omnipotence. No life was characterized as good or bad. The soul represented an experience of a life to be absorbed into and learned from by The God of Many Arms. Even in his dream state, Dar enjoyed the concept of no good or evil, even though he could not agree with its postulation.

Another setting panned across the theater screen of Dar's mind, showing a Lantius much removed from the inception of religious beliefs. A people of high intelligence, they had completed the exploration of their home planet a thousand years before the first caveman on Earth decided cooked mastodon tasted better and was much easier to chew. Social structures were fully in place and incorporated by the entire planet. Lantius had never known war, poverty, starvation, nor any of the depredations his world was to know. They were reaching for the stars. Space was the next frontier to be conquered. With the advent of space travel, Lantius, as an inhabited world, became known to other races with totally different cultures. This proved disastrous. Like Earth, there were worlds with cultures bent on warring. Though few planets supported races capable of traveling the stars, much less invading another world, one did. Lantiusians knew nothing of weaponry, nor had the knowledge for the waging of an intergalactic war, making them easy prey to a predatory world. The Womongly invaded.

Dar watched the war unfold, feeling the pain inflicted on the unsuspecting Lantiusians. An entire civilization was being destroyed by the Womongly. The word, Womongly, meaning . . . *creators of death*. He tried to hide from the terrible death scenes flashing across the cinema of his mind. Then, when all seemed lost, the Lantiusians developed and built an antimatter shield. The shield surrounded their planet, providing a virtual protective screen . . . impenetrable to all but a Lantiusian with a key.

Though asleep, Dar felt the safety the shield provided, and was relieved that he no longer had to witness the devastation the Womongly were capable of inflicting. He relaxed, letting his dream carry him forward.

With their safety secured, Lantius' political base made a bold move. Lantiusians would strive to protect other worlds from the Womongly and other would-be despot worlds. However, they would hold true to their ancient religious precepts. The Lantiusians would warn, provide guidance, and even produce weapons when asked, but they would not physically participate in the destruction of an enemy. The God of Many Arms would not allow them to kill, and to that belief they would hold true.

To accomplish this vast undertaking, the first Nanta, meaning *Keeper of the Peace*, was built. Since that time, five Nanta-like ships had patrolled the vastness of space, seeking worlds threatened by the Womongly.

The dream began to fade, then ended as abruptly as it had begun.

Reluctantly, Dar rolled over, slowly opening his eyes. He fought the desire to wake and lose the continuity of his dreams. The dreams were so wonderfully vivid, both in action and in color. Images swirled through his mind, propelling him through a lifetime of experiences, none of which were his own, but filled with meaning nonetheless. He carefully scanned his new surroundings, comfortable in the knowledge that he was safe from harm.

Wiping the sleep from his eyes, Dar sat up on his pallet of air. The bed, nothing more than a cushion of temperate air blown from tiny ports recessed in the deck, silently supported his weight, shifting its intensity as he moved about its unseen surface. For a covering, there was a beautifully embroidered sheet which felt like cotton, but was more akin to an electric blanket. Without the clumsiness of cord or control, the sheet noted shifts in body temperature, then self-regulated for his comfort. He threw the covering off, swinging his legs over the cushion's edge. The moment he stirred, iridescent light cast a pleasant glow throughout the room.

The room was not large, but provided the austere comforts he'd known aboard the aircraft carrier Eisenhower several years before. Attached to the bulkhead, directly across from his bed, stood a small desk with an executive style chair. To the right of the desk there was a strange looking wash basin, cabinet, and closet. Next to the sink, a hatch led to a toilet and what appeared to be a shower. In the corner, two comfortable guest chairs sat next to the bulkhead. Spartan, but adequate, he thought with pleasure. Dar had always enjoyed shipboard life, and this appeared little different.

"Major Fantin, are you awake?" Littia's voice filled the room.

"Yeah, come on in," Dar said, as he grabbed the embroidered bed covering, wrapping it around his still naked body.

The door slid open, disappearing into the wall. Littia, dressed as Dar last remembered, stepped into his quarters. "Autmb numabi cstilltus bemeria, Major Fantin," Littia said. The smile on her face beamed welcome back from his long sleep.

"Thank you Littia. I must say it was an experience," Dar answered, not the least bit surprised he'd understood the alien words she had spoken. He effortlessly adopted to the new language, which seemed as familiar as good-old down south English and equally adaptable to his accustomed phraseology. "Quite a ride you gave me in that Educator of yours. You people are something else. I understand what you do, but not why. My God, your planet was practically destroyed over a thousand years ago."

"Yes, we understand your question, and that too shall be answered at the mass briefing for you and your contemporaries later today. Are you hungry?"

Dar thought for a moment. "I could eat a horse," he said, realizing he had not eaten for sometime. "How long was I in the Educator anyway? Contemporaries?" Dar fired the questions.

"Four of your Earth days," Littia said. "Yes, there are several of your kind aboard. Twenty-four to be exact. We shall give you a moment to dress, and then we shall take you to the dining hall." She turned and slipped gracefully out the still open door before he could ask for further clarification.

Dar considered her answers, running his fingers through rumpled hair. *Why would they want twenty-four humans aboard Nanta*, he wondered. *What had she meant by contemporaries?* Rising from the bed, he moved to what he took to be the shower. To his surprise, the sonic mist felt refreshing as any water shower he'd ever taken. Just the routine of preparing for the day was comforting, real, something normal in a very abnormal situation.

Dar finished shaving. All his customary toilet articles, it appeared, had been reproduced and stocked in the cabinet above the hydrosink. Turning to the closet, he opened the single door to find a flight suit modeled closely to the one he'd worn aboard. On the left breast pocket, embroidered in gold lettering:

Commander Dar Fantin
  Keeper of the Peace

Though he wondered at the "Commander," the suit felt familiar over the light blue skivvies he'd been provided. Socks and boots were at the bottom of the closet. Again, he felt everyday intimacy.

"We have returned," Littia's voice brought Dar to reality. "Are you prepared," she paused, "I mean dressed?"

It was the first time Littia had stammered over the proper usage of words. Dar smiled and said, "Yeah, come on in. Not that you haven't seen me in my birthday suit already."

"We beg your pardon. Your birthday suit?" Littia looked confused as she entered.

"Yeah, birthday suit, you know . . . naked." Dar smiled a bit sheepishly.

"Oh," Littia returned the smile, "We understand. If you will follow, we shall dine."

The corridor was more of an enclosed street than a true passageway, Dar noted, close on Littia heels. Lights moved playfully around the curved tunnel, giving it a living feeling, which was pleasant to the mind and eye.

"Why do you find me so attractive?" Littia asked. She didn't slow her pace.

"Damn it, you did again," Dar said. "Can you read my mind or something?" In fact, that had been exactly what he'd been thinking about.

"No. Not exactly. We just get feelings from you. Does this displease you, Major Fantin?"

"It's a bit disconcerting, but I'll live with it. I guess if anybody else could pick my mind like you I would be upset, but I'm getting kinda used to you doing it."

She stopped in front of a moving ribbon of floor and turned to meet Dar's eyes. "Thank you, Major Fantin. Your compliment we accept with pleasure. Please step on the PCT, er, personal conveyance tape."

Dar followed her lead, and for the first time was among others. Nanta was a huge ship, filled with Lantiusians. Right now, Dar thought everyone of them must be trying to crowd this moving ribbon Littia had called the PCT. Though they appeared to pay little attention to him, with the exception of a nod of greeting, he felt nervous.

"We are quite used to having aboard other planet inhabitants, Major Fantin," Littia said. "Please, be not concerned."

"Yeah, right." Dar said. She'd done it again. What bothered him was not so much the numbers, it was their beauty. "Is everyone so perfectly beautiful on Lantius?"

"We are as we are," Littia sighed. "Here we are," she said, stepping from the tape.

Across the wide passageway stood a broad entrance from which Lantiusians streamed in and out. Tantalizing smells drifted through the entrance as well. Dar's stomach growled with anticipation. The dining hall was expansive, and filled with sounds of eating, laughing, and pleasant conversation. Dar swept his eyes over the crowd.

"I'm not believing this," Dar said to no one. "Hey, John! John Cannaly, you scoundrel," he yelled over the din of noise. "Hey, Snake, over here!"

John Cannaly looked up from his plate, spotted Dar, and smiled at his waving friend. "Cuda, you old son-of-a-bitch, what are you doing here?" Cannaly rose and started fighting his way through the throng. Coming together, the two men shook hands and embraced.

"Damn, Dar, it's good to see a friendly face. You got any idea why we're here?" Cannaly asked.

"Only an idea. Did you go through the Educator?"

"I think we all did," Cannaly said. "I guess that answers the question. It's the Womongly, huh?"

"Why else would they bring us up here? That's what they do, and I guess Earth is next." Dar said. Littia moved next to him. "Pardon my manners, Littia, this is one of my best friends, Major John Cannaly. Those of us who really know him call him Snake."

Cannaly offered his hand. "Pleased to meet ya, Littia."

"We are pleased to meet you as well," Littia said. She smiled with delightful charm. A look of perplexity filled her eyes. "Why do they call you Snake? We do not understand."

Cannaly looked at Dar. "You always were lucky. My guide is a guy. He's nice enough, but leave it to you to get this gorgeous creature as a guide." He turned back to Littia. "They call me Snake, because I steal girl friends. It's like a hobby of mine."

Littia shook her head, then brushed the hair from her face, "We have much to learn about Earthling men," she sighed.

"Come on, let's eat. Get some grub and join me at the table," Cannaly said. He pointed to the buffet line. "The food is darn good, even if we don't have any idea what it is. See you in a minute."

Dar and Littia moved to the line. The food, served on plates the size of a Thanksgiving turkey platter, was plentiful, wafting delightfully appetizing aromas. Though he hadn't a clue what any of the dishes being served were, his empty stomach cared less whether he filled it with a crimson meat dish or thick leaves smothered in thick green gravy. He was hungry. Not as hungry as Littia though, he thought, looking at her over-sized plate heaped with as much food as it could hold without dribbling to the floor.

"Do you always eat that much?" Dar asked, as they moved to join Cannaly.

"We metabolize food rapidly, Major Fantin," Littia answered, flatly.

The two friends talked through their meal. Their experiences were nearly identical. It was the same for all the abductees, it seemed. Cannaly explained that all twenty-four guests of the Lantiusians were aviators. Most were from the U.S., but others arrived from Russia, France, Israel, and England. All were specialists in fighter tactics, with a solid background in air-to-ground bombing as well.

"One interesting point," Cannaly said, "everyone of us came aboard in our aircraft. This ship must have one heck of a hangar deck. Every state-of-the-art fighter in the world is aboard the Nanta."

"Have you heard about a mass briefing?" Dar asked over a mouthful of meat. He was hoping Cannaly knew more than Littia had told him. "Damn, you're right, this is good chow."

"Told you it was. The briefing is supposed to be this afternoon," Cannaly said. "I guess we'll be filled in then. Regardless, they certainly have us here for a reason, and chances are, it ain't gonna be good."

Littia, listened to her guest's conversation, but said nothing. As was the case with all Lantiusians, food was important, and one did not waste time talking when one could eat. The last crumb scraped from her plate, she said, "The briefing will be in two hours. We will leave you here to talk with your friend, Major Fantin. Please excuse me. We will return for you at the appropriate time." She left before either could answer.

Dar and Cannaly were joined by other pilots from Earth. After introductions, speculation on what was going to happen to them ran the gamut from being the main entrée on the evening's menu to fighting a war. All were nervous. All were anticipating action. And all wore flight suits with Commander embroidered on their left breast, regardless of the rank they had held in their respective military services.

CHAPTER 4

Conversation among the pilots ended abruptly as Lantiusian guides streamed through the dining hall door. Dressed as they were, in identical tunics, Dar still had little problem sorting through the gaggle for Littia. She moved gracefully through the crowd, golden hair shining like a halo and stepped to his side.

"We are ready to escort you to the briefing, Commander Fantin," Littia said. Her creamy white face reflected an intent seriousness. "Will you please follow me?" She stepped off, not waiting for an answer from her charge.

Dar nodded. "I'm right with you," he said. "What's up? You look like you just swallowed something sour. Something I did?"

Littia turned to look at him with intense interest while walking swiftly to the transport tape. "Something sour? No, we do not believe so," she said softly, not understanding the question. "We must hurry. Viceroy of Peace is to speak. We must not be late."

"Viceroy of Peace? He must be an important man for you to look so upset."

"Viceroy of Peace is not a man," Littia spoke rather brusquely. "She is one of the most important Lantiusians aboard Nanta. She is the supreme guide to us all, for it is she who determines those we shall help and when. Viceroy of Peace is the reason you are here. The fact that she wishes to speak to you personally is most irregular. We must not be late."

The PCT moved them swiftly down a corridor. At one point, Littia directed him off one tape lane and onto another. The moving ribbon began to crowd with ship's personnel clothed in a variety of colored tunics. The style and cut remained the same, identical to Littia's for the women, and full-bodied for the men. However, the spectrum of colors must delineated duties and rank, Dar thought, viewing the traveling rainbow. There was little discourse among the growing throng, other than an occasional greeting between friends. This surprised Dar. He would have been more comfortable if a din of voices filled his ears. The Lantiusians' quiet sobriety caused him to feel uneasy about the upcoming briefing. Whatever was drawing them in such numbers was not something one joked about. Even during the Gulf War, when pilots gathered for mass briefings, there was always a great deal of loud talk and good-natured gibing prior to the actual brief.

"Here we are, Major Fantin," Littia said, stepping from the tape. She gave a light tug on Dar's sleeve.

Dar started at the touch. It was the first physical contact she had made since he'd come aboard. It somehow reassured him against the brooding thoughts spinning in his mind. "Lead on." He smiled at her, neither expecting nor receiving a smile in return.

They entered a room the size of a football stadium. *My God! This ship must be mammoth*, Dar thought, taking in the sights. The auditorium was awhirl with color. Every hue, tint, and shade of the spectrum, plus some he could not describe, blurred before him. Hidden lights cast colorful beams on the walls, ceiling, and floor, creating ever changing artistic designs. Dar felt like he had been led to the interior of a giant kaleidoscope. *Damn, it's enough to boggle the mind*, he thought.

"We are to move to the front row for seating," Littia said. "Viceroy of Peace is speaking for your benefit. The others come to listen as well. It is a rarity for us to hear her thoughts in such a personal manner."

Guides led their charges to the front of the huge room. Littia indicated two front row seats at center stage. Dar tried to arrange his small frame in a seat that all but swallowed him. It was obvious most Lantiusians required different seating arrangements than did humans. His comrades, he noticed, were having the same problem, yet, Littia's smaller frame conformed somehow the large seat. The front row, which could have easily seated two hundred, was occupied with twenty-four humans and their guides.

A sudden hush consumed the hall, as a stately woman, dressed in a light red tunic and standing close to seven feet tall, walked briskly onto center stage. Dar studied the Viceroy of Peace, realizing she was much older than Littia, but just as beautiful. The colorful light show filling the auditorium faded to a single blue light which highlighted the tall speaker, yet still allowed a comfortable radiance throughout the huge enclosure.

"Welcome, Commanders," the Viceroy began. "You have been educated, and know much about us. Unfortunately, through your education, you know more of us than we of you. Nanta found your world less than two years ago, which has provided us with little time to adequately categorize Earth and its inhabitants. We do know of your species' violent nature, that your world is divided into many different nationalities speaking varied languages, and of your vast differences in political ideologies. This is not unusual. We have encountered numerous similar societies in our travels. Your petty sociological differences have little meaning to us or any race who routinely travel space. What your world has in quantity, and this is vitally important, is an abundance of natural resources. Resources sought by the inhabitants of many worlds."

Dar was captivated by this woman. Her voice had a hypnotic affect, each word seemed drilled into his brain with importance. He glanced at his fellow captives. They, too, were under her spell.

"You are now familiar with Lantius' fate hundreds of years ago. You know how we survived. Now, the Womongly are here, with their sights set on the planet you call Earth. Believe me, please, Earth has no defenses capable of withstanding a Womongly onslaught. Nothing whatsoever. The life forms of your Earth will cease to exist if the Womongly are allowed into attack position. We have brought you . . .." She paused, making eye contact with each pilot in turn. "Yes, *brought you* among us, granting you this knowledge, and helping your planet by doing so. The God of Many Arms has sanctioned our will to provide enlightenment of the Womongly, but we may not fight with you."

At the mention of the God of Many Arms, the crowd hummed softly. *An "amen,"* Dar thought.

"It was for that reason you were chosen. We repeat, chosen to protect your planet against the Womongly. As we speak, your aircraft are being blueprinted so that true space fighters may be built incorporating technology far beyond anything you presently know. However, though your craft will be fitted with weapons capable of fighting the Womongly, and though each will be capable of flying in open space, the craft will maintain the operational 'feel' of the Earth fighters in which you were brought aboard. Having helped many worlds from the ravaging of the Womongly, we know this to be important to your success."

Dar looked at Cannaly, several seats to his left. Their eyes met in disbelief. Dar, shrugged, running his fingers absently through his hair.

"We can give you guidance and encouragement, but the choice is yours, and yours alone. You may not elect to fight. If that be the case, your education shall be erased, and you will be returned to Earth unharmed, where you may await your inevitable destruction with the rest of your race. If you decide to attack the Womongly, before they reach a tactical position for an assault on Earth, you will remain our guests until it is over. Nanta will be your home base, a safe refuge from the fighting. We must warn you, the combat will be vicious, and many, if not all, may have their lives terminated. If the battle is lost, we shall cry for your world, but we will not personally intercede in the fighting at any time. The God of Many Arms forbids it. The choice to fight for your world is yours, yours alone, and individually. It is the will of The God of Many Arms." She paused.

"Before I go on, are there any questions you would like to ask?"

Silence for a moment, then a young French pilot blurted out, "Why are we all Commanders?"

Dar thought the question to be 'so French' ~ to be concerned about rank at this stage of the game.

"You have all been given the same rank for now. You will sort out who will lead amongst yourselves. We shall not influence your decisions. It is our hope--."

The Viceroy of Peace sprouted a six inch hole in her chest. The ruby red glow passing through her disappeared, as she crumpled to the floor.

The arena went from total silence to chaos in a split second. Dar dove for the floor, as did all the pilots. Their combat reactions were taking control. Red blasts of light sought standing living targets. Lantiusians either stood frozen with fear, or ran from the red death. Fleeing for exits, they knocked companions to the floor, rapidly intensifying mass confusion and hysteria.

Four hotdog shaped creatures, each supported by three stumpy legs and holding short tapered tubes in sinewy arms, were blasting Nanta's defenseless audience. In seconds, the enormous hall was awash in dead and dying.

Littia stood staring at the attackers. She did not scream or try to flee. Like a doe caught in the headlights of an oncoming truck, her feet were rooted to the deck. The expression on her face exemplified absolute horror. "Womongly, it can't be . . . how . . . never . . . not here," she uttered softly over and over. Her people were dying, the red beam blasting closer to her with each passing moment.

Dar rolled under his seat, catching his breath, he tried to assess the situation. Bodies were beginning to fall near his position, when he noticed Littia still standing.

"Damn it," he muttered, rising from the protection of the seat to grab her around the hips. He pulled hard, knocking her off her feet. "Get down," he yelled, rolling on top of her.

Littia said nothing. *She's in shock*, Dar thought, looking franticly for Cannaly. Their eyes met. "These idiots are being slaughtered, "Dar yelled over the screams.

"Yeah. What can we do?" Cannaly yelled back.

" You go right, I'll go left. I don't think these things are expecting anyone to fight back. Go!"

Cannaly turned to his right and began running for an aisle. Dar did the same to his left. Other pilots, overhearing Dar's commands, followed them. By the time Dar and Cannaly had reached an aisle, half the pilots were close on their heels, ready to help. Dar waved the groups forward, went into a crouched position, and began duck-walking toward the enemy.

The attackers were murdering indiscriminately, completely immersed in their killing. The movement of several crouched humanoid figures struggling up the aisles on either side went unnoticed. Dar gave Cannaly an arm signal for the rush. Dar and his group poured over the Womongly as suddenly as the small creatures had begun their own attack.

The attacker, to Dar's surprise, as he threw a roundhouse punch to the midsection of the closest alien killer, had soft bodies. The killer's weapon clanged to the deck, flung from his arms by the force of Dar's blow. Dar expected them to be much stronger.

Each of the strange creatures wore a breast plate, designed to withstand low level thrumber fire, but its pliable metallic properties provided little protection against human fists, feet, and elbows.

Dar realized, as he and the others beat the small creatures with little mercy, without their weapons they were no match for the larger humans. In less than a minute the three Womongly lie dead. The killing of Lantiusians ended. The screaming did not.

Dar took in the pandemonium, nodded to Cannaly to standby, and tore off for Littia. She had not been hit when he'd knocked her down, but he was not sure she had stayed under the seat. Crashing through the confused and dazed crowd, Dar reached the front row moments later. She was still huddled where he'd left her minutes before.

"Littia, Littia, are you okay?" He knelt, gently rolling her over.

Littia's eyes opened sluggishly, their grey-green effervescence lost. Slowly, she focused on Dar. "Commander Fantin, we . . . .." Her voice trailed away.

Dar sat, drawing her onto his lap. "Hey, lady, don't you go and leave me now. I've just begun to get used to having you around," he said softly. Then yelling at the top of his voice, "Get medical help down here, NOW!"

A few of the Lantiusians, their wits returning slowly, began helping others. Within moments klaxons sounded throughout the ship. Kneeling beside him, a stately silver-haired Lantiusian assured Dar medical help was on the way.

Littia's eyes flickered opened, to look straight into Dar's. "We hope that you are all right, Commander Fantin."

"Littia, damn it, call me Dar," he said softly, as he gently squeezed her hand. "How are ya doing?"

"We shall be fine. What of the others?"

Dar could feel the horror of what she had witnessed pass through her mind. "Never mind that now. Are you okay?" He hugged her closer.

"Yes, we will be fine." She wiggled from Dar's arms. "Please, see if others need your help."

A blue tunic bent to Dar's aid. "We are a doctor, can we be of assistance?"

"I think she'll be okay, Doc, but please check her over anyway," Dar said. He let the doctor take her from his arms, standing to see what else he could do.

Cannaly, banging his way through the crowd with several of the pilots in tow, reached Dar's side. "What the hell have we gotten ourselves into, Dar?"

"I don't know, but it looks like we're into a fight whether we want it or not. We have got to have a meeting of the minds, ASAP."

"Okay, but . . ."

Before Cannaly could finish, a group of green clothed Lantiusian men gathered around them, "Please follow us, we shall take you to your quarters."

Dar saw that other pilots were being herded together as well. It was time to call it a day, relocate, readjust, and rethink the situation. "Just a minute, buddy, let me check on my guide." Without waiting for an answer, Dar knelt again by Littia.

"Littia, they are taking me back to my room. Will you come see me when you're feeling better?"

"We shall be there, Commander Fantin." A weak smile formed on her beautiful face. "We thank you, Dar."

Dar gave her hand a squeeze, rose, and followed the greenies out of the coliseum of death.

CHAPTER 5

The PCT ride through the ship was mass bedlam. Frightened Lantiusians swarmed in every direction. There appeared to be little aim or direction in their hubbub of activity. However, Dar felt sure there was definitive intent in the chaos. Emergency procedures of some sort, he imagined.

Their green clothed escorts remained on the tape, signaling the pilots to return to their rooms. Stepping from the PCT, Dar motioned to Cannaly, "Hey, Snake, join me in my quarters."

Cannaly flopped into a guest chair, while Dar arranged himself at the desk. "Damn, I haven't had so much fun since the hogs ate Willie," Cannaly said. "Just what's going on, Dar?"

"Your guess is as good as mine, but it's for darn sure, these tunic-clad hosts of ours aren't able to react to violence. Did you see them? They just stood there." Dar picked up a pen from the desk and flung it across the small room.

"Must have something to do with this God of Many Arms they talk about," Cannaly said, watching the pen roll to a stop. "Regardless, who in hell were those little bastards? Christ, they couldn't have been more than three feet tall, and soft as marshmallows. Where did they come from?"

"I think they were as big a surprise to the ship's crew as they were to us." Dar said. "My guess is, we've been rudely introduced to the Womongly. If there are anymore of the little SOBs around I'd say our lives are going to wind down very rapidly. The ship's crew won't fight, that's for sure." Dar stood and began pacing.

"You can say that again." Cannaly paused, looking around the room in thought. "Dar, what did you make of the lady's speech?"

"If we are to believe her, we're supposed to be the salvation of Earth. Sounds like something even a terrible science fiction writer would throw-up over." He stopped in mid-stride to face his friend. "These Womongly characters don't sound like the nicest of down-home folk to me, and, frankly, I wonder what a handful of fighter pilots can do about it."

"Damn it all, I could use a beer," Cannaly said.

A sharp rap sounded on the door.

"Come," Dar said. The door hissed open. "I'll be dipped. The thing opened at the sound of my voice."

Five pilots streamed through the open hatch, crowding into the small quarters. "Well, what the bloody hell's eyes are we going to do?" A British pilot spit out.

"Yeah," another of the group took up were the Brit had stopped. "I think this is pure crazy. Some of us have families. Wives and kids to think about. If they'll send us home, let's go for it."

Dar recognized the Brit as one of those who had helped subdue the Womongly. "I'm not going to do anything until I've got more information," he said, responding to both men. "I have a feeling the Viceroy of Peace had more information to relate than she was allowed time. Regardless, I need a few questions answered before I'm leaping into the breach one way or the other. What are your thoughts?" Dar questioned the remaining pilots.

"Yes. Agreed. Bloody hell, this is a mess though," the Brit retorted.

"Yeah, you're right about that. What's your name, anyway? I'm Dar Fantin. Dar extended his hand.

"Sorry, old chap. Danny Franklin, Royal Navy." He took Dar's hand firmly.

Introductions began around the room, as more of the pilots crammed into the room. Soon the inevitable questions echoed through the energetic conversations. "What do you fly? What do you suppose they've done to our birds? Do you really believe we can fly F-15s in space?" No one had a hard answer for any of the questions, but in the asking, nerves were calmed and the tentative bonds of a squadron began to form.

Dar had no idea how long the group had been yelling at each other, each trying to be heard, but he had an uneasy feeling he was supposed to have the answers to the myriad of questions firing back and forth like cannon shots. He didn't. He was in a void like everyone else. He was just about ready to start clearing his living spaces when an imposing man of well over seven feet appeared outside the door, obviously trying to gain the attention of the obstreperous group.

"Yo! We have company." Dar shouted over the babble.

The men quieted, as Dar moved through the crowded room to intercept the strikingly handsome Lantiusian clothed in a scarlet tunic. The giant's dark hair hung to his shoulders. Odd, considering he'd noticed that male crewmembers kept their hair short. The man's tunic had a startling amount of gold inscriptions embroidered into its satiny cloth, symbols Dar had not yet seen. It suddenly dawned on him, the educator had not taught him to read Lantiusian. *Darn inconvenient*, he thought.

"Please come in," Dar asked of his impressive guest.

"We thank you, Commander Fantin. We are called Supreme Commander Jicama. We command Nanta."

The man's words drew an immediate military reaction from the pilots crowding Dar's room. They came to attention, falling as silent as a jet flaming out at thirty thousand feet.

The response of the earthlings had an unusual affect on Jicama. He began to edge way from the hatch. Dar stepped smartly forward and took the surprised man's hand.

"Sir, I am Major Dar Fantin, United States Marine Corps. Welcome to my quarters."

Jicama looked directly into Dar's eyes, and with sudden understanding, smiled warmly. "Yes, now we understand. This formality has to do with your military status. We, on Nanta, are less formal regarding body language." He shook Dar's hand softly.

Dar felt from the light pressure the big man exerted on his hand that the Lantiusian was unsure what this touching of hands meant, but the big Commander did not wish to offend his guest. The pilots relaxed, but, as they would have in the presence of any commanding officer at home, stayed alert.

"Commander Fantin, we would like to extend our warmest thank you for what you and your men have done today. You saved Nanta, and for that, there is not enough we could possibly do for you in return."

"Thank you, sir," Dar said. "Glad we could help. Maybe in return you could fill us in on what's happening. We're pretty much in the dark about what happened this afternoon and why." Dar waved his arm, indicating the entire group needed some answers.

"In the dark? We do not understand. Is our illumination insufficient? I will have it increased immediately."

"Sorry, sir", Dar responded, a huge smile spreading across his face. "In the dark, means we don't know what's going on and would like some explanations," Dar said.

" Ah, yes. Your colorful mixing of Earth idioms with our language has a way of confusing us. We would be happy provide you with more details, Commander Fantin. Would you and your fellow commanders join me for dinner? Perhaps we can explain more profusely over a good meal."

"It would be our pleasure, sir. Just name the place and the time, and we'll be there with bells on, and thank you."

Again, Jicama studied the earthling before him. Dar could tell he was having trouble assimilating the manners and colloquialisms he fired at him. Standing at Jicama's shoulder, an aide, dressed in a lighter red tunic, whispered in Jicama's ear. Understanding twinkled in his dark green eyes.

"Yes, we understand. We shall have an aide here at the next hour to escort you and your pilots to the officers' bar. Of course, your guides will accompany you as well. Dinner will follow after a drink or two. If that will be acceptable, we shall look forward to your company." He smiled, spun on his heel, and trooped off for the PCT. A man accustomed to having his orders and requests followed, he felt no need of a response from Dar.

"Yes, sir." Dar spoke to the retreating figure, then turned to face the men gathered in his room. "Well y'all don't just stand there, get your rears in gear. It's shit, shower, and shave time."

CHAPTER 6

Dar was giving one last swipe over his highly polished boots with a cloth he'd found in his closet, when Littia's soft voice filled the room.

"Commander Fantin, we are here to join you. May we enter?"

Dar smiled. "Of course, come on in." The door disappeared revealing, not Littia, but a goddess. She had obviously spent a great deal of time dressing for the evening's event. The white tunic remained; however, jewels now adorned her neck. A string of roughly cut emerald colored stones hung between her breasts, catching the light in a manner that radiated a pale green aura from her shoulders to her tightly sashed waist. Most of Littia's golden hair had been swirled in tightly braided bands above her grey-green eyes, yet some of the spun gold hung in ringlets cascading down from the braids. The effect was stunning, forming a perfect frame for the most beautiful face Dar had ever witnessed. A touch of coloring on her lips finished the portrait to perfection.

"You look absolutely exquisite, Littia," Dar exclaimed, awe struck. "I don't think I've ever seen a more beautiful woman."

Littia stepped gracefully into the room, her tunic waving slightly with the movement. The light caught the stones differently, and the picture altered. She remained a wondrous work of art, but with subtle changes to the original portraiture. "We thank you, Commander Fantin. This is an important evening for me. We have never had the opportunity to be in the company of the Supreme Commander. We are but a guide." Her eyes radiated expectancy.

Dar ran his fingers through his hair, "You are far more than a mere guide, Littia." He paused, the smile evaporating. "Littia, are you all right?" Her presence had blanked his memory of the afternoon's encounter.

"We are fine, Commander Fantin, and we thank you. It may be that you saved my life. We are indebted to you."

Dar stepped closer, taking her hand in his. She resisted, then relaxed. "Littia, you don't have to thank me for anything. Past history. But there is one thing I do request. Please stop calling me Commander Fantin. I'm Dar." He held her eyes steady, gently squeezing her hand. "Please."

Almost shyly, Littia cocked her head, studying her charge intently. A smile played on her lips, "Very well, we shall call you Dar, if that is truly your wish."

Smiling back, Dar said, "You bet it is."

Voices and the sound of men moving from their quarters interrupted their conversation.

"Hey, Dar, the escort is here. Let's get a move on," Cannaly yelled through the open hatch, giving Dar an exaggerated wink. "Come on. Time's a wasting."

Reluctantly, Dar released Littia's hand, and extended his arm. Littia looked at him curiously, then, with understanding, laid her arm on his. The two joined the group following Jicama's aide.

The tape ride ended at an elevator. At least Dar thought of it as an elevator, since it was as close to his understanding as anything he could describe. The aide stepped from the solid deck of the passageway into a tube of soft light. The party-goers, looked questioningly at each other, then one by one, with gentle urging from their guides, tentatively followed Jicama's aide.

Dar's initial reaction, even with Littia on his arm, was to leap for the safety of the deck he'd just left. There was nothing but yellowish light, with nothing to indicate a top or bottom. Dar noticed he was not alone in his surprise and uneasiness. Others caught their breath in surprise when they stepped aboard. As more entered, the tube seemed to expand to accommodate their numbers. When all were loaded, the aide touched a symbol inscribed in the light.

There was little feeling of movement, yet the aide assured his guests they were smoothly rising twenty-one decks. Characters, flashing continuously on the wall of light, reflected from the occupant's eyes.

In what seemed to be but a moment, the aide stepped forward, signaling his charges to follow. *How*, Dar wondered, *did their escort know when we arrived? Apparently, their education wasn't as complete as it could have been. Was it the strange symbols flashing on the light? If he was to move about the ship with ease, he'd have to soon solve that problem.*

Turning to Littia, he started to ask her about the operation of the elevator, but was cut short with surprise.

Beyond the size of the room, which, like everything else he'd seen aboard Nanta, was gargantuan, the loud buzz of voices startled Dar. This was not like the auditorium, where talk had been subdued. Here, he felt he had just walked into the "Dirty Shame" smack dab in the middle of a Friday night Happy Hour. High pitched laughter filled the room, as a combo of musicians played loudly in a far corner of the vast enclosure.

"Commander Fantin, we are so pleased you have joined us," Supreme Commander Jicama said, suddenly appearing from the center of a nearby group of Lantiusians clothed in red tunics.

"Thank you, sir. Glad to be here," Dar answered. "Looks like you have quite a gathering this evening."

"Yes, we suppose we do. These are my officers who are not on duty. Most wish to express their appreciation for your heroic actions earlier today. We hope you do not mind."

"On the contrary, sir. Flattered would be more like it," Dar said, nodding at Earth's delegation. His eyes caught Littia's. "Supreme Commander, do you know Littia?" Dar felt the hand on his arm tighten.

"We have not had the pleasure," Jicama said, a smile forming on his handsome face.

Dar registered Jicama's smile as genuine, and that he obviously appreciated Littia's beauty as much as he did.

"We are Littia, Guide 3rd Class, Supreme Commander," Littia shyly interrupted. "We feel diminutive in your presence." She gave a slight bow to the tall Commander.

"We all are needed in the eyes of the God of Many Arms," Commander Jicama said still smiling. He turned from Littia to face Dar. "Would you and your companions join me at the bar?"

"Sir, I thought you would never ask," Dar said. "Lead on."

As the group moved for the bar, the guides formed into a group, leaving their charges to their own devices. Dar captured Littia's eye as she released his arm. He'd hoped she would not leave his side; however, to his disappointment, was left with nothing but a flash of a knowing smile.

"We shall be close by, Dar, and we shall join you for dinner," Littia said softly.

"There you go again." Dar returned the smile. "Reading my mind."

Before he could say more, he was swept to the bar with Cannaly and the others. The drinks were powerful and tasty, though a good old rum and coke would have been more to Dar's liking. Still, the company was excellent, the conversation furious, and the drinks free. *What more could a fighter pilot ask for,* he thought, as he met yet another of Nanta's officers, then turned to the Nanta's leader.

"Supreme Commander," Dar started his question. "How many of your people died this afternoon?" He knew the question was a bold step, but what the heck, he'd been known a firebrand for years among his superior officers in the Corps. Why let the big Lantiusian cower him.

Jicama's smile faded. "Ah, we are afraid that thirty-three of us have been received by our God of Many Arms this day. Had it not been for you and your men, many more would have died."

"Well, sir, I must admit that there was a thought or two of self preservation running through my mind at the time. I just don't get it, sir, why your people won't lift a finger to save their own lives. Plus, I just flat don't understand how your security, if you have any, could possibly allow the enemy aboard."   Dar knew he was treading on thin ice. His education clearly told him of the non-violent nature of the Lantiusians. He watched Jicama's face darken.

"Commander Fantin, it is just our way. Please let us talk of happier things."

Captain Langos was furious; all three and a half feet of him. His normally pinkish complexion took on a definite red tinge around his yellow, owl-like, eyes. If he'd had a neck, his head would have been jutting forward in anger. Langos had been the captain of the Dectima for ten years, and the report just given by his First Officer infuriated him. "Failed? Failed? Is that all I get out of you? Tales of failure?" Langos stomped forward on three stubby legs, waving thin muscular arms. The four frightened officers he was facing backed away from his fury. "I do not want to hear of your inept attempts. Success is the reason we are here, not to be brought down by a few humans." The sibilant sound of the s's his language required, resembled that of a rattlesnake trying to speak.

"Captain, we had no knowledge of the fighting characteristics of these earthlings," the First Officer whined, fearful of the small captain. Desperately, he continued. "As yet, we are not totally defeated. There is still one of us aboard Nanta. He may well succeed where the others failed."

Captain Langos stopped his fuming, reflected a moment. "True. All may not be lost. Has Combat Operations devised a plan?" A normal pinkish hue spread over his face, as breathing flaps stopped fluttering in frustration.

"They have," the First Officer answered, with more confidence than he felt. "A diversion, giving the remaining member of the insertion team an opportunity to take Nanta off guard. One Womongly against the entire Nanta's crew is sufficient. They refuse to fight."

"Yes, yes," Captain Langos said, irritation welling up once more. "What of the earthlings? We now know they will not just stand to be exterminated like the Lantiusians." He spat "Lantiusian" out as if his tiny oval mouth had been filled with rotting meat.

The First Officer shrugged. "What can they do against a blast from a thrumber or sub-particle beam? They have no weapons, though we now know they will fight back. Our remaining Rage Warrior will be more careful this time. His intentions are to kill the earthlings first, then start on the Lantiusians."

"I like it," Captain Langos hissed. The plan pleased him. The blue planet would yet be his. Such a beautiful world, and so filled with the resources desperately needed on Womongly. Earth was perhaps their last chance of survival.

"Our home planet equates time much as your Earth does, by its revolutions about our two suns. However, by a Lantiusian calendar, two of Lantius years are but six months by Earth standards." Commander Jicama was explaining to Dar what the Viceroy of Peace had meant by their short evaluation period of Earth.

The two were sitting side-by-side at the head table in a banquet room the size of a blimp hangar. Dar was pleased to find the chairs had been modified to accommodate the rears of he and his comrades. Hundreds of tables were strung in lines before them, each filled to capacity with Lantiusians eating quietly. Cannaly, along with the remaining pilots and their guides, sat to Jicama's left, as voluminous amounts of food was served from carts pushed by yellow clad men and women.

"That is why we chose to, ah, how to phase this correctly, *borrow* your world's finest fighter pilots." Jicama continued. "By our calendar we had little time to learn your languages, let alone negotiate with the multiplicity of governments your world supports. Of course we had to train a few of our guides in the languages of the pilots we brought aboard, but that was to put you at ease as you came aboard. Once educated, language was no longer a problem." The big Lantiusian paused, then sighed heavily in thought. "Your abduction, we are sad to say, was the cause of the deaths this afternoon, and it was my orders that brought you here."

Dar's temper flared momentarily at the thought his being aboard Nanta might be the cause of so many deaths. "We did not ask to be here," he said irritably. With his comment, he saw a change in Jicama's disposition.

"My apologies, sir." Jicama lowered his eyes to the table. "We did not mean to offend. We assume this small enemy force came aboard along with one of your Earth's fighters. It seems unlikely, but it appears the Womongly fighters, have now been modified for jump flight, allowing them to follow our shuttle to Earth. Apparently, the Womongly were able to slip aboard with one of your aircraft. We have yet to discover how, but we shall."

Littia nervously watched the two men exchange words. No one ever questioned the Supreme Commander. She tried firing a "mind" warning at Dar.

Dar sat upright, startled by a sudden flash of color across his central nervous system. He quickly scanned those around him, catching Littia's eyes staring intently at him. She nodded slightly. She's warning me, he realized with utter amazement. He turned back to his host. "My apologies as well, Supreme Commander. It is just, well, this whole thing is hard for us to swallow, but now that we're here, I think I can speak for most of us when I say we will stay and fight. We'll need your help and some time to get organized, but we *will* fight."

The tense exchange had gained the attention of Cannaly and others near by. "We'll fight," Cannaly spoke loudly.

Captain Langos nodded to his First Officer, "Fire!"

Minutes later, four thermal nuclear torpedoes struck Nanta's protective shield simultaneously. The explosive force of just one weapon comparable to a dozen of the most powerful nuclear weapons known on earth detonating at the same instant. Nanta rocked savagely from the blow, but her shields held.

Confusion reigned throughout the hall, as the great ship's artificial gravity generators hiccuped from the blast. Groans, grunts, and cries for help surged from every corner. Bones snapped as bodies piled up against chairs, tables, and bulkheads. Food flew throughout the hall, covering the walls and floor.

A cart, weighted with food, toppled near the head table, its bright covering stripped away by a waiter flying six feet into the surrounding mayhem.

The Womongly wiggled free of the cart's lower tray where he had hidden for several hours, waiting for the torpedoes.

Dar, thrown from his chair, landed in a heap against the bulkhead. He caught a glimpse of an airborne Supreme Commander Jicama a split second before the wind was knocked out of him by the big man's weight. Dar doubled up in pain.

Once free of the confines of the cart, the Womongly, his dark breast plate reflecting the room's light, spun in a circle, taking in the room at a glance. He found what he wanted ~ the head table. Advancing around tangled bodies, he approached the table searching for targets. He raised his thrumber rifle and fired.

Cannaly rolled to his left and coughed green soup from his throat. He'd been thrown face down into his own bowl when the torpedoes impacted. Unhurt, he struggled to his feet, to look smack-dab into the owlish eyes of the Womongly. He dove for cover. A red blast sliced a gash in the table where he had been a heartbeat prior.

The rifle barked softly once more. A Russian pilot fell dead, his arm smashing Cannaly's right eye as he hit the deck. The deadly light flashed again further down the table, and another pilot's chest disappeared.

Rolling Jicama aside, Dar realized the big man was unconscious. Relieved of the Lantiusian's weight, he gasped for breath and heard the first blast of the rifle. He had no trouble recognizing the weapon's dissonant discharge so soon after the afternoon's killings. Frantically, he searched for Littia. With some relief, he spotted her lying under the table with a chair canted on her legs, apparently as unconscious as Jicama.

"Christ, not again," Dar yelled in disbelief. Still struggling for air, he crawled toward Littia, his peripheral vision catching Cannaly diving for the deck. Then the Russian went down. "Snake, you all right?" Dar screamed over the din of noise and confusion.

"Yeah, I'm okay for now," Cannaly yelled back. "Dar, the damned thing is going after *us*."

Cannaly's words took a moment to register. Then it hit him. They had no weapons, nothing to fight back with, and *they* were the targets, not the Lantiusians. The Womongly had learned their lesson well, and planned to kill them before exterminating Nanta's crew.

Two more blasts from the thrumber ripped through the table forty feet away. One shot missed. The other took an arm off the young Frenchman who had asked the rank question during the afternoon's briefing. Dar stared in astonishment. There was no blood. The arm was cleanly severed, but there was no blood. The man crumpled to the deck in shock. Dar's mind raced. He grabbed a plate, and stood.

Dar saw the Womongly immediately. The little killing machine was a lone predator among terrified sheep. He was concentrating his fire at the far end of the table. The shots burned holes through the wooden table looking for flesh hidden behind its formidable structure.

"Hey, asshole," Dar howled, hurling the plate at the small creature with the big gun.

A beam of red light sizzled over Dar's head as he dove for cover, rolling over several times when he hit the deck. Two more blasts, a pause, and then the Womongly returned to his systematic blasting of the far end of the table.

"Throw and roll," Dar yelled at Cannaly. "Throw and roll."

"Throw and roll, " Cannaly yelled back, picking up a plate.

Danny Franklin watched in horror when Dar stood with a plate. Now, hearing Cannaly and Dar's exchange, he understood as well. He started passing the word down the line, "Throw and roll," demonstrating as he yelled.

Plates, bowls, and mugs were their only ammunition, but there was no lack of these items, Dar realized.

Cannaly stood, heaved a plate and dove for the deck, rolling as he hit. A red slash of light melted the bulkhead above him. Danny threw his bowl, and the rifle barked in his direction.

Dar scuttled like a frighten crab for the far end of the table, checking Littia as he passed. She appeared to be breathing, but he couldn't stop to check. Moving rapidly, he scrambled over unconscious and terror frozen Lantiusians. He rounded the end of the table, never slowing his pace, his knees and arms pumping furiously.

Their attacker was being pummeled with food and tableware, confusing him just enough to hinder his violent attack. Bewildered or not, the Womongly continued his offensive on the head table.

Dar was twenty feet behind the assailant. He had stayed low, always keeping cover between himself and the Womongly, but now he was in the open. He began running, legs driving like a fullback's.

Dar tackled the Womongly dead center. The little, soft-bodied, three-legged creature's innards turned to mush. It died before he and Dar hit the floor. The rifle went airborne, landing near the head table. Dar untangled himself, stood, and kicked the remains several times squarely in the face. Slowly, still full of adrenaline, he walked to the weapon. Scooping the rifle from the floor, he looked up to see Cannaly grinning at him.

"I think I'll hang on to this thing for a while," Dar said. "I just hope I can figure out how to use it before this happens again."

CHAPTER 7

Dar rolled off his pallet of air, groaning as sore muscles let him know, in no uncertain terms, they were not impressed by his recent activities. Sitting on warm jets of air, he leaned forward, letting his arms dangle to the floor. *I've got muscles where muscles shouldn't be*, he thought. He stood, glancing at the ship's clock over the desk. It told him nothing, as he again realize he could not read Lantiusian. *Still, it felt like early morning*, he thought, and walked slowly to the shower.

Twenty minutes later, Dar felt almost human, shaking off a poor night's sleep. The long, hot sonic shower loosened tight muscles, putting a semblance of life back in them. Slipping on his flight suit, he reflected on the prior evening, thankful they had lost only four pilots. The Frenchman, Dar tried to recall his name but memory failed him, had been removed to the ship's infirmary, with assurances from both Littia and Jicama of a rapid recovery. He'd been guaranteed the arm would be replaced with a prosthesis more powerful and capable than the original flesh and blood. Littia suffered bruises, but no concussion from the lump on her head. On the other hand, Jicama's seriously split forehead would take him out of commission for a few days. They had been lucky, darn lucky.

"Hey, Cuda, you in there?" It was Cannaly.

"Yeah, come on in," Dar said. The door slid open at his words. He rubbed his fingers through his hair then shook his head. *A wonderment,* he thought, *this device which seems to know precisely when to open and close.*

"Get your rear in gear, Cuda. We're having a meeting of the minds outside in the corridor. Come on, let's go."

"Meeting of the minds? What are you talking about?" Dar struggled into his boots.

"All the pilots are gathering to decide what we're going to do, geez, man, it's not every damned day you have to do battle twice with some gawd awful aliens." Cannaly responded.

Now that Cannaly mentioned it, Dar realized there were voices engaged in excited discussions just outside his quarters. "My mind was a thousand miles away," Dar said. "I didn't even notice. I'll be right there."

Moments later, Dar stepped from his room into the large hallway, the door closing behind him. The chaotic chatter immediately fell silent as if the group had been waiting impatiently for his arrival. Taken aback by the intense stares directed in his direction, Dar finally asked, "All right, what's going on? Did I miss something, or do I have a banana in my ear?"

Cannaly, grinning maliciously, slapped Dar on the back, "About time you joined us, *boss,*" he said.

Dar glared at Cannaly. "What are you talking about, Snake? I think you've lost what few marbles you had left in your brain housing group. What's this boss crap?"

"While you were trying to shake the sleep out of your eyes, the rest of us sort of --" Cannaly smiled again. "Well, we all got together and elected you squadron commander. Hell, boss, every fightn' outfit has to have a leader, and you, my friend, are ours. Congratulations."

"Right. Since when did we become a squadron?" Dar asked, slouching against the wall, while giving Cannaly a who-do-you-think-you're-kidding look.

"Since we bloody hell decided to stay and fight," Danny Franklin said. "If we're taking on the Womongly, we need proper military organization, and the first order of business was a squadron leader." A grin spread across his thin face. "And, old chap, you're it." He stepped forward to take Dar's hand. My congrats as well, Senior Commander. Good show, I'd say."

"Senior Commander?" Dar came upright off the wall. Danny had his full attention.

"That's right. Since everyone here has been dubbed a Commander by our hosts, we had to conjure up a proper title for our Commanding Officer. We --," Danny waved his hand, indicating the group, "hereby christen you Senior Commander. What the bloody hell, you don't even have to kneel to receive the title."

The group laughed, a hearty laugh of rudimental unity. The humor dispelled a small portion of the tension the band felt since their arrival.

"What other momentous decisions have you ragtag, no count aviators made in my absence?" Dar asked. "I don't suppose you thought to ask my opinion?"

"Well, let me put it to y'all this way," Tom Bennett, the F-16 pilot from Texas drawled, "your unit is formed. Commander Cannaly here is your Executive Officer, Franklin will be Operations, and the rest of us will fly hell out of whatever they are makin' out of our jets."

"That's right," Cannaly said. "We don't figure we'll need more command structure until we know for sure what's in store for us. We'll determine flight leaders later, after we get a chance to see what each of our talents are."

Dar looked around at his newly formed squadron. He felt humbled by the entire situation. Never placed in the position of squadron command before, it was nevertheless something he'd dreamed of since pinning on the gold bars of a Second Lieutenant. Now he was being thrown into the position under very unusual circumstances. *Was he ready?* Dar wondered.

"Okay then, that's settled," Cannaly said. "What's the first order of business, boss?"

Dar thought for a minute. "Eat. Let's get some breakfast then regroup back here. I have some thinking to do. One thing you can count on though, and I mean this, I'll try not to let you down."

"Attention," Danny ordered.

The gathering of Earth's finest young military aviators came to attention. They had familiar structure around them now. It felt reassuring to take action and have a leader they trusted, though untried.

"Dismissed," Danny ordered.

As men headed for the tape, Dar grabbed Cannaly's arm. "Wait a minute, asshole. You did this. I know you did."

"I just helped them see the light, that's all. Seriously, Dar, you are the best man for the job, so stop your bitching and let's get on with it."

"Okay, Snake," Dar said, smiling for the first time. "But first, what the hell is wrong with your eye? And don't give me, 'you should see the other guy' nonsense."

Cannaly's smile faded. "That big Russian's elbow clipped me when he went down yesterday. Damn, what a mess that was."

"I'm sorry, I should have known." Dar meant it, he was sorry and he should have guessed. "Have you had it looked at?"

"Nah, it's fine; not to worry. So what have you got in mind for this new command of yours?"

Dar thought for a moment. "Well, for starters we need to know that we aren't going to be surprised by those damnable little hotdog Womongly again. Plus, on the same line, I'd sure as hell like to have a sidearm of some sort. Then we'll need access to the elevators, or whatever those light tubes are, and instructions on how to operate them. We need the freedom they will give us to move around the ship and meet Nanta's crew on a work-a-day level. Finally, if we are going to take this unit into combat, we need to prepare physically. I want Danny to have his guide arrange for an exercise area where we can start PT. We'll need PT gear ~ shoes, shorts, T-shirts. In the meantime, you and I are going to get some answers. You know, little things, like where in hell are we in relationship to Earth, how long do we have before this war begins, where are our aircraft, and when can we start flying."

"Christ all mighty, Dar, where have you been hiding? Anyone would've thought you knew you were going to be the CO."

"It never crossed my mind." Dar said, with complete sincerity. "But I realized early on if we were to stay and fight, we'd have to organize, and start training, like yesterday."

"Right, but we don't have a clue where our planes are, much less the engineering required for their refit."

"That's our task for today. I'll talk to Littia. I think she trusts me enough to help get the ball rolling. What about your guide, could he be of any help?" Dar rubbed his hand over his eyes in concentration, trying to think of anything he might have missed.

"I honestly don't know," Cannaly said. "We certainly don't have the rapport you and Littia have, but he's been helpful and friendly. I'll see what I can do."

"Good. How about some chow before we leap into the breach?"

The two men walked to the PCT, each filled with germinating hopes about the future.

Captain Langos stared through the large view port on his command deck. To an outsider, the small man-creature might have appeared at peace with his world. In actuality, the tranquil countenance displayed by the captain was light years apart from his raging internal turmoil. Langos took no notice of the view ~ thousands of sparkling diamonds suspended in the panoramic beauty of cold space. Dectima's crew had failed once again. An intolerable defeat. He could feel the anger welling within his chest, making it difficult to breathe the heavily moisture weighted air required by the Womongly.

Dectima, floated motionless in space, maintaining a distance of several hundred thousand miles from the Lantiusian ship. Langos, shifting his third leg into a more comfortable position on his command stool, irritably reflecting on previous events. The torpedoes, though deadly to every ship in the known universe, had no more effect on the Nanta than if he'd tried to slap her with a norpeswatter from the planet Mentbols. Of course, he'd known that would be the case when he'd given the order to fire, but his agent inside Nanta was to coordinate the distraction with the annihilation of the Lantiusians. His hatred of Lantiusians bubbled deep in his gut. What right, Langos fumed, did they have keeping him from resources so desperately required for the survival of his race?

The insurgent, equipped with a micro-broadcaster embedded at the center of his breastplate, had given Langos vicarious pleasure as he watched the earthlings die on the VID screen. Viewing the killing field, his growing anticipation changed to alarm as the sandy brown haired human moved from the cover of the overturned table. His Rage Warrior died easily at the hands of the earth man. Rodinium breastplates gave little protection when engaged in hand-to-hand combat. What tenacity these humans have, to attack a Warrior carrying a thrumber rifle armed with nothing but one's wits and brawn, Langos thought. It was pure madness, and their lunacy gave him little comfort now. Dectima would have to face whatever the Lantiusians had planned for Earth's defense, and any defense would involve the few demented earthlings aboard Nanta, of that he was sure.

"Sir, you asked to see me?" Dectima's First Officer asked tentatively, interrupting Langos' introspection.

Slowly, Langos turned to meet his second in command. Saying nothing, he stood, untangling his third leg from behind the command stool. "Ah, First Officer, thank you for coming," Langos crooned.

"What can I do for you, sir?" The frightened officer asked, his breathing flaps fluttering. He had seen his captain's exceeding cool composure on two occasions. In neither case did it bode well. When Captain Langos emanated total calm, there had to be a solar storm raging within.

"You failed me once again. Is that not so?" Langos' round mouth hissed the words with honey dripping from each syllable.

"Sir, we tried." He took a step back, his polymorphous facial tissue subtly changing to yellowish fear. "The earthlings are fighters of some magnitude. Who would have guessed they would put themselves before the blast of a thrumber?"

"Yes, yes, who would have guessed? Still, you failed, and I have grown very weary of your operational miscarriages." Langos straightened his breastplate, hiked up his blue pantaloons, and pulled a twelve inch tube from his belted waist.

Before the unfortunate First Officer could react, Langos tripped a small switch on the tube. A seven foot whip of fire curled wickedly from the tube's mouth. With lightning speed, Langos raised the whip and slashed out. There was no report from the whip, as it missed the cowering First Officers' large right ear by inches. Langos drew his arm up for another strike, then slowly lowered the still sizzling weapon to his side. "You are relieved of all further duties aboard Dectima," he hissed, letting the whip extinguish. "Confine yourself to your quarters until further notice."

Langos turned, walked stiffly to his command station, settling once again on the stool. He stared, undisturbed, into the reaches of space.

"I've got to see what we are up against." Dar was imploring Littia for aid. "Can't you arrange for me to see Supreme Commander Jicama, or at least his second in command?"

Dar had noticed Littia, totally absorbed in eating, sitting at a table as he entered the mess hall. She looked as beautiful as ever in a fresh white tunic with golden hair cascading to her waist. He grabbed a plate of yellowish green goop from the serving line and chose a seat with Cannaly across from her.

"We are but a Guide 3rd Class, Dar. We do not operate in the same circles as the senior officers." Littia said with resignation. She wiped a small fleck of food from her lightly lavendered lips, not looking at Dar.

With some desperation, Dar pleaded, "Look, I have been chosen as the leader of this gaggle of fighter pilots. You brought us here to fight. To fight, we need weaponry and information. I have to talk to Jicama." He laid his hands flat on the table between them. "I need your help, I've got nowhere else to turn."

Littia smiled warmly, her eyes lighting up with pleasure. "Dar, you are their leader? We are so pleased. My senses told me something of importance occurred involving you. That is what the Supreme Commander has been waiting for ~ a leader, selected by your own. We shall talk to my supervisor immediately, and we are sure you will be asked to an audience with Supreme Commander Jicama shortly after his receiving knowledge of this matter."

"Thank you," Dar said, relief clearly evident. "By the way, how do you feel? You took some pretty hard knocks yesterday."

"We are fine. Lantiusians heal rapidly," Littia answered. "We shall go and make your request now."

"Sit down, Littia. You haven't finished your second plate yet, and I've noticed how much Lantiusians love their food." Dar smiled. "See, I'm learning."

Littia returned his smile. "Yes, you are learning a little, we suppose," she said, and touched his hand gently.

CHAPTER 8

Pacing between the bulkheads of his small room like a young bull, Dar was ready to blow propriety and charge off to find Nanta's bridge on his own. He'd been waiting in his quarters, where Littia suggested he remain until she or an aide came for him. That was at breakfast, and he'd skipped lunch as the hours ticked by, but there had yet to be a summons. Patience, he knew, was never one of strong suits.

Danny Franklin, his newly elected Operations Officer, had just left, after passing on the first welcome news of the day. His guide was making arrangements for both a physical training area and provisioning of proper PT gear. The pilots would be outfitted by evening.

Cannaly remained with Dar until his friend's impatience and ill humor grew thin, then took off to find out about the elevator situation. Alone now, Dar plopped down at his desk, threw one leg over the back of his guest chair and fumed.

"Senior Commander Fantin?" An unfamiliar voice asked from outside his door. The question was followed by a soft knock.

"Yes. Come in." Dar's voice clearly reflected irritation.

The door slid from sight, revealing a giant of over eight feet, tall even by Lantiusian standards. The titan's short cropped golden hair and brown eyes were accented by a shamrock green tunic of an officer's aide.

Dar was still irritable. "Well, just don't stand there, y'all come on in," he said, and untangled his leg from the chair. "I hope you've come to take me to see the Supreme Commander."

Ducking through the door jamb, the visitor entered looking questioningly at Dar. "We do not understand, 'y'all'. Please explain."

"What? It's nothing but a southern colloquialism, for Pete's sake." Dar was still ill-tempered from the waiting. "What can I do for you?"

"Senior Commander Fantin, we have come to escort you to the Supreme Commander," the tall man said quietly. "We did not mean to offend."

"Forget it," Dar said contritely. "I didn't mean to snap at you. You're just doing your duty. My apologies. Just give me a moment to clean up a bit." He made his way to the small head, leaving his visitor momentarily alone.

"We are sorry, Dar," The voice was soft in his mind, but distinct. "Please do not be angry with Aide 1st Class Dimara, it was my fault you have had to wait so long. We could not see my superior until an hour ago."

"Littia? My God, you can read my mind from anywhere?" It was a question more than a statement. "Where are . . . .?" Dar stopped in mid sentence, realizing he was talking to himself in the mirror. *This 1st Class aide must think I'm nuts*, he thought.

"Perhaps, but then most Lantiusians think all of the earthlings are crazy. We have never seen anyone attack a Womongly without weapons."

"Stop it, Littia. "Where are you?"

"We are with Supreme Commander Jicama. He is awaiting your audience, and Dar, you do not need to speak aloud. Just think your words to me."

"Damn it all, I hope you're the only one reading my mind. Tell him I'm on my way." This time he thought the words, picturing Littia as he did so.

"That was well done, Dar. We shall be waiting."

Dar's mind cleared as suddenly as it had been filled with Littia's voice. *How does she do that, for that matter, how in hell am I doing it*, he thought emphatically, leaving the head for the main room. He nodded to the big man, "Please, Dimara, I am ready."

The giant looked quizzically at Dar. "Excuse me, Sir, but how did you come to know my name? We do not believe we provided you that information."

Dar stammered for words. He wasn't sure he should reveal his source. Instinctively, he decided to down play the situation. "Oh, ah, I must have heard it at the dinner. You're a hard man to miss."

His quick answer appeared to placate the bulldozer of a Lantiusian, as he turned to lead Dar toward the PCT.

Dar followed the aide through a maze of corridors, tapes, and light tubes. He was completely lost by the time they reached a section clearly designed as a medical facility. To enter, both men passed through two distinct isolation areas, where once again, Dar felt the tingle of an electrical charge passing over his body. Reminiscent of his first hours aboard Nanta. They were greeted by a nurse dressed in a medical blue tunic, who immediately recognized the big aide. With a brief nod, she indicated that they should continue down the long passageway.

"Come in, Senior Commander Fantin," Jicama's command voice resonated through hall. "We can't express enough our pleasure at your being selected leader of the Earth pilots. We believe it is appropriate for earthlings to touch hands on such occasions?" In good spirits, Jicama offered his hand.

"Thank you, sir," Dar said, taking the offered hand, and noticing Littia sitting quietly in a back corner of the large room.

"We have much to discuss, my friend," Jicama said. "Please have a seat, that we might talk."

The aide slid a chair under Dar, and was waved away by Jicama. As the big man took his leave, Littia rose as well.

"Please, sir. If it would be okay with you, I'd like Littia to remain. She is my guide, as you know, and may be of some help, besides she reads my mind and will know what we talk about anyway."

"What? This Guide is reading your mind. This should not be so," Jicama sat upright, the air bed shifting to accommodate his weight, his surprise and anger evident.

Littia took a step back, as if hit. Dar came rapidly to her defense. "Sir, she has my permission to do so. We talked of this early in our acquaintance. Please, it is not her fault. Just an oddity"

"I see. Still this is highly irregular, and, for that matter, quite unusual. Normally, mental joining is rare among Lantiusians, but to have such a link with an alien species is practically nonexistent."

"Well, sir, to me *you're* the alien, not me." Dar was smiling.

For several seconds, Jicama looked intently at the earthling and then started laughing. "I like you, young Earthman. May I call you Dar?"

"Certainly, sir," Dar responded, somewhat flattered.

"Again, the Nanta is in your debt. There is no one in our known universe who would dare call the men from Earth cowards." Jicama praised, then turned serious. "We are indeed sorry for your losses. The Womongly's intent was clearly evident, and if it were not for fast thinking on your part, I fear all would have been lost. We and the crew thank you."

"Thank you, again sir, but I assure you I was not thinking so much about saving the Nanta as my own rear end,"

"Own rear end?" Jicama asked, his eyes clouded in question and thought.

"My ass," Dar said, and patted his buttocks.

With understanding, the Supreme Commander again laughed. "We have much to learn about your language and its translation to Lantiusian. Now down to business. My First Officer will be joining us momentarily. He will take you to the bridge, where you may ask any questions you desire. We have instructed all personnel to help you in every matter you require."

"Thank you sir, that will be helpful. My first questions are to you, however. With your permission, of course." Dar paused, rubbing a hand through his hair in thought. Are there going to be any more little surprise encounters with these Womongly?"

"Right that you should ask," the injured Supreme Commander answered softly. The answer is no. The ship was in the process of being searched when the second attack occurred. Every compartment and cupboard has been cleared. We should not expect another attack aboard Nanta."

Dar nodded. "I accept you confidence, sir, but would it be possible for myself and my officers to be provided with side arms just incase? Quite frankly, I don't wish to meet another Womongly unarmed."

Jicama sat quietly in thought for a moment before responding. "You have the thrumber rifle, we believe. At least that was the information we were given. I'm afraid that will have to suffice for the moment. Nanta's engineers are absorbed in the construction of you fighters. We do not wish to deviate their efforts. Please be assured there will be no further attacks. We shall, however, have a technician explain the use of the rifle to you. Will that surfice?"

Dar grimaced with displeasure at Jicama's answer. "Yes, that would be most helpful. Thank you." Sighing with resignation he asked, "How long do we have until this war begins, and where are we going to fight ~ here or closer to Earth? I'm presuming we are far from Earth."

Again, Supreme Commander Jicama did not respond immediately, taking a moment to think his answer through. A naturally cautious man, he did not wish to give this earthman unverifiable information. He gently smoothed the reddened bandage over the gash on his forehead. "We are not sure. Womongly are extraordinary strategists and have destroyed or enslaved hundreds of worlds. As we understand their problem, they must evade Nanta to pull closer to Earth, and they are aware that is impossible; our surveillance is far superior to the Dectima's. Still, the captain clearly understands we will not fight, so that leaves one unknown to him ~ the Earthlings. He undoubtedly has some respect for you and your men. We found a mini-broadcaster on each of his insurgent agents, so this captain has seen you in action, and that might have him shaken. My guess, and this is just a guess, is that he will not wish to begin a fight without further knowledge of the capabilities of you and your men. If that is the case, I think you should have up to two Earth weeks in which to prepare."

Dar nodded understanding. "And the where?" He asked.

Jicama, unaccustomed to long speeches or being interrogated, drew a breath. "We think he will maneuver to a position behind Earth's single moon. This would provide him natural space concealment from which he could fly his attack craft." He paused, brow raised in thought. "Yes, we are sure that is where he will take the Dectima --."

"POOF"

Before the Supreme Commander could finish speaking, there was an audible popping sound, and, to Dar's amazement, the ugliest creature he'd ever seen appeared on the air bed next to Jicama. Adrenaline flowing, Dar immediately took a fighting stance, surprised at the broad smile appearing on Jicama's face.

"Well, there you are. Where have you been these last few days?" Jicama intoned, reaching out to lightly stroke the hideous little brown beasty.

Relaxing, as he watched Jicama caress what appeared to be a tiny kangaroo with a frog-like head, Dar asked, "What's that?"

Dar felt Littia tickle his mind with mild laughter, as Jicama ruffled the animal's scaly surface and crooned softly as if speaking to a child.

Still grinning, Jicama glanced up at his guest. "Loto, meet Dar, Dar this is Loto. She's an utapotus. Come, give her a stroke, she loves to be petted."

Unsure about the small scaly animal, Dar tentatively reached out to touch the ugly utapotus. "She's soft as mink," Dar exclaimed in surprise. "I would have thought she'd feel reptilian."

Jicama laughed, as did Littia. She moved from the corner to join the men, reaching down to stroke Loto with Dar. The utapotus rewarded their ministrations with pleasurable bubbling sounds, and curled tighter next to Jicama.

"Well, if this don't beat all. Where did she come from?" Dar drawled, still stroking Loto.

"We have no idea," Jicama answered. "They have been native to Lantius since time remembered. Our scientists have never been able to discover where they come from or where they go. They just are. Still, they're wonderful to have around, and every Lantiusian would love to be chosen. Unfortunately, very few of us are ever graced with a utapotus's company"

"Chosen? I don't understand," Dar looked with bewilderment at the grotesque little pet.

"*They* choose whom they will grace with their company," Jicama answered, "and once favored, the utapotus will remain until their chosen companion's death. There can be tangible rewards with having been singled out as a companion as well."

"Really? I'm almost afraid to ask what those might be," Dar asked, still lightly brushing the soft scales.

"They can warn of personal danger, or good tidings; in some cases they can even communicate the future arrival of a visitor, things of that nature," Littia said. She was smiling. "But their greatest quality is that of creating a calming influence and a relaxing atmosphere."

Dar noted how the pressures of the last hours seemed to melt into oblivion as he massaged Loto. He felt as if he had not a care in the world. *What a marvelous creature to have as a pet*, he thought.

"May we enter?" It was First Officer Tamus.

"Come," Jicama ordered, but the tranquility in the inflection betrayed his relaxed mood. "Dar, this is my second in command,

Tamus. He will escort you to the bridge, and again, he will answer any questions you have."

Dar stuck out his right hand to the handsome Lantiusian. "Nice to meet you, sir."

The First Officer stared at the earthling questioningly.

"Tamus, take the man's hand," Jicama explained. "It appears the touching of hands has some importance to our guests."

"It is one of our formal ways of greeting," Dar explained, taking the offered hand, shaking it firmly. He turned to Littia, who still stroked Loto with noticeable pleasure. "Littia, will you accompany us to the bridge?"

"We would be most happy to do so," she responded. With reluctance she shifted her attention from the utapotus.

"With your permission, sir, I would like to begin the tour. Would it be all right for me to return later this evening, should I need more information?" The question was directed to Jicama.

"Of course. You have direct access to me at any time. In fact . . .," Jicama turned his attention back to the First Officer . . . "Tamus, please issue Dar, and his second in command, we understand they call him an Executive Officer, with a VVCom." Jicama returned his attention to Dar, "With the View/Voice Communicator you can reach me instantly from anywhere on the ship."

"Thank you, sir, that would be helpful." Dar directed his attention back to Tamus. "I'm ready if you are, sir."

The three left the hospital, passing once again through the electrostatic entrances. *No germs in, no germs out*, Dar thought on the short PCT ride to the nearest light tube. The elevator whisked them up thirty decks to the Nanta's upper most level, followed by another much longer tape ride to the entrance of the bridge.

Stepping through the large doorway, Dar's face turned ashen, he caught his breath, and jumped back. Nanta's bridge appeared suspended in a void, with nothing more than a grating as a deck. An unexplainable fear of heights had long plagued Dar; something he'd kept well hidden from Navy Flight Surgeons for years. He didn't like being placed on a one story roof, much less hanging in mid air; it gave him vertigo. Stepping on to Nanta's bridge was like standing on the uppermost parapet of the Empire State Building.

"What is wrong?" Littia asked, with genuine concern. "Are you okay, Dar?"

Moving rapidly to Dar's side, thinking his charge had suddenly taken sick, Tamus's face reflected trepidation as well.

"I'll be okay," Dar said softly without conviction. He leaned forward, placing his hands on his knees and began taking deep breaths. "Just give me a minute." Get control of yourself, dummy, he whispered to himself, using the technique he often used to talk himself out of a tight situation while at the controls of his Harrier. After slowly filling his lungs several times, he stood upright to face his anxious attendants, still visibly shaken. "Sorry. I don't do heights very well, and the way your bridge is suspended took me off guard."

"We do not understand," Tamus said. "Are you not a pilot?"

"Yeah, but that's different. Don't ask me why, cause I don't know, but when I'm strapped in a cockpit, I'm fine. It's just places like this that give me the heebie-jeebies. I'll get over it." Shaking off the dizziness, he spoke with little conviction, "Come on, let's go."

Dar crossed the threshold once more, this time keeping his eyes high, but there was little need, the sight before him took all thoughts of vertigo and flung them away like so much extra baggage. His jaw went slack in awe at the panorama before him. Indeed, the magnitude of the vista overwhelmed his senses. Nanta's mammoth command center was dumbfounding. No fiction writer had ever visualized anything close to the magnitude, complexity, or functional simplicity exemplified by the control station atop the Nanta.

One man commands all this, Dar thought in awe, estimating there were at least two hundred men and women seated at as many consoles. Display screens reflected subdued lights and symbols on the faces of their operators, who were encased on three sides by an array of lit panels, and control sticks. Others were physically wired to the panels before them, their hands deftly fondling the air while their control screens changed with each stroke. However, what at first glance appeared to Dar as professional tranquillity, was overwhelmingly destroyed by the complete chaos created by hundreds of globes darting in all directions between stations.

Two meters above the seated operators, a twenty-five foot high plasma screen surrounded the entire bridge, giving a panoramic view of space. Multi-colored worlds, pink moons, and vast orange stars winked upon the screen along with instantaneous navigational information, threat icons, and a multitude of data Dar perspicaciously knew he would never understand. Above the plasma screen, there was nothing, or so it appeared. A bubble of milky green haze, the size of a football field, covered the uppermost reaches of the bridge. Dar craned his neck back, spotting several yellow-orange flashes slash through the green firmament.

"Small meteors or asteroids hitting the shield," Tamus answered Dar's unasked question. "What you see is our only defense against the rigors of space travel and our enemy's weapons."

"It's awesome," Dar said, and ducked a globe rushing past his head. "What are they? There must be hundreds of them flying around."

Littia and Tamus smiled at Dar, both near laughter.

"Don't worry, they won't hit you." Tamus said. "Their programming would not allow such an occurrence. Still, we understand your concern. It must be disconcerting to one who has not encountered such a device. They are called DataSpheres, and, though they may appear to be in disorder, their importance to the operational capabilities of the Nanta can not be over emphasized." Waving for his guests to follow, he led them further into the confines of Nanta's nerve center.

Dar watched as a DataSphere hovered silently next to an officer operating a complicated looking keyboard. Nonchalantly, the Lantiusian snatched it firmly, and placed it in an opening to his right. The display on his screen changed immediately.

"DataSpheres ensure reliable communications between stations during an emergency, but, more importantly, all of Nanta's computer data is transferred from and stored in each sphere according to its programming. Should any of Nanta's computers fail for any reason, the free floating, preprogrammed DataShperes automatically activate to continue operations uninterrupted." Tamus explained, without further details.

Work continued on the bridge with little regard to their presence ⁓ no notice was paid them as they neared the heart of the massive bridge. Without warning, the deck gave way, allowing ascent of a long console, complete with four comfortable chairs. Its sudden appearance reminded Dar of his Harrier's evaporation into the hangar deck days before.

"Welcome, First Officer Tamus. What service do you require?" A feminine voice emanated from the commander's work station.

"We request nothing at this time," Tamus answered, as he lowered his lanky body into the chair to the right of a larger center seat, and indicated that Dar should sit next to him. "We are now prepared to answer what questions you might have, Senior Commander Fantin."

Seating himself next to Tanus, Dar was still trying to gather his wits together. "Where are we?" He stammered.

"In respect to what?" Tanus returned the question.

"To Earth," Dar said, returning to the realities of his situation. "Where are the Womongly? What are their capabilities? Where are our aircraft? When --?" The questions, so long repressed, spewed like a fire hose.

Littia touched his mind, "Dar, please slow down. First Officer Tamus will answer your questions."

"Er. . . , ah . . . my apologies, sir," Dar said, rubbing fingers through already tangled hair. "How far are we from Earth?"

"Shortly after leaving your planet's atmosphere, we jumped several hundred light years away to the last know position of the Womongly ship, Dectima. Translating the mileage by your Earth standards would be exceedingly difficult."

"I don't understand. Why jump, as you put it, into enemy territory? Isn't that just asking for trouble?"

Reading Dar's thoughts, she said, "To jump is the term used to travel hyperspace from one point in space to another instantaneously," Littia stroked his mind, answering the question he had not put to Tamus.

"The Dectima is limited to the length of a jump, and once accomplished, it must replenish its power source to jump once more. This normally takes three weeks or more. You are aware the weapons aboard Dectima are useless against the Nanta, and therefore, we can track her movements with little fear."

"Tell that to my pilots," Dar snapped, his blue eyes shooting fire with his words, and was immediately sorry for the cheap shot.

"We are sorry for your losses. We, too, lost many. It was an unexpected occurrence. How the Womongly were capable of placing their insurgents aboard Nanta while we circled Earth is still an enigma.

Our best estimate ~ they have now incorporated hyperspace drives in their fighters. This is a new development."

"Great. You're telling me Womongly fighters can travel faster than light at will. How in God's name will we be able to take the battle to them if we don't know where they might be?"

"Now that we know they have the ability, we will enhance our surveillance techniques to track smaller vessels. Rest assure, you will have the ability to jump as well as pursue Womongly fighters." Tanus stated flatly, evidencing little concern over the matter.

"Speaking of our fighters, when will we get a chance to start flying?"

"We understand your desire to begin training, but it will be another two days before your ships will be ready." Tanus paused, turning to the console, "Hanger deck seven, resolution three point one."

A holographic display, shimmering forward of the console, immediately appeared in response to Tanus' command. Several men hovered over what Dar estimated to be a twenty meter aircraft of a sort he had never before imagined, much less seen. "What's that?" Dar asked, almost afraid of the answer.

"It is one of your fighters," Tanus answered. "Is it not to your liking?"

"The Viceroy of Peace told us, before she died, that you were modifying our aircraft. Well, my friend that ain't no Harrier, and that's for damn sure." Baffled at every turn, his frustration was clearly evident.

"Yes, in a way it is," Tanus said, not the least bit disturbed by Dar's discord. "The feel of your Harrier has been engineered into this fighter. When you are at the controls, your senses will respond as if you were flying a familiar aircraft. Electronic displays will be similar, as will ninety percent of your old switchology. However, you will be aided by computers far more sophisticated than anything you have known. Once in the cockpit, with your helmet on, you will be 'one' with the craft, each working for and with the other."

"Sounds as if we have a lot to learn in the next couple of days," Dar said, staring hard at the stubby winged fighter. Mentally, he noted the general features of the craft for later discussion with his squadron. "Where are the Womongly?" He asked.

"There." Tanus pointed to the massive, overhead plasma screen. "Sector B-7, 250,000 miles, bearing 4 low. View, increase 200 percent."

At his command, the holograph disappeared and a section of plasma screen rapidly zoomed magnification, showing a ship of monumental size suspended in a black void.

"Dar gasp. "My God, it's huge."

"No, not really," Tamus stated flatly. "Only about a sixth of the size of Nanta. Dectima is but one point five miles long and about a mile wide. Nanta is over six miles in length and four across. Still, Dectima is a very dangerous advisory, carrying armed fighters and thousands of Rage Warriors.

Every question I ask raises a dozen more, Dar thought. "What's a Rage Warrior?"

"We believe you have already been introduced to the Womongly Warrior class," Littia spoke for the first time. "Bred for their ferocity, they are those who live for but one purpose ~ combat." Liquid contempt oozed with her words.

Dar studied the plasma depiction of his upcoming adversary. *How could twenty pilots hope to win against such strength*, he wondered, rubbing fingers through tangled hair. After several silent moments he asked, "Which do we fight, Dectima or the fighters?"

"Both," Tanus said. "If you destroy only the fighters the Dectima will jump to Womong, their home planet, for re-supply and attack Earth at a later date. We would not hazard a guess when that might be, but return they would." He paused in study, then continued, "Yes, in the end, we must find a means of destroying the Dectima."

CHAPTER 9

Dar, Cannaly, and Danny Franklin sat on overly tall stools, more meant for Lantiusians than earthlings, sipping reddish concoctions of unknown origin. The Officers Bar was not crowed, but pockets of laughter and loud talk rose above the strange music being piped in over hidden speakers. Chatoyant light swept walls and ceiling, creating pictures of serene space scenes, constantly changing, each as spectacular as its predecessor.

"Well, it worked," Cannaly said, and took another sip from his drink. His lips smacked with pleasure. "It isn't beer, but I've got to admit, this stuff is good."

"Yeah, good work, Snake. Finding out how to use the light tubes will be big help. Did your guide issue you a VVCom?"

"Sure did, and I talked him into passing one on to Danny. I figured as long as our hosts are being so amenable, why not ask for what we want." He winked his blackened eye at Dar, letting a devilish smile spread across his round face.

"Good thinking." Dar was about to continue, but was interrupted by a group of tall men dressed in red tunics of senior officers.

"Please, excuse us," a dark haired man, standing just short of seven feet, said. "We are Zentao. Are you not the one called Senior Commander Fantin?"

Dar turned to meet the officer's eyes, catching a glimpse of yet another extraordinary light portrait flashing on the far wall. "Yes, I'm Fantin. What can I do for you?" A warm welcoming smile flashed across his face.

"We understand it is polite to touch hands when meeting, may we do so in appreciation for what you have done?" The big man stuck out his hand.

"Word spreads fast around here," Dar said, thinking about Jicama's reactions to the hand shake, and chuckled. He took Zentao's hand. "These are two of my officers, Cannaly and Franklin."

Introductions followed, with a major production made out of shaking hands with each. "We--" Zentao nodded to his companions -- "we're working on the construction of your fighters, and unable to attend the Supreme Commander's dinner." Upon mentioning the disastrous evening, a somber mood immediately prevailed ~ faces fell, and shoulders slumped. "What we have heard, however, has made it clear you are to be thanked in every way possible. Is there anything we can do for you?"

"Damn right," Cannaly piped up. "Take us to our fighters. We are dying to see these machines Dar has been telling us about. Our CO got a glimpse at them on a holograph a few hours ago, but nothing more."

"Of course," Zentao said, a broad smiling returning to brighten his face. "We would be more than happy to escort you to your fighting machines. Shall we finish our drinks, and go?"

"That'll be great," Dar said, taking a slug from his glass. "Would it be possible for me to have my guide join us?"

"Certainly, that will not be a problem. Should I send an aide for him?"

I don't think that will be necessary, Dar started to respond, then stopped. "Yes, please, and would you have her stop by my quarters to pick up the Womongly thrumber rifle."

Mention of the rifle brought a frown to the Lantiusian face. "Excuse me, Senior Commander Fantin, but weapons are not normally carried aboard Nanta. It would be highly irregular."

"Irregular or not, I'd feel more comfortable have something to shoot back with, should the need arise," Dar said crisply.

"Very well," Zentao said, motioning to his aid to be on his way. "You men from Earth are unusual in many ways," Zentao said, a good natured smile returning to his lips.

"Come on, Boss," Cannaly interrupted. "Drink up, and let's get this show on the road."

"Hold your horses, Snake," Dar said, picturing Littia in his mind's eye. "Littia, you there?"

Following a short pause, Dar felt the now familiar mental prick. "I am here, Dar."

"Are you busy for the next couple of hours, or have I caught you at a bad time?" Dar thought the words.

"We are not busy."

"There is an officer aide on his way to pick you up and escort you to hangar deck seven. I've met a few of the engineers who are refitting our fighters, and they are going to give us a tour. I would like you to be there. If you don't mind, that is."

"We shall be there, Dar. We are pleased that you should ask."

"Thanks. Oh, by the way, stop at my room and get the thrumber rifle. See you soon," Dar sent his message, and turned to the group.

"Damn it all," Cannaly said. "Where did you go? You looked like you just up and drifted into oblivion."

"Oh, just talking to Littia," Dar said casually.

"Right. You're a weird dude, pally. You do know that, don't you?" Cannaly smiled at his friend.

"Weird or not, it's all in a day's work," Dar answered. A feeling of satisfaction rushed though him at the thought of actually being able to make contact. "And, yeah I know I a weird dude, but don't give my little secret away to these guys," Dar said, nodding to the Lantiusians moving for the light tube. Let's do it," and polished off his drink.

Cannaly displayed his newly acquired talent as the group stepped aboard the light tube. Adroitly, he selected the necessary symbols for hangar deck seven, greatly pleased with himself. "Nothing to it, once you get the hang of it," he said, as they dropped forty-two levels.

The light tube opened directly into the hangar, where Littia stood waiting, the rifle hung from her right hand. Handing the gun to Dar, she shyly, accepted her introduction to the senior officers, greeting each with the politeness of one unaccustomed to mingling with higher ranking officials.

"Bloody hell, I don't frigging believe it," Danny said in amazement, his brown eyes the size of saucers. "Chaps, look at those." He slapped Cannaly roughly on the shoulder.

Dar sucked a breath. "Holy shit," was all he could say. The mile long hangar held twenty-four fighters identical to the one he'd seen earlier on the holograph. Now, regarding them en masse, and up close he felt overwhelmed. The beautifully sleek flying machines represented the stuff of dreams, but only dreams. Here, he was looking at a squadron of apparitions straight from a good night's sleep.

"Come, follow me," Zentao said, and stepped on the PCT leading from the light tube.

The small group followed silently, the earthlings eagerly drinking in the near tangible flavor of their new birds. Zentao, obviously pleased with the reactions of Dar and his companions, stepped from the tape as it passed behind the first fighter. The others followed his lead.

"This is one of your F-18 Hornets," Zentao said. "And there," he pointed to the next in line, "is a Harrier."

Dar looked closely at both. "What's the difference? They look identical to me."

"Quite so, Commander Fantin," an engineer spoke from behind Zentao. "Externally, each is indistinguishable from another, but that is where much of the similarity ends. Cockpit and computer configurations are designed around the type of aircraft brought here from Earth."

"So I understand," Dar said, with some disbelief evident in his voice. "I won't ask how you accomplished such a feat, I'll just take you at your word." He drew closer to the transformed Harrier, examining its exterior features closely. The big fighter sat firmly on large ski-like skids, obviously designed for rough terrain landings. Stubby wings of no more than six feet extended from each side, and practically no control surfaces were evident at the tail. Touching the fighter's skin, he found it to be smooth as silk and its cool surface without the slightest mar. It was as if the skin had been molded from a single sheet of metal. Dar noted with gratification, the cockpit bubble sitting high atop a down-sloped nose, allowing the pilot 360 degrees scan capability."

"You are impressed," Littia stroked silently. "We are pleased."

"Impressed would hardly be the word I would use," Dar thought back. "Stupefied would be more appropriate."

Zentao moved to the front of the deep space fighter Dar was tenderly caressing in obvious astonishment. A self-satisfied smile creased his handsome face. "Console," he commanded.

From the deck rose a large maintenance console, and with its appearance, the big bird began to hum with life. Dar stepped quickly back in surprise, only to hear the Lantiusians laugh quietly.

"We have only brought the computers on line," Zentao said, soothing Dar's alarm. "From the console we can operate most systems for maintenance purposes. Watch ~ Extend flight wings."

There was a slight delay, then slowly the stumpy wings began to expand until they extended 20 feet on either side, forming a familiar delta wing design with sufficient lift characteristics for flight in an atmosphere. As the wings emerged, the tail of the fighter changed configuration as well. Three amazed pilots watched as a vertical stabilizer grew from atop of the fighter's tail and a tail plane sprung from either side of the fuselage.

"Your fighter is capable of far more than just space flight," Zentao instructed. "Should it be required, you may fly in practically any condition presented to you ~ space, planetary atmospheres, even land on an asteroid if you desire. Control is accomplished by light pulses directed from ports located on either side of each wing, nose, and tail. Much like your Harrier puffer ducts. There are hundreds of pulse ports located in the skin as well which enhance the overall flight characteristics while in space."

"Jesus H. Christ," Cannaly exclaimed. "What a machine. I think I've died and gone to heaven." He laid his hand against the fighter's smooth silver side, cocking his head in admiration. "What's she got for speed and armament?"

"The Induced Light power plant will allow you to accelerate to around fifty thousand miles per hour. We are not sure as yet, but that is our design estimate. Engaging hyperdrive will jump you to whatever destination you desire instantaneously. As for armament, your Thrumber Gun extends from the nose and is sufficient in power to damage most known space vessels, fighters and mother ships."

His eyes still wide in admiration, Dar asked Zentao, "What in the name of heaven is a Thrumber Gun anyway? This thing," he rasied the rifle, "is called a thrumber whatever too."

Zentao thought for a moment before responding. "It is very difficult for me to explain, as your scientists are far from developing this type of weapon. Imagine, if you will, a ball of lightning. The energy in a single lightning strike on your planet produces hundreds of thousands of amperes, and generates heat six times hotter than the sun. We have been able to harness that sort of power and direct it at an enemy. The name comes from the distinctive sound the blast produces leaving the gun when fired in an atmosphere. It thrrrummbs"

"Is that the bloody gun?" Danny asked, pointing to the 15 foot tube extending from the extreme nose of the fighter. His small frame was near shaking with excitement. "How much ammo does she carry?"

Zentao smile down at the little Brit. "Yes, Commander Franklin, that is the gun, but you have no need to 'carry' ammunition, as you put it. Power from the Inducted Light Drive Engine in diverted to a condenser generator. The condenser is charged at a rate of six hundred thrumbs per minute, a little less if the pilot requires maximum acceleration of the fighter. However, the Thrumber is not the extent of your armament."

"Damn, what more do we need?" Cannaly asked in awe.

"Internally, there are four thermal nuclear torpedoes, which will destroy a fighter on contact, and incur significant damage to a ship the size of the Womongly, Dectima," Zentao instructed. He paused, turning back to the console. "Armament, all."

The smooth belly skin of the fighter appeared to liquefy, allowing four torpedo shaped cylinders to flow silently into view. Each of the ominous looking weapons were attached to a substantial mounting that disappeared into the fighter's underside. There was a discernable 'clicking' sound as the mounts locked into place. The skin then reformed around each of the readied torpedo suspension racks, forming a smooth surface once more.

"Wow," Cannaly said. "I'm gonna to love this thing. Will you have a look at that, Dar? What a machine! Kick a skid, light a light and we'll brief at the next moon down the line."

Dar smiled at his friend. "We've got to learn to fly the damned thing first. We sure as hell ain't in Kansas anymore, and clicking your heels together isn't going to get you in the cockpit."

"Oh, Commander Fantin, learning to fly this fighter will not be difficult for you and your men. Not only do you have a computer which links directly to your brain, you will feel as if you are flying one of your own aircraft." Zentao said nonchalantly.

"Hey, mate, what's this about hooking into our brains? I don't like having my head messed with, not by a bloody long shot." Danny was indignant.

Dar felt much the same, nodding agreement to Danny. This brain tap thing worried him.

"It is in the helmet." Dar felt Littia's stroke. "We are sure you will adjust rapidly to its help."

Dar nodded to Littia. "Can I see one of our helmets?" He asked Zentao.

"We are sorry, no. Your helmets are yet to be finished. In fact, fitting will be done tomorrow, if we remember correctly."

"That is correct," Littia said. "The guides will take their pilots for fittings in the morning. My supervisor's instructions were passed to us earlier."

"Okay," Dar said, and paused, studying the fighter for a long moment. "What about a shield of some sort? First Officer Tamus explained that Nanta has to have a shield to survive in space. Do the fighters have something for external protection?"

Zentao's smile radiated as he spoke. "Ah, a very wise question, and very perceptive of you, Commander. Yes, of course you must have a protective shield, and though it is not of the magnitude surrounding Nanta, it is sufficient in strength to withstand multiple Womongly weapon blasts. Here, let me show you ~ if you will please stand back."

The group moved several feet from the big bird.

"No. Further away please. Ah, that will be good," Zentao said as the group moved a greater distance from the fighter. Turning his attention to the console, he commanded, "Shields."

Immediately, a soft green glow encapsulated the fighter, appearing much like that Dar had seen on the bridge, though, in this case, the coloring was not opalescent. Good, Dar thought, looking through the clear verdant shield, his pilots wouldn't have to fly using a plasma screen.

"This colored outer shield, will provide protection from external sources, such as small asteroids, space dust and debris, and though it will withstand enemy thrumber bursts for awhile, repeated hits will erode its functionality. However, there are two shields, an inner and outer."

"Two?" Dar was surprised. "Why two? If the outer is similar to the protective shield Nanta uses, why do we require an additional inner one?"

"It has to do with mass and acceleration forces." Zentao's face tightened in thought, as he paused to think. "Senior Commander, you are well aware of the effects of gravitational forces while flying. We believe you use the term 'pulling G's'. Well, these fighters pull many more G's than you or the machine could possibly withstand in space. The inner shield will compensate for accelerations in any direction through computer induced reversal of the gravitational field in the opposite direction, thus neutralizing the inertia created during extreme maneuverings."

"Bloody hell, except for G's I didn't understand a word you just said," Danny whined. "But I don't much care, so long as it damn well works."

"We assure you, Commander Franklin, the fields work very well," Zentao said with incredulity that his work should be so questioned.

"He meant no offense," Dar assured. "We're all pretty much overwhelmed by these machines, Zentao. After all, we are mere earthlings. What say we call it a night and head back to the bar?"

The group relaxed in laughter, as Zentao shut down the shield and ordered the console to retract.

CHAPTER 10

Leaning on each other for support, the three pilots stepped from the PCT still singing an old fighter pilot song at the top of their collective voices:

I don't want to join the Army.

I don't want to go to war.

I just want to lay around

Piccalilli underground and

Fornicate me bloody life away.

"Damn it to hell, what's in those red sippers anyway?" Dar asked his companions, with a noticeable slur. "My God, those Lantiusians can down a dozen and it doesn't do a thing. Me? I have three, and I feel like I've been on a week long drunk."

"Don't worry about it, boss, just think how damned awful you're goin' ta feel in the morning." Cannaly jibed, and gave Dar a slap on the back, nearly knocking his friend down.

"Yeah, bloody right. And, you," Danny stabbed a finger into Dar's chest, "ordered us to PT at oh-dark-sparrow fart. We might have to get us a new CO."

"Yeah, right," Dar said. "I reckon you'll be wantin' the job?"

"No way, old chap. I'll leave leadership to you hero types. Me, I'm heading to bed and dream of Lantiusian lovelies, all of whom desire my wonderful body for their bloody own." The Brit staggered off in the direction of his quarters, waving his goodnight.

"Night, boss," Cannaly said. "We've really got our work cut out for us, don't we?" He asked, more soberly.

"Think so, Snake. But what the hell, we're the best there is. Ain't none finer. We'll pull'er off someway. Nite, pally."

The two men went in opposite directions down the passage way. Dar reached his door, "Open!" The wall gave way, and he stepped across the threshold. Effects of the drinks faded immediately, replaced by adrenaline.

"Do not be afraid," a barrel of man said quietly. He had a face that looked like it had been busted one too many times by a fast moving Mac truck. "Please, I mean you no harm."

Dar, the thrumber rifle steadied on the strange visitor, stepped into his room. The door slid shut behind him. "Who are you and what do you want?" Dar asked, anger boiling inside him like a blast furnace. He'd had just about all the surprises he needed for a lifetime, and this red faced, thick chested goon was the last straw.

"Who I am is unimportant. I come with a warning, not to harm."

"Warn about what?" Dar asked, noticing for the first time how the man seemed to shimmer in and out of focus. Then it hit him, "You're a holograph!"

"Yes, a holograph transmitted with much difficulty and little time. I am sent to say, 'All is not what it seems. Beware your ties.'"

"What in God's name is that suppose to mean?" Dar's shoulders slumped. Suddenly, he was tired. Tired to the bone.

"Remember the words." The holograph disappeared in a blur of opaque light.

Alone, the adrenaline buzz dissipating rapidly, Dar tried to focus on the event. "I'm just to damned tired too worry about it now," he said to the empty room. Struggling out of his boots, he threw the rifle and his flight suit into the corner by the closet, and fell onto the warmth on his bed. "Lights out," he called, pulling the cover up to his neck. The room dimmed slowly into blackness. Dar slept.

"Are you sure?" Supreme Commander Jicama asked of his second in command. "Do we know from where it was transmitted, and to where in Nanta?"

"We are sad to report, no in both cases. The transmittal was too short in duration for a triangulation of either. All we know for sure is that it was beamed into the Nanta." The tall officer was in obvious distress. He'd awakened Jicama in the middle of the Supreme Commander's sleep period to pass disturbing news.

"Very well, Tamus. Thank you for letting me know immediately. Perhaps the beam was of such a short duration, it did not reach the intended recipient. Heighten surveillance of hyperwave transmissions just in case."

"Very well, sir. Will that be all?"

"Yes, leave me now," Jicama commanded. As Tamus departed, the tall commander rubbed at his bandage and wondered what and who would be transmitting a holographic message into his ship. More importantly, how was it accomplished? Who besides the Womongly even knew the position of the Nanta?

CHAPTER 11

Dar sat next to the wall in a sweaty heap, with nineteen pilots huddled before him grunting and sucking air into their lungs. It had been a hard work out, ending with enough laps around the gymnasium-sized room to constitute three miles.

"We're going to be fitted with our helmets this morning," Dar began. This was his first All Officers Meeting, or AOM, as a Commanding Officer, and he wished he felt better. Hangovers were something with which he rarely had to deal, but the powerful Lantius drink was stubbornly hanging around in his system. "These helmets have some means of connecting us directly to an on-board computer. Don't ask me how, but that's the story I get from my guide and the engineers working on our fighters. Snake, Danny and I got a chance to see our new aircraft, or should I say, spacecraft, last night, and, gentlemen, you're gonna be impressed."

A hand shot up near the rear of the group. "Sahr, are they really the same es our bird?" A young Russian pilot asked in broken English.

Cannaly laughed. "Son, you ain't gonna believe it when you see it."

Dar smiled. "I would say they are definitely not our Migs, F-16s, or whatever you brought up here with you. I'm not sure how to describe them, but I can't wait to give one of them a try. Zentao, one of the engineers, assured us they'll fly like our airplanes, but damned if I know how. Any other questions?" Dar paused, waiting. "Okay, then. The Executive Officer here has broken the code to the light tubes. He's going to give us instructions. XO, it's all yours."

"Thanks, boss." Cannaly rustled a small stack of papers he had stuck in his shorts. "Here, Danny, pass these out for me." He paused long enough for Danny to take the papers from a plastic bag and start handing out the symbology he'd scribbled on the sheets. "Study these symbols, guys, and you'll be able to operate the light tubes. There's really nothing to it, and they open up the ship to you."

"Thanks, Snake," Dar said, taking the forefront once more. "If all goes well today, we'll plan our first sorties tomorrow afternoon. Commander Franklin, our Operations Officer, will select a couple officers to act as his assistants and scheduler. I plan to be leading the first section and the OpsO will lead the second. Whenever possible, Commander Cannaly and I will never be scheduled during the same time frame. That way, if I buy the farm, he'll take over as CO without interruption. Schedules will be posted in the quarters area each evening. Until we can arrange for some office spaces, we'll use individual quarters for routine work. Anymore questions?"

"What about a logo?" Cannaly asked. "Every squadron has to have an emblem of some sort."

"Yeah, you're right," Dar said. "Y'all come up with suggestions and we'll vote on them the next AOM, which will be tomorrow morning after PT." A deep moan rose from the crowd. "Hey, don't all of ya feel noble, having hurt your body so badly this morning? I know I do." Wiping beads of sweat from his brow, he grinned at the group. "Now, get out of here. I'll see y'all at breakfast."

"Snake, hold up a minute. I need to talk to you," Dar said, putting a hand on his friend's shoulder. The others ambled for the far door, talking excitedly about their fighters and the upcoming flights. "Snake, I had something happen last night that I'm not sure about. Hell, it could have been a hallucination for all I know. I was drunk enough."

Cannaly studied Dar for a moment, and winked his still blackened eye. "What was it? Did Littia appear in your bed?"

"No, I wish it was that simple." Dar passed fingers through wet hair. "I had a very strange visitor when I got to my room last night. It looked like a reject from a morgue after a six car pile up, and as big around as a keg of beer."

"Sure ya did." Cannaly was laughing loudly. "I think you'd better lay off that red stuff."

"No, damn it, I'm serious," Dar emphasized, shaking his head at his own disbelief. "It was a hologram of some sort, and the apparition was sitting in a chair when I opened the door."

Cannaly, with concern evident in his face, considered Dar for a long minute. "You're really serious, aren't you? What did this thing want?"

"To pass a message, and for the life of me, I can't figure it out. He said something about all is not what it seems, and to watch my ties, then just disappeared. But, damn it all, Snake, I was pretty drunk. Maybe it was nothing more than a reaction to the drink. What do you think?"

"I think I'd keep my mouth shut about it. Folks around here liable to find a padded room for you. Honestly, I'd store the information away in that brain housing group of yours, and wait. If it's important enough, he'll be back."

"Yeah, I suppose you're right, but I got a very strange feeling about --" Dar stopped in mid sentence, feeling the now familiar stroke in his mind.

"Dar, we are waiting for you in the dining area. Please join me here. The engineers wish to start fitting helmets."

Littia's words formed clearly in Dar's conscious, bringing a smile to his lips at how the words sounded exactly the same as if she was standing next to him. "Give me thirty minutes, I've got to shower and change," he thought in return.

"Are you okay, Dar?" Cannaly asked. "You look zoned out or something."

"I'm fine, pally. I was talking to Littia. They want us at the mess hall for helmet fittings."

"Dar, you're one weird dude, you know that," Cannaly said, and slapped his friend on the back. "Let's get some food, and start preparing to take to the sky, or space, or nothingness whatever the hell it is."

No more than fifteen minutes had passed until, freshly showered, Dar began slipping on his scarlet flight suit. It was new, and how or when it had been placed in his closet he had no idea. The patch, sewn neatly to the left breast, was new as well . . . Senior Commander Dar Fantin, Commanding Officer. CO of what, Dar wondered ~ SFS-1.

"Hey, that's not bad," he said to Cannaly, who'd draped himself across Dar's desk. "Space Fighter Squadron – One."

"Yeah, I like it. For sure the name fits the situation. Now all we need is a proper emblem, something really different," Cannaly said, and unwound himself from the desk, standing. "What do you think about these new flight suits? You realize, only yours is scarlet? Mine and Danny's are a lighter red, and the others gray."

Dar looked up in surprise. "Looks like Jicama has dressed us like his own staff, perhaps even placing us on the same level, at least for the sake of appearance."

"Yeah, that's what I thought. Are you ready yet? Stop preening yourself, and let's get going. You trying to impress Littia or something?" Cannaly asked, an evil twinkle in his blue eyes.

Dar slid the flight suit's long sleeves up to his elbows. "Snake, you're a certifiable asshole, you know that?"

"Yeah, I know, but you love me anyway."

Their good natured teasing brought laughter, the kind of guffawing true friends enjoy between themselves.

"I'm ready," Dar said, still smiling. "Let's go."

Minutes later, Dar spotted Littia at a table filled with guides and pilots engaged in animated conversations between bites of breakfast.

"We understand you had an exciting evening," Littia stated flatly, as Dar wiggled into a seat next to her, his plate filled with what he thought might resemble eggs and sausage.

Dar turned to stare at her intently, wondering if she knew of his nocturnal visitor. "What do you mean?" Dar tried to sound nonchalant, while blocking his mind from her.

"We understand that after my leaving, you spent most of the evening at the bar with Zentao and his friends. We have been told that you became slightly inebriated. Is this true?" She asked, with a perfectly innocent smile shining Dar's way.

"Oh, that." Dar tried to mask the relief in his voice. "I confess to the truth of the matter," he said, hanging his head in mock shame. "I did have fun at the time, but whatever y'all put in your whiskey is lethal. I think further education might be necessary."

Her smile radiating, Littia touched Dar's hand saying, "We understand, much is left to be learned about our ways. When you are finished with your breakfast, we shall take you to have your helmet fitted."

Dar looked around, realizing for the first time that he and Cannaly were the only ones still eating. He hurriedly began gobbling his food, noting with displeasure that what had looked like eggs and sausage tasted more akin to mush and crackers. Still, the heaviness of the cuisine began overriding the affects of the night's alcoholic escapades.

"I'm ready," Dar stated, then polished off a glass of purple liquid Lantiusians took for juice.

The entire assembly, earthlings and guides, pushed their way into the expanding light tube and dropped seventy decks to be greeted by an ensemble of anxiously waiting Lantiusian engineers dressed in a variety of colored tunics. Dar and the others were quickly sorted and hustled off to individual cubicles.

A tall, powerful looking woman with a face that belonged on the cover of a weight lifters magazine led Dar and Littia down a long corridor to a room filled with electronic gadgetry. In the back corner of the tiny enclosure stood a chair with so many contraptions attached to it, Dar suspected the contrivance was imported straight from the trials of the Spanish Inquisition.

"Please, Senior Commander Fantin, sit down and make yourself comfortable," the dark haired technician said, her face radiating a broad smile.

"In that," Dar said in astonishment. "What have you got in mind? You planning to pull my fingernails out, or drive spikes through my elbows?"

The smile faded from the woman's lips like water hitting a hot skillet. "We would never do such a horrible thing, Senior Commander Fantin. How could you ever think we would be so cruel?"

Dar smiled innocently. "I'm just teasing," he said and wiggled his body into the surprisingly comfortable chair.

"We apologize for his strange behavior," Littia said to the obviously upset woman. "We have come to understand some measure of the earthlings manner of speech. We believe they call it 'joking around'." To Dar she mind blasted, "Dar, behave yourself, she is just doing her job."

Dar flashed both ladies a dazzling smile. "My apologies as well," he said to the technician, who appeared to be placated. "Please, I'm ready if you are."

"Very well," the technician said tentatively. "We are called Medula, and we shall first make a mold of your head. This will entail covering your entire head to your shoulders. You will not be capable of sight or speech during this process, however we shall insert a breathing tube for the short duration the process requires. You must remain perfectly still while we pour the mold, and during that time, you will feel some heat generated.

"Sounds like fun," Dar said.

Thirty minutes later, Dar spit the breathing tube from his mouth. "I take that back. That wasn't fun at all. I sure hope we don't have to do that again. What's next?"

"We need a moment," Medula said, as she busied herself with the still warm mold. Carefully, she inserted the perfectly shaped likeness of Dar's head into a scarlet helmet shell. Once encased, she trimmed the edges to fit the exact form of the shell. "There, now, we may proceed to the next step."

Dar watched, fascinated by the large woman's dexterity, as his helmet took shape. He noted two distinct electrical connections protruding from the upper right hand side of the shell. "What are the connectors for?"

"Those will be used to connect you to the onboard computer," Littia answered. "Inside the helmet are four electrodes which will rest tightly against your skull."

"I'm still not sure about being directly wired into a computer. I've heard about research being done back home, but I've never conceived the notion that you could fly a fighter that way."

"The computer will not fly your fighter, Senior Commander Fantin," Medula said, walking to Dar's side. "The computer will only function as you direct. It will respond to no one else, not even Nanta's bridge. However, should you become incapacitated, it will fly the fighter back to the Nanta. One last thing, once connected to your computer, you must speak aloud to give instructions."

"That's a pleasant thought," Dar said. "Guess you want the fighter back and not the pilot."

"Dar, we would want you back, not the fighter," Littia stated flatly. "Why do you skirmish with us so? We are only trying to help."

"I know, Littia, but I've always fought the concept of anything that took flying out of the hands of the pilot. I just don't like the thought of a machine overriding my decisions in the cockpit."

"Oh," Littia seemed surprised. "We understand now, but we think you will learn to trust this system as an enhancement to your personal capabilities, and not a detriment."

"We are ready, Senior Commander," Medula said. "On first activation, you will feel a slight tingling sensation around your scalp, but it will occur only during this inaugural connection. After the initial link-up, you will be able to communicate with your fighter's computer without discomfort."

"Are you suggesting I'll be hooked up with *my* bird right now?"

"Oh, yes, of course. We have tapped into your fighter on the hanger deck," Medula responded, lowering the helmet over Dar's head.

The helmet conformed comfortably, the inner shell soft as silk, and as it touched his shoulders, a clear golden face plate deployed covering his face. Medula stepped back, examining her handiwork with satisfaction. Nodding silent approval, she moved to a console on the far side of the cubical and began waving commands on a large lightboard.

"You will feel the connection momentarily," Littia tickled silently.

Barely audible, resonating throughout the entire helmet, the buzzing of hundreds of bees filled Dar's auditory range. The sensation grew in intensity, until all else disappeared, leaving Dar stunned and unaware of his surroundings. He felt nausea swell in his gut as the discord continued to increase its tenor. The buzzing grew to a crescendo, ending abruptly with a thunderous clap, followed immediately by an electrical shock racking muscles and tendons. Dar sat rigidly upright, eyes bulging from shock and fear.

"Good morning, Dar," a soothingly pleasant female voice echoed through the link. "I am Nan, and it is my distinct pleasure to finally be working with you."

In mild shock, Dar shook off the sensation of vulnerability which wrapped a cloak about him like cloudy darkness. "Where are you?" Dar asked, groping for understanding.

"I am with you. We are one."

"We are one?" Dar mumbled, the clouds drifting apart with returning awareness.

"I am here to serve you and you only. You are the reason I exist, and I exist only through you. I am Nan, and together we shall see the stars."

As rapidly as the fog had settled on his mind, it now dissipated on curls of smokey wisps. "Nan, you're my fighter aren't you?" Sudden perception surged through him. "Well, I'll be damned, I'm talking to a machine."

"We are one. I am Nan and we are one," Nan spoke with mild contempt, responding to Dar's lack of understanding. "May I instruct?" She spoke more softly. "It will take but a moment."

"Sure, why not," Dar said with little conviction. "Does this fry me as badly as the connection?" It was a flippant question, more to bolster his confidence than for any other reason.

"No, you will not feel pain, only a gratifying filling of your mind. Please, close your eyes and relax." Nan paused, waiting. "Good. Now take a deep breath and let it out slowly."

Dar followed the instructions, letting the breath slowly expel in relaxation. A dot of light appeared directly before his closed eyes, expanding rapidly until it became his entire universe. A warming glow passed over and through him, infusing feelings of love, concern, and understanding into very fabric of his existence. As the last slender puff left his empty lungs, the gentle radiance melted away, leaving a cold hollow void behind.

"Nan," Dar whispered. "Nan, are you there."

"I am here, Dar."

"I understand, Nan. We will truly be one while flying. I am very glad to have you with me. Did you know that Nan is my Mother's name?"

"Yes, that is why I named myself Nan. Are you disappointed?

"No, Nan, it is perfect. Wait one, Littia is trying to get my attention." Dar realized for the first time in several minutes that both Littia and Medula were staring into his face with genuine concern. He smiled, and gave a thumbs up sign with his right hand. "I think Medula wants me to go off line now. I'll see you tomorrow afternoon, Nan, and we'll take our ship for a spin. Whatdaya think?"

"I'll be here waiting and anxious to fly with you, Dar."

Still smiling, Dar raised the helmet from his head. "Wow! That was the best Disney World ride ever invented," he said, passing the unit to Medula.

"You wished to see me, sir," Littia intoned shyly, her head bent obsequiously.

"Guide 3rd Class, is it not?" Jicama asked flatly. "Yes, it is my desire to speak briefly with you." Jicama sat comfortably in his command chair on the bridge of the Nanta. His scarlet tunic draped to the floor, its folds doing little to hide his tall powerful physique. "We wished to ask you about Senior Commander Fantin. Were you able to ascertain if he received a visitor last night?" Jicama did not glance at the beautiful woman standing demurely next to him. His interest was the Nanta, and on the bridge his power was unlimited.

"We are sorry, no. Senior Commander Fantin made no mention of anything unusual, other than having enbided too many Lantiusian drinks at the officers bar."

"We understand. If you should find out further information, you will report directly to me. Is that understood?"

"Of course, Supreme Commander, that is clearly understood."

"You may go," Jicama said, already turning his attention to another officer and contemplating the likelihood of Dectima jumping within the week.

"Well, what do you think?" Dar asked Cannaly.

Both men relaxed in Dar's quarters, Dar with feet up on his desk and legs crossed, while Cannaly, lounged in the guest chair, legs dangling over the arm rest.

"I think I can't wait to get airborne. Plus, I really dig this computer thing. After the initial shock, Tess sort of drained my fears of her and flying the machine."

"Yeah, I know what you mean. Yours called itself Tess. Interesting. Do you know anyone by that name?" Dar asked with more than a little interest.

"Sure. Tess is my sister's name. She's just a couple of years younger than me. We're close, always have been." Cannaly's interest was up. "Why?"

"My computer called herself Nan, my mother's name. It probably doesn't mean a thing, but it does imply they have more knowledge of us than I originally thought. The only thing I can figure is that they did it in that damned 'Educator' cylinder we all went through. Looks to me like it not only gave us background on the Lantiusians, but took something in return."

Cannaly absently took a sip from a bottle he'd brought from the bar. He and several squadron mates had 'done' themselves a happy hour after the evening meal. "What difference does it make? The mission remains the same? Besides, in a way, it makes perfect sense to have a computer link with something familiar."

"Yeah, I suppose you're right, it's just another interesting facet surrounding this whole affair, that's all I'm saying. By the way, have we gotten any suggestions on a patch design?" Cannaly unwrapped himself from the chair, a grin spreading across his boyish face. "You bet. The guys have narrowed it down to three choices. We can vote on which is to become our final selection in the morning. One suggestion is a real hoot. I think it will be the one, but we'll wait and see."

Dar waited, but Cannaly did not continue. "Well, Snake, y'all gonna tell me about it or not?"

"Hell, no. You're going to have to wait and see for yourself." He stood, and took a step to a recessed panel next to the desk. Pressing the center button, a hole appeared in the deck, and he tossed the now empty bottle into the void. "I'm heading for the rack, and I suggest you do the same, boss. Gonna be a long day tomorrow."

CHAPTER 12

The tension around the squadron area was thicker than used engine oil, Dar thought, returning from a meeting with Jicama and Tamus. It was perfectly understandable, considering their newly formed SFS-1 was going to fly for the first time. Dar shifted a neatly tied bundle from his right hand to the left and banged on Cannaly's door, "Hey, Snake, you in there?"

The door slid open at the command "come" from Cannaly, who stood stark naked, still dripping from the shower. "Hey, boss. You ready for the big event? I understand you're flying with Bulldog, that big Texas, F-16 pilot."

"Reckon I'm as ready as I'll ever be," Dar said, and slouched into a chair throwing the package on the desk. Without thinking, he rubbed his fingers through neat hair, destroying any hint that it had ever seen a comb. "Jicama explained how we leave and return to the Nanta . . . doesn't sound like a big deal. In fact, the launch officer controls ninety percent of both the departure and recovery, which is a-okay with me."

"So give, you tell me what we have to do, and I'll get it out to the rest of the squadron."

"Not much to it, really. Strap the bird on, put your helmet atop your gourd and let the launch officer initiate the start sequence. The launch officer pretty much controls the fighter until you're clear of the shield."

"How do we get through the shield?" Cannaly interrupted, still toweling water from his legs.

"Snake, I have no idea how they do it, but the shield folds in on itself, creating a passage not much larger than the craft departing the hanger deck. The folding has something to do with maintaining the shield's containment integrity. First Officer Tamus tried, I mean really gave his all, to explain it to me, but it was way over my head. The shield extends for three miles outward from Nanta, and the flight through the gap will be slow compared to what we would consider a normal takeoff. Once clear, the controls are returned to the pilot, and you're on your own."

"Once clear Nanta, what do we do then, dash off to the next star on the right and on into morning?"

Dar laughed, shaking his head. "Snake, you're a wonderment. No, the Nanta will direct us from the bridge, much like the Combat Information Center aboard an aircraft carrier. Directions will be given by voice command and tactical information is transmitted to our plasma or holographic displays."

"I thought they told us the birds would be similar to our own. What's with this holograph and plasma crap?"

"Actually, as Jicama explained it to me, the holograph takes the place of our Head-up Display, and a plasma screen replaces the Digital Data Indicators. Plus, the computer can switch the holograph to a scan mode capable of zooming in on objects up to 125,000 miles away."

"Damn, we've got to start thinking in thousands of miles instead of hundreds. That's going to be hard getting used to," Cannaly whispered in awe. "Any other secrets you need to tell me?"

"No, that's about it, I think." Dar paused in thought. "Oh, yeah. Here are the patches. Man, they're fast around here. I asked Littia at breakfast if she could have these made for us, and Tamus gave me the package not two hours later."

"Have you seen them yet?" Cannaly asked.

"No, but I'm sure they're perfect, just like everything else around here. Let's open them up," Dar said, retrieving the packet from the desk. "Littia told me all we had to do was stick them to our flight suits. They have a self-adhesive on the back. She commented that as fast as we were changing names and name tags, it was easier to just stick them on rather than have them embroidered "

Ripping the heavy outer covering, Dar chuckled to himself as he remembered the voting earlier that morning. The group had just finished their run, and the first thing on the agenda was the selection of a squadron emblem. Three possibilities had been submitted, but it had been unanimous when the actual vote had been taken. SFS-1's badge of honor, their squadron's emblem to the known galaxies, was a four inch circle with a light blue background. At the center of the circle, stood Yosemite Sam of Looney Tune fame, his bright red mustache hanging past his waist, and a dark blue forty gallon cowboy hat cocked back over bulging eyebrows. Ole' Sam stood atop Earth with his right hand resting casually on a six-shooter strapped to his side. Legs crossed, he leaned jauntily to the left, using a fair facsimile of a Womongly thrumber rifle as a staff. The cartoon character was known by all the pilots, no matter from what part of the world they came, and as a cartoon, held international status. Two flying ribbons were attached, the one on top of the patch read, Space Fighter Squadron – One, and at the bottom a larger ribbon proclaimed, Saviors of Earth, Our Home. The entire emblem was surrounded by a golden ridge.

"Damn, will ya look at these, Snake. They're just what the doctor ordered."

Cannaly slipped his skivvies on and joined Dar at the desk. "Perfect, absolutely perfect. I'll finish dressing and pass them out to the guys right now." He grabbed up one of the newly made patches for himself. "And, I'll get the word spread on how takeoffs and recoveries will be executed at the same time. You, boss, had better get ready to kick a skid."

"Yeah, I'm on my way," Dar said, and picked up a patch for himself. "Oh, by the way, would you tell Bulldog meet me in my quarters in fifteen minutes."

"Will do, and Dar, you be careful out there. Don't try anything stupid, just give her a spin and get on back to let us know how it feels."

"Yeah, right," Dar said, as he walked out the door for his own quarters.

Minutes later, Dar stood staring into his bathroom mirror. He splashed a handful of cold water from the tap into his face, allowing it to drip into the sink. "Admit it," he said to his reflection, "you're scared shitless. Big bad Dar Fantin, pride of the Marine Corps, is about to step into a deep space fighter and lead a squadron into combat, but I'm terrified about the whole idea. A hero type? Not!" Splashing more water, he snagged a towel and rubbed his face red. "Get a grip, dummy. Can't let the others see you this way."

A distinctive "poof" sounded behind him. Startled, Dar spun and quickly crouched into a fighting position. "I'll be --." A smile spread across his face in pleased astonishment. On his desk sat a utapotus, smaller and an off-colored orange instead of the brown pet that joined

Jicama in the hospital, but unmistakably a utapotus. Slowly, Dar walked across the small room, reaching out to touch the small animal.

"Hey, little buddy how are you today, huh? Are you lost or something?"

The grotesque little creature's eyes melted at his words, as if to say, "Why no, I'm not lost. Such a question is nonsense." With little warning, the orange ball of silky soft scales leaned back on it haunches and leaped into Dar's arms.

Dar fell back, as the animal hit him full in the chest. "Whoa, little fella, you mean to tell me you decided to choose me. Well, I must say I'm surprised and honored." Crooning the words, Dar stroked the soft neck of his new friend, feeling the tension and fear that had been plaguing him drain away like a river on a dry desert floor.

"Well, we've got to have a name for you, now don't we," Dar murmured. "Let's see ~ I have it. Pete! We'll call you Pistol Pete, the other name Yosemite Sam uses. Is that all right with you?" he asked a bit shyly.

The utapotus snuggled closer in Dar's arms, his saucer eyes filling his ugly frog face with nothing but love for his chosen.

"Then it's settled. I'll call you Pete, Dar said gently, continuing to caress Pete's soft back.

"Sir," an abrasive voice called simultaneously with a knock. "It's Bulldog."

To Dar's astonishment, the utapotus disappeared from his arms with the first tap. "Come," he said with disappointment. Pete had been an appreciated guest, one he hoped would return soon. "Hey, Bulldog. You ready for a romp in space, or what?" he said, welcoming the big Texan.

"Yes sir," the entering tank of a man said with enthusiasm. "I'm your man. Ya wanna brief here, sir?"

Dar could hardly contain his mirth, there was little doubt how this Air Force pilot had gotten his call sign. Drooping ears, flapping like a flag in a breeze, were pinned to a football sized head. A short powerful neck held the head atop a six foot, two inch frame which sprouted arms and legs the size of tree trunks. What else could they call Tom Bennett? Everything about him gave the appearance of a giant bulldog. How the big man ever crammed his big chassis into the cockpit of an F-16, Dar had no idea. "Yeah. We'll do a quick brief here, and then finish off on the hanger deck."

Forty-five minutes later, Dar led Bulldog off the light tube and into hanger seven. Both men stopped. Staged forward of the remaining fighters sat the two silver machines they were about to strap on and fly into the nothingness of space.

"Sir, I've got to admit, I'm about ready to mess my trou'. I guess I never really thought we would actually blast one of these things into space."

"Don't feel like the Lone Ranger, Bulldog, I'm not sure this is a fantastic idea either, but what the heck? You only live once," Dar said, with more confidence than he felt.

"Oh, I don't mean I don't want to. It's, well . . . hell, I'm just plain scared," the big man said.

Dar slapped his wingman on the back and gave a nervous laugh. "Well, Bulldog, so am I. So, what ya say we climb aboard and see if we can show these Lantiusians what flying is all about?"

"Yeah, let's do it," Bulldog almost yelled, and started walking briskly for his fighter, leaving Dar staring at his back, a twisted grin on his face.

Zentao stepped from a group of engineers busying themselves around the two silver skinned deep space fighters, intercepting Dar as he struggled to catch up with the full striding Bulldog. "Ah, Senior Commander Fantin, are you ready to fly?"

"About as ready as I'll ever be, I guess," Dar answered. "Are they ready to go?"

"In perfect readiness. Please, let me explain what will happen during launch and recovery."

"That would be nice," Dar responded with a bit of sarcasm. "Hey, Bulldog," he yelled after the big man. "Get on back here. Zentao is going to brief us on launch and recovery."

Zentao wasted little time beginning his descriptive dissertation as Bulldog returned to stand next to Dar. "Once you are strapped in and have your helmets on, we shall initiate the start sequence using the maintenance console. As the drive system powers up, it will bring your avionics," he paused momentarily, "I believe that avionics is the term with which you are familiar." Accepting Dar's nodding acceptance, he continued. "Very well, the drive will bring your avionics online and you're computer will acknowledge your presence." Zentao paused, anticipating questions. He continued when none were forthcoming. "After your computer is on line, it will direct you through the remaining preflight preparations. When you are ready, communicate with me, and we'll take it from there."

"What do you mean, 'you'll take it from there'?" Dar asked.

Zentao smiled at the two. "Please, Senior Commander, do not worry, We are not going to fly the fighter for you. When you signal readiness, the area around the two spacecraft will be cleared of personnel so that an airlock may be created."

"An airlock?" Bulldog asked. "Of course, I wondered how they were going to get us out of here without sucking the whole squadron with us."

"You are, of course, absolutely correct, Commander Bennett. A wall will form around your craft, and an outer door will open. My computer station will then lift you clear of the deck and allow the shield to fold in around you. You will see the shield open to free space as it fabricates a passageway, but it will not lose its integrity."

"I won't pretend I have a clue about what you are talking about, but I presume we'll pass through this fold in the shield?" Dar asked without enthusiasm. He was becoming a bit blasé about the wonders of alien technology being exposed to him on a daily basis.

"That is correct. Once clear of the shield you are on your own." Zentao looked at each man with concern. "You do understand, we control the launch from the maintenance panel. Please, do not attempt to override our control."

"Yes, we understand completely," Dar said flatly. "What about recovery."

"It is much the same, only in reverse order. You must only fly your craft to the appropriate side of the Nanta, in this case, the starboard and command your computer to link with us. We shall do the rest."

"Bulldog, enough of this idle chit-chat, let's kick a skid and get on with it." Dar was ready to fly, wearing his impatience clearly on his sleeve.

"I'm ready, boss," Bulldog said, spinning on his heel and walking off in direction of his fighter.

Climbing up the ladder to his cockpit, Dar felt a flood of excitement pour over him like a river. He'd flown his entire adult life, but this was different ~ this was alien technology and deep space, not a training hop in the sky over North Carolina. The cockpit felt comfortably familiar, as he settled into the exact replica of his Harrier's ejection seat, and a quick scan of the instrument panel confirmed the truth of Zentao's engineering capabilities. He was going to fly a spaceship with a Harrier's cockpit. He slipped his helmet on down to his shoulders, closed his canopy, and signaled Zentao he was ready.

Moments passed with little more than a slight humming noise surrounding him, then he felt a rumble in his seat ~ the drive was coming to life.

"Good afternoon, Dar. It is good to be with you," Nan said, pleasantly.

"Hey, yourself. Glad you're here," Dar cheerfully said, and meant it.

"Are you ready for departure, Dar?" Nan asked quietly.

Dar looked over his right shoulder at Bulldog's fighter. The big Texan was holding a thumb up, signaling Dar that he was all set and waiting.

"Yes, Nan, I'm ready," he commanded. Heart racing in his chest, he took a deep breath as the ship was surrounded by a wall materializing from the ceiling. No sooner than the wall had banged shut, a large opening appeared in the bulkhead forward of his ship. Dar asked, his voice shaking slightly, as he depressed the "press to talk button" on his throttle, "Bulldog, what ya think?"

"I think I'm about to have second thoughts about this whole damned thing, boss."

"Yeah, me too." Dar's fighter lifted, and folds of green mist poured through Nanta's shield breach, enveloping the two craft. "Here we go!" Dar felt little motion, but his fighter was passing slowly through the hanger door and on into the tunnel through the shield. He glanced in his starboard rearview mirror, and saw Bulldog close behind.

"Senior Commander Fantin, is everything all right?" Zentao sounded worried. "Your pulse rate is over 140."

"I'm fine, Zentao. Perfectly normal for me when I'm scared to death. Kinda like landing aboard a carrier."

"A carrier?" Zentao questioned.

"Never mind, I'll explain later," Dar said. The fighter was clearing the shield.

"We do not understand, but will wait for your explanation later. You are now clear to maneuver on your own. Good luck to both of you. We will expect you to return within three hours."

"Roger that, Yosemite One is clear to maneuver." Now on his own, the stick and throttle in his hands, Dar was a professional military aviator. "Yosemite Two, you clear?"

"Roger, Yosemite Lead."

"Join in Loose Cruise, and we'll see what we can do with these babies."

"In position, Lead," Bulldog radioed.

"Roger," Dar said, and eased the throttle up to 70 percent, checking his speed. "Holy, Christ were doing 1500 knots already, and accelerating."

"Roger that, but it hardly feels like we're moving," Bulldog excitedly responded.

It hit Dar like a sledgehammer. They were flying at a right angle away from the Nanta, there was nothing but open space before or beside them. Speed had little or no meaning without something to give it references.

"Yosemite Lead, this is Nanta Control, do you hear?"

"Loud and clear, Control," Dar answered.

"Yosemite Lead, turn port to 345.6 Bravo.

Dar put the fighter into a hard left turn, and almost did a complete aileron roll. "Holy shit! Bulldog, are you okay?"

"Still with you Lead. What was that? I 'bout lost my cookies."

Straight and level once more, Dar said, "Standby one." He paused, thinking. "Nan, we have a problem."

"I do not understand, Dar, all systems are working properly. What is the problem?"

"The inner shield, the one that neutralizes mass and acceleration forces is too effective."

"Explain. It indicates perfection," Nan stated with a questioning tone.

"I need *feel,* something to tell my body what is happening with the ship. The stick should harden as the forces build. I'm used to G forces on my body when I'm climbing or turning. Do you understand? These *feelings* help me fly."

"I comprehend your requirement," Nan said. "Standby, I will adjust the field so that you might have *feel*."

"Yosemite Two, ask your computer to adjust your inner shield so that you get a feeling of G's, and have it harden the controls for proper feel."

"Roger, Lead."

"Try a turn now, Dar," Nan said.

"I'm ready to try it again, Lead," Bulldog radioed.

Dar put the ship into a port turn; slowly, he increased pressure on the stick. He felt the G's build, but not uncomfortably, and the stick hardened as more pressure was applied. "Much better, Nan. Thanks." To Nanta Control he radioed his intentions, "Entering sector B, for a speed run."

Owlish eyes hooded with the first real rest he'd had in days, Captain Langos stood rigidly in his sleeping corner. Leaving the bridge several hours earlier, he'd dimmed the glow lamps in his Spartan quarters, set his third leg in the sleeping position and drifted into a deep slumber. Langos' much needed rest was now being cut short by the incessant knocking at his private entrance. He awoke abruptly, and in foul humor.

"Yes, yes, what is it?" Langos yelled, the hissing sound of the s's whistling impatience.

"Sir, you asked to be wakened should anything new develop aboard Nanta," Senior Lieutenant Bezal said with some urgency. With the recent dismissal of Dectima's First Officer, Bezal had been promoted as his replacement. Though the rise in status was an accomplishment, he felt less than pleasure at the reward, in fact, the thought of his friend's recent suicide brought blotches of off-coloring to his pink skin. Being number two in command to an ill tempered captain was not something he had anticipated during this tour of duty.

"Well, don't just stand there goggling, come in and report." Dectima's captain loosened his third leg and straightened his breast plate.

Bezal stepped through the opening door, surveying the austere conditions his captain kept his quarters. Little beyond a desk, communications equipment, and a stool decorated the gray room, with one notable exception . . . a holograph picture stood squarely in the middle of the desk. The graphic colors of the holo showed a Womongly woman, strikingly beautiful to Bezal's eyes, and a small child.

"Well, I'm waiting," Langos interrupted his First Officer's fleeting examination.

"Sorry, Captain. Nanta has put fighters out. Only two at this time, but I expect we shall see more before this day has passed."

"Ah, so it starts," Langos said quietly, more to himself than to his second in command. "How soon until Dectima is ready to jump?" He, as Dectima's captain, knew the answer, but in the asking he was rapidly reviewing his possible courses of action.

"Three day cycles, Captain," Bezal answered abruptly.

"Yes, yes, of course," Langos said absently. "I shall join you on the bridge momentarily."

Bezal bowed stiffly, recognizing he'd been dismissed, and backed slowly from the small cabin, passing a small hand over the door's actuator as he left. Alone, Langos rubbed tired yellow eyes, thinking for the hundredth time in as many hours, how vehemently he hated the Lantiusians.

"Captain on the bridge," a young Rage Warrior announced as Langos took his place in Dectima's command center.

"Give me VID," Langos commanded, his small frame settling on the command stool. Instantly, a holograph depiction of Nanta's sector filled his view. Several thousand miles closer to the Dectima, two small fighters flew in loose formation at better than sixteen thousand miles an hour. "Launch ready pad, and put the ship on combat alert."

Claxons sounded, glow lamps dimmed, and computers came alive throughout Dectima's multiple decks. With in minutes, Langos watched as five Strike Dragons departed an upper hangar bay, and accelerated toward the enemy fighters.

"Tell those pilots to not approach any closer than hundred thousand miles. Have them assume a line abreast defensive posture and wait for aggressive action from Nanta's fighters," Langos spoke loudly and with determination. "I want to see what these earthlings can do before we engage them."

"Shackle, go," Dar commanded. The fighters turned toward each other in a long arch, crossing and resuming the same relative positions at ten miles apart with Dar stepped ten thousand feet above his wingman.

"Good," Dar radioed Bulldog. I think we'll use combat spread as our basic fighting formation, it gives both of us excellent maneuverability and we can constantly check each others six. What do you think, Two?"

"Roger that, Lead, I agree."

"Dar, we have five enemy fighters bearing 46.89Alpha, fifty thousand miles," Nan informed softly. "Weapons are armed, and they appear to be setting up in a Womongly fighting line abreast."

Dar's eyes flashed to his head's up holograph, catching his first glimpse of the enemy. The Womongly fighters were lined up side-by-side with approximately 200 miles of separation. "Got 'em Nan. Thanks." Dar scanned his instruments quickly. "Bulldog, we have visitors."

"Tallyho, Lead. Ya want to take them on?" The excitement in the big Texan's drawl evident.

"Not today, Bulldog. Let's get a couple more hops under our belt before we leap into the breach. One eighty starboard, go!" Dar ordered.

"Yosemite Lead, this is Brit Lead. Just came out of the pipe. Need some help up there?" Danny's flight was space bound.

"Negative, Brit. We're heading for home plate now. Leave those Womongly fighters to themselves, ya hear."

"Roger, understood, Boss. But wouldn't it do my bloody little heart good to shoot that bunch down."

"I hear ya, Brit, but not today. Break. Yosemite Two, let's push her up and see just what these babies will do." Dar pushed his throttle to its stops, and the fighter leapt forward. Passing thirty thousand miles per hour, Dar asked, "Nan is this thing holding together?"

"We are doing just fine, Dar. I'll let you know if trouble develops."

"Holy shit, boss, we're doing over thirty-five thousand, and it feels like were crawling. I'm loving this." Bulldog radioed.

Dar could hear the thrill coursing through his wingman's veins. "Yeah, I know what you mean. Let's pull the power back to 85 percent." He paused to adjust the power, reversing hundreds of small light drives on the fuselage. "Nanta Control, were heading home. Request vector to hanger deck."

"Yosemite Lead, take up 234.2Alpha, slow to approach speed of one thousand knots.

Nanta grew in size until its immensity completely blocked the vastness of space. The green shield provided only a general sketch of the mighty ship it protected, but, to Dar, returning from his first venture into space, Nanta seemed as large as Earth itself.

"We have control." Dar recognized Zentao's distinctive voice.

"Roger, you have control," Dar radioed, and released the stick. Minutes later, the fighter lightly settled on its skids within the confines of hanger seven's airlock.

CHAPTER 13

"Dar, I enjoyed the flight, and will be looking forward flying again soon," Nan said softly.

"Me too, Nan. Probably see you tomorrow," Dar said, just as the recovery officer shut down his fighter. Nan went off line along with the remaining avionics, and he could feel the drive system begin to unwind.

With surprising swiftness, Nanta's wispy green shield disappeared and the hanger door slammed shut, followed by the airlock walls slipping, with a discernible clang, into the ceiling. Dar removed his helmet, unlocked the canopy, and stood to look out on a sea of faces cheering SFS-1's first flight. The entire squadron, plus dozens of Lantiusian engineers, were clapping and yelling at the top of their lungs. Dar turned to face Bulldog, seeing a colossal smile spread from one large ear to the other on his wingman's face, as he too stood receiving the adulation of his fellow fighter jocks. Dar gestured their triumph with a thumbs up.

"What do you think, Bulldog? Want to terrorize space again tomorrow?" Dar yelled over the din.

"You bet your sweet ass, skipper. Anytime, anytime at all," the big Texan screamed back.

The two crawled out of their machines and joined the crowd, only to be inundated with questions fired at them with the sound and rapidity of a 30 millimeter chain gun.

"Hold on," Dar bellowed, over the bedlam. "Try it one at a time." He was laughing along with Bulldog, and both were being slapped on the back with congratulations. "It was great . . . fantastic," was all he could get out above the reverberating voices of his squadron mates.

Cannaly pushed his way through the crowd, taking Dar by the arm. "Okay, boss, I'm next. First thing tomorrow morning. Right?"

"You're next Snake. Standby for the ride of your life.

"Congratulations, Dar," Littia titillated his mind with her thoughts. "We have prayed for you during your first flight. We are pleased it went well and you have returned safely."

Dar stood on tiptoes, scanning the hanger for her. "Where are you," he thought, just as he saw her standing near the light tube, well away from the main body of well wishers. She looked more stunning than ever, her white tunic revealing every curve of her beautiful body, with golden hair, in braids, strung to her waist. "Thank you for your concern. I'm fine. Will you join us later? We've got some celebrating to do."

"We shall be there," Littia said, and stepped into the light tube. She was gone in an instant.

"It's just like flyin' my F-16, 'cept we were doin' better than forty thousand knots. Shoot, thar ain't nothin' to it," Bulldog addressed the crowd, his Texas drawl overly evident. "Just 'member to have your onboard 'puter modify the inner shield to compensate for control feel and g forces. We 'bout lost it durin' our first attempt at a turn." His hands were awhirl with animation, showing what had happened during the first few minutes of his flight.

Dar grabbed Cannaly by the arm, leading him away from the rest. "Snake, Dectima has fighters out, five of them about fifty thousand miles from here. We may not have much time for training, which may be okay in the long run. The fighters really do fly like our own planes. Hell, if I hadn't known better, I could have been flying a Harrier over Cherry Point, only a lot higher."

"Yeah, that's what Bulldog's saying. Heck, boss, maybe we just ought to take the Womongly fighters on. We all have a shit load of combat training in our own birds. Why not apply it to what we have now and go for it?" He waved, indicating the space fighters of SFS-1.

"We may have to." Dar's tone was poignantly serious. "I doubt those Womongly fighters are just going to sit tight and let us train for very long."

"Well, what do you want to do?"

"Tell, Danny, when he gets back, to schedule familiarization flights for everyone tomorrow. If we can get those hops flown without any trouble from the Womongly, we'll take the next step toward getting this fight underway," Dar instructed, running his hand through rumpled hair.

Captain Langos watched his fighters take position. He found it mildly interesting that the first section of enemy fighters turned about, accelerating away from the Dectima. "They don't wish to engage the Strike Dragons. I wonder why? They certainly showed little fear while taking out our agents on the Nanta." Langos spoke quietly to Bezal standing at rigid attention at the captain's right elbow.

"It is my thought, Captain, that they are just testing these new fighters, and do not wish to over extend their capabilities."

"Perhaps," Langos mused. "Ah, look, two more fighters have left the Nanta's shield."

The two Womongly watched silently, as the new fighters accelerated toward the Strike Dragons, while the first section returned to Nanta. Langos admired the seemingly effortless manner with which Nanta's fighters executed formation maneuvers.

"These earthlings are very good," Langos said, absently. "See how each fighter is continually able to clear the others rear sector, even while turning. With that sort of mutual support, it will be difficult for our Strike Dragons to engage their rear quadrant without being seen."

"Do not our fighters fly this type of formation as well?" Bezal asked. Not a Strike Dragon pilot, he had little knowledge of the intricacies or nuances of fight tactics.

Langos complexion shifted slightly, taking on a reddish hue of anger. "First Officer Bezal, you should be quite familiar with how our fighters engage the enemy, you are number two in command. I suggest you begin studying fighter tactics."

Bezal noted Langos' anger rising, not just in his captain's pigmentation, but in the tone of his voice. "Yes, sir. I will begin my studies this very evening," he said, in a weak attempt to appease.

"Yes, yes. See that you do," Langos said, in a more even manner. As he spoke, his eyes were taking in the action on the VID. The enemy fighters were executing a crossing turn, changing their direction 180 degrees. The two fighters now presented their six o-clock to his Strike Dragons.

"Fighter Director," Langos commanded. "Have the lead Strike Dragon engage the enemy. Tell him to take one shot, and return to the defensive line."

"Fighter Director Aye," the captain of Dectima heard an acknowledging voice behind him.

Moments later, the center Strike Dragon accelerated from the defensive line, moving rapidly toward Danny Franklin's flight.

"Danny, we have a single enemy fighter closing our rear quadrant," Danny's computer, Clara, intoned softly.

Danny swiveled in his seat, rolling his fighter slightly to the left, visually searching for the closing threat. "Damn, what am I bloody well thinking," he said aloud. "Old practices die hard, can't see something that far away. Clara, can you pinpoint the target on my DDI?"

"It has been done, Danny," Clara responded softly. "Suggest we turn to meet the danger, or accelerate rapidly on our present heading."

"Brit Lead, this is Nanta Control, you have enemy fighter closing rapidly. Recommend you return to Nanta."

"Not bloody likely, mate," Danny spoke excitedly. "Brit Two, port 180, go. Let's see if these assholes can fly." He slammed his stick the left and began a shallow climb, allowing his wingman to pass well below his own flight path. Rapidly scanning his instruments, noting the speed and distance of his adversary, Danny commanded, "Okay, two, let's push 'er up to 100 percent."

The two fighters lunged forward, closing the distance between the enemy at a combined speed of over 90,000 miles an hour.

"Attention on hanger deck seven," a voice echoed throughout the mammoth work space. "A Dectima fighter is engaging our active flight."

Voices stopped in mid sentence, as the information sank home among the men of SFS-1. Danny's flight was in trouble. Dar visibly paled at the words, and stared blankly at Cannaly.

"Damn it all, I was afraid this was going to happen," Dar said. "Let's hope Danny's smart enough to return to base and not take the bastards on."

"Fat chance," Cannaly said, and smiled. "Come on boss, you said yourself, these fighters are like flying an old friend. Danny ain't about to let the opportunity like this pass him by . . . you can bet on it."

"Yeah, I know," Dar said with little enthusiasm.

"We shall pipe fighter communications to the hanger deck," Flight Control spoke over unseen speakers.

"Not bloody likely, mate ...," confirmed Cannaly's prediction.

"Two thousand miles and approaching firing range," Clare updated Danny.

"Roger," Danny said, scanning both his holographic weapons display and the plasma screen for relative positions of the five enemy fighters. Only one appeared willing to take on his flight of two. "Clara, confirm, only one fighter engaging."

"Confirmed. One thousand five-hundred miles. We are now in thrumber firing range"

"Brit Two, I'll go high after the head-on pass, you go low. We'll catch the bastard in a scissors."

Danny's fighter lit up like Las Vegas on a Saturday night, an iridescent luminescence rapidly shifting colors through the entire spectrum. The Womongly thrumber strike pounded his shield with focused energy, bouncing his craft like a basketball.

"Holy, bloody shit. What was that?" Danny was surprised to be alive.

"We have taken an enemy hit. Our shields are holding," Clara spoke in an even, soothing voice. "Two hundred miles and closing. Crossing in point five seconds.

At better than 90,000 miles an hour, the three closed and passed one another. Danny snapped his stick hard to starboard and pulled his fighter into a steep climb. Brit two followed his lead in the turn but in the opposite direction, and pushed over to go low.

Intending to meet Danny's flight with another visual head-on pass, the Strike Dragon began a long, sweeping turn to port. Rolling wings level, the Womongly pilot was amazed to find his forward quadrant void of opponents.

"Got you, you son of a bitch," Danny said aloud. He was high over the Womongly fighter and decelerating, forcing the enemy to pass beneath him. He dumped the fighters nose, rolled up on his right stub wing, and pushed the throttle to the stops.

The Strike Dragon snap rolled first to the right and then to the left. The pilot was frantically trying to locate Danny or his wingman. Seconds ticked by before he saw a silver dart closing at his five o-clock. He yanked the yoke to the right and into his lap, flying his fighter into an unbelievable turn, but it was too late.

Danny came out of his screaming dive level with the Womongly fighter, and closing fast. A grin spread across his face, as he pulled the trigger on his stick. Orange-yellow light flashed from the gun's muzzle, extending from the nose of his spacecraft. Balls of death streaked across the void, catching the Strike Dragon just as it started its turn. A ghostly glow momentarily enveloped the doomed fighter, then there was simply nothing. With astonishment, Danny flew through the place in space where his enemy should have been.

Captain Langos watched silently as the fighters engaged, seeing his Strike Dragon fire the first shot. The Nanta's fighter glowed with the hit, bringing his excitement up a notch, which caused his skin to change to a greenish tinge. He shifted slightly on his command stool, feeling notable tension from the bridge officers laboring efficiently around him. His mild elation was short-lived. The enemy fighter, though obviously hit, was still flying.

"They have protected their fighters with the same shielding as defends the Nanta," Langos spoke aloud to no one in particular. "It will take several hits to break the shield's power." His small hands unconsciously fondled the fire whip hanging on his right hip.

"Captain, look! What is the enemy doing?" Bezal exclaimed excitedly. The fighters had crossed, and Danny split his flight high and low. The three-dimensional holographic display clearly outlined the traces each fighter had taken.

Langos quickly assessed the situation, realizing his pilot would face open space when he completed his turn. "Fighter Director," he screamed. "Instruct our pilot to look high and to his right. Do it NOW!" Langos' color turned scarlet red as the fury in his chest took hold, strangling further words. Enraged and helpless, his breathing flaps fanning the air in frustration, he watched Danny maneuver into firing position,. The Strike Dragon blossomed and disappeared.

As quickly as anger had overcome him, Langos became fearfully calm, his color returning to a healthy pink. "These earthlings are good, very good," he spoke to Bezal, who, out of personal fear, had backed several feet away from the command stool. "Yes, Captain. Very good," Bezal agreed tentatively.

Ignoring his First Officer, Langos slipped from his stool, straightened his pantaloons and breastplate, and without a word strode purposely off the bridge.

Exhilaration, fueled by adrenaline, coursed through Danny. He'd been flying British Sea Harriers for twelve years, training hard to become the best, and it had all come to this one moment in time. He'd shot down his first enemy in an air-to-air battle, nothing could take that away from him, and nothing in his life would ever match the feeling of power he now felt.

"Nanta Control, Brit flight returning to base. Battle Damage Assessment, one enemy fighter torched."

"Roger, Brit Lead, take up heading 235.44Bravo, and congratulations."

Danny could hear shouts of celebration roaring on Nanta's bridge as the controller spoke. "Turning to heading and slowing to recovery speed," he radioed over the cheers.

Still flushed with success, Danny saw and heard the airlock walls disappear into the hanger's overhead. If Dar's welcome had been warm and loud, Danny's was a torrent river of voices and cheers. Before his left leg cleared the canopy rail, SFS-1 officers physically pulled him from the fighter and passed him shoulder to shoulder within the wildly exuberant group.

Above the roar, Danny screamed, "To the bar, chaps. The bloody drinks are on me."

CHAPTER 14

A kaleidoscope of motion, noise, and light filled the expansive interior of the bar. The first successful flights, coupled with Danny's kill, energized Nanta's entire crew, and galvanized the small group of multi-national pilots into a combat-ready squadron. It was party time, time to blow off pent-up emotional steam, and the "boys from Earth" were defusing real and imagined apprehensions held since being abducted.

Cannaly fought his way through the throng, trying to get to the bar. For the past hour, he and several squadron mates had been teaching Horse to a group of enthusiastic Lantiusian officers interested in Earth's bar games. Fast learners of the dice game, the Lantiusians were nonetheless losing on a regular basis. Cannaly was first out, having rolled four sixes, which no one had been able to beat. Having been the winner now had him struggling, elbow to elbow, through a living throng, to the crowded bar.

"Let me have five of those red things," Cannaly said to a robotic bar tender. He would rather have given his order to one of the many Lantiusians working behind the bar, but with the huge crowd screaming for drinks, the robots, who resembled his mom's upright vacuum cleaner, had been pressed into duty.

"As you wish, sir," the electronic gadget answered in a metallic voice, and clanked off to fill his order.

As he waited, Cannaly surveyed the huge room. Unlike any bar or lounge he'd ever frequented on Earth, this one, he noticed, had no smell. The air was almost antiseptically clean. Unconsciously, he looked around the ceiling for a filtering system. None was visible. Shaking his head, he directed his attention to his left, at the opposite end of the bar from the entrance light tube, a band played on a raised stage overlooking a large, recessed dance floor. Cannaly presumed it was a dance floor.

He couldn't see the actual floor, but there were several dozen couples gyrating to the strange euphony the musicians were blaring out in full force. Cannaly did a little dance step to the music, and wiggled his rear. Not a bad beat, he thought, and felt a touch on his shoulder.

"We would ask you to dance, Commander Cannaly," a sensuous voice requested.

Cannaly's jaw visibly dropped, and he fought for words as he turned to face the woman asking him to join her for a dance. Dressed in the pale pink tunic of a junior officer, her light brown hair fell to her shoulders, and she had the brightest blue eyes he'd ever seen.

"Ah . . . dance? Er . . . sure, I'd love to," he finally stammered out.

With a dazzling smile, she said, "We are pleased." Taking his hand, she led him to in direction of the band like a lamb to slaughter.

Cannaly forgot about the mechanical bartender, the drinks, and his thirsty, dice-playing companions. His hand in hers, he followed with a foolish grin on his face, absorbed in the music, the lady, and thoughts of how he was going to seduce his beautiful dance partner.

Dar sipped his drink, the sweet tasting liqueur burning pleasantly on his tongue, and answered Supreme Commander Jicama's question. "Yes, sir, I think we can fight with very little training. Your technicians did a wonderful job designing likeness to our own aircraft. It will be more difficult adjusting to flying with each other and in the vastness of space than learning how the Dart handles." He paused, chuckling at Jicama's expression. "Yes, sir, that's what we've dubbed our fighters. Darts. Bulldog, one of my pilots, came up with the idea."

Jicama appeared to mull the name over for a moment. Finally, he said, "We like it. Dart. Most appropriate, we think.

"Thank you, sir." Dar responded, then turned his attention to Littia, who sat across the table looking uncomfortable. "Littia, have I told you how beautiful you look tonight?"

Golden hair, flowing in curls to her waist, framed an ethereal face touched with just the right amount of makeup. Exquisitely cut from a bolt of snow white cloth and tailored specifically for Littia, her couturier had designed the garment with a deeply cut "V" which barely concealed Littia's ample breasts. Revealing by any standards, yet so natural for the alien setting, the frock gave Dar the feeling he was in the presence of a Greek Goddess.

Littia rewarded his remark with a smile. "Yes, we believe you have, several times over, but thank you once again."

Jicama looked hard at both Littia and Dar, "Why don't you two dance. We have a matter to discuss with First Officer Tamis."

Tamis, who had been listening silently to the conversation since joining the group earlier in the evening, sat upright at the mention of his name. He knew of nothing important Jicama needed to discuss.

"A super idea, Supreme Commander," Dar said, his face brightening with anticipation. "Littia, would you be so kind as to dance with me?" he asked, standing to offer his hand.

"We would be most pleased," she said quietly. "But we are not a very good dancer," she said apologetically.

Dar took her hand and led her around the table. "I'm not a great one on the dance floor either, so don't worry," he said, though he knew himself to be an accomplished dancer, who had, on more than one occasion, wooed young ladies with his rhythmic prowess. "Let's give it a try and see what we can do to help each other." Blue eyes sparkling, he smiled encouragement and steered her from the table. "Please, excuse us, Supreme Commander."

Jicama nodded, and gave a wave of his hand. He said nothing, but studied the two as they made their way through the crowd. "What do you think, Tamis? We believe our guest has more than a work-a-day liking for Guide 3rd Class Littia."

"We are sorry, sir, we have not noticed," Tamis answered, not sure if he fully understood the question, and wondering why such a beautiful Lantiusian woman would be at all fascinated by an inept earthling.

"Ah, it is a small matter, but could prove to be useful in the future," Jicama mused more to himself than to Tamis. "Very useful indeed."

Forcing his way through the swarming jam-packed bar, Dar, with Littia at his side, bumped painfully into a table filled to capacity with pilots and Lantiusian officers. The group had pushed several highly polished tables together forming one huge gathering place, now littered with glasses and mugs.

"Yo, skipper," a familiar voice screamed over the cacophony. "Come join us."

"Can't, Bulldog, I'm heading to the dance floor. Maybe later," Dar yelled back, noticing Danny several seats further down the table. The

Brit's hands flayed the air with exuberant animation, as he told of his battle and first kill, probably for the hundredth time. Dar bent down, still holding tightly to Littia's hand, and shouted in Bulldog's ear, "I'll bet Danny has darn near taken on Dectima's entire fighter force by now."

Bulldog looked up at Dar and broke out in laughter. "Yeah, and half the of the known universe as well," he said.

Dar slapped his wingman on the back, laughing at Bulldog's extension of his own attempt to poke fun at Danny. . . then became silent and serious. There was a sudden mood shift in the crowd packing the bar. Near the entrance, Lantiusians were strangely silent, slowly edging into tighter groups, their eyes riveted on something just out of Dar's view. He gripped Littia's hand harder, wishing he'd remember the thrumber rifle, and pulled her closer to his side.

"What is wrong, Dar?" She stroked his mind with an edge of fear.

"I'm not sure," he thought, then added, "stay close to me."

"Skipper, what the hell is going on?" Bulldog asked, standing slowly, pushing his chair away so he could move without hindrance, should the need arise.

More of the throng backed away from the light tube. Danny stopped waving his arms in mid stroke, and went mute.

Hiiiiii . . . Hoooo!

Dar's face registered incredulity, then slowly a boyish grin slipped across his face. Releasing pressure on Littia's hand, he said, "It's okay, though I'm not sure how your people are going to react to this."

Hiiiiii . . . Hooooo!

This time the call came from further to the right, nearer the bar. Dar began to chuckle, then laughed out loud. "Hiiiii . . . Hoooo!" he sang out at the top of his voice. Littia stared at him in disbelief, thinking he'd just lost his mind.

"Not without me you don't," Bulldog yelled, leaping on top of the table. As drinks spilled and glasses rolled to the floor, he jumped into the crowd and started forcing his way in the direction of the first *hi ho*.

Hiiiiii . . . Hoooo!

"Another call echoed through the now silent group of astounded Lantiusians.

"Hi, Ho

Hi, Ho
It's off to work we go.
With and knife and fork,
And a belly full of pork.
It's off to work we go.
Hi, Ho"

On knees they marched, their flight suits turned around backwards, cloth napkins wrapped tightly around their foreheads, and a right hand on the right shoulder of the man in front, four of Earth's finest fighter jocks singing boisterously.

"Hi Ho . . . .." the verse reverberated again, as Bulldog fell to his knees, linking with the line and picking up the song. Two more squadron mates joined moments later.

"Dar, have they gone crazy?" Littia asked.

He smiled at her and shook his head, "No, they're just having fun blowing off some steam. You might say, it's an Earth thing."

By the time the knee-marching troupe reached the bar, more fighter pilots had joined in on the fun. Shocked Lantiusians were shaking off the initial surprise at seeing grown men on their knees singing, and one, braver than the rest, joined the band. Laughing men and women stepped back to let the growing chain pass, many falling to their knees, joining the singers as the last man neared. The band stopped playing.

It was fifteen minutes before the revelers finally called it quits, standing to rub sore knees. Giggling like school kids, the entire group headed back to the bar for refills and loud talk. The Lantiusians who had joined in were dragged along by their human counterparts in a show of comradery.

Still confused, but impressed by the way her people had participated in the foolishness, Littia asked, "What was that all about? Is this normal play on your home planet?"

Dar squeezed her hand. "It did just what it was intended to do," he said. "Bring people together. Just look at them, Littia. That one little song, sung with complete abandon, has accomplished, in five minutes, more to solidify my pilots and your people than all your Lantiusian technology could in a year."

Watching those now gathered at the bar, Littia thought a moment. "We agree. It seems we still have much to learn about each others societies," she said thoughtfully, as the band began playing once more.

"Well," Dar said, and smiled. "Let's hope we keep learning. Now, how about that dance?"

Thirty minutes later, Dar dripped with perspiration from exertion. The hard beat of the music reminded him of disco, though the strange weavings of the melodies were like nothing he'd heard before. Tentative at first, Littia watched him with respectful amazement, but barely swayed to the rhythm. With Dar's encouragement, she began to succumb to the beat of the drums, and began following his lead. By the time the band brought their tempo back down to a slower pace, a small group of admirers was cheering them on to more and more complicated exchanges. Dar was used to having others watch him boogie, but for Littia it was a totally new experience. She was enjoying the attention, and even hitched her tunic to mid thigh so she could have more freedom to move.

The music slowed, and Dar moved close, putting his hand around Littia's waist, and taking her right hand in his left. He immediately realized that she had never danced in such a manner, but she slid naturally into his arms, pressing close to his chest. Heat radiated from her pale soft skin. Laying his head next to hers, he began swaying to the melodious tune, letting the sweet smell of her lift him, drug-like, into a pleasurable high.

"Can you tell what I'm thinking?" he whispered. He felt totally alone with her. The crowed noisy room was nothing more than a background of muted energy, present and audible but unable to transgress the mood woven by the nearness of her.

"Yes," Littia whispered back. "You are wanting to take me to your quarters, that we might be alone."

Dar drew back sharply. "And you're not angry with me?"

"No. Look into my mind, Dar." Her eyes were pools of sensuality. Concentrating, Dar saw Littia's thoughts, "When can we go? We are ready." A warm gentle smile played at the edges of his lips, as he sent a mind wave back, "Now. Just let me grab us a drink at the bar, I'll met you at the light tube."

Littia gave a slight nod. "May we finish this dance first? It is wonderful to be held to the music."

Dar drew her closer, continuing to move slowly until the band stopped playing momentarily, then their instruments shifted into high gear once more.

With two glasses in hand and a bottle of Lantiusian wine under his arm, Dar met Littia at the light tube, a smile radiating across his handsome face. "Shall, we?" he said lightly.

The ride down the tube was a silent one. Only their shoulders touched and for both of them it was enough. They had no need for words. At his quarters, Dar commanded, "Open." The door slid back silently. He stepped aside, allowing Littia to enter, and was about to ask for "lights" when he was hit hard in the chest by something heavy and very much alive. Littia gave a yelp of surprise as the overhead lamps flashed on, then gasped in amazement at the sight of Dar laying flat on his back with an orange utapotus curling up on his chest.

"Pete, you darn near scared the life out of me." Dar laughed, and began stroking his friend tenderly. At Dar's touch, a gurgling of pure pleasure rumbled deep from Pete's scaly throat.

Littia, her hand at her mouth, found it difficult to utter words appropriate for the moment. She started to giggle uncontrollably, and then to laugh.

"If you can contain your mirth at my misfortune," Dar said in mock indignation, "I'll introduce you." With gentleness, he plucked the utapotus from his chest and stood. "Littia, this is Pistol Pete. Pete, I would like you to meet Littia."

Trying to contain her giggling, Littia finally caught her breath, and reach out to stroke the scaly animal in Dar's arms. "Hello, Pete. We are very pleased to met you." Suddenly the enormity of situation hit her like a shock wave. "Dar, you have been chosen by a utapotus. But this can't be so. Utapotus' accept only us," she touched her chest, "Only Lantiusians. How can this be? Not, you Dar, please not you."

"What's wrong, Littia? I don't understand, I thought you would be pleased." He tossed the wine bottle on the guest chair, and putting his arm around her shoulders, eased her into the room, letting the door close behind them. Pete squirmed to the floor, jumped up on the airbed, and laid down. Dar felt the utapotus, its yellow eyes whirling, react to the sudden emotional charge filling the room between his chosen and the woman called Littia.

Littia, near tears, could not take her eyes from Dar. "Our religious teachings speak of a day when our society will end, and that its destruction will be proceeded by a remarkable event." She paused a moment to recall the words. *"It is written, from the mouth, mind, and heart of the God of Many Arms,"* her lids closed slowly, and she sat clumsily on the bed next to the loving utapotus, *"that one day a man, not of Lantius, will come, and in the one hand he will hold the flame of peace, in the other the lashing sword of destruction. This man, known by his caring nature and warrior's blood, will be accepted by the one that is not one."*

Stupefied, Dar paced the room. "What are you talking about. What's this 'one that is not one'?" He ran fingers nervously through his hair. As Littia met Dar's gaze, he could feel the pain and sadness in her heart.

"The 'one that is not one' is a utapotus," she said despondently. "No living entity but a Lantiusian has ever been chosen by a utapotus, at least not until now."

Dar moved to Littia, kneeling in front of her and taking her head gently in both hands, "Littia, I may have been chosen by a utapotus, but, trust me, I'm not 'The One'. I'm no savior or destruction monger, I'm just plain old Dar Fantin, and right now I'm much more concerned about you, and your feelings for me, than some legend."

"But, Dar the words of our God of Many Arms are the very essence of Lantiusian culture, the ethos of our society. We are taught from birth to know, respect, and live by His teachings."

Raising slightly, Dar tipped his head back and brushed Littia's lips with his. "Hush, now. We'll keep Pete's acceptance of me a secret. That way we won't upset your companions, and what they don't know can't hurt them."

A weak smile traced across Littia's delicate face, as slowly she reached out to encircle Dar's neck with her arms. A single tear ran from her right eye, a lone line of sadness etched by its existence. "Dar, make love with me."

Without a word, Dar scooped her into his arms, tenderly easing her back on the air bed, and bent to kiss her long and deeply. Littia responded as a woman falling in love, receiving his attentions and storing the moment in her heart to be remembered later.

The kiss lingered until Pete stirred, moving from bed to chair, where he wrapped comfortably around the forgotten wine bottle, only to resume his watchful vigil. The utapotus' manner broke the melancholy of the union, forcing reluctant smiles from both Dar and Littia.

"Dar, we see your mind, and no not that way. My people have not made physical love in hundreds of centuries. Let me show you our way first. Later, we may, if you still desire me, try it yours. Please, let me do this for you, and for me."

Dar nodded acceptance, not sure what she meant, and not really caring, just as long as he could be with her. She was so beautiful. He had to admit, he had not had such feelings of concern or attachment for any woman in many, many years. His heart was near critical mass with the want and need of her . . . his guide into a new world. "Whatever you want," he whispered.

Littia slowly untangled herself from Dar's arms and sat up on the bed, crossing her legs in a loose Lotus position. "Please sit facing me, Dar." She waited for him to assume a similar position. Taking his right hand, Littia placed it on her heart, then moved his left to her inner thigh. When she was satisfied with the proper position of his hands and fingers, she reached to touch him in the same areas. "Close your eyes and think only of me, nothing else but me sitting here next to you."

 Dar closed his eyes slowly.

"Think only of me, think only of me . . . think only of me."

Heat, like the welcome warmth of a potbellied stove on a frosty morning, wound its way through every sinew, muscle, and nerve. Dar reached for the warmth, needed it, desiring its resplendency with all his heart. He could not exist without its temporal mantel of compassionate trust. From the warmth, a flare of light formed as a pinpoint moving through the golden firmament in which he now drifted. The light was the heat, the heat was Littia, and she loomed larger, closer to his center in the ever expanding heaven of gold. He had to reach the light; nothing in life must hinder his ascent to the light, to be one with the light. He felt her radiance wash over him, felt his blaze wash over her, and in the joining the universe exploded, forming images of all the good things in his life, and the marvels of hers. He saw suns and moons circling thousands of planets, giving life to races of beings not unlike his own. He felt the miracle and pain of birth as if he was giving a new child life. He witnessed Littia's love for him growing deep in her heart, and knew she was visiting his secret places as well. Like a balloon being filled with helium, his mind expanded to accept the wonders, pleasures, and fears that modeled the very fabric of a woman giving her all to him, and only him. So swollen with warmth and light that he could receive no more, the aerostat burst in a shower of colored light, and then, darkness.

Dar passed out cold.

CHAPTER 15

Dar woke from a dreamless sleep refreshed, senses alert, but with the distinct feeling something was wrong. He lay staring at the blank white ceiling and tried to gather his thoughts into coherent meaning. Something was missing. There, just beyond his grasp of understanding, existed a void in his memory. He'd been dancing with Littia, completely absorbed by her beauty, and feeling, for the first time in years, a genuine need for emotional evolvement with a woman. Then nothing. A black hole swallowed his memory from the moment he'd held Littia in his arms swaying to the music until the instant he awoke.

The cover sheet moved slightly and something soft rubbed lightly against his thigh. "Well, good morning, Pete," Dar said, pulling the cover sheet back to expose the little utapotus. Smiling, he stroked Pete gently under his ugly head. "Little buddy, what went on last night? I seem to have to have misplaced a goodly portion of the evening's events."

Pete's green eyes scrolled back in his head, as if to say, "Don't you know? What have I chosen, an idiot?"

Dar rolled to his left, looking up to check the clock over his desk. Still plenty of time to get dressed for PT, he thought, throwing the bed sheet back. As he slipped on his shorts, he still tried forcing memories of the past few hours back into consciousness. The only thing he knew for certain . . . he felt wonderfully full of life, ready to take on whatever the day might have in store. One vague recollection began to take shape through the fog; Pete was to be kept a secret. Why, he couldn't recall, but he intuitively knew that should Pete's existence become common knowledge, major problems would follow.

"Boss, you ready?" Cannaly asked, beating on the door.

Dar finished tying his shoes. "Yeah, I'll be right out."

PT went smoothly, though much of the squadron looked as if they had been catapulted off the bow of a carrier without benefit of an aircraft. Paying a heavy price for the quantity of Lantiusian spirits imbibed during the merry making festivities the night before, they trudged rather than ran the last two of the three miles Dar led them on. Their skipper was feeling fine, staying well ahead of his companions during the run, debating whether or not to discuss his apparent memory loss with Cannaly. Finally, he resolved to keep his latest episode involving the bizarre to himself.

Flying started after breakfast, with two flights leaving Nanta by mid morning. On the bridge, Dar sat in a command chair next to Jicama watching the operations on a holographic screen. He'd hoped to run in to Littia while eating, but she had not shown up, and apparently could not hear or was ignoring mind blasts directed at her.

"We admire the dexterity with which your pilots fly the Darts," Jicama offered, breaking into Dar's daydreaming.

"Thank you sir. I wish I could take credit for their training," Dar said, absently. He shook his head slightly, clearing stray thoughts from his mind, and concentrated once more on the screen. "No sign of our friends from the Dectima this morning. I wonder what they're up to?"

"We speculate on Dectima's actions as well," Jicama answered. "Will you be flying today, Dar?" Supreme Commander Jicama changed the subject.

"Later this afternoon, if all goes well with the remainder of our familiarization flights. In fact, my plan is to tickle Dectima's defenses by flying into their sector of space. Nothing real extravagant. Just push them a little."

"Is this wise? Should you not spend more time training?"

"As I said last night," Dar paused, remembering his conversation with Jicama. Littia was there and so was Tamis, and the Supreme Commander had suggested that he and Littia dance. His face tensed as he tried to recall more.

"Are you feeling ill?" Jicama asked with some concern. He'd turned in his chair to look worriedly at Dar.

"Sorry, sir. My mind drifted, thinking of the last night's fun." He smiled reassuringly at Jicama. "As I mentioned last night, your engineers have created the Darts so perfectly, they are like flying our own aircraft. I'm sure, as you can see from the way the familiarization flights are going, that we're ready."

"We are pleased it is so. I believe the Dectima may be very near 'jump' capability. It would be best if we might manage to engage them before they move into Earth's space."

Silence ran deep on Dectima's bridge. The only sound was the humming electronics operated by sixty-two Womongly officers seated in rows behind their captain. Captain Langos sat comfortably on his stool, his third leg loosely dangling behind him, studying the VID screen with close scrutiny. His enemy's fighters, four of them, were engaging in mock battle, fighting each other. Their maneuvers were far more complicated than any he'd ever witnessed during his long tenure as a junior bridge officer, and now, captain of the Dectima. Pigmented skin changed colors rapidly, as Langos' mood changed from excitement to anger . . . excitement over what these strange earthling pilots could accomplish in their small space fighters, and anger that the Lantiusians had brought them here to fight his Strike Dragons, delaying his acquisition of the resource-rich planet these misguided alien upstarts called home.

"How long until we can jump?" Langos snapped.

First Officer Bezal looked up from the hyper-drive control panel he'd been monitoring. "Seventeen hours and nine minutes, Captain."

"Yes, yes, that is good," Langos said, hoping he could safely move Dectima behind Earth's moon before engaging these men and their Lantiusian fighters. There, in full view of Earth, his Strike Dragons would cut them down, one by one.

While Dar sat discussing strategy with Supreme Commander Jicama, Jon Pierre Coe'tte stepped out of a light tube and into a passageway he had not as yet explored. A Mirage pilot, known throughout the French Airforce as the very best stick and rudder man the Force had to offer, he was now grounded, all because of a blast from a Womongly thrumber rifle. Jon Pierre was adapting rapidly to his new prosthetic arm, but the medical personnel attending to his healing would not recommend that he be allowed in the cockpit of his Dart until they were certain of his ability to control the new appendage. The afternoon of his third day in sickbay, he'd told the nurses that he was going for a walk, and since that time, had spent most of his waking hours roaming Nanta.

This could be interesting, he thought, sniffing the rather foul odor permeating the passageway. Nowhere on the ship had he smelled anything but clean fresh air, but here, in this passageway, the mild stench caught his attention immediately. The passageway extended out of sight, which Jon Pierre did not find unusual, but three things were definitely out of the ordinary. No doors leading off the passageway, the PCT located in the center rather than off to one side, and practically no lighting, he noted absently, letting his eyes adjust to the dimness.

Cautiously, he took a step for the tape, then stopped. Strange, he thought, no Lantiusians. The place looked deserted. He took a deep breath, trying to relax, and shake off growing anxiety. With gathering determination, he moved to the tape, and stepped aboard the moving ribbon. Unlike the many PCTs he'd ridden on various decks, this one moved no faster than a man could walk.

He'd gone only a dozen or so feet, when, to his right and left, reflective screens suddenly shimmered in the semi-darkness. Curiosity aroused, Jon Pierre side-stepped off the tape to more closely examine the ten meter long oddities. Pale luminescence cast back a shadow of his face. Thinking it resembled a mirror, he reached out to touch the smooth surface. Instantly the dark mirror turned transparent. He stepped back, jaw slack in amazement. Before him was a small town, consisting of several ovoid buildings with circular doorways and windows. Unconcerned by his sudden appearance, small upright reptilian-like creatures moved around the structures on hard packed mud trails. As he watched, three of the "things" came together, tipped their oversized heads toward each other, and extended a single antenna. The spidery antennae intertwined for several moments, before the three separated to go its own way.

They were talking, Jon Pierre realized with a start. He tapped loudly on the mirror, but no notice was given him.

An idea began forming in Jon Pierre's mind. He walked swiftly to the opposite panel, and touched it lightly. A totally new expanse opened before him. A prehistoric jungle of heavy vegetation filled the enclosure. Brightly colored flowers bloomed around the trunks of gnarled tree-like growths, while strangely shaped flying insects, the size of his fist, darted in and out of two foot tall blades of feathery red grass. Captivated by the wild beauty of the scene, he didn't notice the humanoid-like animal moving from the far right of the forest. The three foot lanky biped seemed to appear from nowhere, walking straight at Jon Pierre. He

backed away, then realized its single black eye was focused, not on him, rather something on the ground just under the mirror. It bent down, picked up a small baby replica of itself, and tucked the babe into the sack-like garment it wore loosely around its body. Nestling the child, it turned and walked into the dense foliage, to be
swallowed from view.

Jon Pierre shook his head in disbelief. With a flash of insight he realized where he was. "A zoo!" he said aloud.

"What are you doing here?"

Jon Pierre spun to his left and came face to face with a scowling seven foot Lantiusian. "I . . .er, I mean, I'm just exploring the Nanta, nothing more," he stammered out.

"This is a restricted area. You are not allowed here, nor are any of the earthlings. We ask you to leave. Now!" the big man ordered, in a tone that left little doubt as to his meaning.

"Sure, I'll leave," Jon Pierre said, backing away from the Lantiusian. "Sorry. I thought we had the run of the ship. It won't happen again."

"We trust it will not," the Lantiusian responded harshly.

Jon Pierre ducked into the light tube and hit the symbol for the hospital deck. As he was whisked upward, he thought about the ramifications of a zoo aboard Nanta.

Dar walked swiftly to the PCT outside the dining hall. He'd eaten little, spending more time shoving food around his plate than actually eating. His morning with Jicama had gone well. Both were pleased with how the flights were being conducted . . . Jicama with the flying abilities of the men piloting the Darts, and Dar with the superb flight control the bridge personnel were providing. After dumping a strange looking protein dish, smelling of almonds, on his plate, he chose a table well away from others. He wanted to contact Littia, and tried several times with no success. "Where is she?" He asked himself a dozen times.

Now, hurrying for his quarters to brief with Bulldog, he felt strangely alone. He stepped from the light tube, and ran smack into Cannaly.

"Hey, Snake," Dar's mood brightened. "I wanted to talk to you about this afternoon's flight. We're both leading sections at the same time, which may be a breaking tour initial flying rules, both of us out at the same time, but I guess there just isn't enough pilots in the squadron to worry about it who might be the follow-on CO."

"Yeah, I know, and I agree. Now that's settled, what'cha got in mind?" Cannaly asked. "Something special I hope."

"Nothing spectacular, but yeah. I thought we might join as a division after we get warmed up and go stir the pot a little."

"Really?" A smile spread wide across Cannaly's face. "I like the idea already."

"I thought you would," Dar said, returning the smile. "Let's get our wingmen together and brief in my quarters. Meet you there in ten or fifteen minutes."

"Sounds good to me. You want me to scout up Bulldog for you?"

"Sure. I'd appreciate that, thanks," Dar said, slapped his friend on the back, and headed for his room.

Pete lay contently on the bed, his large orange eyes spinning with affection as he caught sight of Dar entering the room.

"Hey, Pete," Dar spoke softly. Moving to the bed and bending down, he began stroking the scales under the utatpotus' chin. "How ya feeling today, huh?"

Pete leaped into Dar's arms knocking him back into the guest chair. "What's this?" Dar asked Pete, reaching into the folds of the chair, he retrieved a wine bottle. Dar studied the lavender liquid with curiosity, trying to determine where and when he'd gotten a bottle of wine. More importantly, why? He wasn't even very fond of wine, Lantiusian or not. *Littia. It had something to do with Littia.* Holding the bottle in one hand and balancing Pete in the other, he could almost smell the sweet scent of her nearby.

A loud knock, followed by, "Ya in there, Skipper?", interrupted his concentration.

"Come on in, Bulldog," Dar said loudly.

Pete disappeared with an audible "poof," as the door slid aside.

"The XO and Boomer will be here in a minute," Bulldog drawled.

Moments later Cannaly and Boomer appeared at the door. Boomer, a small, twenty-nine year old Russian Mig-29 pilot, bowed slightly to Dar. It was the first time he'd been in his Commanding Officers quarters, and he was hesitant. "Y'all come on in, and let's get started," Dar said, nodding pleasantly to the reticent Russian.

The briefing went quickly. Each section, one led by Dar the other by Cannaly, would leave Nanta as separate flights, do a few warm up maneuvers, then join as a four plane division with Dar in the lead. Dar explained his intentions. They would test the water around the Dectima by flying within firing range, each shoot a torpedo, and head flat out back to the Nanta, for recovery. Nothing fancy, just tickle the stress level of the Womongly, with no intention of trying to cause major damage to the huge spaceship.

"We'll fire simultaneously on my command and from maximum firing range," Dar briefed. "Any questions?" He paused, giving the three a chance to speak. He looked at each man. Reflected in their eyes was determination mixed with the knowledge that for the first time they were taking the fight into enemy territory. No one spoke. "Okay, then, we'll see y'all out there." Dar ended the briefing.

Alone once again, Dar went to his desk to scribble a note to Littia, intending to give it to one of his officers for delivery. As he reached for a pen, "We are here," formed clearly in his mind.

"Where have you been? I tried all morning to talk to you," Dar asked uneasily.

"We have been in Guide Training. We are sorry we worried you. Can we be of service?" Littia's tone was coolly professional.

"What's wrong? You don't sound yourself." Dar asked, a furrow etching his forehead with concern.

"We are fine," she thought softly. "My instruction was difficult and long. That is all, please do not worry, we are fine." She did not tell him of her early hour interview with the Supreme Commander, nor that *he* had been her instructor.

"Okay," Dar thought, though he had doubts about her explanation. "I'm just leaving to fly. Can I talk to you later, maybe after dinner?"

"Yes, we believe that will be possible." Her thoughts hesitated, then continued. "Dar, please be careful. We shall worry while you fly."

"Thanks, Littia. I'll be okay. Trust me."

"We shall, Dar," the thought was strong and honest.

Littia's thoughts left him ill at ease. Something was not as it should be. He knew it in his heart. Dar sat down in his desk chair to think it through, but Pete popped in, demanding immediate attention. For the next several minutes, he stroked the utapotus, and found his worries draining away. "Thanks little buddy, I feel better now," he crooned to his friend, then stood, "see you in a while." He smiled at Pete, and headed for hanger deck seven.

"Dar, it is good to be together once more," Nan spoke softly. "Are we going out?"

"Yeah, just as soon as we get everything online. We're going to do a little gunnery practice today. How does that suit you."

"Just fine, Dar," Nan said, adding, "all systems are up and operating normally."

Dar thanked the computer, and signaled a thumbs up to Bulldog. Minutes later, both Darts were leaving the green protective shield surrounding Nanta. Newly decorated with his name, Senior Commander Dar Fantin, printed on either side of the canopy rail, and the squadron's Yosemite Sam insignia boldly coloring either side of the fuselage, Dar idled the fighter along the outskirts of the mammoth mother ship. During his first flight, he'd been so preoccupied with flying the machine, he had not really noticed the majesty of his new environment. Space, he suddenly realized, was beautiful, a huge void with pinpoints of bright burning suns, spectrum filled nebulas, and stars by the billions.

"Bulldog, its magnificent out here. Have you noticed?" Dar spoke into his mike.

"Not really, Lead. Too busy flying your wing, but now that you mention it, you're right. Don't think I've ever seen so many stars."

"Yeah. Well, let's push'er up and do a few combat turns. Move it into combat spread," Dar commanded. To Nanta Control he relayed, "Control, we're taking up a heading of 245.0Bravo. Please inform me when the second flight has launched."

"Yosemite Lead, understand. Snake flight should be flying within the next three minutes," Nanta Control radioed.

"Roger that," Dar said, pushing his throttle to 85 percent, and watched Bulldog expertly assume a position ten miles off his right wing.

"Yosemite Lead, you out here somewhere?" Cannaly asked eagerly. "Me and Boomer are raring to go."

Dar leveled his wings from the ninety degree turn he'd just completed, glanced over at his wingman to ensure he was in position, and answered Cannaly. "Roger, Snake. Gotcha on holo. Take up a heading of 200.3Bravo, and we'll rendezvous a hundred and twenty-five thousand miles from Nanta."

"Roger, Yosemite. Meet you there."

The two flights pointed their noses at each other at better than 20,000 knots, and had visual contact in short order. "Have you in sight, Snake. Hold your heading and we'll join on you," Dar ordered. "Yosemite Two, starboard one-eighty . . . go!" Dar led his flight over the top of Snake's section, arriving in perfect combat formation outside and fifteen miles above Cannaly. "Snake, have Boomer slip into fighter wing ~ Break ~ Bulldog, same for you, move into fighter wing on me."

The two wingmen flew rapidly into position behind their lead Darts on a forty-five degree angle and stepped down several hundred feet. In effect, each section was now a single fighting unit, but having combined the two sections into a division of four Darts, the same combat spread formation was maintained.

"Let's go kick Womongly ass," Cannaly yelled, as the formation settled down.

"Roger, kick some ass," Dar responded, laughing to himself. "Nanta Control, request vector to the Dectima."

"Take heading 275.5Delta," Control answered. "Distance to target seventy-five thousand miles, and closing."

"Roger, Control ~ Break ~ Snake, push it up to ninety percent," Dar transmitted, pausing momentarily, then pushed his throttle to 90 percent.

"I have Dectima on both the holograph and plasma screen, Dar," Nan said. "Shall I arm weapons?"

"Arm weapons, and keep me informed about enemy fighters."

"No enemy fighters seen as yet, although it will be surprising if they do not try to engage us," Nan said flatly.

Captain Langos slumped on his command stool. The fatigue and stress of the last

few days were beginning to take their toil both physically and mentally. His normally bright pink skin now appeared dull and lusterless. He'd not spoken a word since asking First Officer Bezal the time until a hyper jump could be executed. Riveted to the VID screen projecting the flights of Nanta's fighters, he silently counted the hours until he could free Dectima from this untenable position.

Without comment he watched two more of the enemy leave Nanta's protective shield, followed shortly by yet another pair. It had been the same all day, fighters leaving, practicing formations and mock battle, then returning to the Nanta. These new fighters were no different, Langos thought. He actually was debating if he should not return to his quarters for a much needed rest, when he noticed the two flights join, and take a heading straight for Dectima.

The Captain's skin suddenly turned a bright green, at the realization of what the four enemy fighters might be contemplating. "Fighter Control, launch Grecatin Squadron from the port side, and have them wait for orders in the shadow of the Dectima."

"Sir. The entire squadron?" an officer at the Fighter Control station asked.

Langos spun around on his stool, fire whip in hand, "You question my order?" His voice was hard with anger.

The young officer stood, knocking over his stool, his skin becoming a bright yellow as fear rushed through him. "No sir. Sorry sir. Launch Grecatin Squadron, port side. Yes sir."

Slowly, Langos composed himself, as he replaced the whip on his belt, and turned his full attention back to the VID. "If these fighters get within tactical strike distance, have the Strike Dragons engage them at full drive," he ordered.

"One hundred twenty thousand miles and closing. Thermal torpedo range in two point five minutes, thrumber range in six point three minutes," Nan calmly said.

"Roger," Dar said. He could clearly see the outline and features of the Dectima on his plasma screen, and his heart pounded with anticipation of his first shot. "Yosemite Flight, arm torpedoes and stand-by for my firing mark. Target the bridge bubble on Dectima's nose". There was no response from his wingmen. He expected none.

"Thirty seconds to torpedo range," Nan said.

"Yosemite Flight, standby to fire. Standby. Standby ....."

"Ten seconds to firing range," Nan ticked off the time.

"Standby, MARK, MARK," Dar loudly radioed to his flight, simultaneously squeezing the trigger on his stick. He watched in awe as four purple streaks of flame sped for the Dectima, then screamed, "Port, one-eighty go!"

Grecatin Squadron Leader, Akama, watched the enemy on his heads- up VID screen. There was little doubt in his mind what the four ships were about to try, and without waiting for orders from Fighter Control aboard Dectima, he commanded his squadron to make a short hyper jump. Fifteen Strike Dragons accelerated a short distance away from the Womongly mother ship, made jump, and disappeared in a blinding flash of orange light.

Captain Langos, a veteran of many battles, anticipated Dar's torpedoes thirty seconds before the devastating weapons were fired. "All available power diverted to the shield," he commanded, his voice completely lacking emotion.

Three thermal torpedoes struck Dectima seconds later. The ship shook violently under the impact, causing minor damage on four decks, but no deaths. The shield held. Langos watched the fourth torpedo pass harmlessly forward of the bow.

"Now it is our turn," Langos said aloud. His tiny circle of a mouth attempted a smirk.

The one-eighty turn completed, Dar checked Cannaly's position on his right wing. "Let's take'er home, Yosemite Flight." His transmission barely had time to reach his wingmen when a blast of violet-red struck his shield.

"Fifteen enemy fighters in rear quadrant," Nan intoned quietly. "Shield holding, all systems operating."

"Holy jumping Jesus, where did they come from? Break right, Break right," he screamed to his flight as the surrounding area blossomed with flowers of violet fire. He slammed his stick to the right, pulled the nose up, and jammed the throttle to maximum. "Snake, there's a bunch of bad guys on our six," he grunted, fighting the g load.

"No shit, Sherlock," Cannaly managed to transmit. "Got any ideas?"

Dar gave a quick scan of the holo and plasma screens. The enemy fighters, closing fast, were flying line abreast, and firing indiscriminately. "Too many to fight as a unit. It's bee-in-the-bonnet time," he radioed, all the while jinxing his Dart.

"Roger, understand," Cannaly transmitted. "Boomer, you're on your own, good luck."

The four fighters split formation. Now they were individual Darts taking on far superior numbers. It was the only way each fighter had a chance of maneuvering freely, but it left each without mutual support.

"Recommend we hyper jump, Dar," Nan said.

The computer sounded hopeful that Dar would heed her advice. "No way, lady," he yelled. "This is what we're here to do. Fight! Just keep the thrumber full of bullets." He yanked back on the stick as his Dart slashed by a Strike Dragon, then stomped bottom rudder to slice the bird down on top of his prey. The gun spoke . . . yellow-orange balls traced to its target. The Strike Dragon disappeared instantaneously.

To Dar, the fight seemed to go on forever, but he knew only minutes ticked by. Constantly yanking and banking, avoiding fighters trying to engage him, and still keep pressure on the Womongly pilots. Two more Strike Dragons turned to space dust under his thrumber.

"Shield holding at eighty-five percent," Nan intoned softly. "We can sustain another ten hits before failure."

The Dart had taken hits, but was holding its own. "Roger, Nan." He pushed into a nose down, negative g turn, barely avoiding one of those ten hits left the machine.

"I'm hit, shield failing," Boomer cried out, the fear in his transmission evident. They were his last words. Boomer's Dart exploded in a fiery shower of lavender particles.

"Bulldog, break left," Cannaly screamed. "You've got two at your six, break left."

Bulldog felt the jarring blow of two thrumber blasts slam against his shield. Instinctively, he pulled hard on the stick, then without thinking, pushed it full forward. The Dart stuttered under the maneuver, but the nose dropped and Bulldog felt the negative g's build. He completed an inside loop, arriving at his opponent's six. With a grin, he pulled the trigger. First one then the other Strike Dragon evaporated.

"Seven enemy fighters remain," Nan said.

"Thanks, Nan. The odds are better now, huh?" Dar rolled wings level at the top of an outside loop, completing a Cuban-eight, then dipped his wing down and flew back into the enemy nest below. Suddenly, they were gone, leaving behind a flash of orange light.

"Enemy has hyper jumped," Nan informed Dar. "Do you wish to follow?"

"Not this time, Nan. Maybe next. Think I've had enough fun for one day." He paused, scanned his holo, finding Cannaly and Bulldog several hundred miles away. "Snake, Bulldog, join on me. Think it's time to go home."

"Roger, Yosemite Lead," Cannaly said, his voice sounding revved, but tired. "I have you on holo. Take up a heading for the ship, I'll grab Bulldog and be with you in a minute."

"Nanta Control, this is Yosemite Lead. We had a little trouble out here, but will be ready for recovery in approximately twenty minutes."

"Understand, Dar," Jicama transmitted. "We have never witnessed such flying. You, all of you, were magnificent.

"Thanks, but we lost Boomer," Dar transmitted sorrowfully.

"Yes," Jicama responded. "But one for eight is a fair exchange, though a sad one."

"Coming aboard," Cannaly radioed.

Dar glanced over his right shoulder, and watched the two Darts maneuver into position.

His entire small body shaking with frustration and anger, Langos slumped on his stool staring at the now blank VID screen. Silently, bridge officers closely watched their captain, waiting for his next command or acrimonious outburst. It was a time to be silent. Eight Strike Dragons and pilots had been lost against a force a quarter in size. Never had such a defeat been handed the Womongly.

"They are insane, these earthlings," Langos spoke quietly. "There can be no other explanation. Yes, yes, completely crazy, but such good pilots. They out maneuver our Strike Dragons at every turn." He stood, rubbed sore eyes, and turned to Bezal. "I will be debriefing with the returning Strike Dragon pilots, should I be needed. Inform me when it is time for our jump."

First Officer Bezal snapped to attention. "Yes, sir, I'll tend to it personally."

Langos left his bridge slowly, body erect, discouraged but not defeated.

CHAPTER 16

A small crowd had gathered on hanger deck seven when Dar and his wingmen returned to the Nanta and started shut down procedures. The cheering was real, but subdued. SFS-1 had lost one of their own in combat. Boomer, a quiet unassuming man, was well liked and respected, making his loss deeply felt by all. The memory of this small Russian would not be soon forgotten. Dar waved, without smiling, acknowledging the praise they were affording him, but was nonetheless profoundly saddened by Boomer's death. He was the young man's Commanding Officer, and as such, ultimately felt responsible for the tragedy. He knew it to be one of the many burdens of command, but intellectually acknowledging it was not his fault did little to fill the hole seared in his soul. Dar fully realized Boomer's death was not going to be the last, particularly, if the Womongly continued to engage his squadron with four times the fighters he could launch to meet them. He wondered, how long his unit could fight with so few pilots and Darts.

He leapt to the deck, where Cannaly was already waiting for him. "Dar, I lost my wingman," he said with dejection. "My God, I watched him blow into absolute nothingness."

"It wasn't your fault, Snake," Dar voiced with compassion. "Boomer was the first, but I don't think he'll be the last to die in this war."

"Damn it all, I know you're right, Dar, but I've never lost a wingy before. It's hard. It sucks."

As Cannaly finished, Bulldog, along with most of the crowd ringed the two tired fighter pilots. Dar wrapped an arm around Bulldog's big shoulders. "Ya, done good out there," he said, smiling sadly at the Texan.

"You too, Skipper. Hell's own fire, ya nailed four of the bastards by yerself. One more and you'll be the first 'Space Ace'."

Bulldog's comment lightened the tension as talked turned to the battle. Dar asked, "Has anyone heard if we damaged the Dectima?"

Zentao, who stood outside the circle of well wishers, spoke above the chaotic chatter of anxious pilots. "Senior Commander Fantin, the bridge passed the word not more than five minutes ago. Your flight struck Dectima with three of the four torpedoes, causing minor damage amidships."

"Thanks, Zentao," Dar yelled back. "Wish it had been more." Turning his attention back to Bulldog and Cannaly, he said, "Join me in my quarters in fifteen minutes for a debrief and some straight talk about the fight. I have a problem. I'm hoping you two can help me clear it up."

"Okay, boss," Cannaly replied. "What's the matter?" He looked at his friend with concern.

"I'm not sure, but I got a gut feeling about something and I'd like to pass it by you two. See ya in a few minutes." Dar didn't wait for a response, but began pushing his way in the direction of the light tube.

Head down, his thoughts still locked in mental, mortal combat against superior odds several thousand miles away, Dar almost bumped into Littia waiting patiently for him by the tube. "Littia," Dar said quietly, reaching out for her.

Littia drew away, then, as if some hidden wall of resolve crumbled within her, she stepped lightly into his arms, tightly wrapping her own arms around his neck. "Oh, Dar, we were so frightened. It was so terrible to watch. The enemy fighters, so many of them, and you in the middle shooting and dodging . . . oh, we are to thankful to have you back." She held him tightly to her, not wanting to let go, as tears slowly formed in the corner of her eyes.

Dar gently stroked her long golden hair. "I'm here now," he said gently, and bowed his head to kiss her cheek. "Come, we should go." He took her hand and led her into the light tube. "Would you join me in my quarters this evening after dinner? I seem to have a bottle of wine and a couple of glasses we could put to good use."

Littia looked long and hard into Dar's eyes. "We shall be there." She hesitated, holding his hand tightly. "And, Dar, this time you shall remember." Smiling at Dar's confused look, she stepped from the tube as it stopped near her quarters. He stood staring at her with astonishment. "Until this evening," she said teasingly, moving to the PCT and disappearing around the corner.

It only took a few minutes for Dar to reach his room, but during that short time his mind whorled with bewilderment. *I'll remember this time.* Now what the blue blazes is that suppose to mean, he wondered, slipping out of his sweat drenched flight suit. He looked for Pete, but the utapotus was not making himself visible. Damn it all, he thought, stepping into the warm sonic shower.

"All right, we flew a good mission," Dar finished the debriefing. Bulldog and Cannaly had been waiting for him when he left the steaming sonic. After he'd slipped on a fresh flight suit, they had spent the last thirty minutes discussing the entire hop.

"Now, here is what I really wanted to talk about. Did either of you notice the way the Womongly pilots were flying?"

"What do you mean, boss," Cannaly asked. "Hell, I wasn't overly concerned about their flying abilities. Just flat ass staying alive was good enough for me."

Dar stood, kicking back his desk chair, and began pacing the small room. "They aren't maneuvering, at least not like I would expect experienced fighter pilots. They make flat, almost lazy turns, and very rarely move into the vertical. Didn't you notice?" He stopped in mid stride and looked questioningly at both men.

Cannaly's thoughts appeared to turn inward for a moment. "You're right." he spoke thoughtfully. "Now that you mention it, not one of those turkeys pulled into the vertical when I'd drop in on their six. They'd just start a hard turn. Made it easier for me to get a firing solution, but it doesn't make any sense."

"Exactly," Dar exclaimed. "It doesn't make any sense. Jicama and Littia both told me that Womongly warriors are trained from birth. My God, Snake, these guys looked like they just came out of flight training."

"They sure knew enough to surprise the crap out of us," Bulldog interjected.

"Yeah, that's right. No question we got caught with our pants down, but if they had popped out of hyperspace in a staggered formation rather than on line, we might all be nothing but glittering space dust right now. No! I'm thinking these pilots are relying on numbers, not tactics. That doesn't add up to a 'warrior' race, alien or not."

"Okay, boss, I agree, but what are you implying?" Cannaly asked.

"Hell, I don't know. That's why I wanted to bounce it off you. What do you think?"

"I think we're darn lucky," Bulldog drawled. "If those dudes aren't for shit as pilots, it's just fine with me."

Dar laughed with Cannaly. "That's bringing it back to square one," Dar choked out. Catching his breath, he added, "You're right, Bulldog, it's probably nothing, but think on it anyway. Let me know if you come up with an idea."

"Ya got it, skipper," the Texan said, getting up to leave. "I'm off to shit, shower, and shave, then I'm gonna eat half the chow in the mess hall. Shootin' up Womongly is hungry work. I'm starved."

"Not so fast, Bulldog," Dar said, chuckling at the Texan's comment. "Snake, I want you to roundup the squadron and have them meet me in the gym. I need to talk to them all at the same time and the gym area is the only place we have large enough to get us altogether. Y'all need time to clean up, so let's make it in an hour."

"Sure, no problem," Cannaly responded. "We'll meet you there."

The two men left Dar with his thoughts. If he was going to lead SFS-1 into an all out fighter war in space, he needed tactics that would help even the odds. He could still remember his flight school instructors, back at Pensacola, telling him tales of the Russians having ten fighters to every one the U.S. forces or NATO could muster. During that period of Cold War history, American pilots trained hard to fight a multiple bogey air war. Now he was faced with the same situation, but there was nothing "cold" about it.

Pete still had not shown his frog face, when Dar left for the gym.

The small personal VID screen sitting on Langos' desk blinked twice then reflected First Officer Bezal sitting at the hyperdrive control panel. "Join me in my quarters," Langos commanded. " I have new orders."

"Yes, sir," Bezal said, his color taking on a slightly yellowish cast of fear. "Immediately."

Langos switched the screen off and stood stiffly, rigid in body and thought. His debriefing with the Strike Dragon pilots had confirmed what he had recognized . . . the Earthling pilots were maneuvering in a manner his warriors had not hereto encountered. To offset such wild abandoned flying techniques would require his pilots to think differently about their engagement methods. He needed time; time to think and retrain.

"Enter," Langos said, responding to the soft knock at his door. Bezal entered slowly, obviously nervous at being ordered into the captain' presence. "Sit and listen carefully, First Officer." He pushed a padded stool in the direction of the younger officer.

Bezal hesitantly walked to the stool, cocked his third leg and took a seat as he'd been instructed. Facial breathing flaps sucked moisture filled rapidly and his saucer eyes focused on the captain with concern.

"First Officer," Langos began, recognizing the anxiety Bezal displayed. His First Officer's deportment was that of a small child who was afraid he'd had done something wrong, but not sure what the offense might be. "Dectima will be jumping soon, and I want new coordinates programmed for our destination."

"Yes sir. That will be done," Bezal said, taking on a more natural color. "What are the new coordinates?"

"I want the Dectima to be put in a geostationary orbit around Earth, just outside of the planet's heavy gravitational pull. Is that possible?"

Bezal took a moment to think. "Possible, I believe so," he mused, more to himself than to answer Langos. "Yes sir, it is possible, but difficult." He spoke with building confidence. "We will have to calculate the hyper jump with extreme accuracy. If we misjudge by the slightest margin we could dump the hyperdrive inside the planet's atmosphere. If that were to happen, there would be nothing we could do to keep from flaming the ship."

"Yes, yes. I understand. Can you make the calculations?"

"I believe so, sir. It would take me a short while, but, yes, I can do it."

"Then do so. Immediately," Langos commanded.

"Sir, may I ask why?" Bezal asked. "It was my understanding we were to position on the backside of Earth's moon until contact could be made with the planet's inhabitants."

"Yes, yes." Langos spoke impatiently. "The Nanta and their Earthling pilots have changed all that. We must find a way of defeating the fighters without undue losses to our own Strike Dragon force. To accomplish this task, I need time and some form of protection. I may not be capable of escaping that damnable Lantiusian mother ship, but

I can help protect us from the fighters. By establishing an orbit at the edge of Earth's atmosphere, Dectima is free from attack from the planet side. The fighters can't surprise us by hyper jumping into the dense atmosphere, just as we can't."

Bezal nodded his understanding. "The fighters will be hesitant to fire thermal torpedoes at Dectima from the moon side for fear of a miss," he said with admiration for his captain's strategy. "The weapon would bypass us and hit their home planet."

"Exactly," Langos said. "Dectima will still be a target of course, but we have effectively narrowed the angles from which the enemy can engage the ship, yet we can return fire in any direction."

"Excellent, Captain. I understand your orders. May I say, sir, it is a brilliant twist of strategy on your part."

"Of course." Langos accepted the complement as natural. The added benefit is our fighters have less space to protect and, therefore, we can increase the number of Strike Dragons in each patrol sent to cover our most vulnerable quadrants."

"What of Earth? Do you anticipate attack from the human element remaining on the planet?" Bezal questioned.

"No. There is no indication the humans have the technology capable of being a threat. If there were, why would the Lantiusians abduct pilots to fight us?"

"Of course, sir. You are right."

"Very well, start your calculations." Langos ended the conversation.

"Attention on deck," Cannaly commanded, as Dar walked through the door to the gym. The tightly gathered group of young Earth pilots snapped to attention in unison.

"As you were," Dar said, striding purposefully to stand before them. "I called this AOM for several reasons, not the least is the death of our friend and comrade, Boomer. We will have a short memorial service for him tomorrow morning, prior to physical training. I wish we could do more, and we will when this thing is over, but for now, we must say our good-byes and get on with flying missions." He paused long enough to look closely at the men he commanded. Each was wrapped in individual thought. No doubt contemplating their own immortality, Dar realized, then continued. "What I really wanted to talk to you about are tactics and formations. I know you're all aware how we were bushwhacked from behind this afternoon. If things had been different, Boomer wouldn't be the only one of us to mourn tonight. As it was, the enemy emerged from hyperspace formed online, abreast, and firing. If our two sections hadn't been staggered in combat spread, that first barrage could have taken us all. This is the second time we've seen this online, abreast mass formation, isn't that right OpsO?"

"Yes, sir," Danny answered. "That one fighter I took out came from the same bloody type of formation."

"Right," Dar emphasized. "I've already talked to Bulldog and the XO about this, and they agree. The Womongly sorely lack in talent, but more than makeup for it in pure numbers. Assuming they will continue to attack us en masse and using much the same tactics we have seen so far, we can enhance our lack of fighters with good strong tactics." He paused once again. What he was about to say, he knew would be upsetting and possibly demoralizing. "Men, there is little doubt that more of us are going to die out there. The odds against us are just too great. We can't expect to be as lucky on every mission as we were today. For that reason, if for no other, we have to make every life and Dart count."

Every eye watched Dar intently. Nods of silent understanding acknowledge his emotionally filled words.

Dar continued, "the Lantiusians have made it clear we are the 'only' defense Earth has against a race of aliens wishing one thing . . . total annihilation of every man, woman, and child on Earth. As for me, I'm not going to let that happen as long as I can slam a stick or push a rudder."

"Don't worry, skipper, we all feel the same way," Cannaly spoke passionately for the group. "As long as there's one Dart to launch, one of us will be at the controls. Count on it."

Dar nodded in acceptance. "Yeah, I know that, but thanks for the support. Okay then, here's what we're going to do. First, OpsO, I want no less than four Darts launched per mission, more if we can arrange rest time between flights. Second, I want the flights led by a division leader to coordinate the attacks on Dectima, but that leadership stands only until Womongly fighters are engaged. If they keep attacking en masse, the only way we can defeat them is one against many. I know separating the flight into singletons will break down mutual support between our fighters, but there are just too many of enemy ships to fight as a two plane section tied together in tight formation. Third, and this is very important, our formations must be staggered and spread out. In-other-words, the entire flight will be at different altitudes and maintain separation of at least five to ten miles, more when possible. Again, I'm assuming the Womongly will, at least for the time being, continue to use the online, abreast formation, so our best bet will be to engage them with separation both vertically and horizontally."

"Skipper?" Abe Goldenstien, an F-18 pilot from Israel interrupted. "What about the vertical? Bulldog has been telling us the Womongly don't use it."

"That's correct, or least we haven't seen them use the vertical effectively, so that's where y'all want to be. Once engaged, go vertical and stay there." Dar paused, then asked, "Are there any other questions." There were none. "Okay, then, I'll see you all here in the morning. Get some rest."

"We'll need it," Cannaly added quietly.

Supreme Commander Jicama and First Commander Tamis sat in their respective chairs studying the mammoth plasma screen suspended before them. "He's getting ready to jump," Tamis spoke, not taking his eyes from the screen.

The view of the enemy's ship sharpened, as Jicama touched a small recessed light on his control panel. "Yes, there is no doubt the ship is spooling energy for hyperspace." Dectima appeared to shimmer with iridescent light, then accelerate at a right angle from Nanta. "Tracking," Jicama commanded, "keep a sharp eye, I want to know the exact coordinates Dectima ends this jump."

Dataspheres danced around the Lantiusians tending Nanta's tracking devices, as more and more information flooded the master computer to be collated and analyzed. "Yes, sir. We have them locked on," A young officer acknowledged his orders.

Dectima continued to accelerate, then, suddenly where the ship had been displayed an instant before, the plasma screen flared with an explosion of white light. "We shall follow you soon," Jicama commented absently. "Very soon indeed."

CHAPTER 17

John Westmeyer took a long swig from his coffee stained mug, the one his wife had given him ten years ago as a joke. The giant cup held darn near a half a pot of coffee and took two boys and a small elephant to lift to his lips. He smiled inwardly, remembering how she would forever nag him about the ponderous amounts of black java he'd consume each day. But that was in the past. Diana had died in a car accident two years prior, and with no children, John had thrown himself into his work at NORAD's tracking station, Peterson Air Force Base, Colorado.

Bespectacled, with prematurely graying hair, he took another sip of strong brew and adjusted his tactical radar screen to a higher resolution. "Holy shit!" The ten year old mug went crashing to the floor, splashing hot liquid and scattering broken glass. John came out of his seat like a shot, dumping the chair over to slosh in the coffee. "Christ, Jonesy, come look at this . . . it can't be for real."

"What'cha got, John?" Jonesy said, as he ambled over to John's station.

John stood staring at his radar screen, mouth hanging slack, and noticeably bulging eyes. "It's huge. It just popped out of nowhere and set itself there." He pointed to the screen, where a blip, many times the size of anything else presently being displayed, shone through the green haze.

"Got to be an anomaly of some sort," Jonesy said nonchalantly.

"Trust me, pal, that isn't any anomaly. It's real, and its bouncing back a signal like I've never seen before. God, I don't believe it. Its taken up an orbit around the equator, just like some damned satellite."

"Well, if it's not an electronic abnormality, what would you suggest? Maybe an alien spaceship just dumped itself on our doorstep." Jonesy laughed at the thought. "You're not trying to suggest something like that could be for real are you?"

"Christ, Jonesy, I have no idea what the hell it is, but whatever, it for damned sure didn't originate from Earth. We would have tracked it long before now." John shook his head, still heedless of the spilled coffee and broken mug. "I think we had better get on the hook and check this out with other stations."

"Yeah," Jonesy said, beginning to think this thing was for real. "Let's hit the red." He was referring to the direct warning hot line to Washington D.C. and Space Network (SN) in White Sands, Newe Mexico SN) in White Sands, New Mexico.

Within five minutes of Dectima's appearance on strategic radars throughout the United States, Canada, and Western Europe, the planet known as Earth realized for the first time they were not alone in the cosmos. A new era had begun, and where the new epoch would lead not a living human soul knew.

Littia looked stunning, standing in the doorway with the back lighting of the corridor sensuously silhouetting her curves through the tunic's fine white cloth. She smiled with gentle shyness, as Dar rose from the air bed, where he'd dozed for the last hour, to take her in his arms. He pulled her into the small room and he pressed his lips to hers.

Littia responded to Dar's touch with a soft sigh and returned the kiss with passion welling from deep inside her. Desire ripped away barriers of emotions long trained to be hidden in the caverns of her mind. Littia's body cried out for the physical, needing tactile contact with this man from another world. She reached out to Dar with her mind, intertwining, their thoughts screamed out desire each for the other.

The magic of the moment was broken by an audible "pop." "Darn you Pete," Dar said, as he pulled back from the kiss. "You pick the damnedest times to show up." He laughed lightly at the sight of Pete sprawled on his desk. There was no hint of real chastisement in his voice.

Littia smiled at the small utapotus, touched Dar's face gently, and moved to the desk. She began stroking Pete under his chin. "Come to save me, Pete?" She asked, looking at Dar with smiling eyes. "We are not at all sure we wish to be saved, but thanks anyway."

Pete's eyes rolled back, and he voiced his complete contentment with the entire situation by gurgling musically.

"Would you like a glass of wine?" Dar offered. "I'm not sure how the bottle or the glasses got here, but I figure it was for a good reason."

"We would enjoy a glass. Thank you," Littia said, a sly upturned smile on her face.

Dar looked her smile questioningly. "You know something I don't?" he asked.

"Oh, no. It is nothing," she answered, continuing to fondle Pete throat.

Dar handed her a glass of shimmering emerald wine, touched his glass to hers and took a tentative sip of the heavy liquid. "Mmmm! This is really excellent," he said appreciatively and with some surprise. He looked over the rim of his glass, as Littia, still smiling, sipped her own drink. "I still think your hiding something from me." He quickly scanned her mind, but there was nothing to indicate she was not telling the truth.

"Stop that, Dar," Littia chided. "It tickles when you stroke my thoughts in such a manner." The smile never left her face. She felt happier at this moment than at any time in her life, and she wanted the feeling to last forever.

Dar took another sip of wine, then set the glass down next to the utapotus. Looking directly into Littia's eyes, he stepped close and took the glass from her hand, setting it beside his own. Taking her face in both hands, he bent to kiss her once again, cautiously probing her mouth with his tongue as her lips parted to meet his own. Slowly, smoothly he slipped a hand to her shoulder, caressing the softness of her pale skin. Littia stepped back just far enough so their bodies no longer touched, letting the tunic slide delicately to the floor as he pushed it from her shoulder. Lips still clasped hungrily to each other, Dar swung her into his arms and carried her to the bed. There, he carefully laid her down, pressing himself to her.

"This is so new," Littia spoke huskily, breaking the warmth of the kiss. "We are not sure what we are to do."

Dar spoke tenderly. "Let your heart lead you. The rest will follow."

Their lovemaking was a time of opening universes for Littia. A new age of physical wonderment filled with sensations she never thought possible.

Cannaly shook his head in disgust, throwing his cards on the table. "I can't believe it," he lamented. "That's the fourth straight hand you've won. Damn it all, Zentao, how did you get so lucky?"

Zentao reached across the table, scraping a pile of multicolored stones into the mounting pile already before him. "We are not lucky, my friend," the tall Lantiusian quipped. "Just very good."

Danny began laughing. "You're bloody right about that, old chum. I think you've damn near cleaned me out. Besides, it's getting late. Think I'll head for my quarters."

"Yeah, it's gettin' on to my bed time too," Bulldog interjected. "We've been playin' fer near four hours, and I've got a flight with the skipper in the morning."

Cannaly looked around the officer's club, surprised to see it nearly empty and the bartender leaning on the bar dozing. "Darn, I didn't realize it was getting so late. Zentao, I want another chance at you tomorrow night, ya hear?"

Zentao smiled pleasantly. "We would be glad to play again with you, my friend. The winning of this game you call poker is so easy."

A high pitch squeal interrupted the friendly teasing, startling Earthlings and Lantiusians alike. "What the bloody hell," Danny said, fighting for the VVCom jammed in his flight suit pocket. By the time he had the small communicator in hand, Cannaly was turning his on as well.

Supreme Commander Jicama's face appeared in the upper right hand corner of Cannaly's VVCom, with Dar and Danny taking up the remaining portion of the screen. Dar, obviously without clothes and looking as if he'd just rolled from bed, peered sheepishly into the small Vid camera.

"Ah, we believe we have everyone one online now," Jicama said pleasantly. "We have called to inform you that the Womongly ship has jumped. We thought you might wish to join me on the bridge while Nanta makes hyperspace to your home galaxy."

"Thank you, Supreme Commander," Dar responded, rubbing his eyes purposefully, pretending to clear them of sleep. "It would be an honor to join you."

Jicama smiled. "Say, in ten minutes then." He clicked his full scale VVCom screen off, but not before taking careful note of Littia lying on Dar's bed. "We thought so Tamis. Our Earthling friend, it appears, has been smitten by our young female guide."

Tamis had drunk in the scene on the screen as well. His face wrinkled with disgust at what he had seen. "Sir, could this Guide 3rd Class possibly resorted to such grotesque physical pleasures as that scene indicated? No Lantiusian female would ever stoop to such vulgar self-abasement."

"We are not too sure of that, my friend," Jicama chided. "We have heard rumors that others of our females have joined with these pilots from Earth. It appears they may have a quality which awakens long since forgotten physical needs once enjoyed by Lantiusians as well. He paused in thought. "Hmm, perhaps we shall have to keep closer watch on our guests. We do not want something as distasteful as coupling to interfere with the nature of our society or the mission at hand."

"Certainly not sir," Tamis said. "I personally will tend to the matter of ensuring closer scrutinization of the Earthlings."

"Please see to it, Tamis," Jicama said, turning to meet the three pilots just stepping on to the bridge. "Ah, Dar, we are pleased that you could join us."

"Thank you, sir. What's the latest status?" Dar asked politely.

"Dectima made her hyper jump just before I called you," Jicama said. "We will follow shortly."

"Do we know where they jumped?" Cannaly asked. "Are they in a position to attack Earth?"

"The computer is calculating the Dectima's ultimate position as we speak. As soon as we have the coordinates, we will make our run as well."

Dar noticed the cold stare Tamis directed at him without concern. *If looks could kill, I'd been long buried,* he thought, returning a questioningly glare. "Is something wrong, Commander Tamis?"

"No, nothing is wrong. Should there be?" Tamis answered, his voice dripping with sarcasm, then turned his attention back to the symbols flashing across his monitor.

Dar kept his eyes on the tall First Commander for a moment more, then turned back to Jicama. "Sir, how soon could we launch a Dart attack after our jump?"

"Hmm. We see no reason why you should not be able to fly within minutes after we stabilize Nanta's systems. Tamis, what do you think?"

"The Darts could launch without problem, as you say sir, but why?" He again directed his attention to Dar.

"I would like to attack the Dectima the first moment we have the opportunity. I figure they will expect us to wait several hours after Nanta jumps to launch an attack. This way we might have an element of surprise."

"We very much doubt you will be able to surprise the Dectima, but we suppose it might be worth a try. How soon could you be ready to fly?"

"Give us an hour before you jump. We'll have the Darts ready and waiting. All we'll need is a vector and distance to the Dectima." Dar said rapidly, excitement building with each word. He ran fingers through his hair in thought.

Supreme Commander Jicama reflected on Dar's request for a moment. "We will delay the jump until you are ready. Tamis, alert the crew and have launch officers report to hangar deck seven."

"Aye, sir." Tamis was already directing Dataspheres to start putting operations in motion.

"With your permission, sir," Dar said. "I need to roust my squadron from the rack and get this thing organized."

"Rack?" We do not understand 'roust from the rack'."

Dar smiled at the Jicama. "Get them out of bed, sir."

"Ah. Another of your strange metaphors." Jicama shook his head in wonderment. "Yes, you have much to do. Go!"

"Thank you, sir." Dar said, spinning on his heel. "Let's do it, Snake. Get the squadron up and moving. I'll meet you on the hanger deck." The three were moving at a trot for the hatch and light tube.

Sally Morrison, CB handle Roses, barreled down highway 95. Heading south, she was driving her sixteen wheeler ten miles over the

Florida speed limit, drinking a warm cola, and talking on her CB. "Yeah, Tuna Man, not a Smokey in sight from Jacksonville south to me. I got the pedal down, and I'm about twenty miles from Space City."

"Roses, honey, y'all wanna pull 'er in at the next bean palace? I'd even buy the coffee."

Sally checked her watch. Three fifteen. "Tuna Man, I'd plumb love that, but gotta have this load in Miami by mornin' and there ain't no time for stoppin'. Catch you on the flipside, if yer' still around."

"Ten-four, Roses. Ya have a safe trip, ya hear."

"Ten-four back to ya," Sally said, dropping the mike to let it swing freely from a hook on the center of the dash. She grabbed the half empty soda can from its holder, lifted it to her lips, tilting her head back to let the semi-warm liquid slip down her throat. "Christ!" She dropped the can, grabbed the wheel, and slammed on the brakes. Tires squealed, as retreads melted rubber on the rough pavement. Her eyes still fixed to the sky, Sally vaguely felt the overloaded trailer begin to lose traction, its momentum continuing as the tractor slowed. She screamed, as reality of the truck came instantly into focus. The huge rig jackknifed at fifty miles per hour, rolling six times down the open four lane. Sally Morrison, became Earth's first casualty of a war she knew nothing about, and never would.

Nanta exploded out of hyperspace trailing hundreds of miles of full spectrum light behind her. The southern sky over Florida filled with fireworks.

CHAPTER 18

Dar tightened the shoulder straps holding him against the backrest of his seat. "Littia," he mind blasted. "Littia, are you there?"

"We are here. Where are you? We've been waiting." Her thoughts were strong and concerned.

"I'm sorry. I'm in my Dart. Nanta is going to jump. After our hyperspace ride the squadron is going to launch an immediate attack. We're just waiting for the go ahead from the Supreme Commander." There was a long pause. Dar wondered if his thoughts had gotten through to her. Softly, like a whisper, he felt the familiar tickling of his mind.

"Dar, please be careful. We shall be here when you return." A pause. "My heart will be flying with you."

Dar smiled inwardly. "I'll try to keep it safe, Littia."

"Senior Commander Fantin," a young engineer yelled up to Dar from the launch console. "The bridge has relayed they are preparing for hyperspace. We recommend you button up."

Dar gave the man a thumbs up and nodded his understanding. "Got to go, my love," he directed the thought to Littia, without thinking. Then the realization of his statement struck home. *Well, just maybe he was falling in love,* he recognized for the first time. Not waiting for Littia to respond he tugged his helmet down to his shoulders, the face plate slammed home, as he signaled for drive start. The Dart rapidly came to life.

"Are we going out?" Nan asked her standard first question.

"Yes, Nan. Are we ready?

"All systems online, armament up and waiting for arming instructions, shield one hundred percent. We are ready, Dar," Nan said quietly.

Above the rumbling vibrations of his Dart, Dar could feel the Nanta gather power around her like a living monster preparing to spring. Engineers and launch officers stopped their work and sat down, grabbing anything that might provide support. A deep growl rose from the bowels of the huge ship, as the vibration grew in intensity. "Nan, what's going on?" Dar asked, holding tight to the canopy rails.

"It is the hyperdrive system, nothing more," Nan responded without concern. "Nanta shall jump shortly."

The growl grew to ear splitting intensity. Then, like a stretched rubber band, Nanta let go her power. One second she was millions of miles from Earth. The next, she flared the black void with kaleidoscopic light between Earth and its moon.

"Jesus," Dar whispered aloud.

"Please, say again," Nan questioned.

"I said Jesus H. Christ, that was something," Dar said, noting the sudden silence now permeating the hangar. "Are we there?"

"Yes, Dar. I expect we shall be launched very soon." Nan's soothing tone did much to calm Dar's rattled nerves.

As if on Nan's cue, launch officers and engineers rushed to their stations in preparation for a mass Dart exodus. Interior walls came sliding down, and tunnels formed through the outer shield.

"You are cleared to launch," Supreme Commander Jicama radioed Dar. "Dectima is 235Bravo at 17,350 miles. We wish you success and much luck."

"I think we'll need as much luck as we can muster to succeed," Dar signaled back, jotting down the directions on his kneeboard. The Dart lifted clear of the deck and began its slow passage through the shield.

As the fighter left the confines of the green tunnel, Dar caught his breath at the sight before him. Earth, a beautiful blue globe, swirling with white cotton candy clouds, and suspended in a field of black, hung on an invisible string directly on his ship's nose. *Home,* he thought, *that's home. The reason we are here.*

Dar looked over his right shoulder, watching seven Darts suddenly appear from the shield one by one. During the mass briefing, he'd ordered radio silence, yet he desperately wanted to break his own orders to comment on the wondrous sight of Earth. He shook the feeling off, returning to the mission at hand, and shoved the throttle to ninety-percent. The Dart gathered speed rapidly, as Dar turned to the heading Jicama had passed him. "Nan, time to target?"

"At present speed, eleven minutes. Be advised we are now well within weapons range."

"Roger, understand. Arm torpedoes and bring target up on screens," Dar ordered.

"On screens. Weapons armed, and operational," Nan said quietly.

Dar glanced at the Darts flanking his lead. They had positioned themselves as briefed, spread out on both sides for fifty miles and staggered at various altitudes. Nodding satisfaction, he turned his attention to the holographic display. "Shit!"

"Say again, please?" Nan asked.

"They've placed Dectima directly on line with Earth. A torpedo miss could be disastrous. We've got to attack from one end or the other." The decision made, he hit the stick to the left, banking the Dart hard to port.

Fifty Strike Dragons, their drive engines idling, sat at "ready launch" positions on three separate hangar decks deep in the bowels of Dectima. Excited anticipation of the coming battle coursed through the Womongly manning the fighters. This was to be their moment of triumph. A time to gain back their honor by showing the upstart Earthlings what numbers versus tactical capabilities really meant.

Captain Langos paced the bridge like a nervous colt. First Officer Bezal had positioned Dectima perfectly, as was expected of him. Yet Nanta hadn't followed immediately, not falling out of hyperspace till nearly an hour after Dectima's jump. *What were his enemies up to this time*, he wondered.

"Fighters out of Nanta," Bezal called to his restless captain.

"Yes, yes. It is about time." Langos hurried to the command VidScreen. "Only eight? They are going to attack with only eight fighters," Langos said. "I would have thought it would be a full scale attack . . . unless." He paused in thought. "They don't have more," he said. The very idea caught him by surprise. "We shall end this tiny war today," Langos gloated to his bridge officers. "Launch the Strike Dragons," he commanded.

Eight Darts flew an arc 15,000 miles from Dectima. In the lead, Dar began a lazy turn to starboard, sweeping his formation into the Womongly mother ship's rear quadrant.

"Enemy fighters approaching from the right," Nan calmly voiced to Dar.

"How many?"

"Forty, no, fifty fighters out. Intercept in one minute, Nan said.

Dar's mind raced. Things were happening too fast. Distances were too little, the speeds too great for him to calculate. "Can we fire torpedoes without fear of hitting Earth?" Now, both the fighters and the Dectima were clearly visible. *The dumb bastards are still using a line abreast formation*, sped through his mind.

"No. Probability of a miss on Dectima hitting Earth is near one-hundred percent, Nan said softly.

The first Thrumber blast hit Dar's Dart head on. "Okay, guys," he radioed, breaking radio silence. Its time to fight. Good luck . . . break, break . . . Snake, get your ass out here. *now!*"

"Already on the way," Cannaly said, as if he had not a care in the world. On his wing flew the remaining nine Darts.

Fifty Strike Dragons, flying line abreast, passed head on with eight staggered Darts. Dar pulled his stick into his lap, zooming his bird vertically away from the horizontally spread Womongly. He held the stick tight in his crotch, forcing the Dart into a huge loop, the apex of the maneuver three hundred miles above the Dragons. Dar grunted against the g forces, as the nosed dropped on the far side of the circle. The bird screamed down the chute directly on top of the Womongly. A lone enemy, his luck all but run out, flew across the Dart's holographic cross hairs. "Arm the thrumber," he commanded.

"Thrumber armed," Nan said.

Dar pulled the trigger. Fifty yellow-orange balls of super charged death shot across the distance, blasting the Strike Dragon into dust. He noticed other explosions all along the Womongly line. SFS-1 was shooting from every direction. The Womongly formation began to fall apart, as Dar leveled his Dart on yet another unfortunate Dragon.

"Enemy in rear quadrant, and closing," Nan said

Dar banked hard to starboard and stepped on the left rudder pedal. The Dart skidded into an eight g turn, destroying the Womongly pilot's firing solution. The blast skimmed Dar's shield as he pushed the stick forward, staggering the Dart into a negative g maneuver. The Dragon sped by his six, disappearing among the fighting throng.

Everywhere Danny looked, a fighter was either in his sights or he in theirs. The pride of the British Navy leveled his wings momentarily, pulled the trigger, flaming his third kill, then yanked back on the stick. The Dart sliced into the vertical.

"Enemy rear quadrant," Danny's computer said.

"Holy bloody shit . . . .." Danny never got the chance to complete the sentence. His Dart evaporated under the well aimed thrumber fire of a Womongly.

"Into the fray we fly," Cannaly radioed cheerfully.

"About damned time, Snake," Dar chided, lighting up another Dragon with yellow-orange heat. He scanned the mass confusion of the fight, seeing a Dart disappear far off to his right. *Too God damned many of them*, he thought dispiritedly.

Like deadly fireflies, Cannaly's Darts flew through the fight, thrumbers torching astonished Dragon pilots, but not before three more Darts met their end at the hands of the Womongly.

The battle area spread two thousand miles across space, each Dart fighting for existence against three to one odds. Playing "bee in the bonnet," Darts fought as singletons, dashing into the thickest part of the fight to shoot at any available target, then streaking for relative safety outside the kill zone. It worked most of the time, but not always. Dart shields were being slowly decimated by repeated hits from the Dragons.

"Shield at forty-percent," Nan passed the information to Dar. "We can not withstand more than two additional hits before total failure."

"Great. Just great," Dar groaned, slapping the stick to the left in an attempt to shake the son-of-a-bitch who was doing everything he possibly could to put him away for good. The Dart shook under a blast of a super charged thrumber.

"For Christ's sake, jump us, Nan," Dar yelled. The Dart's drive whined loudly before he had finished the order.

Not a cloud obscured the early morning night sky over Kingsville, Texas, as porch lights flicked on at a small frame house five miles from the Naval Air Station. Marine Corps Captain Marty Sims, dressed in his olive green flight suit, slipped behind the wheel of his three year old Ford station wagon. Jane, Marty's very pregnant wife, opened the passenger door and clumsily forced her self next to her husband.

"What time is your doctors appointment?" Sims asked for the third time since the two had rolled from bed. The obstetrician's appointment necessitated Jane dropping him off at the base for an early morning brief. Normally, she would never have been up this early.

"Ten this morning. Just like it was ten minutes ago," Jane said testily. "I wish you'd listen to me when I talk. You seem to think nothing is more important than flying."

"I'm sorry, honey. My mind has been on other things lately. I'm going to become the squadron's schedules officer next week, and I'm not sure I'm up to the task. So much to learn."

Jane reached across the seat to touch her husbands hand. "I know. I'm sorry, but it's just that I'm so darn miserable right now.

Marty patted her hand. "No, I'm the one who is sorry." He smiled tenderly at her, backing out of their driveway. Dropping the shift into drive, he slowly accelerated west down Sam Houston Street for Highway 59.

"What's that," Marty asked, indicating a group of people gathered on the corner of Sam Houston and 59.

"Better slow down, honey. Must be an accident or something."

Marty took his foot off the accelerator, slowing the Ford to a crawl. "I don't think it's an accident. They're pointing toward the sky." He scrunched his six foot frame down over the steering wheel to peer up through the tinted glass. "My God!" Amazement shook his voice, as he braked the car to a full stop. Marty leaped from the car, his trained eyes scanning the fire ridden sky.

Like giant lightning bugs moving at sonic speed on a summer evening, the heaven between the Texas plains and the moon was being lit with colorful streaks of tracer-like fire. Balls of light tracked through the darkness, ending in sudden bright explosions, the detonations silhouetting dark forms moving at incredible speeds.

"My God, look there," Marty said, pointing to a greenish glow hanging low on the horizon. "What the hell is that?"

"Beats the crap out of me," Marty's long time friend, Lieutenant Dale Smith said. Smith had just pulled along side Marty's Ford "But for damn sure someone is playing war up there."

Jane put her arm around her husband, fear of the unknown bubbling to the surface. "What's going on, Marty? I don't understand."

"Neither do I, honey, but the base is going to be the best place to find out."

"I'd say we either have spaceships we don't know about, which is unlikely, or we've got a shoot 'emup war going on out there by something we don't even want to think about," Lieutenant Smith said softly.

Strangely silent, the crowd continued to grow on the corner of Highway 59 and Sam Houston Street. A pervasive primal feeling of incredulity, undermined by horror, permeated the men and women gathered in the Texas predawn.

Dar's eyes began to cage, but just barely. Though he had expected Nan to immediately follow his instructions, the jump still took him off guard. In those short seconds, he felt like his entire brain housing group had dislodged from whatever held it in place.

"Wow! That was something, Nan. Are we hanging together?"

"Yes, Dar. All systems operational, with the exception of the shield. Our shield is presently operating at twenty-percent. The last thrumber hit created damage to the outer hull. I have shored the breach with a pressure gradient. We well hold together for the jump back to Nanta."

"Where are we?" Dar asked, and immediately was sorry for the question as Nan began rattling off a string of numbers and coordinates. "Whoa, hold up there, Nan. Just tell me how far we are from Nanta."

"We are five hundred thousand, two hundred twenty-five, point six miles from Nanta."

"Okay, I guess it was a foolish question," Dar said sadly, pulling the throttle to idle. The reverse drive kicked in, slowing the Dart to a stop. Drifting in the black void, he was suddenly aware of the serenity and calm, compared to the chaos he just left. The surrounding heaven shone with stars shimmering against a dark velvet background. To his right, a huge red globe hung suspended like a child's mobile. *Damn, I hope everybody else got out of the fight in time*, he thought. *Thank God Danny had the foresight to think of a plan if things got out of hand during the attack on Dectima.* On Danny's suggestion, each Dart had been programmed with a designated jump point prior to launch. *That magnificent little Brit's forethought saved my life.*

"Nan, I may not know where we are, but it sure is a beautiful sight. How much longer do we have before we return to Nanta?"

"Fifty-five minutes, Dar. I wish I could enjoy the view with you," the computer said almost sadly.

"Pop!" The cockpit was suddenly shared with a utapotus.

"Holy shit!" Dar exclaimed. "Pete, what are you doing here?"

Pete's big orange eyes corkscrewed in their sockets, as he gurgled with pure pleasure. Dar began stroking his back, as the wonderfully ugly creature snuggled into his lap, wrapping its tail around the stick.

"Dar, what is it? I detect additional weight aboard. Are you alright?" Nan asked.

"It's Pete, my utapotus, Dar answered. "Lord knows how he got here, but he's here nonetheless."

"A utapotus. This is not possible. My memory banks tell me of the utapotus, the one who is not one. They choose only Lantiusians. For such an animal to be with you would be improbable."

"Improbable or not, Pete and I are friends," Dar said with a hint of irritation.

"Dar, where are you? Are you all right," Littia's mind blast nearly split his head in half. "Dar, where are you?" The call was frantic.

"Littia, I'm fine." Dar thought back in complete amazement. "How . . . how is this possibly working? I'm half a million miles from the Nanta. There is no way we could send that far."

"Is Pete with you?" Littia asked, her thoughts softer this time.

"Yes, he popped in just a minute ago. Why?"

"Pete is our link. We told you they are unique with very special qualities. He has been our link all along. I should have realized it sooner, but we never dreamed a utapotus would choose a human, much less immediately on your arrival aboard the Nanta."

Dar smiled down at the utapotus on his lap, stroking him with tenderly "Pete, you little scoundrel, you never cease to amaze me," he crooned to the silky smooth alien pet. The battle suddenly flashed through his mind. "Littia, what do you know of the others? Have any Darts returned to the ship yet?"

"Only one. The pilot you call Bulldog returned shortly after you disappeared. His Dart was so badly damaged he could not achieve hyperspace, but he is well. We Guides were invited to the bridge, by the Supreme Commander, to view the battle. It was terrible, Dar. Only nine Darts were able to jump to safety before the fight ended. Supreme Commander Jicama is trying to sort out who is still alive right now."

"Does he know you are mind talking with me?"

"Oh, no! We would never let him know that you can think talk to me.

"Good! Nan tells me it will be awhile before I can jump back, but don't worry, I'm fine."

"Dar, what went wrong?"

"Nothing went wrong. There were just too damn many enemy fighters. We couldn't get close enough to Dectima to get a clean shot before they're fighters were on top of us. The plan was for my flight to engage and keep them busy while Cannaly's flight took out the Dectima, but he had to join the dogfight just to help us stay alive. All in all, we failed terribly."

"Failed to destroy the Dectima, perhaps, but you decimated their fighter force. Supreme Commander Jicama repeated his admiration for your pilot's flying abilities at least a dozen times during the battle. We counted twenty-four enemy fighters destroyed, perhaps more."

"That's a bit of good news, thanks," Dar thought. *Only ten still alive,* his mood darkened. *I've been squadron CO for less than two weeks, and I've already lost over half my unit.*

"You can not blame yourself, Dar," Littia said, reading his thoughts.

"Damn it, Littia, if the Lantiusians have been fighting the Womongly for so damned long, why didn't Jicama know how many fighters the Dectima carried?"

"We . . . we do not know, Dar," Littia sent back. "It does appear strange, but we are sure there is an explanation."

"Yeah, right. Tell that to my boys who are space dust right now." Dar was getting angry.

"We are sure there is a good reason for everything, Dar. Please calm yourself. You will be able to address the issue with the Supreme Commander on your return."

"You can be damned sure I will," Dar fired back.

"Dar, we can spool to hyperspace at anytime," Nan interrupted.

"Roger. Thanks," Dar spoke to Nan, then shifted to thought. "My computer tells me we can jump, Littia. I'll see you soon."

"We shall be waiting," Nan tickled his mind for the last time.

"Pete my friend, I think it is time for you to pop out to wherever you go. I can't hardly fly this thing with you on my lap, playing with the stick."

Pete's eyes drooped, showing disappointment, then disappeared as suddenly as he had arrived.

I'm never going to get used to Pete's coming and goings, his anger abated slightly, just thinking of the utapotus' antics.

Dar made a final scan of his instruments, then gave an order to Nan. "Let's get this show on the road."

CHAPTER 19

The Dart dropped out of hyperspace fifty miles from Nanta. Dar shook his head, clearing the cobwebs, to peer at the massive outline of the Lantiusian ship's green shield shimmering against a blue planet.

"Yosemite Lead, this is Nanta Control. We are pleased you have returned safely."

"Thanks," Dar spoke harshly, still feeling the sting of being launched against superior numbers. "How many Darts have jumped back so far?" His head continued to clear from the hyperspace ride.

"Yosemite, you are the last, we fear. Nine Darts jumped, one returned on drive power." Nanta Control confirmed what Littia had told him.

"Damn, damn, damn," Dar whispered.

"Please say again," Nanta Control asked.

"Just have the recovery team bring me aboard," Dar spoke tartly.

"Yosemite, Recovery. We have control."

"Roger, Recovery. You have control," Dar answered the command, releasing stick and throttle to an unknown Lantiusian located on hangar deck seven. He let his mind drift, as the Dart slowly passed through the shield's tunnel, executed an in-place one hundred and eighty degree turn and settled to the deck.

"I have confirmed four kills with Nanta Control," Nan said softly. "Will we be going out again soon, Dar? I enjoy flying with you."

"Thanks, Nan. Yeah, we'll be out again soon, but we're gonna have to have the hole in the skin fixed first."

Dar pulled the throttle to the off detent, slid his helmet from his shoulders, and opened the canopy bubble. *No rousing cheers this time*, he noted. The hangar was humming with activity, but empty of squadron pilots. Zentao waited patiently for him on the deck below, his face a mask of sadness. Dar climbed stiffly from his cockpit, slowly stepping down the ladder to the floor.

"She needs some work," Dar said, turning to Zentao. "She's only got a twenty-percent shield capability and a hole somewhere aft."

"Yes, Senior Commander Fantin, we have already taken notes on the hole. We are deeply sorry about your losses. Danny was becoming a close friend."

The thought of Danny being blasted to space dust hit Dar like ten g's. "Oh damn! Danny got it?" He pounded his leg with frustration, feeling the bite of losing a man who had become a comrade and an important member of his team.

"Yes. We thought you knew." Zentao hung his head.

"Who else? Did Commander Cannaly and Bulldog make it?" Dar asked, knowing that Bulldog had returned in a damaged Dart, but not wishing to give any hint of Littia's and his situation.

"Yes, both have returned. Commander Cannaly informed me he was . . . how did he put it? Ah, yes! Going to drown himself at the bar."

"Figures," Dar said, smiling inwardly. "Hell, Zentao, maybe we should join him." He walked to the rear of his Dart. Zentao followed discreetly behind. "How soon can we be fully operational?"

Zentao began scrolling through a paper thin maintenance Vidlog he held in his left hand, while Dar walked down the line of blackened and scarred Darts. The hangar smelled of hot metal and burned electrical wiring.

Jesus, they look like relics from an alien junk yard, Dar thought, letting the sight of dozens of men and women working on the fighters sink dully into his comprehension. Not one of the birds had less than three hits burned into their smooth outer skins. Vesicles of molten metal rippled the surface of three Darts, indications of near total shield failure. *Damn, we were lucky to get back this many.*

"With luck, we should have all the Darts fully operational within twelve hours," Zentao interrupted Dar's dark thoughts.

"You've got to be kidding. Just twelve hours?" Dar asked with astonishment. He had no idea that the damage he was surveying could be fixed in such a short period. "That's fantastic, Zentao."

The tall Lantiusian smiled for the first time. "I think Commander Cannaly would say, 'no sweat'."

Dar returned the smile, running fingers through damp hair. "Zentao, is there any chance you could build ten or fifteen more Darts.

Zentao registered surprise at the sudden question. He paused, obviously engrossed in mental calculations. "If we started the project directly upon finishing repairs," he waved his hand, indicating the damaged Darts lining the hangar. "We think we could have fifteen additional fighters on the hangar deck within four, maybe five days. Of course, we could not undertake such a enterprise without the Supreme Commander's orders."

"Jesus Christ, Zentao, what have you got down here a complete manufacturing plant? How can you possibly have fifteen new fighters ready in five days?"

Again, Zentao smiled shyly. "Oh, the Darts are already built. All we have to do is insert the cockpit, and we have already produced several spare cockpits. It was a move on my part, thinking there might be a need if you and your pilots were incapable of matching tactics with the Womongly."

"Zentao, my friend, you never cease to amaze me. Nonetheless, start thinking about it. I'll take the necessary steps with the Supreme Commander," Dar said with determination.

Zentao nodded his head, acknowledging Dar's firmness on the matter. "We have little doubt that you will," he said, tightly.

Dar looked up into Zentao's dark eyes. "You're a good man, Zentao. It's a real pleasure working with you. I know Danny thought a great deal of you as well."

"We are very sad about his loss," Zentao said, hanging his head as if in shame. "Truly we are sorry."

Dar reached up to slap the Lantiusian on the shoulder. "You have nothing to feel sorry about. You have done your very best and we all know it."

"Thank you, Senior Commander. Still, we feel remorse at what the outcome of the . . . ah, er, I mean the ultimate sacrifices you and your men have had to overcome."

"Dar," Littia's mind blast whipped Dar's head around. She was running from the light tube, her arms outstretched.

Dar slapped Zentao on the shoulder once more, then moved rapidly to intercept Littia, gathering her tightly into his arms. "Hey, lady, I missed you," he said lightly.

"Blessed be the God of Many Arms, you are safe," Littia sighed.

"Blessed be that any of us are still alive," Dar said. "Come on, let's get off the hangar deck. Too many eyes on us here." He took her by the arm and led her to the light tube. "I've got to see Jicama. Right now!"

"We know," Littia said, her voice filled with concern. "Please, Dar, do not become angry at the Supreme Commander. His power aboard Nanta is absolute. It would not bode well for you to attack him verbally."

"Yeah, right. I'll keep my cool."

"Keep your cool?" Littia asked, unsure what he meant.

Dar smiled. "I won't upset your precious leader. I'll be a gentleman."

"Ah, we understand. Where shall we meet you later?"

"Cannaly and the rest of my guys are undoubtedly at the bar. Why don't we plan on getting together there? I'll need to talk with them when I'm through with Jicama."

"We understand." She made a hand gesture over the light tube's symbology, directing it to allow her exit on the O-club's deck. "Dar," she looked at him with concern. "The senior Guides are acting strangely. Something is wrong, and we do not understand what it might be."

"Strangely? How?"

"It is as if something is not going as it should with you and your men. Something they know and will not tell me."

"What could they be hiding, and why?" Dar asked, his interest up.

"We are but a Guide 3rd Class, and this is only my first assignment on Nanta. Third Class Guides are very junior in the rank structure. We are told little but what we must know to accomplish the task set before us."

The light tube opened to the officer's bar. "We'll talk more of this later, Littia. Thanks for sharing your concerns with me," He gave Littia a light kiss. "Meet you back here when I'm done with Jicama."

Littia left the tube, seeing the Dart pilots gathered at a table midway down the long bar. The young men were talking softly, their countenance a reflection of those tired and dispirited. She walked slowly to a lone stool near the entrance. Pushing long hair from face, she took a seat to wait for Dar.

Dar stepped from the light tube, head down in thought, and ran into Tamis. "Sorry," he mumbled apologetically, pushing his way by the bigger man. "I'm looking for the Supreme Commander. I was told he was on the bridge."

Tamis straightened his scarlet tunic. "We ask you to watch where you are going," the tall Lantiusian spoke with disdain, pushing heavily against Dar's shoulder. "Yes, the Supreme Commander is on the bridge, but he is busy. We suggest you speak with him at a later time."

Responding to the big Lantiusian's shove, Dar barely contained his anger flaring to the surface. He turned to faced Tamis, his eyes set. "Tamis, I don't much care for you, and I know damned well you like me even less. I don't give a rat's ass one way or the other, but I'm going to see the Supreme Commander. Now! You can take your suggestion and stuff it where the sun don't shine." Without waiting for a reply, he spun on his heel and made for the bridge, leaving a stunned Tamis glaring after him.

Dar stepped onto the suspended bridge, prepared for the vertigo he'd experienced on his other visits. It came, but with less intensity. He shook it off with a shrug, noting chaotic activity throughout Nanta's nerve center. Hundreds of Dataspheres zipped in all directions, while controllers grabbed them and slammed them into computer receptacles. Monitors glowed, their multi-colored lights reflecting off the officers seated before them. High above, the surrounding plasma screen cast a shining view of Earth and Dectima anchored near the planet's outer atmosphere.

Jicama, seeing his visitor enter, broke from a group of officers, striding purposefully to greet Dar with a pleasant smile. "Dar, you and your men did well. Your flying was superior in every respect. Towering over SFS-1's commander, he stuck his hand out to Dar.

Though his mood did not warrant a hand shake, Dar acknowledged the greeting. "With all due respect, sir, I lost half my squadron. I don't consider the loss superior, but thank you nonetheless." Though his words were pleasant enough, there was an icy edge in his voice.

Jicama nodded sadly. "Ah, yes, it is so. A most distressful situation. Still, we have confirmed that your unit destroyed twenty-seven enemy fighters. Considering the odds, we acknowledge SFS-1 as the overall winner."

"That is what I wish to speak with you about . . . the odds, as you put it." This time there was little doubt of the coolness of the statement. Jicama frowned down at Dar with a look that said, *be careful Earthman, don't overstep your bounds.* Dar caught his mistake. "Sir, I apologize for my tone. Its been one hell'va day, and losing so many pilots has me less than pleased"

Jicama's face softened, his dark eyes reflecting understanding. "We comprehend your feelings of loss. Please, join me at the command module where we can speak undisturbed." He took Dar by the arm, a small gesture of comradery, leading him to the seat next to his command chair. "Now, what seems to be bothering you?" he asked pleasantly.

Dar's sweat laden flight suit clung uncomfortably, he was still stiff from the long period cooped up in the tiny cockpit, and his mood remained sour. Pausing to look at the large tactical holographic screen suspended before the command module, he took a deep breath. "Sir," he began softly. "You have told me that for hundreds of years you have helped many worlds in the fight against the Womongly. Is this not so?"

Guardedly, Jicama studied Dar for a moment. "Yes, that is so. Why do you ask? Your time in the Educator has instructed you on Lantiusian history, has it not?" he purposefully answered the question with a question.

Dar ignored the question concerning his education. "Sir, if for no other reason than I owe it to my men, I have to ask why you did not inform me we might be engaging as many as fifty enemy fighters when we launched a full scale attack on the Dectima."

"Ah, is that the problem. Dar, my friend, we were as surprised as you. We have never seen a Womongly World Destroyer ship with more than thirty fighters aboard. As I explained on our first meeting, the Womongly have upgraded their fighters with hyperspace capabilities. It appears they have modified their mother ships as well. Please believe me when I say, I would have never had allowed you to go into such a fight if I had known of the numbers you'd be facing."

Dar scrutinized the big commander for any sign of deceitfulness, finding none. "Very well, sir, I see what you mean. No matter the reason, we still have a serious problem. I only have ten Darts left, and that sure as hell isn't going to allow me to get close to the Dectima, much less destroy her. I presume you have taken into account how the Womongly ship is positioned."

"Yes. Very clever of her commander to place the Dectima in a manner that an attack can only be made from two directions. We fear we have underestimated this particular Womongly captain. From your intent expression, we assume you have an idea concerning our next course of action."

"Yes, sir. I suggest you allow me to launch a Dart for Earth. Let me recruit fifteen more pilots while Zentao builds additional fighters. I have already spoken to Zentao. He assures me he could have fifteen Darts operational in five days, after repairs are completed from today's battle."

Jicama starred at the holo screen in thought. "We see the logic in your proposal and we agree. There is, however, something we could do beyond recruiting additional pilots from Earth."

Dar waited, running his fingers through tangled hair, wondering what Jicama had in mind.

"We believe you should present a yet another defensive option to your world," Jicama said quietly.

Dar studied Jicama with interest, waiting for him to continue.

"We could build a shield around Earth in a three of four day period. If that were accomplished, Earth's populations need never be concerned about the Womongly again."

Dar, visibly shaken, was completely taken off center by the Lantiusian. "I don't understand. If shielding Earth is possible, why did you want us to fight the Womongly in space. Why bring us here at all?"

Jicama smiled knowingly, the grin spreading slowly across his face. "Ah, Dar, we think your world leaders would have never accepted us. Could they have understood the actual threat? No! Had we approached your institutional political conclaves with such a suggestion, we would still be in negotiations. The very fact Nanta appeared from deep space would have sent your world into general chaos. Is this not so?"

Dar listened closely to Jicama's words, and with each, realized how true they were. No country, certainly not his own, would allow such an infernal machine placed on Earth without significant proof of an outside threat. Jicama was right about the Lantiusian's sudden appearance as well. "Yes, sir, you are correct."

"Very well then. Now the situation has changed dramatically. There is little doubt your battle has been seen by hundreds of thousands on the planet. Governments know of our presence, and the war we rage, yet have no idea why, or, for that matter, who."

A single Datasphere zipped by Dar's head en route to an officer several hundred feet down the line of controllers. "That is true," Dar agreed, ducking unconsciously.

"As our plenipotentiary you could act in the Lantiusian's behalf. Your return to Earth provides an opportunity to explain what Nanta is all about, and how dangerous the Dectima is to the very survival of your species. If your world governments accept our offer, it would be an alternative far superior to continued usage of the Darts. Earth would be protected and no additional pilots must die"

Dar nodded agreement, acknowledging the wisdom of Jicama's words.

"We agree to your recruitment of additional pilots, but must insist you attempt to convince Earth's governments to allow the construction of the shield."

Dar fidgeted in his chair uncomfortably, not sure why, after all, Jicama's suggestion was valid in all respects. "I agree, sir. It's a sound idea, and one that could put an end to this war without further bloodshed." He paused, still uncertain. "Yes, I agree, but I still want more Darts and pilots to fly them."

Nodding, Jicama touched a small symbol on his control panel. Within seconds, Zentao appeared before Dar and Jicama, his face a three dimensional holograph floating above the command module. "Zentao, this is Supreme Commander Jicama."

"Yes, Supreme Commander, we are here," Zentao replied immediately.

"When repairs are completed on the Darts, we wish you to begin construction of fifteen additional fighters."

Zentao's face lit up with a smile. "Ah, we see Senior Commander Fantin has convinced you. Yes, it shall be done." The cube disappeared.

"It is done. Now, what do you require for your flight, and where do you plan to go?" Jicama asked, in a business-like manner.

The questions were those Dar had been asking himself just prior to the unpleasant encounter with Tamis. "The only modifications I need to my Dart are UHF radio capability and wheels to replace the skids as landing gear. The rest I can handle." He paused, contemplating the site he should land, then it hit like a thrumber blast. "I'll land at MCAS Cherry Point, not far from where you picked me up," he said with finality, thinking of General Moore. Shaker would listen to him without catapulting him to some rubber room for interrogation.

"Very well then. When will you depart Nanta?" Jicama asked.

"Just as soon as my Dart is repaired and Zentao tells me she'll make the flight."

"Good, it's agreed. Now, if you have no further questions, I need to return to my command duties," Jicama said, and smiled warmly.

Dar rose from his chair. "Thank you, Supreme Commander Jicama. I appreciate your understanding and help, but there is one other item. Could you arrange for me to transmit via UHF prior to my departure?"

Jicama looked surprised at the question. "Why UHF? Why not microwave? Something with more power and capability."

"Because I want to talk on a channel no one will expect. I want to speak with one man in particular, with little chance of the whole damned world listening."

"Ah, we understand. So be it. I shall make the arrangements."

"I think that's all for now. Thank you for your help."

With a wave of his hand, Jicama dismissed the comment. "No thanks necessary. We wish you good luck." With that, he fluidly slipped from his chair, and moved rapidly for the far end of the bridge, leaving Dar to stare after him.

"Twenty-seven Strike Dragons destroyed by a force less than half our own. They fight like demons. Crazy, but fantastic pilots," Captain Langos spoke quietly to his second-in-command, his admiration for the Earthlings evident.

"The important thing, Captain, is we have destroyed over half their fighters as well. If, indeed, the second strike was the remainder of their fleet," First Officer Bezal commented.

Langos recognized the first officer's attempt to appease his raw mood. "Yes, yes. Of course you would view this, yet another defeat, as a single victory. No, there was little victory and much failure. Still, all is not lost. The Earthlings dare not attack the Dectima again. At least not with so few fighters at their disposal. It begs the question, what will they attempt next?" Langos walked to his desk stool. Cocking his third leg, he sat down to gaze at the multi-dimensional picture of his wife and child. "Nonetheless, set patrols on Dectima's space side and keep them spaceborne until I say differently. I do not want to be surprised."

"It has been done, Captain. I took the liberty of posting the patrols soon after you left the bridge." Bezal stood ram rod straight, waiting for the expected verbal attack from Langos. Never before had he assigned duties without Langos' orders.

"Yes, yes. Very good. Langos said, not taking his eyes from the holographic picture. Fluffing his breathing flaps with his small right hand, he sighed heavily. "When can we start broadcasting?"

"Immediately, sir. We are completing the frequency modulators and setting the various band widths. Broadcasts will be made in five different languages simultaneously."

"Very well. The sooner we can begin communications the better. What defensive preparations are indicated on the surface?"

"Radio and microwave interceptions indicate little preparatory actions beyond what we expected. Two nations, the United States of America and Russia, have put their missiles on alert. Nothing Dectima's shield could not withstand, should the need arise." Bezal answered.

"Yes, yes. That is good. What actions from the Nanta? Have they begun to broadcast?" Langos continued to drink in the picture of his wife and child.

"No sir. Nothing from Nanta.

"Hmmm. Unusual. I expected them to open shield construction negotiations by now. It is more their way." Langos took a second to think of reasons why, finding none. "Yes, yes, very well. Instruct the bridge to keep close scrutiny on the Nanta." Langos slowly swiveled the stool around, his owlish eyes drooping with fatigue, to look directly at Bezal. "You have done well, First Officer. Return to your duties."

Dar held up his hand to Littia as he stepped from the light tube, indicating she should keep her seat. "Let me have a few minutes with them alone," he spoke to her quietly. "I'll wave you over."

"We understand," Littia said. "We do not envy you. It is a sad time."

Dar noted Littia's mask of sadness and nodded, then walked slowly into the bar.

"Boss," Cannaly yelled, as he caught sight of Dar. "Come join the wake. Bulldog, pour the skipper a tall green one."

As Dar approached, the men got quickly to their feet, shuffling chairs and dragging another from the closest table. "Sit," he said quietly to what remained of SFS-1. "Looks like y'all have been sipping a few. I think we all need a couple dozen or so. God, what a day."

"We been saluting the fallen, boss," Cannaly interjected. His face looked tired and strained. He sat down, as did the others. "It's gonna take awhile to drink to them all, I'm damned sorry to say. By the way, boss, I don't think you have met Jon Pierre Coe'tte." Cannaly pointed out the Frenchman sitting across from him. "He's been in the hospital. Got his arm blown off by the Womongly when we were trying to eat. Remember?"

"Sure," Dar said, smiling and offering his hand to the Frenchman. "You look fit now. Can you fly?"

"Yes, sir. Got my up chit from the quacks this morning, but didn't get to the flight deck in time. The XO took off with his flight just before I got there, or I'd been with you."

"Well, we could have used another Dart, but I have a feeling you'll get your chance," Dar said, as a green drink plopped down in front of him.

"Try this, skipper," Tom Hanker said with a grin. "Guaranteed to knock your flight boots into next year."

Dar smiled his appreciation, taking a sip of the tall drink. "Jesus H. Christ," he coughed. "What ya got in this, 200 proof hydraulic fluid?"

"Hell, boss. Gotta say goodbye properly. That there is my very own concoction of most everything I could find behind the bar. Good huh?" Cannaly said, and laughed sadly.

"Yeah, right! Good. Hell, Snake, that shit would stop a sexually aroused elephant in mid stroke. What ya planning to do, market it as paint stripper." Dar recognized the lighthearted banter as a pain easing mechanism against thoughts of friends dying in battle. It was a squadron's normal medication. An elixir to heal mental wounds, not broken bones. Tomorrow, it could be any one of them who might not fly home. He took another sip of the strong brew and choked.

"What's up, boss? We know you went to see Jicama?" Cannaly asked, his tone serious. There were many anticipatory head nods around the table acknowledging the question.

Using the back of his sleeve, Dar wiped rivulets of green liquid from his mouth. "I'll give it to you straight. It ain't all good, but not all bad either." He paused, letting the men settle in. "We lost ten Darts, you know that, but we took twenty-seven of the slimy bastards with us. So the odds are staying about even so far. Still, we don't dare try another attack on Dectima until we can get some reinforcements up here."

The mention of reinforcements took the men off guard. "Where are we going to get fresh troops, skipper? For damned sure the Lantiusians aren't going to fight, what with their God of Many Arms and all" Cannaly asked, with astonishment.

Dar took another drink from his glass, then waved Littia to the table. "Is it alright if Littia joins us?" he said. Several heads nodded at once.

"Sure no sweat, skipper," Cannaly answered for himself and the rest.

The men stood, allowing Littia room to slide a chair next to Dar. She said nothing, but smiled shyly at the group.

Once settled, Dar began again. "Okay, here's the deal. I'm taking my Dart to Earth." He stopped to let his words sink in. To his surprise, there appeared to be no immediate reaction concerning the thought he would be returning home. He continued. "I'll land at Cherry Point and get with General Moore. I trust him not to drag me to D. C. and lock me away with the CIA or whatever. My plan is to tell him the situation, and that we need more pilots. Getting pilots won't be hard. Every swinging dick in the Marine Corps will be crawling over each other trying to get in on the action, but there's a catch."

"Even if you get volunteers, skipper, what are they going to fly?" Hanker asked.

"Good question, but easily answered. Zentao is going to put together fifteen more Darts. Says he can have them done in five days," Dar said with self satisfaction. He enjoyed the whistles of astonishment that followed his remark, remembering his own reactions when Zentao told him of the short time frame necessary to build the fighters.

"Okay, boss, what's this catch you spoke about?" Cannaly asked, with skepticism.

"The Supreme Commander wants me to convince Earth's governments to let the Lantiusians build a shield around the planet."

Littia sucked in a breath at Dar's words. "He wants a shield completely around Earth?" she spoke softly, more to herself than the others.

Attention turned her way. "Yes. Is there something wrong with that?" Dar asked.

Littia looked up in confusion. "Oh, we are sorry. We did not wish to interrupt. No . . ah . . . .. No I don't believe so. It is nothing. We apologize." To Dar, she mind talked, "Do not worry, I must be wrong. Please continue with your men."

Dar grimaced with her thoughts, but returned to his briefing. "Jicama makes a good point. With the shield, Earth won't have to worry about an attack from the Womongly." He went on to explain why the Lantiusians had not proposed the shield earlier, and how he planned to speak to General Moore prior to his departure.

The table was deathly quiet when Dar finished talking. Then Cannaly slapped the table. "Well, it ain't the most perfect plan I've ever heard, but it sure as hell beats a sharp stick in the eye. Let's drink to the dumb slobs who will soon be joining us."

"Yeah, and one more for the men we lost. May every one of them be accepted as heroes when this thing is over," Hanker said loudly.

"Here, here. To the heroes," the table joined in the toast.

SFS-1 was bleeding, feeling the hurt of friends and comrades lost, as a young Lantiusian officer entered the bar. To the tall muscular officer, the small band of men appeared nothing more than a fighting unit solidifying its willingness to carry on against the odds.

CHAPTER 20

Reluctantly, Dar stepped from the sonic mist. He knew the shower water, what little required to cleanse his body, drained to recycling receptacles deep in the bowels of Nanta, however, his tours aboard aircraft carriers had taught him well about saving water. A long hot shower helped knotted muscles relax. More importantly, the heat distilled Cannaly's ungodly alcoholic contrivance through his pores. Hurriedly he toweled, combed his hair, then dressed in clean flight gear. In less than ten minutes, he was to meet Littia at the Relaxation Center on deck seventy-five. She had mind talked to him shortly after his second "green goober." *Green goobers, what an appropriate name for that foul tasting drink*, Dar thought.

Littia mind talked directions to the Center along with a time to meet her there, patted his hand gently. She'd eyed him with a "we hope you will live through this" look, then left for her own quarters. Dar stayed for one more "goober," excused himself, heading straight for a shower.

Pete popped in the moment Dar opened the door to his quarters, to curl up on the desk watching every movement his chosen made. Now dressed, with a reasonable chance of living through the goobers, Dar gave Pete's ugly head a gentle stroke. "You mind your manners, ya hear?" he cooed to his friend. "See you in a bit."

Satisfied he would live to see another day, Dar left his room, took the PCT to the light tube. Stepping aboard the tube, he passed his hand over the symbols for the Relaxation Center.

Exiting the tube on deck seventy-five, he turned right as Littia had instructed and walked right past the Relaxation Center. For the next fifteen minutes he wandered the deck, before realizing his mistake. Thinking, *those damned "goobers" are still killing cells in my brain-housing group*, he finally entered the oval confines of an area that immediately smoothed the turbulent encounters of the day. The room, he noticed, was nothing unusual. Not large by comparison to other gathering areas on Nanta, yet the semi-darkness emanated an atmosphere of complete withdrawal from worldly problems.

He spotted Littia curled up in a large recliner, well away from a dozen or so Lantiusians comfortably recumbent to his left. The room was as silent as an arctic morning. Not wishing to break the serenity of the utter stillness, Dar tiptoed to Littia's side. She lay peacefully, eyes closed against the world. He stood a moment admiring her beauty, then sat next to her, placing a hand lightly on her shoulder.

"Littia, it's Dar," he whispered.

Her eye lids fluttered, then opened. "Dar." She reached up to stroke his cheek. "Lie, she pointed to the recliner next to hers, and dream."

Dar lay back, closing his eyes. Subliminal stimulation immediately transported him to a place and time he loved most. He stood on the bow, as far forward as the lifelines would permit, of the aircraft carrier Eisenhower. She was making twenty-five knots, steaming west into the sunset. The South China Sea was flat calm, not a breath rippled the water as the sky turned reds, pinks and purples . . . the entire horizon a canvas for God's paint brush. He spread his arms, allowing the carrier generated wind to blow through tousled hair, and sucked his lungs full of clean, sweet salt air. Dolphins played in the great ship's bow wake, performing high arced jumps against a multicolored sky.

A shrill ring brought Dar and Littia out of their subliminally induced trances simultaneously. The annoying noise tittered once more at Littia's belt, and she reached for her VVCom.

"This is Guide 3rd Class, Littia," she spoke at the picture of Supreme Commander Jicama, who smiled back at her on the small screen.

"Ah, I see you are relaxing. My apologies, but we wish you to report to my quarters," Jicama spoke lightly.

"Yes, sir. We shall report immediately," Littia said.

"Good! Out." Jicama signed off.

"What's that all about," Dar asked, seeing the concern on Littia's face. "Why would Jicama want to see you in his quarters?" The question reflected irritation, not just for being interrupted from his dream, but a hint of jealousy as well.

"We have no idea," Littia answered. She was as surprised as Dar was concerned. "The Supreme Commander has never asked to see me in his quarters before." No sooner had the words left her mouth, she wished them back.

Dar looked hard at her. "You're telling me these visits are normal? It seems very strange that the Supreme Commander would question a Guide 3rd Class for information."

"Actually, not that unusual. The Supreme Commander or Tamis debrief Guides on a regular basis."

"Interesting. Why? What does he want to know?" Dar asked, still upset with the situation.

"Nothing very important. Mostly how each of our charges is acclimating to life on Nanta and their reactions to the war. Things like that. Nothing more."

Dar rolled her answer around in his head for a moment. "Yes, I suppose Jicama would want to know how we are doing, and what better source of information than our guides. Well, you had better get going. I don't think the man likes to be kept waiting."

Littia smiled sweetly at Dar. "Yes, we must go. I'll let you know when I am finished." She stood, and walked swiftly out of the Relaxation Center.

Dar sat quietly for a moment, noticing that the others in the room had not moved nor appeared disturbed by sounds of the VVCom or their conversation. He felt unfulfilled by the severed dream and disturbed by Jicama's request. He stood, giving the Center one last look of regret, ran fingers through his hair, and followed Littia out the door.

Littia knocked softly on the Supreme Commander's door.

"Come," Jicama commanded. The door slid silently aside. "Ah, Guide 3rd Class Littia, come in."

Littia stepped through the large passage to enter Jicama's private quarters. The grandeur of the spacious room took her breath away. Never had she seen such appointments in any of the accommodations aboard Nanta. Here, in these capacious quarters, were rare items from worlds she had only heard about. Jicama sat in a low slung overstuffed chair, which gave the appearance of molding to his body. A brown utapotus curled comfortably in is lap, which Jicama stroked with slow soft movements. Sandals, stitched with golden thread, rested on a rug of fur many inches thick. She tried to remember where such fur came from, but could not recall the name of the animal, only that it came from a world Nanta had visited many years prior. In front of Jicama sat a large wooden table, its black surface polished to a mirror finish and adorned with vases filled with *living* flowers. Tamis sat at one end of the beautiful table, facing Jicama. His scowl could not extinguish Littia's astonishment at the site of a large cylinder rising from the floor to the overhead behind the First Commander. Resplendent lights played games through the liquid filled cylinder, while brightly colored animals, of a type she had never seen, swam without concern between the large waving leaves growing from the bottom of the tank. With excited recollection, she knew the animals to be fish.

"Come in and sit, Guide," Jicama instructed, breaking her wonderstruck ogling.

She walked slowly to the table, feeling the softness of the rug beneath her feet. "Sir, We have never seen anything like this," she said, breathlessly. "It is all so grand."

"Ah, you like my humble quarters, do you? Yes, they are comfortable. Now, sit." Jicama said, a smile evident.

Littia took a chair across from Tamis, feeling the seat wrap around her, providing perfect comfort. Light pictures shifted designs and hues over the walls of the room, casting shadows of galaxies, planets, and stars all with Nanta drifting near by. *We had no idea anyone lived in such luxury.* Her thoughts filled with fascination.

"What of Senior Commander Dar?" Jicama asked. "What is he thinking?"

Littia startled out of her thoughts said, "We are sorry, sir. Please, what was the question?"

"We asked, what is your charge thinking? Is he having second thoughts about the battle with the Womongly?"

Littia's surprise was evident as she looked at the Supreme Commander. "Why, no, sir. Why would you ask? Dar, er, Senior Commander Fantin is every bit as much concerned about the Womongly and his world as he ever was."

"Ah, I thought as much, but First Commander Tamis feels our young Earth leader is becoming far too fascinated with you to follow through with the confrontation with our enemy."

Littia's face reddened at Jicama's remark. "Sir, is not my private time mine alone?"

Jicama gave Littia a fatherly smile. "To a point, yes, your time is your own. However, should evolvement with Senior Commander Fantin create interference for our mission, then that is another matter. Another matter all together."

"We are sorry sir. We do not understand. Is not Senior Commander Fantin's mission to conduct the fight against the Womongly? If that is so, has he not fought valiantly?"

Shaking his head at her naivete, Jicama laughed lightly. "How old are you, Guide?" he asked.

Littia sank back in her plush chair, taken aback by the question. "Ah . . . we mean . . .. We, we are not sure," she confessed. "We do not understand. Why do we not know our own age?"

A grin of satisfaction creased Tamis' face. "You are a Lantiusian woman, a very pretty one, but a clone none the less. A clone less than a month out of the incubators."

Seeing Littia's face fall with understanding and unhappiness, Jicama interrupted his second in command. "Tamis is far too blunt. We are all clones. All of us. Age is our only difference. You are young yet, not familiar with all there is to understand about the mission our original physical parents directed us accomplish. Much of your education has yet to be programmed within you. Soon, perhaps."

"We know of your demented sexual encounter with the Earthling," Tamis snapped. "Disgusting, yet useful if you can tell us of his plans."

Littia's face turned hard as stone, as she flung herself from the chair. "We will not listen longer," she spoke with a force she had never experienced. "Senior Commander Fantin . . . Dar . . . may not be Lantiusian, but he possesses honor and courage. Something we would remind you about, First Commander."

"That will be enough. Both of you will stop this immediately," Jicama ordered in no uncertain terms. "Sit, Guide!"

Littia slowly sat back into the folds of her chair, while Tamis continued to glare unforgivingly. Slowly, she felt her tension subside. "Supreme Commander, we have nothing to report. Dar is planning to return to Earth for additional pilots. He also plans to propose your suggestion of shielding Earth."

"Ah, that is well. That is what we needed to know. Thank you." The Supreme Commander smiled. "During our conversation, I had doubts he would suggest the shielding of his world to the appropriate agencies. Now we may relax and let it happen."

"Sir," Littia began. "May we ask a question concerning the shield?"

"You may ask. We may not answer, however."

"Was it not the shielding of Lantius which brought about the destruction of our home?"

"So! Your education has taken you that far, has it? Yes, the shield eventually destroyed our planet."

"Then why would we want to shield Earth? Will it not destroy that world as well?"

Jicama studied the woman before him, pondering his answer. "No," he stated flatly. "We corrected the shield's insidious problem long ago, I assure you. No harm will come to Earth. You must trust me on this matter, and speak nothing of it to any of the Earthlings. Do you understand?" His voice turned iron hard with the question.

"We understand," Littia said. "We shall not speak of it again."

"That is well. Now you may go. Return to your duties, but report to me immediately should Dar's plans change. Do you fully comprehend my meaning on this matter?"

"We understand perfectly," Littia said coldly. She rose, gave Tamis a distasteful look, and strode purposefully for the door.

Nearing his quarters, Dar stepped from the tape. The sunset dream still swirled in his mind. *Wow, that was something*, he had to admit. As he approached his door, Cannaly's still tipsy voice echoed down the passageway.

"Hey, boss. I think you better hear somethin'," Cannaly slurred.

Dar turned to see his friend with Jon Pierre in tow. Both men wobbled on their feet, the "green goobers" still coursing through their veins.

Smiling, Dar said, "Yeah, come on in."

Leading the pair into his quarters, Dar made a quick scan for Pete. The utapotus was nowhere to be seen. Dar let out his breath. The last thing he needed right now was to give a detailed explanation about Pete to Cannaly and the Frenchman. "Okay, you two drunks, what's so important that you left the wake to visit me?"

Cannaly gave Dar a hurt expression. "Damn, boss, don't ya love me anymore?"

"Sure I do, but that doesn't mean I'm going to kiss you or anything."

All three men laughed. *It was good to laugh*, Dar thought. *Not much of that lately.* "Well, it's your dime, what ya got?"

"We wuz talking, ya know, drinking goobers and talking up in the bar, when Frenchy here comes out with the damnedest story ya ever heard."

"Is that right?" Dar commented, shaking his head lightheartedly at his friend's obviously inebriated condition. "Well, are you going to just sit there, or get on with telling me what this tale is all about?"

"You tell him Frenchy," Cannaly said, turning the floor over to Jon Pierre.

"Well, sir," the Frenchman began, his tongue thick with booze. "I was just telling them about wandering around the Nanta. I didn't have much else to do while I was in quacksville, so I spent hours just wandering different decks."

"Yeah, I got it, you did a lot of wandering. So?" Dar asked.

"A couple of days ago, I stumbled on a deck that our hosts don't want us to see."

With those words, Dar sat forward in his desk chair. "What do you mean, they don't want us to see?" he asked, feeling uneasy. Too many things were not adding up as of late.

"I can't remember what deck I was on. At the time, it didn't make any difference to me where I went. When I got off the light tube, I could smell something slightly foul, you know, kind of rotten."

"Rotten. That is unusual. The air onboard Nanta is almost sterile smelling, it's so clean," Dar interrupted.

"I know. That's why it caught my attention, but there wasn't anything in the passageway that could have produced the smell. In fact, the passageway was unusual as well. No people and no doors, just these big black panels on the wall."

"Go on, tell him about the panels, Frenchy," Cannaly coaxed.

"Oui, the panels," Jon Pierre continued. "I stepped on the tape, which moved very slowly, which was curious as well. Then I thought to myself, what are those panels for? I got off the tape and touched one of them, and it vanished."

"Vanished? Where did it go?" Dar asked.

"Nowhere, I guess. It just went clear, and behind it was a village with creatures living in huts or something. It was strange. I went to the panel across from the first and touched it. Walla! There was another setting altogether. This one was a forest with a humanoid creature and its baby. Skipper, the damned place was a zoo of some sort."

Dar studied the dark haired Frenchman for a moment. "Okay, Nanta has about everything else aboard. Why not a zoo?"

"That may be, sir, but if it was just a zoo, why would the Lantiusians hide it from us. Before I could open anymore more panels, this big mountain of a Lantiusian darn near kicked my ass for being there. All of our hosts have been very polite and helpful. This guy was a hard-nosed son-of-a-bitch. There's no doubt in my mind he'd removed me one piece at a time, if I hadn't cooperated."

Dar sat back, his face screwed up in thought.

"See! What did I tell you, boss. Somethin' ain't right around here." Cannaly interjected.

"Just because they have a zoo, or something they don't want us to see, doesn't make them less important to the survival of Earth," Dar said. "Hell, I don't doubt we'd hide a bunch of shit from them if they were on Earth."

"Yeah! You may be right, boss, but I'm not feeling warm and fuzzy about this any longer. Neither are the other guys," Cannaly said, his words no longer muddled with green goober. "This afternoon's attack was something I'm not soon to forget. With all the surveillance crap this ship's got aboard, why didn't his supreme highness know about the fighters aboard the Womongly World Destroyer, or whatever he calls it?"

"I already explained that. I honestly don't think Jicama was lying to me. Why should he?"

"Boss, your guess is as good as mine. All I'm sayin' is let's be careful. We kinda accepted these people without much thought at first, probably because of their damn Educator. But now, I think we need to tread softly."

"Roger that, Snake. Read you loud and clear," Dar said. "I agree with you, but we still have to consider the threat to Earth, and that's coming from the Womongly. Regardless of how we feel or think about the Lantiusians, we still have to put some trust in them to defeat the enemy."

"Yeah, I guess you're right, but I don't have to like it. As for this zoo thing, it doesn't feel right. I mean it's weird. I just got this feeling, and when I get to feeling funny about somethin', I get worried."

"I hear ya, Snake. What say I talk to Littia about it? Maybe she'll know something."

"Yeah, good idea, and I'll talk to Monasa. Damnation." Cannaly smiled wickedly. "That gal is sure good where it counts. Met her in the bar during the big celebration a few nights back. She's a bridge officer. Maybe she's got some info she'll pass along."

"Good idea," Dar said. "What about you, Jon, have you got a source you could pump?"

"Regretfully, no. As a Frenchman in good standing, I should have been the first to have a bed partner. Alas, I am still a loner."

Dar chuckled at the sad look emanating from the pilot's face. "Never mind, I don't think it will be long until you uphold the French standard for all to see."

Jon's mood brightened. "Oui, it is so, is it not?"

Dar sat staring at the blank wall above his airbed for several minutes. He had to agree with Cannaly. There were things, in the past couple of days, that just didn't add up. Still, no matter which way he turned, he needed the Lantiusians if he was to fight the Womongly. Hopefully, Littia could fill in answers to the questions he had rolling around in his head.

"Poof!" Pete suddenly appeared on his lap.

Dar immediately felt his stress wash way, as it always did when the utapotus made himself present. "You're just what the doctor ordered," he said, stroking Pete's soft scales. With his friend curled on his lap, Dar thoughts turned to Littia.

"Littia, are you still with Jicama?" he mind talked.

"No. We left his quarters several minutes ago," she thought back.

Even in his mind, Dar could recognize from her tone that she was upset. "Are you okay?" he asked.

"We are fine, but the conversation with the Supreme Commander has upset me. We are sorry to worry you. It is nothing."

Dar thought about her answer for a moment, deciding it would be best not to push the matter. "Very well, I understand. Will you join me later?"

"We could join you now, if you wish," Littia thought.

Dar felt the emotional need for contact Littia's words expressed. "No, not right now. I want to check with Jicama about my radio transmission to General Moore. Give me a couple hours." He felt as if he'd let her down when she needed him.

"Very well. We shall see you later," she thought back. She paused, then asked. "Is Pete with you?"

"Yes. Why?" Dar thought back.

"We can feel him with you, and he is sending me calming feelings. We believe he is linking strongly to both of us now."

"He's a very good friend, and I'm darn glad he picked me over everyone else on this ship." Dar tickled Pete's chin. "See you soon."

"Okay. In a couple hours then," Littia thought, opening the door to her quarters.

Dar felt the tickling in his mind go blank. "Pete, old boy, time for you to pop out of here for a minute so. I have to chat with Jicama."

Pete, eyes whirling, looked with understanding at Dar, then disappeared.

Shaking his head over his friend's antics, Dar reached for the VVCom he'd placed on his desk. Snapping the communicator open, he ordered, "Supreme Commander Jicama."

Seconds ticked by before Jicama's face appeared on the small screen. "Ah, Dar. We were just getting ready to contact you. The UHF radio link has been established, as you requested. The unit should be arriving at your quarters within the next few minutes."

"Thank you, sir. That's what I was calling about. Since the radio is being delivered, is there anything special I should know about its operation?"

"We believe not. The controls were copied from your aircraft's cockpit radio."

"I should have guessed," Dar said, and laughed. "Thanks again. I won't take up any more of your time."

"It was no trouble," Jicama stated, as Dar's screen went blank.

Dar gazed at the black screen a moment longer, then ordered, "Zentao."

The small unit came to life once more, showing Zentao's friendly face. "Senior Commander Fantin, is that you? Your Vid is fuzzy," Nanta's chief engineer said cheerfully.

"Yeah, Zentao, its me. Just wanted to check and see how things are going with my Dart."

A smile spread across the Lantiusians face. "Your fighter will be ready to launch by tomorrow afternoon. We are just now redesigning the landing gear for an Earth airfield landing. The skids would have sufficed, you know, but upon researching the types of fields where you might wish to land, they would have torn long gashes in the material you call asphalt."

"That's great work, my friend. That's why I suggested removing the skids. How about the communications? Have you installed the UHF?"

Again, Zentao's face radiated a smile. "Oh, yes, of course. In fact, we have just finished manufacturing the device you wished to contact Earth with before leaving Nanta. It should be at your quarters by now."

Dar started to answer, when a loud "bong" sounded outside his door. "Hang on one, Zentao," he spoke into the VVCom. The door to his quarters opened without command, and a black, egg shaped box measuring twelve inches across came whirring into his room. Like a Datasphere, it moved without apparent propulsion. "Zentao, I think the radio has arrived." Dar smiled into the VVScreen, "You sure have a way of making things move around."

"All part of our friendly service for our alien guests," Zentao returned.

Dar laughed with the engineer. He could tell Zentao was feeling proud of himself, using conversational bantering just as one of Earth's pilots might. "Watch out, Zentao, you're beginning to sound a lot like Cannaly. Lord, I don't think I could put up with the two of you."

"We could have worse examples than Commander Cannaly, we think," Zentao explained. "Let me know if you need any help with the new communication device."

"Roger, will do. And thanks for your help," Dar said, as the screen went black.

Placing the VVCom in his breast pocket, Dar went to the UHF suspended in the middle of his quarters and grabbed it as he had seen controllers on the bridge do. Taking it to his desk, he sat it down, thinking it would stay where it had been placed. "Jesus," he exclaimed, as it jumped back to eye level.

Pete looked up from the chair he'd just popped into. He looked at Dar with disdain, his spinning orange eyes saying, "just use it dummy."

"Okay, Pete. No need to get rude. I'm still learning, ya know," Dar spoke lightly to his friend.

Dar took a minute to study the black box, noting that it was set up exactly like his Harrier's cockpit radio. He turned it on, and switching the channel selector to 362.0. Red plasma digits appeared in a field of black, indicating he had the channel properly selected. There was no mike, but he realized the unit must to be voice actuated. *Zentao, it appeared, had made a few modifications after all, he thought, grinning.*

"Mars Base, Mars Base, this is Mars Two Two.

First Lieutenant Tim Blair sat behind the halfmoon-shaped Duty Officer's desk. Raised above the Ready Room floor by six full inches, the desk was cluttered with flight schedules, weather reports and pilot's yellow sheets. Three phones hung on the wall behind him, along with two radios. One radio provided direct access to Marine Corps Air Station Weather Office, and the other was used for communication with VMAT-203's airborne flights. Right now, First Lieutenant Blair had eight Harrier's airborne, none of which carried a call sign of Mars Two Two. He knew very well that Two Two had disappeared several weeks ago. The incident was still under investigation.

Blair grabbed his radio's mike. "Okay, smart guy, who are you?"

"Mars Base, this is Mars Two Two, Major Dar Fantin speaking. Please inform your Commanding Officer or the Executive Officer.

"Listen, whoever you are. Mars Two Two isn't with the living any longer, so get the heck off my radio frequency."

"I'm only going to say this once more. This is Major Dar Fantin and I want to talk to your CO. *now!*" Dar's voice transmitted hardened steel.

Officers drinking coffee or playing Acey-Ducey in the Ready Room stopped what they were doing, joining Blare at the desk. One of the officers slugging down swallows of black coffee was Major Simmons, the Operations Officer.

"Lieutenant Blair, have this guy stand-by, I'll get the skipper. I know Dar, and that sure as hell sounds like him," Major Simmons instructed the young lieutenant.

"Mars Two Two. Roger. Stand-by, we're getting Lieutenant Colonel Jackson right now," Blair radioed to Dar.

"About damned time," Dar radioed back. He waited for several minutes before his UHF came back to life.

"This is Lieutenant Colonel Jackson, Mars Two Two. Just what the heck are trying to pull off here?"

"Bill, is that you? This is Dar, for Christ's sake. Please, don't cut me off. I need your help."

"Damnation, Dar is that really you? We thought you were dead, lost over the Atlantic weeks ago. Hell, I'm still running the accident investigation," Jackson said.

Dar registered the surprise in his friends voice. "Yeah, it's me, Bill. Don't be throwing any flowers for awhile. I may need them sometime, but not right now."

"Jesus, where are you?" a very confused Lieutenant Colonel Jackson asked.

"Well, you're not going to believe this, but I'm sitting in my quarters, talking on a radio that is suspended in mid-air aboard a spaceship." Dar paused, letting his words sink in. "Before you call a shrink, give me a chance to explain."

Word of the unusual radio conversation spread throughout the squadron spaces like a wild fire. The Ready Room was rapidly filling with officers.

Dar began his explanation of his situation and the threat to Earth. "Surely, you saw or heard about the battle we fought early this morning?"

"God damn it, Dar, that was you? Every military installation in the country has been put on alert. Yeah, I've seen those things in the sky, but had no idea you were involved. How could I?"

Well, Bill it isn't just me. There were twenty-four of us to begin with, but we only have ten left now.

"You're trying to tell me you're one of the missing pilots. Hell, planes started missing all around the world. I knew about the pilots, but everything surrounding their disappearance has been classified Top

Secret, burn before reading stuff, so the general public hasn't a clue what's happening." Jackson paused. "Did you say only ten left?"

"Yeah. We lost over half during this mornings engagement," Dar said, not wishing to explain further. "I figured information about the disappearances would have a lid put on it tighter than gramma's cookie jar. We can't do anything about that now, but I need some help from you."

"I'll do what I can," Jackson said into his mike.

"Okay, here is what I need. First, clamp a vise on the men I know are hovering around the Duty Officer's desk listening. I don't need for this conversation to get out. At least not yet. Can you do that for me?"

"Sure, consider it done," Jackson said, glaring at his officers.

"Second, get General Moore down to your Ready Room as soon as possible. I'll standby here. I have to talk to him, like now. Understand?"

"Right, I'll get on the hook. Wait one," Jackson said, leaving the radio for the phone.

Dar cooled his heels while Jackson made his phone call. *God, I hope I'm doing the right thing,* he thought.

"Dar, General Moore is on his way," Jackson radioed. "He should be here in about ten."

"Good," Dar said. "I'll wait.

The ten minutes passed slowly for Dar. Everything was riding on this next conversation. If General Moore did not agree to his terms, what was he going to do? The only other option would be to land in D.C. and hope the crazies there would let him return to the Nanta after he'd given them all the information at his disposal.

"Dar, God damn your soul, is this really you?" General Moore's deep bass voice echoed through the airwaves.

"Yes, sir. I'm afraid you didn't get rid of me yet," Dar answered.

"Lieutenant Colonel Jackson tells me you're sitting in one of those spaceships circling Earth, is that right?"

"Yes sir, that's where I am all right, but I want to return to Cherry Point to talk with you," Dar said.

"Gads, man, you mean you can get back here? How? When?" General Moore asked.

Dar smiled. General Moore's voice had risen several octaves higher with each question. "Yes sir. Tomorrow afternoon. I'll arrive in a . . . er

. . ., let's say a rather unusual fighter, around sixteen hundred. Would that be all right?"

"Be all right? Are kidding. Hell, man I'll have the red carpet out and waiting," General Moore answered.

"No red carpet, please. In fact, I want to keep this visit as quiet as possible. I'll give you a full briefing on the situation, but then I need to be able to return here. General, I can't begin to tell you all that has gone on since my disappearance, but trust me, it's vitally important to the survival of Earth that I get a chance to explain the situation up here."

"Jesus, we figured things were bad. Just watching the show this morning has got Washington in total chaos," General Moore said. "Yeah, I think I can guess how important this is? You realize, if you are going to fly in here tomorrow in some damned spaceship, every super inflated ego in Washington will want to talk to you."

"I know, and that really has me concerned. I want to be able to return to the Nanta."

"The Nanta?" General Moore interrupted.

"Yes sir. Nanta is the mother ship I'm fighting from. There the good guys."

"Okay, son, but I'm not sure I can promise anything when it comes to the boys from D.C.," General Moore said.

"I understand, but you have got to comprehend my situation. We have been fighting the Womongly since I got taken. The Womongly are the bad guys. Plus, the original group of pilots elected me their Commanding Officer. I can't stay on Earth."

"What the hell are you talking about Dar. You telling me you've got an entire squadron up there? What in the name of God is going on?" General Moore asked desperately.

"I'll explain everything tomorrow, General. I know you'll have to touch base with Washington, but I would prefer as few people present at my briefing as possible. Just clear the field from around fifteen hundred on. I'll be showing up, probably with every Air Force fighter on the East Coast following me. I just want to get back up here when I'm done. Can I have your word on letting me leave?"

"Son, if that's what you want, you got it. What else?" the General asked.

Dar began a rattling off a list of things he thought necessary for his visit. When he'd finished, "Is all that possible between now and tomorrow, General?"

"Yeah, Dar, I think we can handle it okay. Damn, boy, am I glad to hear your voice again. Sounds like we have a God damned major situation developing. I'll do my best for you," General Moore radioed.

"Thanks, sir," Dar transmitted, realizing the General meant every word. "See you around sixteen hundred tomorrow. I knew I could rely on you." He was pleased with his decision to talk first with Major General Moore.

CHAPTER 21

Littia stirred, moving an inch or so from Dar's back. The airbed reacted immediately with slight puffs of warm jets to accommodate her shifting weight. For the past several hours, she lay snuggled, kitten-like, to Dar's back, enjoying the warmth of his body close to hers. Their love making, hours earlier, had been a wonderful mixture of physical pleasure and sensuous mind entanglement. Two world's eroticisms joining in a single new pleasure for both. After, she lay next to a sleeping Dar with eyes closed, but sleep evaded her every effort to fall into needed slumber. Tamis' words rolled around her consciousness like a wayward comet streaming through space.

She was a clone. All Lantiusians aboard the Nanta were clones, taught, like the earthlings, in the Educator. What concerned her most was not what she knew, but what she did not know. *Jicama mentioned that her education was incomplete. Why?* That was the factor she could not fathom. *Why not provide her with a complete knowledge of her past history, both personal and Lantius in general? What possible purpose could there be for a partial education?*

From the desk chair, a soft gurgling sound reminded her Pete was still watching over his chosen. She rolled completely over to face the desk.

"Pete, please come here. We need you," Littia whispered into the darkened room.

Pete's eyes turned orange and began spinning. Poof! He disappeared, only to rematerialize an instant later on the bed next to her, soft scales brushing against her breast and abdomen. The closeness of the utapotus brought immediate comfort, washing away ill thoughts which had been tormenting her since her encounter with the two most important men aboard the Nanta.

"Thank you, Pete," she cooed. "We could not sleep, but perhaps talking to you might help."

Cuddling Pete, Littia thought of Dar, and how she was not completely honest with him when he'd asked questions about her visit with the Supreme Commander.

"He is a good man. He is the one," a deep baritone voice resonated, filling her mind.

Littia bolted upright, knocking Pete away. "Who's there," she asked aloud. She was frightened by the voice in her mind. Never had she mind talked with anyone but Dar, and this was certainly not the man lying next to her.

"What's wrong?" Dar asked, his voice groggy with sleep.

Concerns flashed through Littia's head. She did not want to explain more to Dar than she had already. Just telling him that the Supreme Commander wanted to know what his plans were regarding his visit to Earth was quite enough. "Nothing, we just thought we heard something. Please, go back to sleep," she said in soothing voice.

Dar wiggled under the auto-sheet, rearranging his legs for comfort, and began snoring gently.

"Who's there?" she thought. She waited. Nothing. *We probably just imagined the voice.*

"A vivid imagination? It is doubtful. You have not exhibited much of an imagination since this presence has known you." The baritone thought filled her mind once more.

"Please who are you, and why are you invading my thoughts?" Littia pleaded.

"This Presence is well known to you and to Dar. This Presence's chosen," Pete answered.

Littia's mouth fell open with surprise. She looked down at the small creature at her side. Pete's eyes whirled, lighting up the edges of his face and tiny grotesque ears. "Pete, is . . .is it really you filling my mind?" she stammered the thought.

"This Presence speaks with no intention of filling your mind, only to say, he is a good man. He is The One. You may trust him."

Taking her head in her hands, Littia groaned. *This can't be. Utapotus do not speak or mind talk.*

"Perhaps never before. There was little need. The need is great now. Much depends on my chosen. He has no idea of the weight he carries on his shoulders. Decisions made by the one called Dar Fantin will have ramifications on many worlds other than his own." Pete's eyes turned red, then yellow, as he passed his thoughts to Littia.

Near tears, Littia struggled with inner turmoil. Too many things were happening, clouding her life with situations she could not comprehend. "We are but a Guide 3rd Class, with little understanding of the meanings of your thoughts. We have just learned we are a clone, no more than a month old, without benefit of a full education. How can we be of help to Dar and my people at the same time? Pete, why do you speak of the importance of this Earthling? He is but an alien to my world, nothing more, except to me. My heart is his, you know of that, but the other, we can not understand."

"You are but a child, where This Presence is of the ages. There is little reason for you to comprehend my thoughts. To be there, to provide support when needed, and to love my chosen is all This Presence will ask. Ask I do. Do not despair, child, This Presence will be close by, always. Now, sleep and let the troubles of the day wash from you. This Presence believes my chosen will require much from you, and you must be healthy with full functioning faculties to be of service." Pete's eyes dulled to an orange.

Like a spring rain falling on parched earth, Littia felt tranquility wash across her mind. She lay back on the bed, placing an arm around Pete's soft middle and fell into a deep, restful sleep.

Dar's eyes fluttered open, invaded by the overhead light flooding his quarters. "Good morning, Pete," he said, reaching out to pet the utapotus lying next to him. He could hear the sonic shower running in the head, realizing, for the first time that Littia must still be with him. "Littia," he called. "How long have you been up?"

Littia's dripping head peered around the corner. "Not very long. We just needed a cleansing," she said, her smile brightening Dar's world. "We shall be out in a minute."

Dar stretched, easing muscles into the day after a long night's sleep. "God, I feel better this morning than I have in a long time," he shouted at Littia, trying to overcome the noise of the sonic mist being shot from its nozzle. She didn't hear him, or at least didn't answer. Throwing the warming, self regulating cover back, he threw his legs over the edge of the airbed. " Well, Pete, today I'm going to be leaving you for a while." He ran fingers through hair tangled from sleep. "Or are you planing to ride with me again today?" Dar smiled down at the utapotus.

Littia came out of the bathroom. "We imagine our friend will be with you," she said. "Has he talked with you yet?"

Dar looked up with a puzzled look. "Talked to me. You mean, Pete? You have got to be kidding. Why would you say that?"

"Well, he can mind talk just like we can. He talked to me last night," Littia said.

"Right! I think you may have been dreaming. I don't think Pete can communicate, though I've come to depend on him to ease my fears and tension." Dar started for the shower. "Are you done, I want to take a sonic as well."

Littia looked at him with disdain. "Dar, we are not joking. Pete can mind talk. Honestly."

"Sure he can," he said, taking her in his arms and kissing her deeply. "You know," he began, "I think I'm falling in love with you." His words came out with a seriousness intended to assure her he was not joking.

"We know," Littia spoke with tenderness. "We feel the emotion within you, and it is one we feel as well."

"Damned straight," Dar said. He slapped her on the rear with affection. "I've got to get ready for my flight to Cherry Point. What's on your agenda for the day?"

"Worry about you, we suppose." Littia laughed. "Why did you have to complicate my life, anyway."

"Ah, you lucky woman you. Having me around has lifted your life from the mundane." He kissed her once more, then headed for the shower. "I'm starving," he said over his shoulder. "Hope they have that hateful 'green eggs and ham' crap for breakfast. The stuff looks terrible, but it taste pretty darn good."

Their bantering was interrupted by a loud bang on the door. "Boss, you gonna join us for PT, or what," Cannaly yelled.

"Damn. I forgot all about PT," Dar mumbled under his breath. "Snake, you lead training this morning. I'm running behind schedule."

"Sure, boss. Littia, you take good care of the skipper for me, ya hear," Cannaly yelled through the door, and laughed.

"Damn you, Snake, get the hell out of here," Dar said. He was laughing as well.

"Commander Cannaly is a good friend, is he not?" Littia asked. The seriousness of the question not lost on Dar.

"The best! I've known him since flight school in Pensacola. They don't come in finer than Snake," Dar said. "If anything should happen to me, you help him anyway you can, Littia. I mean it." His head poked out of the bathroom to emphasize his point.

"Nothing is going to happen to you, Dar," Littia's tone was filled with finality. "But we hear what you are saying. We will respect your wishes."

"Good," Dar said, disappearing once more into the shower.

"Pete, disappear for a few minutes, will ya?" Dar asked the utapotus. He didn't need his small friend lounging around his quarters while he was on the VVCom with Jicama. Littia had kissed him goodbye, after he'd toweled dry from the sonic. Now, dressed, it was time to get more information on the shield Jicama proposed to wrap around Earth. He snapped the palm-sized communicator open. "Supreme Commander Jicama," he instructed.

"Ah, good day, Dar. What can we do for you?" Jicama asked.

"Good morning, sir. I wondered if we might discuss Earth's shield in more detail. I'll need facts on how, where, and when if I'm going to convince anyone about its constructed."

"Of course. Join me on the bridge. We shall try to provide you with all the necessary information you require." Jicama smiled into the Vid.

"On my way," Dar said, snapping the lid shut on the VVCom. "Pete! I'll be back shortly," he said, not wishing to leave the utapotus without acknowledging the presence of his invisible companion.

It took only a few minutes, on the PCT and light tube, to reach Jicama's lofty domain high on the bow of Nanta. Dar stepped on the suspended bridge, fighting the feeling of nausea sweeping over him. *Damn, I'll never get used to this damned place.*

He caught sight of the Supreme Commander slouched behind his command monitor, studying a tactical holograph floating several feet above. Nanta's control center was much quieter than on his last visit, yet there were still multitudes of Dataspheres darting among control stations, where Lantiusian officers worked behind various arrays of screens, scanners, and sensors.

"Permission on the bridge?" Dar asked, loud enough to be heard by Jicama.

The Supreme Commander glanced at Dar's just long enough to wave him in, then returned his attention to the holograph.

Dar walked slowly to the chair next to Jicama's, taking deep breaths to counteract the woozy feeling rumbling in his stomach. *Glad I decided not to eat until after this conversation*, he thought, wiping sweat from his brow with his sleeve.

Jicama waved a hand over his control panel. The holograph disappeared instantly. "Welcome, my friend," he spoke to Dar, taking a long look at SFS-1's commanding officer. "Are you all right? he asked.

"Yes, sir. I'm fine. It's this darn bridge of yours. Being suspended over a field of nothingness gives me a touch of vertigo, that's all. I'll be fine. Has anything new developed with the Womongly?"

"No. We have seen no activity, other than their protective screen of fighters, since the battle yesterday morning. Now, what is it you wish to know about the shield?"

Jicama's question left no doubt he wanted this over as soon as possible. "Well, sir, you said they could be installed in four or five days, so I presume you have the shield generators already prefabricated, and stored aboard Nanta."

"Yes, that is so," Jicama agreed.

"Very well." Dar nodded, pleased he had guessed correctly. "How will you get them to Earth? How many generators will it take to produce the shield, and where will they be located?"

Jicam studied Dar for a moment. "Very well," he sighed, as if he had come to a decision. "It will take six generators to build the shield, one at each of your planet's poles, and the others located around or near the equator. The generators will be transported to designated points by shuttle ships from Nanta. The shuttles are the same craft that transported you aboard."

Jicama's last statement took Dar unawares. "Sir, are telling me it wasn't Nanta that plucked me from the sky over North Carolina?"

"Of course not," Jicama replied, a fatherly smile curling at the edges of his handsome face. "Nanta can not operate within the confines of a planet's atmosphere. We must use shuttles to accomplish 'on world' activities, Nanta is strictly 'off world'."

"Christ," Dar said, shaking his head with amazement. "These shuttles must be huge."

"Quite large, my friend. In fact, they can hold fifteen of your fighter planes with ease. So you can understand that there will be little problem transporting the generators."

"But once they are in place, what's to stop the Womongly from destroying them before they're operational?" "Ah, that will be up to you and your pilots. While we are setting up the shield it will be your sole purpose to keep Womongly fighters from interrupting our work, or destroying the generators. Of course, once the shield is operational, the threat will no longer exist."

Dar took a minute to digest the information. " If that's the case, I'll for sure need additional pilots. We'll have to run a twenty-four hour fighter cap to ensure survival of the shields."

"Yes, we expect that will be the case," Jicama said.

"One final question. When the shield is up and running, what's to stop sabotage of the generators on the ground from a force placed on Earth prior to the shield's readiness."

Supreme Commander Jicama burst out in laugher. "Dar, once the generators are switched on, nothing short of a thermal torpedo detonated in the heart of the generator is going to shut it down. It would have to be place there on the Nanta, as each individual generator has it's own defensive shield once operational. Not even one of your primitive nuclear fission devices will be capable of penetrating those individual shields."

Dar wasn't laughing. "With all due respect, sir, if each generator has it's own shield, how will we accomplish routine maintenance of the system or shut it down, for that matter, should the Womongly threat go away?"

"Ah, a very good inquiry, my friend. Do not fear. We shall provide your world with all the necessary operational information required. How you wish to disseminate that knowledge will be entirely up to your controlling governments."

Dar nodded his agreement. "That seems perfectly reasonable," he said. "Thank you for your time, sir." He smiled. "I promise, I won't bother you again until I return from Earth."

"Ah, Dar, it is no bother. Just make your argument strong for the shield's construction. It may be vital to Earth's survival."

"I understand, sir." Dar felt the raw edges of seriousness in Jicama's comment. "Now, with your permission, I'll run down Zentao. I need details on what he has done to my Dart, and instruction for my reentry into Earth's atmosphere."

"We hope you will not 'run down' Zentao," Jicama said, with a shocked expression.

This time Dar laughed. "Sir, I mean I need to find him, not actually run him down physically."

"Blessed be the God of Many Arms. You and your strange ways and words. Go on, get out of here and 'run down' Zentao," Jicama said, shaking his head with his newfound understanding.

"Captain on the bridge," a Rage Warrior cried, touching his Rodinium breast plate with an audible clank in salute.

Langos let his three legs glide him to his command stool, taking little notice of the activities of his officers. "Carry on," he commanded. "First Officer Bezal, give me an update on our broadcast attempts."

Bezal, slipped from behind his battle station to stand just behind Langos. "Sir, we have been broadcasting for over an hour, but the Nanta is jamming every frequency. Shifting modulation and frequency every sixteen one thousandth of as second has improved our ability to transfer information to Earth receivers, but we doubt they have the UHF or HF technology to decipher such short transmissions."

Langos' complexion grew red, his anger rising. "Have you tried microwave burst transmission as I ordered?"

"Yes, of course, sir. However, the Nanta has apparently developed a method of interrupting our microwave transmissions as well. Sensors tell us of the interrupter's existence, but we have not established a method of circumventing it as yet."

The red deepened in Langos' face. "Helmsman, ahead on quarter. First Officer, establish random orbits, skirting the edge of Earth's atmosphere. Vary speeds and distances, but always keep Dectima in a position which inhibits a fighter attack from the Lantiusian mother ship. We shall see if this microwave interrupter can maintain position with our movements."

"Very good, sir," Bezal said, immediately returning to his battle station to put the orders in effect.

Langos stood for a long moment, staring at the blue planet suspended in a sea of black. *They do not fight, yet the Lantiusians foil my every effort,* he thought silently.

Dar walked out of the light tube onto hangar deck seven. The first thing he noticed was the smell. No longer was the air filled with the sour stench of molten metal and burnt wiring. Once again, the sterile smell that permeated all of the huge spaceship prevailed.

The hangar deck was alive with men and women repairing fighters damaged during the previous day's battle. Machinery whined under heavy working loads, stripping the exterior skin from several of the more extensively damaged Darts, revealing interior frames. The frames gleamed under the hangar's lights like polished bones.

Zentao looked up from his maintenance VidLog, and smiled down at Dar as the smaller man walked to his side. "We thought you might be showing up this morning," he said.

"Hey, Zentao. Yeah, I've got a ton of questions about this afternoon's flight. Have you got a minute or two?" Dar asked.

"Of course. Anytime," Zentao replied. "It is my pleasure to be of help. Oh, by the way, we hope you will like what we have laser burned into your Dart."

"Laser burned?" Dar asked, confused.

"Yes. Have a look," Zentao said, stepping aside so Dar could clearly see his fighter.

A whistle left Dar's lips. At the canopy rail of his repaired Dart, an inscription read:

Senior Commander Dar Fantin
Commanding Officer, Space Fighter Squadron – One
Nine Confirmed Enemy Fighter Kills

On the side, near the center of the fighter, was a four foot high, multi-colored depiction of Yosemite Sam, standing with his thrumber rifle and drooping mustache. It was a perfect replica of the patch adorning his flight suit.

"Damn, Zentao. That's great. Thank you. I mean it," Dar stammered out.

"We thought you might like something to show your standard when you arrive on Earth," Zentao said. "We have to admit, it was Commander Cannaly's original idea. We talked to him last night. Even through his apparent alcoholic induced haze, he seemed capable of some forms of thought. He gave me the idea."

Dar laughed, slapping the bigger man on the back. "Zentao, it doesn't make any difference where the idea came from. This is great," he said. "Thank you for your efforts. With everything else going on, I don't know how you find the time. Do you ever sleep?"

"Sleep is for wimps, we think Cannaly would say," Zentao said.

Dar smiled broadly, recognizing Zentao's pleasure at being able to please him. "Okay, then. Let's get down to business. I see you've installed new landing gear. Are they retractable, like the skids?" Dar asked, turning to the business side of his visit.

"Yes, fully retractable. Actually, the change to wheeled landing stems was the most difficult problem we faced. The skids retracted into a single well. With the addition of a nose wheel, we had to redesign the recess aperture. We assigned fifteen engineers to the problem. After many hours, and some very innovative ideas, we were able to fit your new landing gear into the Dart."

"Ya done good, Zentao. Now what about launch and recovery? Will that remain the same?" Dar asked.

"Oh, yes. Nothing has been changed as far as the Nanta is concerned. However, your landing on Earth will be entirely up to you and your onboard computer."

"Okay. I can handle the landing. Hell, the Dart flies like a Harrier, so no problem there. My big concern is reentry into Earth's atmosphere. I don't know how to keep from burning into a crispy critter."

"Crispy critter? We do not understand," Zentao said, perplexed.

Dar smiled at the taller man. "Zentao, of all people, you should know how we Earthlings talk. Crispy critter, burned to well done, nothing left but a flame. Understand?"

Zentao shook his head, laughing. "Yes, we should know by now how you scoundrels talk. Still, there is much we have to learn. You should not have any problem with entering Earth's atmosphere. Your computer will handle all the necessary equations for a safe trip. Also, the Dart's shield will protect you from all but an out of control reentry."

"My friend, I really appreciate your concern for my safety," Dar said, meaning it.

"Your safety *is* my concern, Dar. We mean, Senior Commander," Zentao retorted.

"Please, Zentao, it's about time you started calling me Dar, or skipper, or anything but Senior Commander. Hell, we've been through enough together to stop all the horse shit crap with rank. After all, I'm the stranger here."

Zentao smiled with obvious pleasure. "Thank you, Seni … ah, Dar. We would like that very much. One additional item. We have added nanites, repair micro-robotics, throughout critical systems. Those systems which are considered safety to flight."

"Nanites? I've heard of those, probably in some science fiction move or other. You mean they actually exist?" Dar asked.

"Oh, yes. They exist. Most of Nanta's systems have been injected with nanites. They really are quite effective. However, your Dart will be the first to have such units aboard. This will be an experimental situation. Is that all right with you?"

"Sure, why not? I always take all the help I can get. These tiny mechanical critters sound like they may come in handy sometime," Dar responded.

"That they might, but let us hope you never require their services," Zentao said. His serious expression said as much as his words.

"I still have a major concern. Until now, you or your officers have handled the startup sequence. What am I going to do when I shut down the Dart after landing?"

Rubbing tired gray-blue eyes, Zentao began to explain. "We have installed a holding function for all systems. When the light-drive is shut down, you will have twelve hours of electrical sustaining voltage. The onboard computer will remain fully functional. When restart is desired, you must verbally direct the computer to initiate the cycle."

"Twelve hours? What if I need to stay longer?" Dar asked, not at all sure how long it would take to brief General Moore.

Nanta's chief engineer thought a moment. "If you are required to remain longer than twelve hours, initiate a start. Let the light-drive run for a minimum of one hour. That should give you another nine or ten hours, but each time it becomes necessary, you will have less time available between run times."

"Gotcha. That makes sense. Anyway, I hope to hell I won't have to spend that much time at the Point before I can return back here." Dar patted the slippery smooth surface of his spacecraft. "When will she be ready to fly?"

"The Dart is ready now," Zentao said, a bit surprised at the question. "We thought you knew."

It was Dar's turn to be caught off guard. "She's ready?" He checked his watch, which he'd kept on Earth time since his arrival. "Okay, we'll plan on a fifteen hundred launch. That's four hours from now. Is that okay with you?"

"Whenever, we shall be waiting," Zentao said, his teeth gleaming with his smile.

CHAPTER 22

Scrambling up the ladder into the cockpit, Dar vibrated with excitement. During lunch, he'd said goodbye to Littia, who accepted his departure with something less than enthusiasm, yet understood the need for his trip to Earth. Later he rested, as best he could, in his quarters, with Pete nestled next to him on the airbed. Now it was time. Time to launch for Cherry Point.

He slid down the back rest, letting his feet glide onto the rudder pedals. The cockpit, the Dart's control center, felt as familiar as a well-worn deck shoe, yet the spacecraft it reigned over remained an alien. As alien as his enemy, the Womongly.

Helmet on, shoulder and lap belts tightly fastened, Dar gave Zentao a two finger start-up signal, exaggerating the twirling movement. Within moments, the Dart came to life, lights flickering as systems came online.

"Are we launching for your home planet?" Nan asked softly.

"Yeah, that's the plan. Think you can handle the reentry without problem?" Dar needled his computer, thinking of it more as a person than a nonentity.

"Of course. There will be no problem passing through Earth's atmosphere. Please ensure you assign the proper landing coordinates," Nan said.

Dar recognized Nan had not understood his teasing comment, but her *get-down-to-business* attitude brought him back into focus. "Roger, Nan, coordinates follow." He rattled off the lat/long, finishing with, "Altitude above sea level thirty feet, and a magnetic variation of zero five west." As he spoke his fingers flashed over the digits on his Up Front control panel, inputting, manually, the same information. A second later, the plasma screen above his right knee winked twice, then displayed Nan's projected flight path from Nanta to one hundred thousand feet above the Atlantic Ocean, southeast of Cherry Point.

"Will this flight path suffice, Dar? Nan asked, her voice light and cheerful.

"I guess so," Dar said, thinking he may have been wrong. Nan might just have a sense of humor after all. "You're the expert. I put myself in your capable hands . . . er . . . transistors or whatever you use."

The fighter rumbled with raw power, as Dar quickly moved through his post start checks. As he finished, the Dart was air-locked from the hangar.

"Once launched, do you wish me to fly the profile, or shall you?" Nan asked.

"Thanks, Nan. I'll fly until we reach the point you need to begin your reentry procedures. When you're ready, she's all yours." The Dart moved slowly through the tunnel in Nanta's shield. "We're on our way," Dar whispered.

"Fighter out, Captain," First Officer Bezal spoke to Captain Langos, who sat quietly before his tactical command holographic screen.

"Yes, yes! I have him. Where are the others?" Langos inquired. He squirmed on his stool, never taking his owl-like eyes from the three dimensional depiction of the Nanta and the fighter passing into open space from a warp in the green shield.

"It appears to be a single ship. We have no indications of other fighters exiting Nanta's hangar bays," Bezal answered.

"Hmmm. What could this lone Earthling have in mind?" Langos mused. He watched in silence, as the Dart flew slowly away from the Nanta, executed a turn to starboard, and began accelerating in the opposite direction from Dectima.

"Sir, do you wish the Strike Dragons to follow?" First Officer Bezal a asked."

Langos thought for a moment, studying the Dart's flight path. "No. Hold our fighters in position. There is no need. By the time the Strike Dragons launch and jump, the enemy will already be entering Earth's atmosphere. I have no doubt he is going to attempt a landing on the planet."

"Very well, sir." Bezal said, turning to an officer standing at rigid attention behind the Combat Tracking Monitor. "Tracking, mark the enemy fighter and follow. Give landing coordinates when calculated."

"Aye, sir," the young Tracking Officer replied.

Dar set the throttle at ninety-five percent, enjoying the view of Earth that grew larger with every passing minute. The Dart was cruising at twenty-one thousand knots, or three hundred-fifty plus miles per minute. As Nan instructed, he flew the line graphically pictured on his plasma screen, holding the Dart dead on flight path. He checked his watch. Fifteen thirty. Another ten minutes and he'd be at the reentry point.

"Dar, it is time for me to take control," Nan said, her voice as soothing as a baby's blanket.

"Roger. You have control," Dar said, taking his hands from the stick and letting his feet fall from the rudders.

"I have control," Nan repeated.

The throttle moved to idle, reacting to a silent command from Nan, causing tiny reversing thrusters to extend from hundreds of points along the fuselage of the Dart. Speed began to fall drastically. Nan corrected slightly to port, then raised the nose twelve degrees to shallow the glide path into the heavier atmosphere surrounding Earth. "Speed five thousand knots. Shifting shield forward," Nan said to Dar, who watched her exacting maneuvers with admiration.

"Jesus," Dar exclaimed with surprise, as a deep green globe surrounded the nose of his fighter. "Is that the shield?"

"Yes. I have concentrated its entire force forward to absorb the heat of reentry. Is there a problem?" Nan asked.

"No. No problem, it just scared the crap out of me when it jumped out of nowhere. Sorry."

Nan corrected the dive angle, compensating for gravitational pull, holding the Dart at reasonable speed. "Two hundred thousand feet, two thousand five hundred knots, heading three-two-zero," Nan rattled off flight statistics. "Extending wings and tail."

Dar swung his head to the right, watching in amazement, as the starboard wing slowly grew from the fuselage. Just forward of the wing, a ring of flames spewed around the super heated shield, the fire casting shadows across cockpit instruments. Suddenly, the red flames extinguished, and the Atlantic Ocean, with defined edges of the North American continent sprang into view.

"One hundred thousand feet, two thousand five hundred knots, heading three-two-zero," Nan droned. "We have safely made reentry, Dar. Do you wish to take control?"

"No, not yet. Let me catch my breath for a minute. I need to orient myself. Keep her level at this speed and attitude," Dar directed.

"Very well, Dar. What did you think of reentry?" Nan asked, her voice sounding even more human.

"Fantastic. You did a great job." Dar praised, scanning his instruments. He switched the TACAN, his primary radio navigational aid on Earth, to Channel 75, Cherry Point's transmitter. Nothing happened. Still too far away, he knew, but the inertial navigation platform was now displaying information on the plasma screen, as well as the Heads Up Holograph. He was twenty minutes and a thousand miles from Cherry Point, thanking Zentao unconsciously for his exact replication of his original Harrier.

"Time to contact someone before they shoot my ass down," Dar told Nan, switching his newly installed UHF to Guard. The Heads Up Holograph displayed 281.1, giving him radio access to every military plane airborne, and practically every ground control station within radio range.

"Any station, any station, this is . . .." *Damn, what should I use as a call sign?* "This is Nanta Fighter," he finally said. "Any station, this is Nanta Fighter."

"Nanta Fighter, Washington Center. Squawk three-two-zero-two and ident. Switch and contact on two-nine-zero point five."

The transmission was weak, but understandable. Dar switched his UHF to the newly assigned frequency and radioed, "Washington Center, Nanta Fighter, squawking ident. Level, Flight Level one-zero-zero-zero, heading three-two-zero.

On the ground in Wilmington, North Carolina, a confused Jeffery Lancaster looked up from his radar scope. The busy room, filled with men and women controlling aircraft passing through the southern sector of the airspace encompassing Washington Center, glowed with an eerie green light cast from a dozen radar scopes.

"Hey, George," Lancaster called to his supervisor. "I've got something strange here. You better have a look."

Flight Supervisor George Hamilton looked up from a scope he was viewing with a trainee. "Be right there," he said. He pointed to the scope, speaking softly to the young woman he was helping, then unplugged his headset to join Lancaster. "What ya got Jeff?" he asked.

"Look at this," Lancaster said, indicating a blip on the lower right hand side of his screen. "Check the speed and altitude read out."

George leaned over Lancaster's shoulder. "Shit! Are sure you're interrogating correctly?"

Lancaster gave his supervisor a sidewise glance. "George, how long've you known me? That thing is for real. He just made radio contact out of the blue and responded to my request for identification. This," he stabbed his finger at the screen, "is what came back. Calls himself Nanta Fighter."

George plugged his headset into the jack next to Lancaster's. "Nanta Fighter, this is Washington Center. Please ident." The blip flashed momentarily in bold script, showing identical information. "Nanta Fighter, where did you come from?"

"Don't ask. You wouldn't believe it anyway," Dar transmitted. "I'm requesting flight following to MCAS, Cherry Point."

"Roger, Nanta Fighter. Are you aware you will be penetrating from international airspace through our ADIZ?" George questioned.

"Roger, that. Understand penetration of Air Defense Intercept Zone, in ten minutes. Recommend you contact the Air Force and tell them there's no need to launch interceptors. Nanta Fighter is one of the good guys," Dar radioed.

"Lancaster, get the Air Force on the hotline. Tell them what we got here." The supervisor paused, thinking. "Nanta Fighter, say intentions?"

"Center, Nanta Fighter. I say again, request clearance present position direct NKT," Dar identified Cherry Point by its TACAN call letters. "And descent to Flight Level two one zero."

"Negative, Nanta Fighter. Can not clear you through ADIZ."

"Look, Center, you can either give me clearance, and we do this with your help, or I'm comin' home on my own. Your call," Dar transmitted.

"The Air Force already has him, and have launched F-15's to intercept," Lancaster told his supervisor.

George nodded his understanding. "Okay, let's see what this asshole has for balls," he said to Lancaster, then keyed his mike. "Nanta Fighter, cleared present position direct NKT. At pilot's discretion, leave Flight Level one zero-zero-zero for Flight Level two-one-zero."

Dar acknowledged his clearance, took control from Nan, and pulled the throttle to idle. "And, Center, tell those fighters to go home. I don't want to be messing around with them. Confirm my arrival with Cherry Point Approach Control. They're expecting me."

The two controllers looked at each other questioningly. "Do it," George ordered Lancaster.

Minutes ticked by, as George waited for Lancaster's land line conformation with Cherry Point Approach. He watched as the blip left one hundred thousand feet, heading for lower altitude, and slowed to mach 2.

"God damn it, George, you're not going to believe this. I just got off the phone with a General Moore. Says he's the Wing Commander. He really is expecting this dude."

"What about the Air Force?" George asked.

"Say's he'll take care of the Air Force. He just wanted to know where the F-15's had been launched from. I told him Langley," Lancaster informed his supervisor.

George checked the scope, watching Dar pass through forty-five thousand feet, still decreasing his airspeed. "Christ, why me?" he lamented. "Okay, let's give him clearance to NKT. Hell, whatever he's flying could out run the interceptors anyway."

Lancaster re-plugged his headset into the control panel. "Nanta Fighter, cleared present position, Cherry Point.

"Roger, cleared direct Cherry Point," Dar radioed, a smile creeping at the corner of his mouth.

The Dart continued to slow, as Dar raised the nose, leveling off at twenty-one thousand feet. He checked his position, noting the TACAN needle was now locked on Cherry Point. "Center, Nanta Fighter, I have TACAN lock on NKT, request switch to approach control."

"Go ahead and switch him," George told Lancaster. "But keep him on the scope so we can track him to the deck."

Lancaster nodded understanding. "Nanta Fighter, contact Cherry Point Approach Control on two-six-eight point seven."

Dar repeated the frequency back, then said, "Thanks for the help Center." He made the radio channel change. "Cherry Point Approach, Nanta Fighter, one hundred-fifty miles, Flight Level two-one-zero, heading three-two-zero. Requesting lower."

In the radar room, two floors below Cherry Point's tower, General Moore sat beside Master Gunnery Sergeant James who made a final tweak to his scope. "Gunny, you got him?" Moore asked.

"Yes sir, right there," the big Marine said, pointing to the blip at the edge of his screen.

"I got him," Moore said. "Bring him home, Gunny."

"Nanta Fighter, Cherry Point Approach. Cleared straight-in approach runway three two, winds three-six-zero at ten, altimeter two-niner-niner-two, call seven miles level at fifteen hundred.

Dar smiled. He could fly this approach in his sleep, having made it dozens of times during his two tours at Cherry Point. "Roger, cleared straight in approach," he radioed, rattling back the information he'd just received, then dumped the nose.

The Dart, landing gear down, hit the cement at four thirty-nine Eastern Standard Time. Dar slammed the throttle to idle, then forward, letting the reverse thrusters along the fuselage slow his speed to no faster than a man could trot.

"That was a very nice landing, Dar," Nan whispered.

"Thanks, Nan," Dar said, soaking up his first look of home in several weeks. He'd expected the field to be alive with activity, but was surprised to see it strangely quiet with practically no movement evident. Crossing the center mat, a "follow-me" truck, blue bubble-gum light flashing, dashed out in front of him. He switched to ground control on the UHF. "Ground, Nanta Fighter, I have the truck."

"Roger, Nanta Fighter. You will be parking in front of the tower."

He didn't need the truck to find the tower, but slowed his taxi speed to accommodate the vehicle's slowness. The "follow-me" truck rolled to a stop. Two men jumped from the cab, dashing back to chock the Dart's wheels. "Nan, I'm going to shutdown the light-drive. Are the systems all okay?"

"Systems all one hundred percent, Dar," Nan said. "When shall we be leaving?"

"I'm not sure, but I'll be back before the twelve hour limit runs out. Are you going to be all right?"

"Yes. I will monitor and maintain systems while you are away."

"Thanks, Nan. See ya in a little while," Dar said, then pulled the throttle to off.

CHAPTER 23

General Moore walked through Base Operations then opened the double glass doors leading to the flight line. As he stepped out into the Carolina sunshine, his jaw went slack as the enormity of the situation hit home. There, sitting before him, was an honest to God spacecraft, designed to fight in the vast voids of space. The afternoon sun reflected brightly off the Dart's polished skin with a near blinding effect, causing the heavy set, muscular general to squint brown eyes against its glare. He took two tentative steps in the direction of the alien fighter. Wind, blowing across the airfield's expanse, tussled his silver-gray hair, as he raised a hand in greeting to the younger man encapsulated in the first known ship to land on Earth which had been built by another world.

With an audible "pop," General Moore watched as the canopy opened allowing Dar to stand in the seat and present his senior officer with a formal salute. Moore returned the junior officer's courtesy, then walked rapidly toward the Dart.

Dar jumped to the ground, grunting under the force of his landing. Recovering, he turned to meet General Moore, a man he deeply respected. Their association extended over many years, though he could hardly call him a personal friend. Moore was a general after all, and he only a major, but he nonetheless valued and personally respected the big man's leadership abilities. "General, good to see you," Dar said, extending his hand in greeting.

"By God, it's good seeing you as well," General Moore said, smiling. "Son, that's one helluva machine you're flying. How many of them do you have?"

Dar's smile faded. "We had twenty-four, but there's only ten left. Yesterday's fight took a real toll. I lost eight pilots." As he spoke, a major dressed in full combat gear marched to the General's left shoulder. Dar did not recognize the man, but immediately understood why he was waiting to report.

"Dar, this is Major Mike McCulley," General Moore began the introductions. "He'll be in charge of security."

"I figured," Dar said, extending his hand. "Hope you understand how important this fighter is to me."

A thin smile traced its way across the tall major's face. "Nothing, I mean nothing, is going to mess with your aircraft, Major Fantin. I personally guarantee it." He turned back to the general. "With your permission, sir, I'll position my men."

"Do it," General Moore ordered.

Major McCulley walked away a few steps, raised his right arm, and gave a pumping motion. Immediately, tail gates clanged open on the back of four military trucks parked inconspicuously next to the tower. Marines, dressed in full battle gear and armed with M-16's streamed silently from the trucks, running in formation to establish a shoulder-to-shoulder cordon around the Dart. Facing outboard from the fighter, the young Marines came to attention with weapons at port-arms.

Major McCulley looked with satisfaction on the formation. "Lock and load," he commanded. The silent flight line suddenly filled with the sounds of ammo clips being slammed home and safeties snapped on. The sound faded away as rapidly as it came. McCulley turned back to face Dar. "Nobody is going to mess with your bird."

Dar grinned. "I can see that, Major. Thanks." He turned back to the General. "Sir. Where is everyone? I Don't think I've ever seen the field so quiet."

"I had them stop all flight operations at fourteen hundred. Didn't want you to have any interference. Didn't give a reason, just ordered 'em to stand down and send everyone home."

Dar looked around. Not a plane moved, nor was there any activity on any of the various squadron flight lines. "Well, sir, they took you at your word. If I didn't know better, I'd think it was holiday."

"We'd better get goin', son," General Moore spoke sharply to Dar.

"I'm ready, sir," Dar said. "Where is the briefing going to take place?"

"In my conference room at Headquarters. I have a staff car waiting. Would have had it right here for us, but darned if I was sure what this space craft of yours was going to look like. Thought it might burn the damned car up if I had them park it here."

Dar smiled. "That's fine General, I need to stretch my legs some anyhow. The two men walked for the doors leading through Base Operations. "Sir, who's going to be there? At the briefing."

"Well you'd thought God All Mighty Himself had just rung up the Pope or something from the reaction I got when I briefed the Joint Chiefs. Dar, you've created quite a hornets nest."

"Yes, sir, I figured as much. Are they going to let me return to the Nanta?"

"Far as I know. None of the 'suits' from Washington have brought it up and neither have I. I told them your request, so it's not like they don't know."

"Good! I have to get back. You understand, sir. It's my command."

"I know, son. I'll do my damnedest to get you back."

Dar realized the older man was telling him the truth, but the real test would be when he actually tried to return to his Dart. They reached the olive drab car which had the flag of a two star general flying from a small staff attached to the front bumper. A sergeant, dressed in camouflaged utilities smelling heavily of starch, held the rear passenger door open for them, shutting it softly once they'd settled inside.

"We've got General Westerly, head of the Joint Chiefs as the senior military representative. Secretary of Defense Gladmyer, Chester Kinton, who is the President's Chief of Staff, a bunch of other Washington high mucky-mucks, and the Secretary General of the UN are all waiting to hear your tale," General Moore informed Dar as the car pulled away from Base Operations.

Dar heard the words, but his thoughts were racing on a different tangent. He watched trees pass, smelled the green grass mixed with the ever present aroma of jet fuel which permeated everything near the airfield. A small goldfinch fluttered by his window, bringing a smile of pure pleasure to his lips. His emotions sucked in the familiarity of being back on Earth.

"Did you hear me?" General Moore asked.

"Ah, er. Yes, sir. I'm sorry. It's just great to be back, even for a little while.

The car turned off A Street into the circular drive leading to the two story, red brick building which housed the Second Marine Aircraft Wing Headquarters. Pulling up to the General's private entrance, a Marine corporal, decked out in Dress Blues, rushed to open the door. Dar and the General slid from the back seat, returning the corporal's picture perfect salute.

"Well, let's get this over with," Dar said with a sigh. "I can't say I'm looking forward to it, but what's decided here just might save or destroy everything we know." The full magnitude of his burden fell like a hard Harrier landing on his shoulders. On Nanta, he could put 'end of the world' thoughts out of his mind, but here and now, these thoughts sneaked in like weeds.

General Moore escorted him into the first floor conference room, filled with men talking in muted voices. All conversation stopped, eyes shifting to get their first look at the young major bearing a message from an alien race.

Dar could feel the heavy stares, but more importantly, he could smell the coffee. On the long table, which filled most of the room's interior, sat six silver pitchers filled with *real* coffee. Coffee cups, with saucers, were neatly arranged at each seating position, along with a pad of lined paper and several pens.

"General," Dar whispered. "Could I get a cup of coffee? I haven't had cup of real coffee since I left."

General Moore began chuckling. "Hell, yes, you can have a cup of coffee. You can drink the whole damned pot if you want to." He lead Dar to the head of the table, where a chair had been placed next to his own, grabbed a silver pot and poured a cup, handing it to Dar.

Dar took a sip of the hot brew. "Oh God, that's good." His face lit up with pleasure, as he looked around the crowded room. Some of the faces he recognized from the evening news, but most were unfamiliar. What struck him was the intensity of the group. Their dispositions emanated tension, filling the room with uncertainty.

"Gentleman, this is Major Dar Fantin, as I'm sure you are all well aware," General Moore began. "Yesterday, after the major's first contact with me, I passed along everything I knew about the situation to the Joint Chiefs. Hopefully, the Major will be able to fill us all in on what's happening. If you will have a seat, we'll begin." Chairs scuffed quietly on the thick carpeting, as the group took their seats. Papers rattled, briefcases opened and closed, yet quiet pervaded the room. He waited for the room settle then continued. "Major Fantin, let me introduce you to our gathering." General Moore made the introductions one by one around the entire conference table, then took his seat, turning the floor over to Dar.

Dar stood, taking a deep breath, trying to calm the nervousness he felt. These were important men. Men who could, at a glance, make or destroy careers, start wars, or establish peace.

He began with his abduction and the first few days aboard Nanta. Describing the Nanta proved harder than he thought, as was the Educator. *How do I describe a space ship so alien to what even I understand*, ran through the back of his mind as he spoke. Once he started explaining about the formation of his squadron and the Darts, he was on firmer ground. He told of the first battles with the Womongly, both on the Nanta and his squadron's first encounter with their fighters. From Jicama's descriptions, he tried to press home the realization that for hundreds of years the Lantiusians had been battling the Womongly by using others to engage in the actual fighting, and why. He ended with a complete description of the last battle, where Space Fighter Squadron - One had lost eight pilots. He'd been his feet for over two hours. Finished, Dar took another slug of coffee, long since cold, and took his seat.

The room remained silent, it's atmosphere cold and unrelenting.

"Major Fantin, that's the wildest concoction of horse shit I've ever heard. If that spacecraft of yours wasn't sitting out on the flight line, I'd have you carted away in a sack," Chester Kinton, the White House Chief of Staff, stated sarcastically.

Dar's temper flared as he turned to face the smallish man with shifting black eyes and paper thin lips. "Well, sir, the Dart *is* sitting on the flight line, isn't it? I've lost fourteen good men fighting the Womongly. I assure you they didn't think any of this was a fairy tale."

"That's exactly my point," Kinton interrupted. General Moore informed us that you want more pilots to help fight this fearsome Womongly of yours, yet, you admit to having lost fourteen men already. Why should we send more pilots when, under your leadership, you're obviously getting an ass kicking?"

Dar watched the little man settle back into the leather bound chair with self satisfaction. Slowly he stood, looking directly into the dark eyes of one of the most influential men in the country. "You self serving, egotistical son-of-a-bitch." He spoke softly, but a venomous warning echoed in each word. "I may be an officer in the Marine Corps, with sworn allegiance to my country, but this thing up there is more important than loyalty to the likes of you."

Kinton sat forward on the edge of his chair. "You watch your mouth, Fantin. Who do you think you're talking to?"

"No one is questioning your story, Dar," General Moore interrupted before the two men could continue their feud, his look of disapproval held intently at Kinton. "Sounds to me like you've been up to your ass in alligators and they've chewed most of a leg off. However, what good will more pilots do against the Womongly?"

Dar stared hard at Kinton, not wishing to let the bastard off the hook, then slowly sat back down. "Sir, my squadron has taken quite a toil on the Womongly force. I'd say we've destroyed three of their fighters to every one we've lost. But your question is a good one. I can best answer it by explaining the strategy Supreme Commander Jicama advises would be in the best interest of Earth."

"Wait a minute." Kinton slapped the table as he spoke. "Now you're suggesting this alien Supreme Commander is going to take over the defense of our country."

"Weren't you listening?" Dar said, his anger flaring once again. "I think I explained that the Lantiusians have been protecting worlds, worlds not countries, for hundreds of years."

"Mr. Kinton, I believe it is time for you to shut your mouth and listen," General Westerly said. As the most senior general in the United States Armed Forces, his words did not fail to meet their mark.

"Poof!" Pete appeared on the table in front of Dar, curling around the now empty coffee cup. His whirling eyes surveyed the room casually.

"Jesus, what's that?" General Moore said, scooting his chair away from the table in surprised apprehension.

Smiling, Dar reached out to stroke the utapotus. "Damn you, Pete." He smiled down on the little animal, feeling his anger drain away at the mere touch of his friend. "This is Pistol Pete, General. A utapotus. Perfectly harmless, I assure you. I know he looks uglier than a three hundred pound woman in pink tights, but he's about as good a pal anyone could ask for." As he spoke, Dar could feel the tension dissolve in the room. Pete's timing had to have been intentional, achieving the desired affect. "Here, General, try petting him. He's surprisingly soft.

General Moore reach out tentatively to touch Pete's neck, then stroked his back. "I'll be damned, he's as smooth as a baby's bottom," he said with a smile spreading across his face.

"Well, Major Fantin, you certainly have our full attention now, General Westerly spoke for the entire gathering. "Please continue."

"Yes, sir. As I was saying, Jicama recommends he be allowed to construct a defensive shield around Earth. This shield would be similar to that being used on Nanta. An identical one also protects their home world. It will require ferrying six shield generation units to Earth. One generator at each pole, and four scattered around the equator. With your go ahead, they can be in position and operational within four or five days."

"And these generators will provide us full protection from an invasion by the Womongly?" Westerly asked.

"That's what I'm led to believe, and if you decide to allow its construction, I need more pilots to act as escorts for the shuttles hauling the generators to Earth.

"Who controls these generators, Major? These aliens or us? General Westerly asked.

"Supreme Commander Jicama assured me the operation of the shield will be turned over to whoever we wish.

"How long do we have to make this decision?" Secretary of Defense Gladmyer asked.

"The sooner the better. In fact, I don't understand why the Womongly haven't started their attack already, unless they are waiting to see what the Nanta is going to do."

"Are you aware, Major Fantin," Gladmyer interrupted, "that we have been receiving radio signals from this Womongly ship?"

It was Dar's turn to be surprised. "No, I did not know of any radio transmissions. What are they saying?"

"We have been unable to decipher them. It appears there is some sort of jamming going on, plus the duration of the signal is much too short. We're working on it," Gladmyer responded.

Thinking about what Gladmyer had just said, Dar fondled Pete, wondering what was going on. Why would the Womongly try contacting Earth? It didn't make sense. Suddenly, his mind filled with the baritone thought, "Trust yourself." His hand stopped in mid-stroke, realizing the mind blast had come from Pete.

"Dar, are you all right?" General Moore asked. "You look like you've just seen a ghost.

Shaking his head in confusion, Dar looked at Moore. "Er . . . ah, yes sir. I'm fine."

"Good. Now what type of pilots do you need?" General Moore asked.

"It doesn't make much difference F-15, F-18, AV-8, just so long as they are good."

"How soon?"

"Like yesterday," Dar said, causing the room to relax and chuckle at his remark. "You just let me know where and when and I'll arrange a shuttle pickup from Nanta.

"Major Fantin, you have certainly filled our plates to overflowing," General Westerly stated flatly. "Perhaps you could give us a couple of hours to discuss the ramifications of your request and suggestion."

Taking Westerly's lead, General Moore turned to Dar. "Wait in my office, and get yourself something to eat."

Dar smiled a thank you. "About a ten pound medium rare steak would be nice."

"Tell my aide to get it for you," Moore said, standing with Dar. "I'll get back to you."

"Thank you, sir. Come on Pete, we're not needed for awhile."

Pete raised his frog-like head, looked up at Dar, surveyed the men surrounding the table one last time, and disappeared.

The mere thought of a real steak had Dar salivating, but the aroma of the charcoal grilled steak drove him over the edge. Dar ate alone, sitting behind the huge mahogany desk normally reserved for the Commanding General of the Second Marine Aircraft Wing. The aide had taken him at his word. Within thirty minutes of indicating his eating preferences, the lieutenant had plopped a huge slab of meat, with all the fixings, down in front of him. Now, using a hunk of fresh bakery bread to sop every last morsel, he wiped the plate clean. Chewing this soggy bite, he sat back in the leather chair, with a sigh.

Two hours had passed since he'd left the conference room. During that time he'd struggled with inner questions concerning his conduct. Had he convinced them? Had he made a terrible mistake when he'd gotten upset with the Presidents Chief of Staff? He was a jerk, but a very powerful jerk. Then there was the question of Pete. Had Pete really mind blasted him? It had to be. Who else could it have been? And, besides, Littia had asked him if Pete had talked to him yet. The utapotus was a never ending source of amazement.

Dar glanced at a small clock sitting on the highly polished desk, smelling the lemon oil used to keep its mirror finish. Two A.M. Only two and a half hours left before he'd need to crank his Dart back to life.

As another hour passed, he was getting worried. He wanted to leave, to return to Nanta with some news, good or bad. The door to the office swung open, just as he was about to call the aide for more coffee.

"Well, Dar, you did it," General Moore boomed. "You'll have your pilots tomorrow. As far as the shield goes, they're still trying come to some final consensus. There is a lot to be considered and God knows how many politicians to convince." The big man dropped down onto his office sofa, waving Dar to remain seated.

Dar let his breath out with a sigh. "That's good news, General." He paused, thinking. "Sir, will they let me return to Nanta?"

"Whenever you're ready, son. It's been a long night. You want to get some sleep before you leave?"

"No, sir. I've got to start the Dart within the next hour anyway, or I lose power to my on-board computer. So I might as well head back. Heck, I'm to keyed up too sleep anyway.

"Yeah, I know what you mean. Okay, I'll have my driver take you to the flight line. I've got to get back to the meeting." Moore stood and stuck out his hand to Dar. "Have a safe trip, son. I'll be standing by the radio."

"Thanks for everything," Dar said, taking Moore's hand.

"We should be thanking you. Now get out of here before those yo-yos in there decide they want you to stick around."

"Say no more, General. I'm on my way."

The two men left the office, Dar to his bird, the General to more round tabling of the possible options left open to a world rapidly approaching harm.

Dar settled into his cockpit with thirty minutes to spare. He waved to Major McCulley, indicating that he should clear the Marines from around the Dart, then slipped his helmet on. "Nan, are you there?" he asked.

"Yes, but I was getting worried," Nan said immediately. "Are we going to fly?"

"Yes, we're going to fly. Let's get this bird started and head back to Nanta."

CHAPTER 24

Space Fighter Squadron – One waited for Dar to shut down, and the airlock walls to open. As their skipper scrambled down from the cockpit, they crowed around him with questions, each trying to out shout the other.

Dar laughed. "Give me a break, guys," he yelled over the general mayhem. "Let's go to the bar. I need a drink."

"Now you're talkin', skipper. Hell, it's zero six hundred. What better time to open the bar." Cannaly screamed back. He grabbed Dar by the arm and led him to the light tube, where all ten Earthlings shoved their way in for the ride.

Settled at a table near the center of the deserted Officers Bar, Dar related his story from the beginning, ending with his uneventful landing back on the Nanta. It was pushing seven, when he said, "That's enough for now, guys. I'm tired. It's going to be a busy day tomorrow, er, I mean today. I need some rest." The group groaned, but began to break up, heading for their quarters or the mess hall. Dar reached for Cannaly's shoulder. "Meet me in my room. I didn't tell them everything. We've got some talkin' to do before I speak to Jicama."

"Roger, that," Cannaly said, with a look of concern. "Figured as much. We've known each other too long to try and fool the other. I could see you were keeping something pretty damned tight to the vest. See you in a minute." He walked off to join the others, leaving Dar to stare at the cluttered table.

"Littia, I need to talk to you," he sent the mind blast with intensity.

"Oh, Dar, it's good to hear your voice. What's wrong?" Littia's thoughts filled his head.

"I'm not sure. Will you meet Snake and me in my quarters?"

"We are all ready here. We've been waiting for your return, but knew you would talk to your men first."

"I'll be right there," Dar said, racing for the light tube.

Several minutes later, Dar sat at his desk with Cannaly sprawled on one of the guest chairs, and Littia comfortable on his airbed. Littia looked worn, as if he'd wakened her with his mind blast, but she was fully alert. "I'm not going to beat around the bush. We may have a problem. The Womongly ship is trying to contact Earth. Problem is their transmissions are being jammed, and their bursts are so short that military intelligence can't decipher them. Why would the Womongly be trying to talk to Earth, and who is jamming the signal?"

Cannaly let out a whistle. "Damnation, Dar, I haven't got a clue. Doesn't make any sense, unless they're trying to surrender." He laughed lightly at the joke. "And that's not likely."

"What do you think, Littia?" Dar asked, then moved quickly to her side. Her pale white face had turned ashen. "Are you all right?" he asked with genuine concern.

"We are fine. We just feel weak suddenly. Do not worry for me."

"Littia, do you know something we don't?" Dar asked.

"Dar, we know nothing, we only feel." Tears slowly formed at the corners of her eyes. "We did not wish to bother you with my problems, but we know you want my help, and we so desperately want to be of some service."

"What are you talking about, Littia?" Dar asked. He was completely confused and concerned about her sadness.

She wiped a tear for her cheek. "We are a clone, Dar. Nothing more than a clone who is but a month old."

Dar took her hand in his, patting it gently. "So what?" he said softly, knowing she thought her revelation would shock him. "It doesn't make any difference to me."

She looked up into Dar's eyes, wiping a tear from her cheek. "You really don't mind, do you?"

"Hell, no! Why should I?"

"We want to help, but they did not fully educate me when we came out of the incubator, that's why, after my conversation with the Supreme Commander, we were so upset. We don't think many of your guides have been educated. There must be a reason for this, but we just don't know what it is. Don't you see? We want to answer your questions, but we don't have the knowledge."

"I thought you told me the guides were hiding something from you. If they haven't been educated, what would they hide?"

"It is the guide trainers and senior guides that are holding back information, not the guides assigned to your pilots," Littia said, her voice becoming stronger with each word.

Dar sat back down, glancing at Cannaly, who just shrugged at his look.

"What else did Jicama tell you?" Dar asked. He could see she was struggling with his question, as if she was fighting with an inner demon.

"Nothing."

Both Dar and Cannaly waited, but the beautiful face was a blank. It was obvious she was not going to tell them more. "All right, I want you both to think about this latest development. Snake, don't say anything to the others. At least not yet. There's been enough going on without causing more problems. Littia, will you see if you can dig something up on these transmissions?"

She nodded.

"Good. I'll be talking with Jicama when we are finished. I'll see what I can find out from him, but more importantly, I've got to get those new pilots up here and start planning the next stage of this crazy war."

Cannaly got up, stretching. "Okay, boss. I'll see you later. I'll get the guys together and come up with a crash training program for the newbies."

"Good thinking. I'll talk to you as soon as I'm done with Jicama," Dar told Cannaly as his friend left for his own room.

Dar was waiting for Jicama when the tall Lantiusian stepped from the light tube for the bridge. "Good morning, Supreme Commander," Dar said respectfully. "I wonder if I might have a few words with you before you get too involved in today's activities."

Jicama looked down on Dar. "We would be pleased. Join me on the bridge."

The two walked in silence to the command station. "What is it today?" Jicama asked.

"Several items, actually," Dar said. "Besides, I thought you'd want to know how things went on Earth yesterday."

"Ah, yes, we were informed of your return. We thought you would have reported to me much sooner than this hour. How did your meetings go? Were you able to convince your leaders about the shield."

"We won't know until later today. When I returned to Nanta, General Moore, my contact, was still meeting with the officials who will make that decision. Which brings me to a new problem. I'll require access to a microwave radio with secure, burst voice communication capability. Can that be arranged?"

"Certainly. We will have such a unit delivered to your quarters. It should be there by the time you get back. What else?"

"When and how will the new pilots be picked up? I forgot to ask you that question before I left."

Jicama thought for a moment. "Can you have them loaded in a container of some sort? Something like a trailer."

"Yes, that shouldn't be a problem. Why?" Dar thought he knew the answer, but asked anyway to make sure.

"We'll send a shuttle, using it to tractor beam the container aboard. Will that be satisfactory?"

"Yes, sir, quite satisfactory. I recommend we use the center mat at Cherry Point. The mat is where four runways come together. It should be plenty large enough and is well away from buildings."

"Perfect," Jicama said. "That will be quite acceptable. When shall we send the shuttle?"

"I have to talk with . . ." Dar stopped mid sentence, ducking a Datasphere that stopped inches in front of his face. Jicama yanked it from the air, placing it on his command module. "Damn things," Dar whispered. "I have to talk with General Moore again this morning. I'll VVCom you with a time."

"Ah, that will be fine," Jicama said, a bit impatiently. "What of the shield? Will we know it's status when you talk to this General Moore?"

"I really don't know, but let's hope so. How much time do you think we have before the Womongly start their attack on Earth?" Dar asked the question in an off-hand manner.

"Actually, we are surprised they have not begun their attack. Certainly they have the necessary weapons aboard. It is strange, but this captain of theirs has been unpredictable."

"Why would they be trying to communicate with Earth?" Dar asked, trying to sound casual.

Jicama studied Dar, his look hard. "Ah, yes. The radio transmissions. We know of these, of course, but have determined they are actually using radio and microwave frequencies to pinpoint targets. The Womongly have done this sort of thing in the past." He paused. "We assume your military has been unable to actual decode these transmissions."

"That's correct," Dar responded, trying to discern any misinformation the Lantiusian might be stuffing down a dumb Earthling throat. "Strange way for them to range targets, considering the sophistication of which they are capable. Still, I guess it would be one way of doing it that would not rouse suspicion from a less technological standpoint."

"Ah, there you have it. You have answered your own question, and of course we have been jamming their transmissions to prevent pinpoint targeting on their part. Now, if there is nothing more, we have much awaiting my attention," Jicama said.

Jicama's dismissal was evident. "Thank you for your time," Dar said, leaving the bridge for the light tube. He arrived at his quarters minutes later, finding the new microwave radio floating along side the UHF above his desk. He snapped on both radios, studying the microwave closely. He'd never used a radio quite like it, but it appeared simple enough.

"General Moore, this is Dar," he radioed, using the UHF.

"Dar, General Moore. I guess you got back safely last night," the general responded immediately.

"Yes, sir. No sweat. Sir, do you have a microwave radio handy?"

"Roger," Moore responded. I've had my office fitted with just about every imaginable type of radio gear the communication's squadron has at their disposal. Why?"

"Well, sir, I thought it might be best if we switched to microwave and use burst transmissions. More privacy that way."

"Understand," Moore said, passing a frequency to Dar.

The two Marines talked for thirty minutes. The General informed Dar that Washington and the United Nations accepted the shield as the most logical method of defending Earth, and that the pilots were standing by for pickup. Dar told the General of his conversation with Jicama, and that the Womongly transmission may be a targeting method.

"When can they start the shield?" General Moore asked.

"I'm not sure, but I think Jicama may start shuttles moving your way within the next couple of days. Actually, he seems very anxious to get them in place, so it may he may be much sooner. Tell you what, General, I'll have him contact you personally. That way I'm taken out of the loop as a middle man. I need every free minute to get my pilots ready. Will that be okay?"

"Sounds good to me. I'll be sitting next to these radios until this thing is over."

"Expect a transmission from the Supreme Commander within the hour. Have the pilots handy as well. I expect the shuttle will be on its way as soon as I tell Jicama of our conversation."

"Roger that, Dar. Talk to you later then. Moore out," the General closed their conversation as abruptly as Jicama had.

Dar sat quietly for several moments thinking. Things were happening rapidly, outstripping his ability to keep up. He was dead tired, but had to make arrangements for the new pilots, plus work out a method of escorting the shuttles carrying the shield generators. Littia was hiding something, and Pete could mind blast him. "Damn, I've got to get a handle on this mess," he said aloud, trying to shake the uneasiness surrounding him. No sooner than the words left his mouth, Pete appeared on his lap.

"This presence believes you are handling the difficult situation with competence," a baritone voice invaded Dar's mind. "This presence requests you touch him."

"Pete, is that really you? Dar asked, reaching out to pet his friend. The touch instantly drained his fatigue away, leaving in its place a feeling of renewed vitality. "You never stop amazing me. Thanks, I need that."

"This presence is here to assist you any way possible. You must now speak to the Supreme Commander. Is this not so?"

"Yeah, this is so." Dar smiled down at the utapotus. "How long have you been reading my thoughts, you little scoundrel?"

"This presence has been with you since your arrival on the Lantiusian ship, Nanta. It was ordained to be so. So it is."

"Ordained or not, I don't know what I'd do without you. I wish there was someway I could thank you for all your help."

"No expressed gratitude is required. This presence is here to assist and guide 'the one.' Now, do as you must." Pete's eyes whirled like a barber's pole, and then he disappeared with an audible pop.

Feeling like a new man, Dar ran fingers through tangled hair, then dug the VVCom from his pocket. "Jicama," he commanded.

Seconds later, the Supreme Commander's face appeared on the tiny screen. "Ah, Dar. You have talked to your General?"

"Yes. The pilots are ready for pickup, as we agreed." Dar continued with the coordinates outlining Cherry Point's center mat. "How soon will you be sending the shuttle?"

"It shall be launched within the hour," Jicama said, and paused. "Can you supply an escort for the pilot shuttle? We would think four Darts would be sufficient.

"That shouldn't be a problem," Dar said, after a moments thought. "I'll have my executive officer arrange it with Zentao."

"Ah." Jicama smiled. "That will be quite satisfactory. By the way, did your General Moore also have further information about the shield?"

"He did," Dar said, "The United States and the United Nations have elected to allow its construction."

"Ah, that is good. We shall begin preparations for the movement of the generators immediately."

"Sir, I'll need a few hours to brief the new pilots. Perhaps even try to give them a quick familiarization flight before we move the generator shuttles. Is that possible?"

Jicama studied Dar for a moment. "Yes, we will provide you with the interval you request. However, time may be of the essence. There is no tactical reason why the Womongly should not begin their attack anytime now."

"I understand. We'll do the best we can. If all goes well, we should be ready to escort your first shuttle by tomorrow afternoon."

"Very good. We shall count on it, and arrange our operations accordingly," Jicama said, and smiled.

"One more thing, sir, please have another set of radios, like those you sent me, brought to you. General Moore will speak to you personally concerning where the generators should be delivered on Earth. Is that acceptable?"

"Certainly. We will be pleased to talk to your General. However, my friend, does this General Moore possess the officialdoms to make decisions?"

"He does. Washington, ah, that is, the President has given him operational control of the present situation."

"Very well, we shall have a translating device attached to my radio and contact the General immediately. Is there anything else?"

"Not right now," Dar said.

"Very well then," Jicama transmitted, and flicked his VVCom off.

Captain Langos paced his bridge, his titanium pantaloons fluttering rhythmically against the fire whip hanging at his side. Freshly polished, his breast plate reflected the dim blue lighting that illuminated the bridge. Lost in thought, Langos' chameleon skin continually changed colors with each shift in mood.

"Captain, we are intercepting another UHF transmission from the Nanta," First Officer Bezal reported.

"Yes, yes. What is it?" Langos asked, his voice tight with tension. He'd fought the Lantiusians before, and knew what was about to happen. The question was, would these Earthlings fall prey to his enemy's request?

"It is the same Earthling whom we intercepted yesterday. He is once again talking to a General Moore. This Earthling, Dar, apparently is the leader of those abducted by the Lantiusians."

"So, what are they saying?" and impatient Langos asked. He marched to stand directly before his second in command.

"They are sending more pilots," Bezal said, placing a small ear piece next to the side of an oversized ear. The muscular lobes folding inward to hold the speaker in place.

"How many?" Langos demanded.

"They do not say, but they are to be picked up within the next few hours. A shuttle will be launched to the same coordinates the fighter landed yesterday."

"Hmmm," Langos mused, his skin turned redder with each bit of information. He rubbed his breathing flaps with small fingers.

"Sir, they are going to send shield generators as well. This General Moore has spoken of approval by governing bodies on the planet."

Langos noticed Bezal's oval mouth attempt an expression of concern. "Yes, yes. It had to be so. Our enemy operates much the same wherever we engage them. He spoke softly, more to acknowledge his own acceptance of what he'd been fearing would happen.

"What are your orders, sir?" Bezal asked. "Do you wish the Strike Dragons to engage the shuttle sent to retrieve the additional pilots? It will have an escort of four fighters."

"No," Langos said with determination. "Save our resources for the shuttles delivering the generators. This Earthling will surely put his force out to protect them. He does not have many experienced pilots left, and the additional Earth men will be untried in battle. No, hold the Dragons until I give the command."

"It shall be done as you say, Captain," Bezal said, giving Langos a stiff bow, his hand tapping his breast plate.

Dar sat eating with Cannaly at a long table they occupied by themselves. The dinning hall was almost empty, and what few tall Lantiusians were eating paid little attention to the smaller men stuffing their faces with a vegetables grown in Nanta's "hot" rooms.

"Damn, Dar, you look like you had a full nights sleep," Cannaly managed to say between bites. "I don't know how you do it."

Dar smiled, wiping a string of wet leafy yellow plant from the corner of his mouth. The food smelled like sweet potatoes, but tasted like home cooked collards. Something his mom boiled down when he was a boy, and he loved to eat with fresh ham. "I have a secret weapon," he told his Exec.

"Yeah? Well how do I get one?" Cannaly asked.

"Ya can't. It finds you. Don't worry, I'll tell you all about it soon." Again Dar's face lit up with a smile. "Besides, if I told you, you wouldn't believe it anyway."

"Keeping secrets from your best bud. Hell, that ain't fair."

"Who ya got flying escort for the shuttle going to the Point?" Dar asked, changing the subject before he was forced to divulge Pete's magic.

"Bulldog is leading the division, with Frenchy flying his first mission as number four. Thought it would give the Frenchman a chance to get some flight time."

"That sounds good. What about the newbies? You got your stuff in one bag for some sort of training program?" Dar asked.

"Stop sweating it, Skipper. You know I've got it under control. By the time that first delivery shuttle leaves Nanta, they'll be every bit as ready as we were on our first flight."

"Had to ask, or wouldn't be doing my job," Dar said, slapping Cannaly on the shoulder. "Did you learn anything more about the zoo?"

"Yes and no," Cannaly said, pausing for a minute to swallow a hunk of something. "I asked my girl friend. The one who works on the bridge. She went white as a sheet, and that's damned hard for a Lantiusian, seein' as how their skin is so pale by nature, but she wouldn't tell me a blasted thing. My guess, they're really trying to hide this zoo thing from us, but I can't figure why."

"Well, we have bigger irons in the fire right now. I reckon we can put the zoo on a back burner. What really bothers me about the whole thing is that Frenchy thought those zoo creatures were intelligent. I'll ask Littia about it again tonight."

"Skipper, I gotta run. The first shuttle escort should be forming up on the hangar deck by now. I want to see them off."

"Yeah, me too," Dar said, scrapping his oversized plate clean. "Let's go."

CHAPTER 25

Dar walked smartly into the room the squadron used for its morning workouts.

"Attention on deck," Cannaly ordered. Twenty-four men snapped to attention.

"At ease. Take a seat," Dar instructed.

He waited for the group to settle down, arranging themselves on the floor. Silently, he studied each new pilot, realizing how strange all this must seem to them. Looks of raw anticipation reflected off most of the new men's faces. General Moore had selected well. These men were champing at the bit for action. Olive drab flight suites displayed patches indicating each man flew the latest model American fighters.

"Welcome to Space Fighter Squadron One," Dar began. "I know most of you must be feeling like you've just walked into Disney World, but I can assure you we are glad to have you with us. Unlike the first group to arrive aboard the Nanta, you weren't afforded the privilege of going through the Educator. It's a delightful device, where you can stand naked for a few days getting all the knowledge you ever wanted to forget about our hosts." His attempt at humor brought a few smiles, but basically went over like a missed approach. "Okay, here's the situation . . .."

He spent the next hour bringing the group up to speed, noting that the group was diversified as far as the airplanes they flew, but all were from the United States. Two he recognized as captains he'd flown with in the Harrier community.

"So there you have it. Since you didn't get the benefit of the Educator, I've had the XO assign one of the original crew to escort you around and show you the ropes. Your Darts are already being prepared by Zentao on hangar deck seven. Trust Zentao. He's a Lantiusian, but you won't find a better man aboard the Nanta. He'll help you, through one of us, get acquainted with your new birds. Hopefully, there will be at least six or seven ready by tomorrow's shuttle launch. Regardless, each of you has to get a helmet fitted to both your head and the Dart's on-board computer. Be prepared for quite an interesting experience during the fitting. My guide informed me, just prior to your arrival, that they are waiting to fit each of you whenever we were ready. We'll try to get together after evening chow, but if not, Commander Cannaly will keep you informed about what's happenin'. Any questions?"

A Navy F-18 pilot stood. "Yes sir. Will we get a chance to fly before the escort mission?"

"I hope so, but I can't guarantee it. Don't worry too much about it if you don't. Trust me, these Darts fly almost identically to the fighters you're used to. Crawling in the cockpit will be as familiar as lacing your boots. The biggest problem is overcoming the spatial relation effects caused by flying in space. It takes some getting' used to, particularly if you're a 'seat of the pants' pilot like me. Speed and distance sensations are very different." He paused, letting his words sink in, then continued. "The first shuttle is scheduled for early afternoon, so we may have time for you to get an hour or so flight time before it launches. Any other questions?"

"Sir, what about the enemy? Are we going to see some action?" one of the Harrier pilots asked.

"Gentleman, I'm not going to play a fool's game with you. We've lost fourteen men since this started. Chances are we're going to lose some more. This war is for real, and we're rolling the dice with the highest stakes possible . . . Earth. The Womongly fighters aren't easy to kill, but they have a basic flaw in the way the handle tactical formations. That's really the only thing that has given us an edge. That and the fact we are better fighter pilots than they are." That brought a few smiles. "Are you going to see combat? Is the Pope Catholic? Yeah, I don't think you'll have to worry about getting a chance to pit your mettle against the Womongly."

"Skipper," Cannaly interrupted. "I best be gettin' these guys down to their helmet fitting. I'll answer any questions they might have on the way."

"Roger that, XO," Dar acknowledge. "Okay then, we'll see you later. Dismissed."

The group clattered to their feet to follow Cannaly out the door. As Dar watched, Bulldog elbow his way into the crowd to hang his gigantic arm around one of the new recruits. *Leave it to Bulldog to gather these guys under his wing,* he thought, reaching for his VVCom.

"Zentao," Dar commanded, as he walked from the room. He wanted to talk to the engineer, having missed him earlier, when the pilot pickup shuttle left with its escort.

The small screen came alive with Zentao's smiling face. "Dar, good seeing you. Did your pilots arrive with few ill effects?"

"Yeah, we got all fifteen of them. They look a bit the worse for wear, but that's understandable. After all, it isn't everyday you get zapped aboard an alien spaceship."

"Yes, we see what you mean. What can we do for you?" Zentao asked.

Dar sensed the Lantiusian was busy, wanting to get back to work. "Sorry to bother you, but I wanted to ask how production is going on the new Darts?"

Zentao's smile returned, lighting up his handsome face. "We just rolled number seven out on the line about ten minutes ago. Right now, we are well ahead of schedule. We know how important these new machines are to your success."

"That's great, Zentao. Yeah, you're right. I need every fighter I can get for tomorrow's launch. The new guys are getting helmet fittings right now, so I expect you'll be seeing them shortly. They'll want to see the Darts. Could you have someone show them around?"

"Consider it done, Dar. We shall tend to their questions personally," Zentao said.

"Thanks, Zentao. I knew I could count on you. See you later," Dar signed off, closing the lid to the small communicator.

The afternoon was wearing thin, as he stepped into his quarters. The extra boost Pete had given him in the morning had all but dissipated. Dar felt like last year's stale fruitcake. He was surprised to find Littia curled up on the airbed asleep. As the door slid closed, she awoke with a start.

"Dar," she said, sleep confusion still scrambling her thoughts.

"Who did ya expect?" Dar said, smiling. "You got another boyfriend I don't know about?"

Littia ran fingers through her long hair, moving it away from her face. "A boyfriend? We do not understand." "Never mind," Dar said. He was too tired to try keeping up an exchange of lighthearted bantering.

Rolling over, Littia exposed the utapotus curled tightly next to her. "Did the pilots arrive on schedule?" she asked.

"Yes. I just finished briefing them. They're down getting their helmets fitted. Hopefully, we'll be ready by this time tomorrow. Zentao has the Darts rolling off his mysterious manufacturing assembly line at a rapid rate. He has seven new ones on the flight line already."

"That's good," Littia said, though with little enthusiasm.

"What's wrong, Littia?" Dar asked. "You look like you just lost your best friend."

"No, we have not lost our friend. Yet! We are just worried about you. We wish you did not have to escort the shuttles. The Womongly are sure to attack."

"Well, if they do, we'll have a surprise for them. The squadron is up to full strength, and these guys are all good. I'm sure of that. General Moore would only send me the best."

"Do you have to fly? With all the new pilots, could you not direct the operation from Nanta's bridge?"

"Not likely, Littia. I'm a fighter pilot. This stuff is my bread and butter. Besides, as the CO, I have to be out there with my men."

"Yes, we know. We just thought we'd ask," Littia said, her voice filled with sadness. "We have come to depend on you, Dar. May the God of Many Arms Protect you."

"I'll take all the help I can get," Dar said, his voice taking on a light air. "Don't worry. I'm too darn mean to die. Besides, I have a secret weapon."

"Secret weapon? What secret weapon?" Littia asked, her confusion evident.

"Why, that little rascal," Dar said, pointing to Pete. "He's my lucky charm. You don't think I'd let anything happen to my utapotus do you?" He move to the bed, stooping to pet Pete, and in the process, gave Littia a light kiss on the check.

Littia's mood brightened noticeably, reaching up to put her arms around Dar's neck. "We hope we shall always be together," she said.

Dar stepped back, taking her face in his hands. "Me too, Littia. I mean that. But we have to settle this thing with the Womongly. Then we can have all the time we need."

Littia nodded, reaching up to pull Dar down next to her. As he fell on the bed, Pete disappeared.

Dar's eyes opened with a snap. He was tangled, arms and legs, with Littia. Their love making had begun franticly, then settled into a slow mutually caring union of mind and body. He'd fallen asleep minutes after. A deep restful sleep. Now, wide awake, he checked his wrist watch. He'd been down for three hours.

"Littia. Littia. Wake up," he said, gently nudging her shoulder. "Wake up."

Green-gray eyes opened to look at Dar. "That was wonderful," she said with a kittenish smile. "We think our races compliment one another quite well, do they not?"

Dar smiled broadly. "Yeah, I think we do just fine." His mood turned serious. "I have to meet with Cannaly and the others. They're probably waiting for me right now. I'm sorry."

"Don't be. We've got to leave as well. If we don't get back to the guide's quarters, there are those who might think something is going on between us." She smiled. "As if it's a secret any longer. We think everyone of you Earthlings have seduced one of us since your arrival. It has offended many ranking officers, but there is little they can do about the situation."

Dar slapped her lightly on the thigh. "Well, we Earthlings may not be as highly evolved as Lantiusians, but we do have some pleasing animal instincts."

"Yes, we've noticed," Littia said. "Go on, get going. We know you have much to accomplish before your flight tomorrow."

They rolled from the airbed together, retrieving scattered clothing. "Littia, have you found out anything about the Womongly transmissions or the zoo?" Dar asked as casually as possible.

Wrapping a belt tie around her white tunic, Littia shook her head. "Not really. The zoo, as near as we can ascertain, is just that, a zoo. Animals gathered from worlds Nanta has visited over the years. Still, of those we have asked, they appear to question why we do not know about the zoo."

"What about the transmissions?" Dar pressed.

"As a Guide 3rd Class, we have little access to that sort of information. No one we have asked knows anything about Womongly transmissions to Earth, or anywhere else for that matter."

"Damn it all. I was sure hoping you could come up with something. Never mind, I'm sure it's nothing. The questions just stick in my craw, that's all. Don't worry about it."

"Thank you, Dar. If we ask too many questions, we might cause more problems."

"I understand," Dar said. He gathered her in his arms. "I may not get a chance to see you until after the mission tomorrow. You be careful, ya hear?"

"It is not for me to be careful. We shall be fine. It is you who must come back."

"Not to worry, I'll be fine," Dar said. "Now, I've got to find Cannaly. We have a lot of planning yet to do." His kiss, promised a safe return.

CHAPTER 26

Eighteen Darts stood at the ready on hangar deck seven. Zentao moved with determination through groups of workers, fanatically completing last minute systems checks. From the light tube, Dar took the sight in with satisfaction. Somehow they'd pulled if off, a near miracle, in his mind. Even the new pilots scheduled to fly the escort mission were able to get a bit of space flight time during the early morning hours. While the newbie's launch spun around the backside of Nanta, away from the Womongly ship, he'd spent two hours with Jicama. Dar remembered the Commander's opening remarks;

"Your political leaders have given me the positions they wish the shield generators to be located. We assured them the locations were perfectly acceptable."

Where do we move them?" Dar asked. Not so much out of curiosity, as for concerns related to the escort missions.

"Ah . . . One at each pole, as we stated. Those two we will shuttle first, as they will be the most difficult to put into service. We can only take one generator aboard a shuttle at a time. We have two shuttles capable of carrying the shied generators, so to locate the four remaining will require two additional launches."

"Yes, sir. I understand, but where are they going to be delivered?" Dar asked again.

Jicama waved his hand over the command monitor. Instantly, a holographic display of Earth appeared, dangling as if it was a huge globe in a museum, but in reality, a world suspended in space. "Here," the Supreme Commander said, pointing to the island of Tarawa. "And here," his finger passed through the display indicating Indonesia, just north of the city of Sumatra." The holograph rotated slightly. "ah, we believe you call this land mass Africa. There in the country of Zaire, and finally," the globe continued to spin, "south of Quito, on the Ecuador."

"As you directed, sir, all of them are along the equator," Dar noted.

After the Dar's conference with Jicama, he had Cannaly and Bulldog put a schedule together, filling the two flights with an equal number of new men aligned with the, now, old hands. Dar's approval of the flying roster was immediate. Now it was the time to get down to business. He stretched his legs, making short order of the distance between the light tube and his squadron waiting for him on hangar deck seven.

"Squadron, atten-hut," Cannaly commanded, as Dar moved to the front of the formation, then turned and saluted, giving Dar a wink.

Dar returned the salute, the ordered, "At ease. Take a seat."

A small portion of the hangar deck had been arranged with comfortable chairs. Each seat had an individual plasma screen, the size of a small laptop computer, attached to the backrest. The screen hung forward and to the right of the occupant. As his men settled into their seats, Dar removed a small opaque box, Jicama had given him, from his breast pocket. He squeezed gently, activating the box, which then projected a holograph of a shuttle in space.

"This, gentleman, is what we're are going to protect. It is a cargo shuttle, not unlike the one used to bring all of us aboard the Nanta. Though most of you did it by consent, and not strapped in a jet as some of us did."

Several chuckles rose from the group, at Dar's weak attempt at humor.

"The ship is about thousand feet long and about the same wide. She's no small craft as you can imagine. By the time we station ourselves around her, we are going to cover a big hunk of space between the Nanta and Earth's atmosphere. She's not as fast as our fighters, but is capable of making a jump if required." Dar paused, then went on "I presume, Cannaly has spoken to you about what and how to my a hyper-jump."

Heads bobbed in answer.

"This afternoon's launches will be heading for the North and South Poles. Therefore, atmosphere re-entry profiles will be quite different for each Dart flight, as will be the flight paths to the re-entry points."

A hand raised in the middle of the pack. "We won't have mutual support between flights then, will we sir?"

Dar remembered his name, Captain Bill Kobs. "That's right, Bill. Once we leave the Nanta, you'll join up in your assigned flights. After assuming positions around the shuttle, each flight is on its own. I'll be leading Yosemite Flight, escorting the first shuttle, which is heading to the North Pole."

"I'm the honcho leading Snake Flight," Cannaly interrupted. "We're headin' south. These guys don't know it yet but we're actually goin' to Australia, where the beer is cold, and girls are hot, all of which love fighter pilots, and me in particular."

The group laughed. "Thanks, Snake, that certainly lowered the level of seriousness." Dar spoke lightly, glad for the noticeable drop in the groups tensions after his friend's remark.

"If you look at your tactical view screens, in front of you, you'll see how we're going to arrange our formations around the shuttles, as well as our projected flight paths. Since each flight has nine Darts, we have a hole in our protective formation. Note, we flank the shuttle in all directions, leaving an opening at the bottom, near the rear. We'd need ten fighters per flight to completely surround each of the shuttles, but since we don't have the numbers, the two rear flanking fighters will continually rotate about the shuttle's axis. This should, hopefully, provide the protection needed under the shuttle. Are there any questions?"

Dar waited several moments, allowing his men to think of any questions they might have regarding their flights. "None. Okay then, we'll split up into individual flights. I'll brief here. Snake, have your guys swing their seats around to face you on the opposite side."

The two flights separated, pulling their chairs into tight groups. Dar began briefing the eight pilots he'd be leading. "Bulldog, you're the second division leader, and will take over the entire flight should something happen to me. I hate losing you as my personal wing man, but you've earned your spurs."

"Who's goin' to save your ass if I'm not around" the big Texan drawled with good humor.

"Yeah, right. Tell you what, I'll watch my rear, you just keep your six clear, ya hear," Dar poked back.

The briefing turned to the serious matters of flight control and methods of stay alive if the balloon went up. By the time Dar finished, over an hour had passed. He checked his watch. Thirty minutes till launch. "Okay, let's man up."

"Captain, a shuttle has just departed Nanta," First Officer Bezal reported.

"Yes, yes. I see it," Langos said, rising stiffly from his command stool to move closer to his tactical command holograph. He sat back on his third leg, letting it stabilize him as he leaned back to view the large screen. "Bring us up to maneuvering speed and move us out of orbit."

"Aye, sir," Bezal answered the order. "Helmsman, move us out of orbit, set course two-four-zero point ten."

Dectima slowly gathered way, moving on a course diagonally away from the Nanta. She lay thirty thousand miles from her enemy, slowly moving further from the Lantiusian ship.

"How many Strike Dragons are out?" Langos demanded.

There are ten Dragons deployed, with fifteen waiting at ready alert," Bezal replied, in a flat monologue.

Langos griped his fire whip, absently taping his breast plate. Deep in thought, his skin softened to a pale pink. "Launch the remaining fighters. Have each of them calculate a short jump between Nanta and the planet. Instruct the flight leaders not to make the jump until I give the order."

"Sir, another shuttle has just appeared. Neither has accelerated to cruise speed as yet. What do you think they are doing?"

"I see them. Continue your present course and speed. It is my supposition they are preparing a transfer of shield generators to they planet. I expect we shall see fighter escorts shortly."

"Your are correct, Captain. Fighters are leaving the shield now." the First Officer informed Langos.

"How many?" Langos asked, returning to his command stool.

"There are ten out, and still they come. How can that be? I thought you said we had destroyed most of the fighters?" Bezal asked, momentarily forgetting how quickly his captains moods could change, when such a question was posed.

"Are you questioning me, First Officer Bezal?" Langos flared, his color rapidly turning red.

"My apologies, sir. Please forgive my impertinence. There are now eighteen enemy fighters out," Bezal said in a a wavering voice.

"Captain, all Strike Dragons have launched," a senior flight director announced.

"Yes, yes, very well. Now we shall wait and let the situation develop," Langos whispered, stiffly nodding his upper body with anticipation.

"Yosemite Flight, check-in," Dar transmitted. He waited while all eight of his fighters answered, then directed, "Join-up. Let's go to work."

Dar eased his throttle forward, accelerating to five hundred knots, as his flight assumed formation on either side of his Dart, then scanned his plasma screen. "Nan, which one of the shuttle is ours?"

"It is the shuttle on the right, Dar. Bearing two-six-four at fifty miles."

"Roger, got it. Arm all weapons."

"All weapons armed. Do you expect to engage the enemy, Dar?" Nan asked, in a calming soft voice.

"Yes. I'd be surprised if we don't see some action, but who knows, this might end up being a milk run. Just keep all those beautiful sensors of yours on full alert, ya hear." He scanned his instruments, noting all indications normal, then radioed, "Shuttle One, this is Yosemite lead, we're taking position on you at this time. You can start acceleration now."

"Very well, Yosemite lead, we are throttling forward," the shuttle commander transmitted.

Dar waited, as his flight took position around the shuttle, then bumped this speed up to take a position below and ahead of the bigger ship. "Snake, were off. Good luck to you and your flight."

"Same to ya, boss. See you at the bar," Cannaly transmitted back.

The gaggle of shuttles and fighters rapidly approached fifteen thousand miles an hour, heading for their respective poles on Earth.

Langos sucked hard through his breathing flaps, causing them to flutter in protest. "There is our target, First Officer Bezal. Have the Dragons jump ahead of the first shuttle."

"Do you wish all the fighters to attack that single target, Captain?" Bezal asked.

"Yes, yes. All the Strike Dragons on the first shuttle. Do it now!" Langos commanded.

Bezal turned to the flight director, and gave the order.

"Enemy on the nose, twelve o'clock," Nan's voice was soft and reassuring. "Twenty-five fighters line abreast."

"Got'em Nan. So much for a milk run, huh," Dar sighed. "We've got company, Yosemite flight, dead ahead at fifteen thousand miles and closing fast. Hold your positions," Dar radioed his flight.

"We're ready, Lead," Bulldog radioed. "Bring'em on, ya hear."

"Torpedo inbound, Dar, targeted for the shuttle. It is a small weapon, the shuttle's shield will withstand the hit," Nan passed her information without concern.

"Roger. Can we hit it with a thrumber blast, Just in case?" Dar asked.

"Targeting torpedo," Nan said. Seconds passed, then his Dart's nose erupted with yellow-orange fire, which streaked across space to intercept the incoming weapon. It exploded in a fiery blast.

"Good shooting, Nan, keep it up."

"Thank you, Dar," his computer answered. "More torpedoes inbound."

"Take them under fire," Dar commanded, then pressed the transmit button on his throttle, "Yosemite Flight, have your computers take the torpedoes under fire." The area suddenly lit up with thrumber fire, as nine Darts sent balls of destruction at the incoming torpedoes that were hell bent on destroying the shuttle. Explosions ignited, hundreds of miles in front of Yosemite Flight, as weapon met weapon. Two torpedoes sped past the onslaught of thrumber fire, crashing into the shuttle's shield. Dar felt his Dar shutter under the blast.

"Approaching thrumber range on the enemy fighters," Nan intoned, in a gentle voice.

"Roger, got it." He keyed his radio, "Okay, guys, this is what were here and get paid the big bucks for. Go for it, and good luck."

The two flights came together at the combined speed of thirty-five thousand miles per hour, thrumber balls filling space like fireflies dancing in the night. Dar felt hits on his fighter immediately, knocking him around in the cockpit like a puppet.

"What's the damage, Nan?" Dar asked, hammering the stick to the right, then pulled the speeding Dart into the vertical. He force himself against his shoulder straps, turning to watch four enemy fighters pass beneath him.

"Shield holding a t eighty percent," Nan droned. "all systems operative"

Dar stepped on the right rudder, causing the Dart to skid into a near uncontrollable turn from the vertical. The nose fell like a stone. "holey shit," he mumbled, seeing enemy fighters everywhere. Pulling hard to port, he brought an adversary into the cross hairs of his heads-up display, and pulled the trigger on the stick. Thrumber fire tore a line in the blackness, hitting the Dragon near the cockpit. He held the pipper and gun fire on the unfortunate enemy, burning through his shield. The Strike Dragon exploded in a ball of purple flame.

Not all of Yosemite flight was doing as well. Dar slammed the throttle full, pulling the nose up to execute a Cuban-eight. At the top of the hundred mile loop, he watched as two Darts disappeared in white light. He swung to the left, and rolled level, bringing an enemy, the one that had just killed one of his squadron mates, into his sights. Balls of yellow-orange spewed in a steady stream from the Dart's nose, sending another Womongly pilot to his death.

"Skipper, you have two on your six. Break right, break right," Bulldog radioed frantically.

Dar heeded the call, slamming the stick to the stops. The Dart strained under the load, as thrumber fire filled the space he'd just left. The two fighters flew past, overshooting Dar's flight path. He rolled to the left, and let the Dart accelerate. "Got you now you bastards," Dar mumbled.

"Please, say again," Nan asked.

"Disregard," Dar shot back, leveling his sight on on of the shooters. A ball of thrumber heat caught the Womongly just as he started a hard turn. The Dragon's shield glowed, then gave way. "That's three," Dar said aloud.

Dar felt his Dart rock under a blast. An enemy had him in his sights and was directing well aimed thrumber, burning through his shield.

"Shield at five percent and failing," Nan exclaimed. "Light drive damaged, Dar we can not jump!"

Dar said nothing. He was too busy trying to shake the killer at his six. He jinxed right and left, desperately trying to destroy the pilot's firing solution. Still the balls of thrumber heat sought the vital innards of his ship. He pushed the nose over, attempting the impossible . . . an inside loop.

The Womongly lost his target, but Dar was completely out of control. The Dart shot out of the mayhem at over eighteen-hundred miles and hour. He dragged the throttle to idle, opening the reverse thrusters to slow his velocity.

"Nan, situation report. What's left?"

There was a pause, the Nan's voice , broken and weak, responded. "We are in serious trouble, Dar. Shield is destroyed, most systems are gone, and the light drive is spooling down. Expect power failure in two minutes."

"Can't you fix it: Damn I all, Nan we'll drift out here forever. Come on, we've got to think of something."

"Light drive fail . . .." Nan tried to say. The Dart went quiet, drifting silently.

Dar stared, dumbfounded, at the fight still raging several thousand miles away.

Thrumber fire cut crisscross lines over the Earth's face. From his position, it looked like finely hand-tooled lace, threads ending in colorfully constructed flowering buds, where the heat of a thrumber sun blasted a ship in to oblivion. He made out the shuttle, still racing to the re-entry point, the Dart rolled slowly, taking the fascinating expose' from his view, replacing it with the cold surface of the Moon. He coughed.

"Damn, I'm out of oxygen," he said to himself, reverting to his tendency to talk to himself when faced with and emergency. Like the engine in his AV-8, Harrier, the light drive powered the on board oxygen generator that allowed him to breath. With light drive failure, the only breathable air would be what was left in the small cockpit. Dar pulled his helmet off, carefully placing it atop the stick. He took a deep breath of stale non-circulated air that remained. "What a helluva way to die," he said to no one in particular.

Silently,Langos watched this tactical situation screen. If his small oval mouth had been capable of stretching into a smile, it would have spread from one oversized ear to the other. Images flashing across the holograph clearly indicated the Dragon's superior numbers were taking their toil. Of the nine enemy fighters entering the fight, only five remained. However, Strike Dragons were flaming as well. He'd counted seven destroyed.

"Instruct the Dragons to concentrate their attack on the shuttle. We must destroy the shield generator," Langos commanded Bezal.

"It has been done, Captain," the First Officer responded.

Look there," Langos exclaimed, as he watched two Dragons fire on a single enemy fighter. "The fools are attempting to follow the enemy through an inside loop." As the words left his mouth, the two Dragons slammed into each other, creating a fireball double the size than that of a single explosion. "Imbeciles! A total waste of men and equipment," the said. His fury initiated an immediate shift in his color from excited green to red anger.

"Sir, the fighter has lost control," Bezal reported. "It appears he is dead in space.

"Yes, yes, I can see that, First Officer," Langos said quietly, his mind calculating his next move. "Bring Dectima around and make heading for the disabled fighter. Increase speed as well."

"Aye, sir," Bezal acknowledge. "Helmsman, turn to the new heading of three-four-two point six, increase speed ten percent."

"Time to intercept?" Langos asked.

Bezal surveyed his monitor, his small hands flashing across heat sensitive controls. "Five minutes, Captain."

"That is well," Langos mumbled, his yellow eyes glowing with anticipation. "Prepare retrieval arms on the starboard side, bay twelve."

Dar looked dully down at his finger nails."yep, turning blue," he said aloud, recognizing the onset of hypoxia. "Gettin' cold too. Probably better if the pressurization had gone all at once. It'd be over in a hurry then. This way, I'm going to die slowly.

He pounded his thigh, hoping the pain would keep him awake for a few minutes more. "Where's a utapotus when you need one?" Dar spoke to his dead heads'-up display. He looked into the darkness. The moon was nothing more than a pinpoint, balanced on the nose of his fighter. "Eyes not working right either."

Dar's head drooped, chin resting on his chest. "We gave it our best shot," he whispered, letting darkness fall over him like death's cloak. He passed out, unaware that his fighter had come alive with tens of thousands tiny robotic nanites.

Captain Langos turned his attention from the tactical holograph, which now displayed the shuttle entering Earth's heavy atmosphere. The space battle was over, and his Dragons had not been able to stop the shuttle. He marveled at the Earthling's tenacity, as he watched the five remaining enemy fighters made a dash to catch the spaceship, still in their care. Strike Dragons, those that survived, were trying to reform for their return to Dectima.

"How many Dragons remain?" Langos asked his First Officer.

"Standby one," Bezal said. He turned to the Fighter Director, bowing slightly as the Director relayed the information to him." Sir, there are fourteen fully function Dragons and two damaged, but flyable."

"Very well. Have them return for recovery," Langos ordered, walking to the starboard view port. He watched as Dectima slowed, drawing along side Dar's Dart. "Begin recovery operations of the enemy fighter. I want the pilot alive. No harm is to come to him. Is that completely understood?"

"Aye, sir," Bezal said. "Captain, should we assume the pilot is an Earthling? They breath a high mixture of oxygen, much higher than we do."

"Yes, yes, I understand your concern. Have bay twelve flooded with one hundred percent oxygen. That should save the Earthling's life. If he, indeed , is still alive.

"Aye, sir," Bezal responded.

Bulldog slammed his throttle to the stop, accelerating to catch the shuttle before it began re-entry. "Snake, this is Bulldog."

"Go Bulldog," Cannaly radioed back.

"Damn it, Snake, there's only five of us left. They got the skipper."

Cannaly felt his heart drop like a hard landing. "They got Dar. Are you sure?" he radioed for conformation. His flight was on the opposite side of Earth, so had not been in view of the battle, but had listened to the rapid fire radio transmissions as the short battle progressed.

"Yeah, they got the Skipper. Hell, Snake, my bird flies like a paper kite, after what felt like a dozen or so hits. My computer tells me I've only got half a shield left, but I'm taking what's left of Yosemite flight back to try and protect the shuttle.

"Roger that," Cannaly transmitted. "Stick with the shuttle for now. I'll send three of my flight around to give you help on your flight back to the Nanta, should the bastards show up on your way home." He was the squadron's CO now, and had to make the decisions. "Hang on, Bulldog, ya hear."

"Roger, that," Bulldog radioed.

Dectima dwarfed the small Dart as it drifted alongside the Womongly ship's starboard aft quarter. Captain Langos watched the bay doors open on the intra-ship HoloCam. He could see several of his crew, clothed in protective suits, struggling to position the control panel that operated the mammoth retractor arm. With difficulty, they locked the panel in place next to the open hatch, then pulled thick cables to the arm.

"Captain, the retractor crew signals they are prepared to attempt recovery of the enemy fighter," Bezal reported.

"Give the order," Langos instructed, as he watched the arm slowly begin extending away from Dectima's starboard bay, its claw-like hand with two articulating digits, opposed by a shorter more powerful rotating hook, opening and closing to warm its operating fluids against the cold of space.

Bezal moved quietly to Langos' side, "Captain, we are prepared to flood the bay with pure oxygen, when the outer doors are closed."

"Yes, yes. Have you arranged for a voice translator package?"

"It has been ordered," the First Officer answered, watching the mechanical claw gently grasp Dar's Dart just forward of its stub wings.

"Very well. You will accompany me to bay twelve," Langos instructed. "Have protection suits and a squad of Rage Warriors standing-by for us."

" Aye sir," Bezal acknowledged, moving to his station to give the necessary orders. After passing the Captain's orders, he hurried after Langos, whose pantaloons fluttered with his rapid departure from the command bridge.

In REM sleep, Dar's eyes rolled as he watched his dream unfold on the screen of his mind. He was trapped in a decompression chamber. Though it was much larger than the one he'd been subjected to during flight training at Naval Air Station, Pensacola, Florida, he knew it to be a chamber nonetheless . . . he thought he could hear the air being pumped out of its enclosure.

His eyes fluttered, then opened with a near audible snap. Completely disorientated, he shook his head, trying to clear the cobwebs that stuck to his brain like cotton candy. *I'm sure as hell not in Kansas anymore,* he thought, still lightheaded from lack of oxygen.

"He lives, Captain," Bezal said without emotion, unsure how he felt about having this man, this enemy, aboard the "Dectima.

"Yes, yes, I can see that," Langos retorted, with some show of enthusiasm. Unlike his First Officer, he was pleased to see the Earthling alive, and appearing well. He had plans for this captive. "Have they translated the scribbling under the fighter's cockpit?"

"They have sir. His name is Senior Commander Dar Fantin, and it appears he has destroyed many of our Strike Dragons and their pilots."

"Yes, yes. It is of little consequence now. Hmm, senior Commander, you say. Could it be we have captured the leader of the Earth's fighter force?"

Dar heard the conversation between the two very strange looking creatures, dressed in red protective suits, but could not understand the garbled words fraught with hissing. As his mind cleared, he noticed the same sound evident in his waking dreams. It's oxygen being pumped into not out of the bays expansive surroundings, he rightful guessed, trying to move for the first time without success. He was on his back, lashed flat to a hard pallet or planking of sorts.

Moving his head forward caused an immediate reaction. Three thrumber rifle barrels were shoved in his face with deadly intent. These he recognized immediately as Womongly. His heart sank, and true fear flashed through him as realization hit with hammered force . . . he was a prisoner.

A harsh sting of words spit from one of the small Womongly, and the rifles were withdrawn. Dar raised his head, trying to locate the man in charge.

"Bring the translation package to me," Langos ordered.

Dar watched as a small console, raised on a pedestal, was rolled next his shoulder. Fear, again washed over him in waves, evidenced by the sweat pouring from his brow.

A red suit leaned over Dar, allowing large yellow eyes to shine down on him through a clear helmet fitted over a hairless head. "You are Senior

Commander Dar Fantin, are you not?" The voice was mechanical in nature, an obvious machine voice speaking in English.

Dar twisted against his bonds, accomplishing little more than cutting a thin line of skin. Warm blood trickled down his wrist. He lay still, looked up at the strange being in the red suit and said, "Yeah, that's me."

He watched with utter amazement as his interrogator turn a bright green, not realizing it was a physical display of excitement on the the alien's part.

"That is good. I am Captain Langos, commander of this ship, the Dectima. Let me assure you, Senior Commander Dar Fantin, we mean you no harm Please try and relax, and I shall have the bonds holding you removed. Do you understand?"

Dar looked up into Langos' yellow eyes. They told him nothing. He nodded his head, then said, "Yes, I understand."

"Yes, yes, very well," Langos replied, then waved two Rage Warriors forward to loosen the straps holding Dar to the pallet.

As the bonds were relaxed, Dar lay still, not wishing to antagonize the small Womongly freeing him. He had no desire to test the remaining Warrior's trigger fingers. Their rifles were still leveled at his chest. Bindings removed, the Rage Warrior stepped away from the pallet.

"Thank you," Dar said, nodding to the Womongly he assumed was in charge, then slowly moved to rub his sore wrists.

With his untethered movement the group took a step back. They had all heard of the fighting skills the Earth men had displayed against their comrades aboard the Nanta.

"Move very slowly Earthling, we know of you fighting prowess," Langos warned.

The voice may have sounded like it was being bounced off a metal echo chamber, but it left little doubt in Dar's mind that he'd just been given a hard and fast order. "Listen, whoever you, I'm not moving from here till you give me the go ahead. I'm not about to try and take on a thrumber rifle on your turf." The metallic voice changed his words into hissing garble. "But, sir, could I please sit up?"

Langos studied his captive for a moment, then said, "Yes, yes, sit up."

Slowly, but with determination, Dar slid his legs over the edge of the pallet, then followed with his upper torso. He was surprised to see his Dart resting in a cradle, not more than twenty yards away. "Where am I," he asked quietly.

"Yes, yes. We understand your concerns. You are aboard the Womongly space vessel, Dectima," Langos said.

"Well that's just great! Out of the fat, and into the fire," Dar whispered.

"What's that you said? The translator could not define the meaning of your words."

"Nothing, really." Dar shook his head, then looked up at the questioner. "What do you want of me anyway? I won't tell you anything." He spoke with confidence, though he wasn't at all sure he could tolerate torture, if that's what they had in store for him. *Lord only knows what methods these creatures have devised to extract information,* he thought.

"I want nothing from you, Earth man. It is far more important that you listen to what I have to say. There is little about your plans I do not already know. The Lantiusians are as predictable as day follows night."

"Why should I listen to you? You and your crew have been trying to kill me and my men since we arrived on the Nanta. More importantly, you are attempting to destroy my world," Dar said, trying to sound indignant.

Langos let out a long sigh, breathing flaps fluttering under the escaping air. "Senior Commander Dar Fantin, we have no intentions, and never have had any intention, of destroying your world. The Womongly only wish to open trade routes with your people, not kill them."

"Who do you think you're kidding, Captain. The very name of you ship means 'World Killer', or Destroyer."

"Yes, yes, the Lantiusians have taught your well," Langos said, making a gurgling sound deep in his throat, meant to be laughter. "Dectima is translated into all galactic languages, except Lantiusian, as 'World Explorer', not Destroyer, my new friend. I think we have much to talk about, is this not so?"

Dar sat back, his surprise complete. Was this ugly little alien telling him the truth? He had no idea, but remembering certain strange events since boarding Nanta focused forward in his mind. Things like the strange being that appeared in his cabin, warning him that all was not what it might seem. Jicama's strange behavior and excuses for not knowing the strength of his enemy he so off had fought, and the strange way he'd suddenly been treated by the Jicama's First Officer. Remembering these, he thought it best to listen to what the Womongly Captain might have to say. "Yeah, maybe we do."

"I have made arrangements for you to be fitted with small breathing tubes, one that can be inserted directly into you breathing apparatus. We require far less oxygen than does your species, and you will find Dectima's atmosphere heavy with moisture. In fact, the amount of pure oxygen we have pumped into this bay would be as deadly to us as one of you fighter's thrumber guns. Will you allow such a device to attached to your body?"

"I don't think I have much of a choice the the matter. Sure, fit away," Dar answered. He sounded flippant, even to himself, but he didn't want to show his enemy the overwhelming anxiety he was feeling. *Or were they his enemy,* he wondered, then asked, "What about my Dart?"

"Your Dart? I do not understand," Langos said.

"My fighter," Dar said, pointing to his fighter.

"Yes, yes, of course. We understand. It appears your Dart, as you call it, will be internally repaired within hours," Langos answered.

The nanites! Of course, I'd forgotten all about those little mechanical bugs Zentao planted in my Dart before my first trip to Earth. "You mean, she'll fly again?"

"Yes, yes, I should think so, and that is well. I think after our conversation, you may wish to fly your Dart at least once more."

Dar registered hidden meaning in the Womongly's words, but couldn't quite put his finger on what it might be. He started to rise, then sat down quickly when thrumber rifles again leveled at his belt. "Captain, please tell your men I'm not going to attack them or you. I'll listen to what you have to say. That's a promise."

After a brief exchange from Langos, the riles lowered, allowing him to stand and stretch. "Okay, Captain, let's get this breathing gadget attached and start chatting."

CHAPTER 27

Steadying the small oxygen generator belted around his waist, Dar ducked under the threshold leading to Langos' cabin. He was finding the labyrinth of corridors and passageways traversing Dectima difficult for his five foot ten inch frame to negotiate. Twice, he'd banged his head on the top of a hatchway. The diminutive Womongly had built their ships to meet their needs, not an average Earthling. Once in the Captain's Spartan-like quarters, he tried to stand, only to end up having to stoop slightly to clear the overhead.

"Please, sit," Langos said, pointing to a three legged stool next to a work desk.

The smooth surfaced desk, Dar noted, was decorated with a single holographic picture of a Womongly and a child. *Must be the Captain's wife and kid,* he thought. He shuffled to the stool, slid it out, then, with caution, took a seat, not sure the small stool would hold his weight. "Thank you, Captain," he said, hearing his metallic sounding words translated into hisses and grunts by the translator package.

For the next few minutes, neither man spoke. Dar felt uncomfortable under the hard scrutiny of the Womongly's stare. Divested of his red suit and clear helmet, the Captain was one ugly looking creature. The one thing he could be thankful for was the tubing running into each nostril of his nose. The pure oxygen, streaming through the opaque tube, helped mask the terrible stench of rotten garbage which permeated the entire ship.

"What do you know of us, Senior Commander Dar Fantin? I am speaking of the Womongly," Langos asked, breaking the long silence.

"Only what I have been told about your race by the Lantiusians," Dar replied. He was uneasy with the question and his answer. From what he'd seen so far, this captain commanded his ship with ruthless authority. He was a commander who ruled from a platform of fear, regardless of the comical impression he'd made on Dar with the alien's oversized ears, gills, and eyes the size of saucers atop a hotdog body.

"Yes, yes. It is always thus, when we engage the Lantiusians. They have been our enemy, our only enemy, for hundreds of years. I suppose they have told you this? Langos inquired.

Dar nodded, "Yes, that's pretty much the truth, though I expect your version of the war y'all been fighting will be quite different."

Langos said nothing for a moment, studying Dar closely. "Did they place you in their Educator Tube?"

"Yes," Dare replied, without elaboration.

"Then you believe, or were educated to believe, the Womongly attacked the planet Lantius. Is this not so?"

"Captain, no disrespect meant, but you implied that it would be you providing me with information. I told you, I would not answer your questions. I consider myself a prisoner of war. In my Marine Corps, that means you get name, rank, and serial number . . . period.

Langos' pink face flared to red. He was not used to anyone talking to him in such a manner. His hand went to the fire whip, before he was able to swallow his anger. "I only wish to establish the breadth of your, so called, education so that I might correct much of the misinformation I am sure you have accepted as fact." He calmed himself, letting the flare of ire pass.

Adrenaline pumped into Dar's system as he saw how his answer provoked Langos. For an instant, he was certain the strange looking loop, draped a the the Captain's waist, was going to be used on him. Years of military training warned him never to let his interrogator manipulate him into providing information on any subject. In this case, however, he could not find hard rational why he should not answer the Captain's inquiries. "The Educator taught me that you started the war," he said without emotion. With his answer, the Womongly's yellow eyes seemed to soften, and his pigment turn more pink than red.

Poof! Pete appeared on Dar's lap, curled and content.

Langos stumbled back on his third leg, drawing the fire whip.

"Captain, please, this is my friend," Dar yelled, covering the utapotus with his own body. The whip, now fully ablaze, lowered an inch.

"What is this? Only Lantiusians have these strange creatures as pets," Langos said, whip still at the ready.

Dar sighed. "Captain, I assure you I am definitely not a Lantiusian, and yes it is a utapotus, normally found only with your enemy, but this little one chose me. I had little or no choice in the matter. He is harmless. Please, I beg of you, put that blazing contraption of yours back on your hip. Pete, here, isn't going to hurt you or anyone else."

Slowly, almost with reluctance, Langos lowered the whip, its fire extinguished.

"Very well, I will accept your word. This is very unusual in all regards, however." He looked closely at the small animal resting on Dar's lap, then replaced the whip to his belt.

"I will tell you a story," he said, planting his third leg to rest upon.

Dar relaxed as well, letting Pete shift slightly on his lap.

"Since the advent of the Womongly's ability to travel the stars," Langos began, "we have been merchants, for we have something very few other planets or even galaxies have, the Last Element. This natural compound, found on Womong, gives every space traveling world the ability to power their ships, and even more importantly, to make hyper-jumps. We may talk more of this later."

Langos paused to let the import of this knowledge settle with Dar.

After a moment, he continued, "The Womongly, from the very onset of space travel, have been merchants. It is true we are a hard and disciplined race. For that reason, to many worlds, many species, we appear uncaring and war like. This could not be further from the truth, though we will and do protect ourselves when necessary, as it has been these last few weeks."

"Then why attack the Nanta?" Dar interrupted.

"Yes, yes, the attack on the Nanta. I shall answer your question in due time, but let me continue. In the course of our space exploration, we chanced upon the planet of Lantius. A gorgeous world, rich with natural resources, not unlike your planet, which we now orbit. We made contact with the Lantiusians, who, at first, welcomed us. Their society did not struggle with the depredations of war, there was no sickness, or food shortages so prevalent on other worlds. Lantius was a utopia of sorts, populated with a race who consider themselves to be superior to every other living thing. However, they were without space travel, which we were glad to share in exchange for raw goods to transfer to our home world. What we did not know, this Lantiusian superiority complex force them to consider the Womongly as barbarians. A barbaric race suitable only for annihilation. Even more so, considering we, the Womongly held the key to their ability to join the space traveling worlds. We had the Last Element, but were considered too barbaric to deserve such wonders.

Much too late did the true intent of the Lantiusians become evident to us. Under the tutelage of Womongly engineers, they constructed their first space craft, fully equipped with weapons capable of waging war. We thought little of providing the technological knowledge involving weaponry, as all our ships are and were fitted like wise.

Dar listened with fascination, as the Womongly Captain unfolded his tale. He wanted to laugh, thinking how totally different the two explanations of past history were. The real truth, he thought, must be located somewhere in the middle.

"The Lantiusians sorely underestimated my world. Though their weapons were sufficient to destroy us, they had never engaged in warfare, and therefore, strategically, were mere children. Retreating to Lantius, they constructed a shield. A shield which surrounded their entire planet. A shield no known weapon could penetrate. A shield of green, generated by perpetual machinery that could not be shut down, once put into operation. The Lantiusians, defeated, retired unto themselves, swearing one day to destroy the Womongly. From their defeat, grew a master plan, as well as their shield.

Dar shifted his weight on the stool, which provided little comfort. The low stool pushed his knees high, forcing him to lean slightly forward. He listened, but with trepidation, thinking about how much truth could the tale actually hold.

"This presence finds the Womongly's story to be true," Pete mind blasted.

Dar sat upright, caught off guard by the baritone voice in his head.

Langos registered Dar's surprised look. "Senior Commander Dar Fantin, are you feeling ill? He asked, discontinuing his historical account.

"I'm fine, Captain. This stool is not the most comfortable seat, but I'm fine. Please continue." He stroked Pete gently.

"Yes, yes, you are large, and the stool is small. I wish I could offer you better," Langos said, his small hands spread before him with the apology. "Now, where was I."

He paused in thought before beginning once more. "First, the Lantiusians developed a religion which forbid the killing of others, swearing never to attack another intelligent race. Second, they designed enormous spaceships which could hold thousands of their people. These ships traveled throughout the know galaxy, and beyond, warning other worlds of the Womongly, spreading lies that we brought war and death, rather than only wishing to trade. Five such ships were built, and I know of three that still exist. One of those is the Nanta."

"But that would make Nanta thousands of years old," Dar interrupted.

"And so it is, my new friend," Langos said. "Oh, it is continually being modified, but it is many thousands of years old."

"How can that be? No ship could last that long, not even in space."

"Nanta has, along with two others. They have been over-hauled, rebuilt, and increased in size many times, as the centuries past. How? Through the mass destruction of entire worlds."

"Dar shook his head. "No way, Captain. The Lantiusians can't kill or destroy worlds. Hell, er, I mean," he stopped in mid sentence, flustered by both Langos and his loosing his temper. "Sir," he started again, under control once more. "I've lived with these people. They can not kill, not even to protect themselves. The God of Many Arms religion won't let them. The Rage Warriors you were able to sneak aboard would have annihilated everyone of them, if it hadn't been for me and my men.

"Exactly so," Langos said, the metallic voice of the translator inflecting his self satisfaction to Dar. "Had it not been for you Earthlings, we might have finally won our war." Langos sighted, his breathing flaps fluttering. " Your violent disposition of my Rage Warriors has brought us to this point, has it not?"

"I don't see how, but I'm still listening," Dar said.

"It is true that the Lantiusians can not directly kill another sentient being, but that does not stop them from having others shed blood on their behalf, or for their purposes. It is the Lantiusian way. But, let me continue.

Lantiusian ships preceded out trading vessels wherever we traveled. Most new worlds, after their initial fear, learned our true purpose, and needing the Last Element for space travel, took us as allies and friends. Others, however, succumbed to the Lantiusian lies, and accepted the Lantiusian offer of weaponry to take us under attack, as you did, Senior Commander Dar Fantin."

"Captain, your version of history is totally different than that of the Lantiusians. I don't know who to believe," Dar said, when Langos paused for a moment.

"Yes, yes, we understand completely, but there is much more to tell. For hundreds of years it was so, Lantiusians having other worlds fight their battles. Then, disaster struck our enemy, creating ramifications which changed everything. The shield, Senior Commander Dar Fantin, don't you see, the shield is the key. They built a shield which could not be destroyed around their planet, nor could it be shut down. Fearful that the Womongly would sabotage their shield generators, the generators themselves were shielded as well. This proved a disastrous miscalculation on their part. It proved to be their total downfall."

"I'm afraid I don't understand how a shield, meant to protect Lantius, could be the Lantiusian's undoing," Dar said.

"It is true the shield protects, but it also blocks all things, including the life giving warmth from a sun. In the case of Lantius, two suns. The planet turned to a glacier of ice and snow. Lantius died."

Dar rocked back on the stool, remembering his first look at Nanta's shield, while standing on her command bridge. A green covering which blocked out any view of space. "Why not just shut down the generators?" he asked.

"As I have told you," Langos replied, with a touch of annoyance, "The generators were designed never to be shut down. They were perpetual running machines, locked in a manner not to be turned off . . . ever. The Lantiusians had produced the perfect shield to protect their planet, or so their scientists thought. It was perpetual, self maintaining, and self protective."

"Jesus," Dar whispered. They killed their own planet. "The five ships had no home, no resources, and nowhere to go. Right?"

"Yes, yes, now you are beginning to understand. Holding to their religious beliefs, the Lantiusians increased their deceitfulness by approaching a new world with more than words. They would arrange to be in the same galaxy as a Womongly ship, prior to our making contact with a chosen world race, convincing the populace that we were there to destroy their planet. How? Exactly the way they duped you and your world leaders. The Lantiusians need your Earth, or so they believe, to continue their existence, but they can't engage in your planet directly in a battle that they would have to engage themselves in combat. By deceit and the use of their Educator, they are able to convenience some that we are the invaders, and not the Lantiusians. It is clever, and it works. Not always but enough times to keep them building

"Holy shit, the shield," Dar exclaimed, slamming a fist on the desk with understanding. The sudden burst of anger caused Pete to jump, his bright eyes spinning. "They set the stage for some unsuspecting world to accept the need for a shield."

"Yes, yes, that is correct," Langos said. "You and your men have accomplished everything the Lantiusians wanted, step by planned step. You were protecting a shuttle carrying a generator to Earth, were you not?"

"God forgive me, yes. The first of six. If what you're telling me is true, Earth will be as dead as death itself when those generators go online. "It is so, I am afraid," Langos muttered.

"What I don't understand, if these generators produce a shield that nothing can penetrate, and they can't be destroyed or turned off, what good does that do for the Lantiusians? They can't break the shield's power to remove Earths resources, once the planet dies . . . the shield would not let them through."

"Yes, yes, we see your understanding on the matter. However, long ago, the Lantiusians developed a key, a micro command, if you will, that will shut down the generators when they have done their job. A planet doesn't just die over night, it takes years, but they have the time, and will schedule a return trip to gather what they need by shutting down the generators."

"It is a wonder they didn't have this 'key' when they built their own generators. I guess they learned the hard way."

"Yes, yes, quite right. The hard way, as you put it.

"That still doesn't explain the transmissions you have been making to Earth? I was told they were for targeting purposes? Now, I doubt that very much."

"Transmissions? Targeting? No, we were trying to contact your world governments to explain our intentions. Nothing more. Unfortunately, the Nanta jammed our signals as fast as we could transmit."

Dar gently place Pete on the desk, and stood, head bent to clear the overhead, and began pacing the small room. His mind was spinning at Mach 1. What Langos portrayed made sense. He'd played right into the Lantiusians and Jicama's hands like some dumb kid. *I should have known,* he thought. *That darn holograph telling me not all was as it seemed was my first go with thinking something was off. Then Littia not being fully educated, Jicama's insistence on the shield, and the zoo.* "The zoo!" Dar said aloud. Captain do the Lantiusians kill everyone on a planet they shielded?"

Langos thought for a moment. "Frankly, I am not sure what you mean. They destroy everything. The only difference between the shield being established on your Earth and the one constructed on Lantius is that they now have a method of shutting it down." He stopped to think a moment. "It is rumored that they do extract several mating pairs of intelligent life, prior to activating the generators, to be put on display for the entertainment of ship's personnel, but that is nothing more than conjecture on my part." "Conjecture my fat rear end," Dar said, his temper rising to the boiling point. "Those bastards have a zoo aboard, filled with alien races from around the galaxy. That's why it was put off limits to me and my crew."

"I know nothing of this thing you call a zoo, but do not be too hard on yourself. Many worlds have died before, and in all likelihood, many more will do so in the future."

"Not if I can help it, Dar said. "Pete, I need your help."

"This presence is ready," the utapotus mind blasted back. "I've been waiting."

"Captain, would you allow me some private time with my friend here. I need a few minutes to sort out what you've told me."

Langos shifted his third leg, drawing it forward. He looked hard at Dar and the utapotus, then came to a decision."I acknowledge your wish. There are duties on the bridge to attend. You will not leave my quarters for any reason, however. This is not a request, Senior Commander Dar Fantin."

"I understand, Captain,"

CHAPTER 28

Dar watched the Womongly captain leave, noticing four Rage Warriors standing just outside the hatchway. He nodded in their direction, giving them a smile. There was no response. He' expected none, but it was in his nature to try and get under, whatever they call, skin. Turning to face the desk, he walked to the stool and sat down. "Okay, Pete it's you and me. I need your help."

"This presence is ready. You are The One. You shall prevail," the utapotus mind sent.

"Yeah, right. I'm 'the one.' That's for sure. I'm the one that got us into this mess. Now I've got to figure a way out. Can you help me?" Dar asked.

"This presence will help where it can, but this presence must not interfere with events as they might occur."

"Okay, I understand, I guess.' Dar spoke aloud, more to himself than to Pete. "I've got some questions."

"Ask your question. If this presence has at my disposal the answers, they shall be answered."

"First, who are you? What are you? Every time I turn around you're getting me out of trouble or soothing my fears." Dar reverted to telepathy with his friend.

"This presence is called 'utapotus.' It is an ancient word, the meaning far removed from today's knowledge. Utapotus describes a 'watcher' or 'protector.' This presence, a manifestation of the entities who are "The Watchers, was sent to keep vigil over The One."

"Darn it Pet, you're talking in riddles." Dar directed his thought to the utapotus. "I don't understand. Entities? Watchers? Me being this , so called 'one' you keep talking about.

Pete appeared non-flustered by Dar's bewilderment. "Recall the warning you received."

"Warning? What warning? Dar questioned, shaking his head with frustration.. The it hit him. "Pete, you're talking about the apparition that appeared in my quarters, aren't you? It was real, and not the alcohol."

"Real? Yes, quite real. The entity known as Dar does not listen well at times, this presence believes," Pete chided.

"Thanks a lot for your confidence. You know, I'm still pretty new at this sort of thing? I have never had things 'popping' in and out of my life until I met you."

"Yes, this presence accepts you have much to learn," Pete answered.

"Thanks, at least for that much," Dar said, pausing to think, then asked, "Captain Langos, this Womongly, do you know him?"

"Know him? No, this presence does not know him. This presence senses his unforgiving of failure, a hard entity, but fair."

"Do you think he's telling me the truth? I mean, his story is one-eighty out from what I have been led to aboard Nanta."

"The entity, Langos, speaks truth as he understands events."

Dar sat quietly for a moment, gazing at the holograph on the desk. *They are one ugly race,* he thought, *but that doesn't make them liars, like Jicama.* Unconsciously, he straightened the oxygen tubes leading to his nose, then ran fingers through tangled hair. Looking around the small gray-colored room, he was struck by just how little was present to give him an idea what Langos' life was like.

"If Langos is telling the truth, why didn't the Lantiusians just find another world to live on when Lantius died? They certainly had the technology." "This presence is unsure of the answer to your question. As you say, they had the technology, but not the desire. Perhaps the cause is linked with their superiority complex in some manner. Most certainly, part of their rational for staying in space was to destroy the Womongly."

"But, why obliterate whole races simply to retaliated against the Womongly? It doesn't make sense." Dar struggled with the dilemma, deprived of a clearly defined answer. He got up, again pacing the small enclosure, head bowed to clear the low overhead.

Pete shifted position on the desk, tucking powerful hind legs under his scaled belly. "There are thousands of worlds inhabited by races of intelligent entities. Intelligence in not necessarily followed by rational actions, for what is rational to you, may be totally irrational to another.

Lantiusian existence presupposes god-like superiority. The eradication of alien worlds means little to them beyond universal cleansing. By using their shielding device, they absolve themselves from directly killing living, sentient beings. The shield is *requested* by those they wish to destroy, and they provide, knowing the consequences."

The utapotus' baritone thoughts washed over Dar's mind like a small school boy being patiently instructed in the ways of the universe. "What you're saying, Pete, is that they won't stop until the Womongly are destroyed, or there are no more worlds to be convince the need for a shield. Then, maybe they'll attempt to find a new home."

"This presence feels that is so."

Dar shook his head, pulling a tube from his nose. Dectima's smell immediately filled his senses. "Geez, this place smells like a dump," he said aloud, replacing the tube, then eyed Pete. "Okay, where do we go from here?"

"The decision is yours. This presence may not interfere with the choices entities make."

"Can I contact Littia through you?" Dar asked.

"Of course," the utapotus answered.

A plan began to form in Dar's mind, but its entire inception revolved around Littia's cooperation. Would she help? It would mean she would have to betray her own people.

"Littia, Littia, are you there?" Dar used his mind to speak, praying his telepathy would reach her.

There was only a moments delay, until his mind filled with Littia's voice.

"Dar, you are alive! Oh, Dar, they told me you were dead. Praise to the God of Many Arms, that you are still with me."

Dar could hear the emotion behind her words. Littia's voice shook with passion. "Told you I had a good luck charm. I'm fine, and Pete's right here with me."

"Where are you? When will you return" are you sure you are not hurt?" Littia asked in a flurry of questions.

"Littia, I assure you I'm just fine," he telepathize with more sternness than he'd wished. "But I don't have much time, and I really need your help."

"Anything, Dar, you know that. What can we do?"

"First, can you tell me what happened? How many Darts returned?" Dar asked, holding his breath for the answer.

"It was terrible, Dar. Only five men returned from your flight. Commander Cannaly's flight all returned safely, but the squadron lost five, no four since you are safe."

"Did Bulldog make it?" Dar asked.

"Yes, Bulldog limped back to the Nanta, though his Dart was all but destroyed. Even Zentao was amazed it had held together long enough to return." She paused, then asked, "Dar, where are you?"

Dar ignored the question. He didn't want to explain his situation yet, not even to Littia. "Can you find Cannaly for me: I need to talk to him, but please, don't tell anyone I'm still alive. Will you do that for me?"

"Yes, I'll find him for you, but where are you?" Littia repeated her question.

"I'll explain everything, but find Cannaly first. I don't want to go through this twice. Please, Littia, trust me."

"We trust you, Dar. Very well, we shall find Cannaly, but it may take awhile."

"Try the bar," Dar sent back, not trying to hide the chuckling his thoughts were sending with his message.

"We shall try the bar first," Littia sent back.

Dar heard the levity in her thoughts as well. "I'll wait for you, and, Littia, I'm deadly serious about not telling anyone I'm alive, not even Cannaly. Just get him somewhere that both of you can be alone and not interrupted," he tried to make his thoughts impart the sincerity of the request.

"Very well, we shall do as you request," Littia thought back.

Dar felt the tickle of her thoughts leave his mind.

Senior Commander Jicama sat slouched in a beautifully upholstered chair, stroking his utapotus, who lay curled comfortably in his chosen's lap. Jicama's feet rested on the thick carpet covering his sitting room, as he watched chatoyant lights radiating off tiny scales of the fish-like creatures swimming in the vertical aquarium. Across from Jicama, Tamis relaxed, sipping a small glass of purplish wine.

"We have done well," Jicama spoke quietly. "In three days, maybe four, we shall have another world at our disposal."

"And with substantial losses to the Womongly forces as well. Though we detest the Earthlings, we must admit they have been valiant in battle. The Dectima's fighter force must be very near decimated," Tamis expanded on his leader's comment.

"Ah, it is so. Do you think the Earthlings will continue to fight with such determination, now that their leader is gone?" Jicama asked.

"Yes, we do not see them giving up, or changing what they have started. This Commander Cannaly has already taken charge and reorganized the unit. Tomorrow's fighter launches will be as large as today's. Zentao has completed construction of the remaining fighters."

"That is good. Then success is within our grasp. Another planet, rich in resources we desire, and a significant defeat of a Womongly spacecraft. Can't get much better than that," Jicama said with satisfaction, taking a large gulp of wine from his goblet.

"Plus, the annihilation of yet another barbaric race from the universe. The God of Many Arms must be pleased, as would our ancestors," Tamis added.

Poof! The utapotus disappeared from Jicama's lap.

The tall Supreme Commander smiled down at his vacant lap, saying, "Wondrous pets, the utapotus," he spoke, while rising from his chair to fill his, now empty glass, with chilled spirits. "We do have a problem, however." He returned to his seat, settling into its deep folds.

"The women?" Tamis asked.

"Ah, yes, the women. Have you maintained a record of those who have had contact with the primitives?" Jicama asked.

"Certainly. Those that require will be fully educated immediately after the Earthling's are confined to the zoo. Of course, we must still acquire sexual mates for the pilots, but that will be accomplished shortly before the shield is operational," Tamis answered nonchalantly.

"We are pleased, Tamis," Jicama said, appreciating the joy Tamis' voice reflected when he spoke of incarcerating the Earthlings. "You have done well." He held his glass out in salute.

"Dar, we are back. Are you there?" Little mind blasted.

Dar had, for the last thirty minutes, alternated between pacing the small quarters and tapping his fingers on the smooth desk. "I'm here, Littia. Have you got Cannaly with you?"

"He is here with us. We are in your room. He knows nothing, and is wary of me," Littia said.

"I can understand that. Okay, tell him who you're talking with and how," Dar instructed.

There was a long pause. "He says we are crazy. That he appreciates that we have lost someone very close, but that we should get some help or much needed rest," Littia's mind sent.

"Yeah, he would," Dar telepathize, laughing inwardly. "Ask him about a certain night in Subic Bay when he pinched the Admiral's wife's rear end, and if it wasn't for some fast footwork on my part, would have ended up in the brig."

Again a pause. "That got his attention, Dar," Littia sent.

"I thought it might. Did you tell him about Pete?" Dar asked.

"We told him, but we do not believe he understands, but is willing to listen to what we tell him."

"Good. Now listen carefully, Littia. What I'm about to tell you will be contrary to everything you now believe. Nonetheless, Pete assures me it is true, and I know you trust the utapotus. Remember, they didn't fully educate you, well, there was a reason. A very good reason! Jicama didn't want you to inadvertently give me any indication about what was actually happening. Can you trust me on this, Littia?" Dar thought rapidly.

"Yes, why should we not," Littia sent back.

"Because the Womongly are not our enemies, the Lantiusians are," Dar sent. There was a long pause. "Did you hear me, it is your people that are trying to destroy my world, not the Womongly."

"We heard. We do not believe. My people will not kill, you of all people should understand that. Why would you make such an appalling accusation?"

"I am sorry, Littia, I truly am, but it is the truth. Please hear me out, and pass my thought to Cannaly," Dar asked, his mind pleading, hoping to make Littia understand the import of his request. He felt her indecision and the terrible hurt he'd inflicted upon her.

"We shall try," Littia weakly replied.

Dar began, telling of his capture and subsequent interview with the Womongly captain, Langos. Leaving nothing to the imagination, his recount covered the death of Lantius, and the flaw in the personality her race possessed. He paused after a every few thoughts, allowing Littia to pass the information to Cannaly.

"Dar, are you sure this is true?" Littia interrupted his thoughts.

There was a shift in her mind's tone, Dar realized immediately. A hardness of strength and resolve. "Yes, Littia, I'm telling you the truth . . . all of it. Pete can confirm my thoughts."

"This presence confirms the truth of Dar's thoughts," Pete interjected to both of them.

Dar finished relating the information he considered important, ending with the explanation of the zoo.

"Commander Cannaly directs us to relay that Frenchy would have liked to have known about the zoo. He was on of those killed this afternoon," Littia passed. "He also wishes to know what you are planning."

"Good! Okay, here's the plan," Dar started, finishing several minutes later. "Does he have any questions?"

"No. Cannaly says he understands perfectly and and can't wait to get space borne. But, Dar, what of us?"

He didn't have a proper answer for her. "I don't know, Littia," he thought, his mind racing for a solution. "I just don't know, but I'll figure something out. Have faith in me."

"We do, Dar. The Supreme Commander will regret his not fully educating his guides, particularly this Guide 3rd Class. My lack of knowledge allows me to side with your people with a clear conscience."

"Thanks, Littia. I know it must be difficult for you," Dar thought. "Tell Cannaly, I'll be watching for the shuttles." He paused, then added," My heart is yours, Littia.

CHAPTER 29

Dar stood with Captain Langos on the bridge of the Womongly vessel, Dectima. Towering over every officer on deck, he felt like Gulliver on a Lilliputian island. The tactical holograph display depicted a different view of space than he'd seen on the Nanta. The Lantiusian ship was now the object of concern, not the Dectima. Plus, through the large bridge view ports, he had a clear view, into the darkness of space, unfettered by the green haze of a shield.

"Did you sleep well, my new friend:" Captain Langos asked his guest.

After his talk with Littia and Cannaly, he'd been escorted back to the hangar bay where he'd first awakened after being hauled aboard the Dectima. "Only fitfully, I'm sorry to say," Dar said. "Not to disparage your hospitality, sir, but I'm more accustom to sleeping on something softer than your pallet."

"Yes, yes. You must understand, Dectima is ill prepared for an Earthling visitor. I trust the food was nourishing, though possibly not to you liking."

"Nourishing? I suppose so," was all Dar said, recalling the bowl of foul looking black worm-like strings delivered to his bay during the early morning hours.

"I am pleased," Langos replied, the translation package changing his grunts and hisses into intelligible words. "I understand you have, with the help of my First Officer, removed your fighter from the retriever arm, and prepared it for flight."

"Yes, sir, that's correct. I checked her out first thing this morning. The nanites have done their job well. My on-board computer has been able to start the light drive, and all systems are up, ready, and on line."

"Very good. I gather then, the plan is on track?" Langos asked, turning to face Dar.

Dar felt the Womongly's yellow eyes search his. "Yes, I believe all is in readiness," Dar replied coldly, thinking of the Lantiusians. He'd explained his plan to Langos shortly after breaking off the telepathic link with Littia. "Now it's up to Jicama."

"Captain, shuttle exiting Nanta's shield," First Officer Bezal said, interrupting Dar and Langos.

Returning his attention to the holograph, Dar immediately recognized the ship leaving the tunnel in Nanta's shield as one of the shuttles. "Come on you bastards, let's dance," Dar whispered.

"You had better be going Langos instructed. "My first officer will lead you back to bay twelve."

"I'm on my way," Dar said, already moving for the exit off the bridge. "Come on, Bezal, show me the way."

Cannaly waved to Littia, as he climbed into his Dart. She had stuck close to him ever since their strange conversation with Dar. It had taken most of the night to individually brief each pilot on Dar's plan, and their individual roles in its execution. The time, he felt, was well spent, if he hadn't aroused suspicions among the Lantiusians.

The real test had come during his meeting with the Supreme Commander. It had been hard to contain his natural instincts to leap on the bigger man and beat the crap out of him on the spot. He'd kept his cool, and the two had agreed to fly much the same tactical formations as the previous day, adjusting flight paths to compensate for delivery of the generators to locations along the equator.

"So far, so good," he said aloud, slipping on his helmet.

"Are we going to fly, Snake?" his computer asked.

"Yep, we're going out," Cannaly said. "let's get this show on the road."

Minutes later, Cannaly exited through the shield, watching as other Darts appeared from tunnels created by engineers operating controls on hangar bay seven. Once the entire squadron flew safely in space, he transmitted, "Bulldog, this is Snake. Join'em up on me."

Flying at five-hundred knots, straight and level, Cannaly watched as twenty highly-polished Darts began assuming formation positions on either side of him.

"Shuttles bearing one-zero-two-bravo," Cannaly's computer said softly.

"Roger, got'em," Cannaly answered, then keyed his radio, "Bulldog, you have the lead. Do your stuff."

"I got the lead," Bulldog transmitted.

Cannaly yanked his stick to the left, accelerating rapidly away from the others, as he pushed his throttle to full drive power.

"What's this?" Jicama asked, rising from his command chair. His uneasiness grew as he watched the fighters move into a single large formation. "This in not how the mission was briefed." "I have no idea," Tamis said, his hand rapidly passing over his monitor. "Snake Lead, this is Nanta Control, what are your intentions? The shuttles are awaiting your escort."

Nanta Control, this is Snake. You know some days are like that. They just don't go like you want them to . .. even in space. Snake out!"

Jicama studied the Dart formation closely. "Tamis, have the shuttles jump. Now!, he screamed.

But sir the shields . . . ," Tamis stopped in mid sentence, watching the plasma screen.

Bulldog led Space Fighter Squadron – One to with two hundred miles astern of the shuttles. "Split and fire," the big Texan ordered.

Nine Darts separated from Bulldog's wing. There were now two flights, one made up of ten ships, the other nine. The the distinctive main flights began moving rapidly into two separate arrow heads. The lead fighters acted as point, with three Darts on either wing, plus three of four forming another arrow head beneath and slightly to the rear of the main flight.

"I've got the shuttle on the left, Kobs, you've got the one on the right."

"Roger, got it," was the transmitted reply.

At one hundred miles, thermal torpedoes began streaking from the Dart formations. One after another, weapons roared for the targeted Lantiusian shuttles.

"Break," Bulldog screamed on his radio.

At Bulldogs command, Dart pilots snapped their sticks, One second there were two flight tied wing to wing, the next, Darts were maneuvering in nineteen different directions, expeditiously accelerating away from the shuttles.

The first torpedo struck, then another, followed by thirty more. The dual explosions ripped space, radiating blast waves with enough intensity to shake the monumental Nanta.

"Good shootin' Bulldog. That ought to rattle a few cages," Cannaly transmitted. "Damn fine shootin'." He was rocketing for the Dectima, accelerating through twenty-two thousand knots.

"Friendly fighter at two thousand miles," his computer informed him.

"Hey, Dar, that you out there?" he radioed.

"Who'd expect, Flash Gordon maybe?" Dar radioed back. "You ready?"

"Dar, my man, I was born ready. This should be a cake walk. Let's do it."

"Roger that. See ya when I see ya," Dar transmitted, turning his Dart for Earth. "Nan, calculate a re-entry point for the North Pole."

"Re-entry point calculated, Dar. Why are we going to the North Pole?"

"We have a little job to take care of down there. Arm the thrumber."

"Thrumber armed. Do you wish me to fly the re-entry?" Nan asked.

"You have control. Let me have it back at one hundred thousand feet, over the pole," Dar instructed, letting go of the stick. He sat back, watching Earth, a blue marble suspended in a field of black, rush toward him.

The Dart's shield lit up with fire, as the wings extended and entry into Earth's heavy atmosphere began. "Passing two hundred thousand feet," Nan said, quietly.

"Roger," Dar said, looking at the northern ice cap. He touched his plasma screen, magnifying the display to its highest scale. "There's our target, Nan. Make corrections as necessary."

The Dart made a nearly indiscernible shift in flight path. "Dar, is that not the shield generator?" Nan questioned.

"Yes, we have been instructed to destroy it, Nan. Is there a problem?"

"No, there is no problem. It is highly unusual for us to target a friendly device, however," Nan said. "Passing one hundred thousand feet. You have control."

"I have control," Dar responded, taking the stick, and placing his feet on the rudder peddles. He pulled the throttle aft, slowing the Dart to seven hundred knots, tweaked the sight on his heads-up display and waited. At ten thousand feet, he pulled the trigger. Balls of light stormed their way to Earth, initially striking just short of the generator, then tracking forward to the target. The generator disappeared into icy dust.

Pulling hard on the stick, he began a sling-shot maneuver, shooting him back toward open space. "Take us to Nanta," he instructed Nan. "You have control."

Cannaly, his face radiating a smile, hurtled his way north from the South Pole, leaving a smoking hole on the ice where a shield generator once sat. "Set course for these coordinates," he instructed his computer, punching in the numbers on the heads-up.

"Snake, you still around?" Bulldog radioed.

"Hell yeah, what ya think," Cannaly transmitted. "What's your status?"

Laughter filled his helmet, with his transmit button still depressed, Bulldog was filling the airwaves with deep laughter. "Snake, you ain't gonna believe the havoc we're causing the FAA, every Flight Center in the world, and Cherry Point Approach. You'd think we just appeared from Mars or somethin'."

"Leave some fun for me. I'm headin' your way. Have you heard from the Skipper yet"

"Not yet, but I saw a bright flash coming from way up north. I figure he got the job done there as well. Ya know there's going to be some heavy partyin' at the bar tonight, Snake. Ya ready?"

"Are you kidding me? Son this aviator and savior of Earth's human race is going

to drown himself in good-ole O-club whiskey."

Nanta loomed ahead, the thick green shield surrounding her like a shroud. "Nanta Control, this is Major Fantin, United States Marine Corps. Request you have Zentao open the shield for recovery.

"Ah, Dar. We surmised you might have survived after all. We imagine the destruction of our shuttles was your handiwork. Was it not?" Jicama transmitted, with sarcasm dripping from each syllable.

"You might say I had something to do with it, you . . .." Dar bit his tongue before he called Jicama what was in his heart. He still hoped to get aboard the Nanta, and the Supreme Commander was his only ticket. "Have Zentao open a tunnel."

"Why would I want you back aboard my ship," Jicama asked.

"I left something behind, something I want to take back to Earth with me," Dar said, enjoying the tension in Jicama's voice. "I mean you or your ship anymore harm, though what you had planned to do to my world, you deserve most anything I can think of."

"You poor dumb barbarian, you actually think you have won, don't you?" Jicama asked, his voice full of hate. "Believe me, you have won nothing, just delayed the inevitable."

"That may be the case, but we've bought ourselves some time. If you come again, we'll be better prepared. Now, may I land?"

"Your arrogance astounds me. What makes you think that we would allow you to leave once you landed, should we grant your request?" Jicama questioned.

"Simple, your Supremness," Dar flippantly transmitted, "From the moment you open a tunnel through the shield, my finger will be on trembling over the trigger. One wrong move, your mistake, my mistake, and a thermal torpedo turns Nanta into scrap metal."

"All the more reason not to let you enter through the shield," Jicama responded.

Look, Supreme Commander, all I want is to retrieve my guide," Dar said, his frustration building."There has been enough killing for my part. I may have the desire to blow you into the next galaxy, but I'd go with you, and I'm not the suicidal type."

"Enough of this," Jicama screamed. "No! You man not land, and you can forget about the one you called Littia. She will sent to the Educator, where I will have every bit of her mind destroyed, leaving only base functions. She'll be sent to the zoo as a reminder to those who think to betray our way of life. You can forget about you guide, she's as good as dead."

Dar's heart hit his heels. "Damn you, Jicama."

Poof! Small body trembling, Pete appeared in Dar's lap.

Dar felt the distress his utapotus friend radiated with thoughts and whirling eyes. "Littia," he screamed with his mind.

"We are here," Littia's voice tickled his mind with sadness. She was being led, along with the other guides assigned Earth's pilots, to the Educator. "Did you succeed?"

The Dart drifted along side Nanta. "Oh, God Littia, I'm so sorry. This is my fault," Dar cried.

"This presence is deeply rooted in your mind, Littia," Pete's thoughts radiated to both Dar and Littia. "Accept the Educator without fear, the future has not been written, and The One has much left to accomplish. He may yet, in time, be with you."

The Nanta began accelerating, moving away from the Earth. Dar bumped his throttle forward, trying to maintain position.

"Dar, we love you. Always remember we shall be with you."

Nanta jumped, leaving Dar alone in the blackness of space.

"You are The One," Pete's thoughts stroked Dar's mind. "This battle has been won, the war is just beginning."